CHASING VICE

CHASING VICE

A Murder Mystery

WALTER GEORGE ALTON

Publisher's Cataloging-in-Publication data

Names: Alton, Walter G., 1941-, author.
Title: Chasing vice / Walter George Alton.
Description: Yachats, OR: Wild Ginger Press, 2024.
Identifiers: LCCN: 2024922251 | ISBN: 978-1-943190-44-7 (print) | 978-1-943190-45-4 (ebook)
Subjects: LCSH Murder--Fiction. | Crime--Fiction | New York (N.Y.)--Fiction. | Mystery fiction. | Thrillers (Fiction) | BISAC FICTION / Mystery & Detective / General | FICTION / Thrillers / Crime | FICTION / Thrillers / Suspense
Classification: LCC PS3601 .L86 C43 2024 | DDC 813.6--dc23

Wild Ginger Press
www.wildgingerpress.com

JETSAM

*The part of a ship, its equipment, or its cargo that
is cast overboard to lighten the load in time of
distress and that sinks or is washed ashore.*

FLOTSAM

*Goods floating on the surface of a body of water
after a shipwreck or after being cast
overboard to lighten the ship.*

1

NEW YORK CITY
1984

AS DARKNESS GIVES WAY to early-morning light in Soho, a solitary dirty white garbage truck moves slowly along the street, like some kind of behemoth, stopping frequently. One man dressed in green, hanging on the side, jumps off when it stops and is joined by the driver. They grab beat-up metal and plastic garbage cans on the sidewalk, dragging or carrying them to the back of the truck, dumping their contents in the truck's open cavernous mouth along with large, full black garbage bags that they sling in. They then roughly return the empty cans to their spots by the buildings. As they approach a big collection of trash near the stairway to the cellar of a newly renovated co-op apartment building, they stop in shock at the sight of the naked, broken body of a young woman.

———

On the fifth floor of an old live-in loft in Tribeca, a tall, dark, unshaven man in his early forties, dressed in a paint-spattered blue denim work shirt, old blue jeans ripped at the right knee, and worn-out leather Stan Smith tennis shoes with a paintbrush handle in his mouth, stares at a large canvas on an easel. He has short dark brown hair, blue eyes, high cheekbones, and is handsome. He looks muscular and fit—athletic. He moves the brush in his hand on the colorful abstract painting. He has been up all night working. Baloo, a magnificent male Great Pyrenees, is lying nearby on the polished maple floor with his head between his paws, watching his master, waiting like a patient polar bear. Near the working area there is an old heavy bag hanging by a chain from a rafter and a full-length mirror for jumping rope. Attached to another beam is a round flat circle of wood with a black leather speed bag hanging from its center. A big TV on a low table is off to the side of the mirror. There are dumbbells on a shelf by the side wall.

The artist finishes his paint stroke and looks at his canvas. He smiles, cleans his brushes, and puts them down. He looks at his dog, who lifts his big white head.

"Okay, big guy, let's go out." Baloo gets up excitedly and shakes his fur. Johnny Colrain walks to the door, takes his worn brown leather bomber jacket off a hook, and grabs the lanyard leash from another. He slips on the jacket, leans over, gives the dog a pat, and opens the door.

Two white-and-blue police cars and an ambulance with their roof lights flashing are parked on the street behind the garbage truck at the co-op on Prince Street where the young woman's body was discovered. Four uniformed policemen are talking to the two sanitation men when a black unmarked Plymouth Gran Fury arrives. The driver, Detective Jim Ashford, opens his door and steps out.

He is the new breed—educated, clean-cut, neat, dressed in a gray tweed sport coat, starched white shirt, blue striped tie, and charcoal slacks. His black plain-toe shoes are shined. He is a slim forty-one-year-old black man, five feet, nine inches tall, who looks in shape. He has a strong pleasant face. Everything about him projects professionalism. The man in the passenger seat is slower to open his door and exit the car. Detective Frank Dugan is sixty years old, balding with sparse gray hair on the sides of his head, overweight, and slovenly. He is five feet, ten inches tall with a big paunch that wants to hang over his belt. His face looks swollen and pink. His nose is a little purplish with some broken veins visible. He has at least one day's growth of his beard so there are white whiskers present. In addition to the stubble, he has bad skin, which is pockmarked. An old-line Irish cop, he is wearing a crumpled brown wool sport coat, a blue shirt open at the neck with a loosened solid navy tie, and tan slacks. His unpolished brown shoes are scuffed. He does not look friendly in any way. Dugan approaches the uniformed cops who are talking to the sanitation men.

"What have we got?" he asks the police officers, eying the blanket covering the body.

Detective Ashford, already at the body, bends down, gently lifts the blanket covering it, and looks at a beautiful young woman.

One of the uniformed officers says, "She must have jumped from a window or balcony."

Ashford says nothing but turns his head and gives the uniform an annoyed look.

"Go and see if you can round up the superintendent of the building," Dugan directs one of them gruffly. He tells another to put out crime scene tape.

Ashford straightens up and looks up at the building. Instinct makes him then direct his gaze up the street, and he sees something of interest. Dugan notices and turns to see Colrain and Baloo walking toward them on the far side of the street.

Colrain crosses the street with the dog, which pulls at the lead and starts barking as he catches Dugan's scent. Dugan backs up a step as they approach. Colrain smiles.

"Hi, Ash, Dugan."

Dugan looks at the artist and his dog with disdain and grunts, but Ashford smiles broadly and steps forward to pet Baloo, telling him to quiet down. As he talks and strokes the animal, Baloo calms down and responds to the attention. He pushes into Ashford's leg and looks up at him. He obviously knows the detective. Finally, Ashford stops petting the dog and looks at Colrain.

"Up kind of early, aren't you, Johnny?"

"Late, actually. What happened here?"

Dugan responds, "A lady who decided to bail out."

Colrain is not amused and gives Dugan a hard look. There obviously is bad blood between them. Ashford jumps in.

"Whoever she was, she was gorgeous; my guess is a model. Want to take a look?"

"Not really ..."

Ashford frowns.

"But I will," Johnny says.

Colrain approaches the body, and Ashford lifts the blanket where it is covering the face of the victim. Colrain is stunned.

"Oh no ..." he mutters.

He kneels down to look closer at the woman's face. There is blood behind her head from her broken skull, but her face is not smashed. Ashford watches and waits. Colrain gets up slowly, visibly shaken and upset.

"You know her?" Ashford asks.

"We worked together once."

Ashford is quietly assessing Colrain, but Dugan speaks.

"I bet."

Colrain's eyes flash, and he takes a step toward Dugan but thinks better of it as Ashford puts a hand on his chest. Ashford turns his back to Dugan as he leads Johnny away and speaks softly to him.

2

CAPE MAY, NJ ~ JULY 1966
COAST GUARD BOOT CAMP

JOHNNY COLRAIN STANDS at attention in front of his double-decker bunk along with the rest of the new recruits in the large barracks. Six feet, one inch tall, 185 pounds of muscle, and in great shape, he looks straight ahead as the boatswain's mate walks up and down talking at the recruits of his new company. Underneath his sailor cap, Johnny's head is shaved, which has revealed a bump that makes him look mean, especially when he has a serious look. He is not comfortable in his blue sailor suit. In fact, he is not comfortable being in this position, an enlisted man restricted by the military training regime. He is a free spirit but also knows self-discipline. As an athlete and someone who has had his share of fights growing up, he looks at the boatswain's mate with cold eyes as the boatswain's mate is threatening the recruits that if someone steps out of line, he will take the recruit into his office and close the door. The boatswain's mate is saying that no one will know what happened in there. Johnny is thinking about this short, overweight Coast

Guard boatswain's mate speaking to them. Johnny's eyes project his thoughts. *You better be pretty damn tough, boatswain, because if you take me in that office and close the door, I will beat the crap out of you.*

The boatswain's mate is a career coastguardsman. He looks at Johnny Colrain and assesses him correctly. He makes him the yeoman of the recruit company. The mate is smart. He knows that this recruit, who is a bit older than the rest of the recruits, who are enlisted teenage boys, will take over and run the unit so he himself will not have to do much. Johnny is fine taking control of the company. He hates to be inspected, and he learns that by ensuring the barracks are immaculate and the unit and its members perform well, there is less inspecting of all of them, which means him.

In the first test of the recruits' physical fitness, the PE instructors run them through their paces, push-ups, sit-ups, pull-ups, and jumping jacks in a large gym. This is considered a physical fitness test. A tall blond freckled instructor from West Virginia with buck-teeth and a Southern accent tells the group to hit the floor for twenty push-ups. He then goes over to Johnny.

"You did not hit the floor fast enough."

Johnny gives him a hard look.

"You have to be kidding," Johnny says.

The tall goofy-looking sailor smiles at him.

"Nope. You have to come back after dinner to take the test again." John Colrain is in great shape. He goes back to the gym and exceeds all the requirements of the PE test. However, he is pissed that he had to do it over again for what he considers a false reason.

Several days later, it is hot and humid as the recruits exercise in their PE class outside on a large concrete slab. They are all sweating. Johnny's sinuses and postnasal drip are running. He is feeling it. He has to spit out a wad of mucus doing the calisthenics while on the ground. Surfer Joe, the West Virginia freckled PE instructor, is running the class, and Johnny is still mad about what happened in the initial PE testing when he felt he was wrongfully singled out. His company is being taken through various exercises. They are told to do jumping jacks, and Surfer Joe instructs them.

"You will all start together and end together; and if not, you will double the number until you start and end together."

Johnny gets an idea. He knows he can do jumping jacks all day long. The group starts to do the set of twenty-five jumping jacks. Johnny waits for a beat at number twenty-five and then does one more, which means that the company has to do fifty more. There is some grumbling. When they reach fifty, he does the same thing, and a loud groan goes up from the group. Now they have to do one hundred. When they get to one hundred, Johnny does one extra again. Now there are loud protests. Surfer Joe is very uncomfortable because time is going by, and another company of recruits is about to arrive. The boatswain's mate in charge of the PE program sees what is going on. He grabs a different PE instructor and tells him to take Johnny to a nearby hill, have him barrel-roll down it, and then climb back up ten times as a punishment for his disruptive actions. That PE instructor, Jim Ashford, takes Johnny up the hill. When they get to the top of the hill, he speaks.

"What are you doing, man?" Johnny looks at him questioningly.

"I want to fight that Surfer Joe. Tell him I will meet him somewhere." Ashford shakes his head.

"You don't get it, man. It's all part of what they do here when you first come in as a recruit. They pick out a few guys, fail them, and then punish them to make an example for the others. It means nothing."

Johnny thinks about this as he rolls down the hill and then runs up it ten times with ease. It does not make much sense to him, but he realizes Ashford did not have to say anything and is trying to help him. He accepts what Ashford said.

The next day when it comes time for the swim test, Johnny dives in and swims a lap underwater doing just the dolphin kick. When he comes up at the far end of the twenty-five-yard pool, Ashford is standing there. He smiles.

"Where did you swim?" he asks.

"NYU," Johnny answers.

Ashford walks to the other end of the pool and into the office of the boatswain who runs the PE program. A few minutes later, he comes out and walks over to Johnny.

"Okay, go see the chief boatswain in his office," he says.

Johnny knocks at the door, is called in, and stands before the boatswain. The boatswain looks up.

"When you get out of boot, after your leave, you will be coming back here as a PE and swim instructor for your active duty."

Johnny is shocked but quickly processes it. He is pleased. No duty on a ship, but instead he will be going back to boot camp in Cape May after he graduates for the remainder of his six months of active duty. That is okay with him.

Johnny gets in a few scrapes as he goes through boot camp but nothing serious. When the recruit company that is working in the dining hall decides to punish him for pitching a winning softball game against them and bad-mouthing them after they disparaged his recruit company on the parade ground by not giving Johnny any food as he is going through the line, he is not fazed. He sees Ashford and shows him the meager amount of food on his plate. Ashford then goes through the line with Johnny a second time, forcing the recruits serving the food to give Johnny a full plate of food. That makes them mad, so they all come out and try to intimidate him by standing around his table. He looks at them and does not eat. He waits. They all start getting itchy because they have to clean up the kitchen and mess hall including his dishes before they leave for the evening. He waits them out. They curse at him, but they finally walk away to finish their duties, and then he eats.

———

Two weeks later when Johnny's leave is finished, he walks into the locker room on the base to start his duty as a PE and swim instructor, and there is Surfer Joe standing by a locker. Surfer Joe sees him and starts laughing.

"I really got to you, didn't I?" he says with a huge goofy grin.

Johnny, who now understands the game, looks at Ashford, who is standing right there, and he can't help but smile back.

"Yup. You did," Johnny says as looks at Jim Ashford, and he opens the door of an empty locker.

While he is working as a PE instructor, Johnny develops a friendship with Ashford, who shows him the ropes. They go to a few bars that have bands that play rhythm and blues. When they have leave, they ride back to New York City together and talk a lot on the long stretches of the drive. Ashford takes him to some of his favorite clubs, and Johnny shares some of his favorite galleries and bars, but after Ashford joins the police force, they do not spend as much time together.

ASHFORD LOOKS at Johnny's face trying to ascertain what is going on with him.

"Johnny, you know better than to take the bait from Dugan."

He gets no answer.

"Right?"

Johnny finally nods.

"What do you mean, you worked together?"

"Her name is Adrienne Wyatt. She is a model, and we worked together on a three-day job."

"What agency did her bookings?" Ashford asks.

"The Gordon Agency."

"Was something going on between you two?"

"No, she was involved, but we became friends."

"We ran into each other at functions once in a while, but that was it. I will tell you, Ash, she dated rich guys but was not like the average model. Adrienne was intelligent, well-read, and funny. I don't see her taking her own life."

Johnny feels terrible and is trying to sort out in his mind what could have happened to Adrienne. He is not coming up with anything. Ashford looks at Johnny waiting. Johnny says nothing.

"You okay?" Ashford asks.

Johnny still doesn't answer. The super shows up with the uniformed cop. Ash notices and continues to address Johnny.

"I am sorry to upset you with this, but she looks like a model, and I thought it was worth asking if you knew her. So, thanks for that, John. I may call you if I need your help with the modeling community." There is an awkward pause. He adds, "If you see Robespierre, tell him that the Mets won last night, and I will be by to collect my ten bucks next week."

He smiles at his friend, and Johnny manages a bit of a grimace back. Ashford bends over to scratch behind Baloo's ear. The dog responds, cocking his head and pushing it into Ashford's thigh.

Johnny and Baloo walk on, heading for the Hudson River. Johnny keeps thinking about Adrienne and their interaction shooting the print job in Florida. She was very beautiful, a tall, slender, big-boned blonde from Iceland with a great smile. He wanted to take her out, but she was dating a rich entrepreneur and doing the party scene. That was not his thing. He is of a different ilk—not a party guy— so it never happened.

The two of them make their way to Pier 25 on the Hudson where Robespierre's is located. It is on an old barge turned into a restaurant, heavily decorated with dark wood beams, brass, and oil paintings. There is a large apartment above on a second story. It is not open, but Johnny knocks loudly on the side door to the kitchen and waits. After a few minutes, he hears a sleepy Robespierre yell, "Yeah, yeah ... I'm coming!"

A short, trim, handsome black man in his forties with close-cut black hair and a little mustache opens the door and looks out. He has a distinctive, expressive face. He is five feet, eight inches tall, wearing a T-shirt, pajama bottoms, and dark brown leather slippers. He is wearing a friendly scowl.

"What time is it, dude? I don't think this is a civilized time to be up."

Johnny is amused by the way Robespierre looks and replies, "Some people have to be. Are you going to let us in?"

From the interior of the building, a strong female voice with a heavy Caribbean accent speaks, "Come in, Johnny. Have you had breakfast?"

Robespierre shakes his head and smiles at Johnny.

"You are her favorite. Although, I can't figure out why." He reaches down and pats the side of the big dog.

"Okay, you two," he says, straightening up.

Robespierre, Johnny, and Baloo enter the kitchen of the restaurant. The dog is wagging his tail. Robespierre's mother, Lucienne, sees Baloo and goes to find a large bone from a walk-in refrigerator. She returns with one and gives it to Baloo. The big dog takes it gently in his mouth and happily lies down to chew it. Lucienne is a big robust woman. She has an open attractive face and, surely, was quite a beauty in her day. Her hair is piled up on her head, and she is in a sleeveless red print dress with black clogs on her feet. Her big strong dark arms show. She projects warmth, but she is not anyone you would want to be angry with you. Her smile is magnetic, and she is very intuitive. She is a force.

"What do you have to say for yourself, John Colrain? You have not come by to see me in a long time," she says with a faux stern expression on her face.

Johnny goes to her and gives her a big hug. He lets her go and watches her magnificent smile appear.

"Sorry, Auntie Lucienne, I have been trying to finish this piece I am doing. You have to come see it."

"No reason to ignore your people," she scolds and looks hard at him. "What is wrong, John?" she asks. Johnny is silent. "How about some pancakes, and we talk?" she asks.

"That sounds good to me. I am starved."

Lucienne puts on an apron, walks to the supply pantry, and comes out with a bag of flour. She picks up a bowl and starts making batter. Robespierre grabs two large cups, turns to the big copper espresso machine, grinds some coffee, tamps the grounds in the silver bowl on the handle, inserts the handle in the machine, presses the button to fill a cup with strong Italian-roast coffee, then repeats it. He takes some milk from a refrigerator and steams it with the nozzle on the espresso machine. He adds the just-steamed milk to the two cups. He brings them over to Johnny who takes one. He and Johnny sit down at a small oak table in a little alcove to the side of the large kitchen, which is occupied by two huge stainless steel tables, multiple pots hanging from steel racks above them, a butcher block, and two industrial ranges with large hoods above them.

Robespierre has known Johnny for a long time. Robby, as Johnny calls him, used to tend bar in the East Village before he owned Robespierre's. For some reason the bar where he worked, The Raunchy Brit, which was a bit seedy, became a model hangout. After he finished his active duty in the Coast Guard Reserves, Johnny modeled part of the time to support himself and afford art classes, and Johnny would sometimes meet up with friends at the Brit. He took Ashford there, and Ash became friendly with Robby. They loved talking baseball. One night Johnny and Ash were standing having a beer when a beautiful model came in with a big rough-looking guy. They both noticed the couple. Although Johnny does not generally find models that attractive, this woman was more his type, and when she walked by and caught his eye, he automatically gave her a friendly smile. Almost immediately the man she was with pushed Ash aside with his left hand and threw a punch at Johnny with his right. Johnny saw the guy at that moment and moved sideways to his right to escape the haymaker. It partially glanced off Johnny's cheek. He moved in at an angle and threw two quick jabs that landed and caused the man to stop his attack momentarily, but then he kept coming. Johnny, who had taken a few karate classes, tried a karate kick to the stomach that just made the man grunt. It surprised Johnny that it did not floor the guy, and he was only stopped for a second or two. At that moment Robespierre appeared with a baseball bat, stood between them, and glared at both of them.

"We'll have none of that in here! It's over!" he shouted with authority.

He then directed the man back to the bar and stood looking hard at Johnny.

"Are you nuts? Don't you see the size of that guy? He obviously is out of his element and clearly very protective of any woman he brings in here with the likes of guys who look like you around."

There was a big pause as the two men looked at each other. Robby then smiled at Johnny. There was something he liked about him.

"Go with Ash to the other end of the bar, and I will buy you a drink."

That started the friendship. Johnny would go to The Raunchy Brit and talk to Robespierre, and Robespierre would go to Johnny's loft where Johnny would cook dinner while the two of them talked, which continued while they ate. Johnny learned Robespierre's story and was fascinated by it.

———————

Robespierre's mother, Lucienne, grew up in Antigua. His father was an Italian sea captain who took advantage of her at a very young age. She was but a girl, only fourteen, when she got pregnant with Robespierre. Not highly educated, she was smart, hardworking, strongly principled, and imparted those principles to her son. She eventually separated from the Italian, whom she had married. When Robespierre was eight years old, she remarried and moved to Harlem. To earn money, she cleaned people's apartments.

Lucienne's second husband was not a nice man and did not treat his stepson well. Robespierre learned to be tough. Being small, he had to use his fists proficiently, and living in Harlem, he used them, but he was also ambitious and intelligent. He was fast, good at baseball, and applied himself in school. He stayed away from drugs. When he got into Howard University on an academic scholarship, he studied literature and then went on to get a master's in education at Columbia University. He was raised with flavorful food and developed his palate from his mother's cooking. After teaching English in the public school system for a few years, he decided he would open a restaurant featuring Caribbean food with his mother doing the cooking. He started working at night at The Raunchy Brit to supplement his income. He was well liked and developed some good connections tending bar there. He also got around town after hours but got tired of it.

With financial help from some wealthy patrons he met at The Raunchy Brit, Robby was able to open Robespierre's. Johnny donated several paintings for the restaurant. The two of them would occasionally go out on the town but often ended up back at Robespierre's with Lucienne making them something to eat. Lucienne took to

Johnny immediately and liked feeding him, especially since he enjoyed her cooking so much. There was always teasing about this by Robespierre, but he got a kick out of it. He loved seeing his mother spoiling his friend and treating him like another son. Johnny felt like family.

––––––––––

Johnny tells them about Adrienne Wyatt and what happened with Ashford and Dugan. Robespierre shakes his head when he hears that Johnny almost went for Dugan. Robespierre knows their history. Dugan had tried to shake down Johnny's landlord because of his certificate of occupancy. The CO was actually legal because it was an artist's loft, and Johnny was allowed to work and live in the space. Johnny researched it and reported Dugan, who then lost a promotion.

"Are you in trouble?" Robespierre asks.

Johnny thinks about how much he loves these two people. They really are not just wonderful friends but also the salt of the earth. Family.

"No. Nothing like that, old friend," he replies.

Lucienne turns from the stove, looks from one man to the other, and smiles.

Robespierre is silent, just thinking. He then speaks.

"I remember her, man! She was aiming high. I never saw her with just anyone. I think she dated a business guy who was an executive at a car company."

"Yup. That's her. She was not your average model, for sure."

Johnny looks over to Lucienne, who is starting to plate the pancakes with Jones sausage. He gets up and grabs two plates and brings them over to the table. Lucienne follows with her own plate. Robespierre freshens their coffee cups, gets a cup for his mother, and makes one for her. He brings her cup and a pitcher of maple syrup that Lucienne has heated to the table.

"I don't get it, Robby. I never saw Adrienne depressed, and she was not a druggie as far as I know," Johnny says.

Robespierre listens and makes a face.

"You don't know what she was into, Johnny."

"You don't think it was an accident, John?" asks Lucienne.

"I guess it's possible, but I doubt it."

They eat in silence. Johnny takes his last bite of pancake.

"Delicious, as usual, Lucienne."

She gives him a big smile, and Johnny busses his dish into the big sink. He walks back to the table.

"I have to go. Thanks ... so good."

He leans over and gives Lucienne a big hug and kiss on the cheek. Robespierre gets up and walks with Johnny toward the door. Johnny grabs the leash from one of the tables. Baloo gets up carrying what's left of the bone in his mouth and goes over to Johnny, who clips the leash onto his collar.

"Ashford says he will be by to collect his ten bucks," Johnny tells Robespierre, who frowns.

"Johnny, be careful with Dugan. He's bad news."

"Yeah, he's a piece of work, all right."

Johnny and Baloo walk out the door and across to North Moore Street.

4

THE FIRST PRECINCT police station is bustling. Detective Ashford is at his desk reading the coroner's report of the death of Adrienne Wyatt. He is startled and whistles. The initial theory of suicide is shattered by the findings. A substantial amount of vomitus was found in the lungs. Adrienne Wyatt died from aspirating her own vomit, not from a fall. There were welts on her back and buttocks inconsistent with a fall. There was also cocaine in her blood.

Detective Dugan is all business as he enters a posh Upper East Side apartment house on Park Avenue. He speaks to the doorman and then shows him his badge. The doorman rings up to an apartment. He nods to Dugan, and the detective walks purposefully through the beautifully decorated lobby to the elevator. He is taken to the twelfth floor. He knocks hard on the door of one of the four apartments on the floor. An exotic woman—tall, thin, dark-haired, and striking, dressed in a white blouse, indigo blue jeans, and sandals—opens the door. She is obviously terrified by Detective Dugan. The obese detective pushes his way into the apartment. He shuts the door quietly and turns to her. He smiles luridly then suddenly lashes out and slaps her viciously across the face. She reels backward from the force of the blow and cowers before him, holding her cheek.

"You will keep your mouth shut, won't you, Renée?"

"Yes. Yes, I will. I promise!"

Dugan stares at her.

"Don't think you can escape from us, Renée. You can't. Not from us. Do you understand?"

"I do. I do."

"Good. Now come here."

"No, Dugan. No. Please."

"Kneel down, Renée."

———

It is a sunny day in Manhattan. Priscilla Gans rushes out of the subway on lower Broadway near Spring Street. She is in a hurry to get to the gallery where she works. She feels good. This is a job she really likes. Dressed in a colorful flower-print dress, she walks fast, and her dress moves in the wind that is blowing. She has a leather bag over her shoulder and stylish green flat shoes on. At twenty-eight, a tad over five feet, two inches, curvy and freckled with reddish-blond hair in a thick French braid, she has a wholesome look and a friendly attractive face. Priscilla was born and raised in Upstate New York. Her dad stoked her ambitions. She went to public high school in Berlin, New York, but decided to attend Barnard in New York City if she could get in. She did and excelled there. Her burgeoning interest in art was fed. She visited all the city's museums during her college years, and this has continued. She shares a large apartment in Peter Cooper Village with three young women who found each other as roommates through the classifieds in the *New York Times*. She runs up the stairs of an old renovated loft building and enters a light airy gallery on the third floor.

"Hi, Robert!" she says as she enters.

Robert Easton is the owner of the gallery. Born in England, he spent many years in Australia, where he learned about aboriginal art, and immigrated to New York from there. He has dark red hair and very fair skin. He wears glasses and has quite a paunch on his large frame. He is about five feet eleven. You can tell from looking at him that he is a friendly man. He greets her with his distinctive accent.

"Hello, Priscilla. This should be an interesting exhibit."

Robert is mounting a new show featuring artists that he has not shown before. Priscilla drops her bag and goes to help him hang a painting. It happens to be one of Johnny's.

"This artist will be in later. I like his work," Robert remarks.

Priscilla steps back and looks at the abstract painting. There is something about the composition and colors that she likes.

"I see what you mean, Robert."

––––––––––

As Johnny and his big dog walk down Leonard Street, an unmarked black car approaches and pulls over to the curb. Ashford is by himself and gets out of the driver's side of the car. He goes over to Johnny and bends down to pet his friend. Finally, he stands up and addresses Johnny.

"Adrienne Wyatt did not die from the fall, John."

"What?"

"She had cocaine in her system, but she died from aspiration."

"I don't understand, Ash. What are you saying?"

"She had vomit in her lungs that killed her."

"And she ends up broken on the pavement, Ash?"

"Someone probably threw her out the window, but she was already dead." Johnny looks askance at Ashford trying to process this information.

"To make it look like suicide?"

"That's what I'm thinking," the detective responds with a grim face.

Ashford goes on to explain what the coroner found in more detail, and he has not been able to come up with any meaningful leads so far. He tells Johnny that he has spoken with Evelyn Gordon, Adrienne's agent, and Dugan spoke with Renée Toulouse, her best and, apparently, only friend. Ash learned that Adrienne had been in New York just eight months. Because of her exceptional looks, she was invited into the social scene of the very rich but had no real girlfriends except Renée. She was born and grew up in Reykjavík, Iceland. After two years studying in Paris at the Sorbonne, she met a modeling agent and started modeling. She decided to come to New York and signed with the Gordon Agency. She stayed with Evelyn Gordon and her husband at their town house on the Upper East Side for two months when she first arrived. During that brief period, she frequented Macquilken's, a well-known watering hole nearby, owned by a former male model, Randy Macquilken. Evelyn Gordon believes that Randy may have dated Adrienne. He might know something.

"I could use your help, Johnny."

"How, Ash?"

"You did some modeling; you can ask around. People in the modeling world know you and will talk to you. Find out more about what was going on in Adrienne Wyatt's life, who she was seeing before her death, whether she was a druggie—that kind of information."

Johnny rolls his eyes.

"You know Macquilken?" Ash continues.

"Yes."

"You could talk to him."

"Dugan won't like it, Ash."

"First of all, he may not find out that you are doing it, and second of all, I don't really care. I need to solve this."

———

A large freight elevator door opens on the street level in front of Johnny Colrain's building. Colrain, mounted on his black Honda V4 Magna motorcycle, roars out into the street. He rides past the courthouses, Police Plaza, and the municipal building to get on the FDR Drive at the Brooklyn Bridge entrance. He guns it as he leaves the ramp and shoots up the Drive, past Waterside and the UN, exiting at Sixty-Third Street. It is dusk, and he parks the gleaming black machine in front of the Gordons' double wide town house not far from the East Seventy-Eighth Street houses. He dismounts and opens the gate that leads to the door to the private residence part of the building. He rings the doorbell and waits impatiently, shifting back and forth in his black leathers. The door opens, and Vlasta Marek, the Czech housekeeper, dressed in a gray uniform with a white collar, looks at him. She has plain gray open-toe shoes on. She is a short, slight, nice-looking woman, about sixty years old with chin-length dyed brown hair and bright hazel eyes. When she sees who it is, she lights up, and a big smile appears on her nice face. She steps forward and gives Johnny a big hug.

"Johnny! How are you? We haven't seen you in a long time!"

"Hello, Vlasta. I am fine. You look lovely as usual."

"Oh no ... we'll have none of that, you charmer!" she says, laughing.

Johnny smiles at her. He has visited the Gordon home several times for a party when he modeled. He always liked Vlasta and would end up in the kitchen chatting and joking with her. He asked her about growing up in Czechoslovakia and how she came to America. The family came to the United States during the 1968 Czech revolution, or Prague Spring. She liked to tease him about not having a date, which was usually the case.

"Is Evelyn or Joe home?"

"Come in!"

Johnny enters and waits in the vestibule of the living quarters while Vlasta calls out to Mrs. Gordon. Looking around, he admires again the beautiful antiques and rugs in this part of the house. Evelyn Gordon, a small, lively woman in her mid-fifties comes from the living room. She is very slim. Her face is pleasant but quite wrinkled. She wears her graying hair short. Her reading glasses are perched on her head with chords attached to the frames draping down to the back of her neck. She has on a light pink twinset with navy wool trousers. On her feet are smooth black leather Ferragamo shoes with a leather ribbon and gold buckle. She knows Johnny because the Gordon Agency represented him on those occasions when he did some modeling. The agency wanted him to do it full time, but it was only something he would do when his art was not producing enough money to meet his expenses. Because his paintings have been selling moderately well, he has not modeled for some time. Evelyn smiles at him.

"Hello, Johnny. What brings you here?"

"Hi, Evelyn. I need to talk to you and Joe."

"Let's go into the study."

Colrain follows Evelyn through the foyer, down the hall to a beautiful room with floor-to-ceiling bookcases and a round center pedestal mahogany table on one side of the room with four mahogany chairs around it. There is a small bar in one of the bookcases. One wall is whitewashed brick with a black fireplace surround and a dark wooden mantel. The other walls are a soft butter yellow. There are two overstuffed drab green cotton velvet sofas in front of the fireplace facing each other with a Mies van der Rohe Barcelona coffee table between them. A small wing chair covered in a faded green and white toile is on one side of the coffee table facing the fireplace. The muted Persian rug on the floor is worn in some places.

Joseph Gordon, a tall, handsome, distinguished-looking man with buffalo horn glasses, who is in his fifties but looks ten years younger than his wife, sitting on a sofa, turns his head, sees Johnny, and gets up. He is over six feet tall and has the appearance of a dean at an exclusive prep school. He is wearing a dark gray sleeveless cashmere sweater over a crisply pressed blue shirt, black slacks, argyle socks, and black loafers. Holding a book, he moves toward Johnny and extends his right hand. Johnny shakes it. Joe ushers Johnny to one of the sofas, and he and Evelyn sit on the other facing Johnny. Vlasta brings in a tray of hors d'oeuvres and puts them on the coffee table. Joe pours an aperitif for himself and his wife. Johnny declines a drink. They look at Johnny and wait for Johnny to speak.

"Do you know about Adrienne Wyatt?"

Evelyn lets out a heavy sigh.

"Johnny, her booker could not reach her, and then there it was on the news! It is awful!

Joseph Gordon adds, "We are shocked, of course. Do you know anything about it?"

"No. We were friends, and I shot a job with her in Miami, which you know. I haven't spoken to her since we returned to New York. I am trying to figure out what happened."

Johnny does not volunteer he is helping Ashford, who has already interviewed them. His talk with the Gordons doesn't add much. Adrienne Wyatt was not gregarious within the agency. She did not hang out with other models, with the exception of Renée Toulouse, whom they kicked out of the agency. Joseph Gordon expresses great upset about Adrienne's death. Evelyn suggests that Randy Macquilken has not told everything that he knows. She is pretty sure that Randy dated Adrienne. Colrain asks Evelyn what happened with Renée. She explains that Renée started missing "go-sees" and having an "attitude" at her bookings, which Evelyn assumed was due to doing too much cocaine. She misbehaved on some jobs. They had to let her go. Colrain thanks them and leaves.

As he checks on his bike, he ponders what the Gordons have told him. Something doesn't sit right with him. He can't put his finger on it. Dusk has fallen on the Upper East Side of Manhattan, and the streets are quite busy. People are hurrying home or on their way for drinks or dinner or both as Colrain walks to Third Avenue. Macquilken's is brimming with customers as usual. Because Randy Macquilken was a popular model, his place became a restaurant frequented by models, which in turn attracted sports stars and other personalities. His place is definitely "in" and always seems to be full. Johnny remembers seeing Cary Grant one time and Reggie Jackson another time in the restaurant. Johnny used to go there after a weekly volleyball game with some friends at the gym in the Spence School when one of the players had a daughter who went there. Randy knew all the players because he used to play with the group on occasion. He would let the group have free drinks with their dinners when they showed up after playing. That did not do much for Johnny since he is not much of a drinker.

As Colrain starts to enter, a young college-age woman stationed at the door to keep out the riffraff stops Colrain because of his leathers. Colrain does not let on that he knows the owner of the restaurant but starts kidding with her, charming her. Randy Macquilken notices and comes over. Randy is blond, medium height, and looks like a handsome prep school guy. He has a high-pitched laugh that Johnny finds odd, is very sociable, and is comfortable glad-handing people, which is an asset as a restaurateur. He sticks out his hand and smiles. Johnny grabs it, and they shake.

"Hi, Johnny, long time no see," Randy says as he ushers him away from the door area into the restaurant.

"Hey, Randy. I know. I've been busy trying to get an exhibition going."

"You have to let me know when you have the opening," Randy says as he takes him to a table.

"Actually, the opening is tomorrow night at the Robert Easton Gallery. You need one of my paintings in here. Sit for a minute. I have to talk to you."

Randy gives him a curious look. Johnny never modeled with Randy when he was modeling to support himself and his art. He knows him from the volleyball game. They are friendly but not good friends. They both sit down.

"What is on your mind, Johnny?"

"Adrienne Wyatt."

Randy reacts visibly and then gathers himself.

"What about Adrienne?"

"You dated her, right?" asks Johnny.

"I tried but didn't get very far. She came into the restaurant with her friend, Renée. I was very taken with her and brought over a bottle of champagne to their table. I spent a lot of time with them, and she gave me her number. I went out with her a few times and thought we were getting along pretty well when all of a sudden everything changed."

"What do you mean 'changed'?"

"We had a couple of nice dinners, and I invited her to go with me to East Hampton for the weekend. She said yes, she would love to go, and then she called me and backed out. She seemed very odd. She did not come into the restaurant at all after that. I called and asked her out a few more times, but she declined. She was polite but completely different in manner."

"Randy, did you get angry? See her again and get physical with her?"

"Of course not. I admit I was upset about the sudden change in feelings and a little hurt since I thought something special was starting. I could not understand why she changed so abruptly, but I never saw her again after she bailed out on going to East Hampton with me. That was six months ago. I am sorry to hear that she took her life. Why are you asking about Adrienne?"

"I have a detective friend looking into the circumstances of her death, and he asked me to talk to a few people I knew in the modeling community about her."

"Why?"

"He said it is routine under the circumstances. As far as you know, was she heavy into any drugs?"

"Not as far as I know, Johnny."

A waiter comes to the table and interrupts them. Johnny orders a hanger steak and a Bass Ale. Randy starts to get up.

"Enjoy your meal, Johnny."

"One more thing, Randy. Do you know anyone else she dated either before or after you?"

"I don't, Johnny," he says as he stands.

"Thanks. By the way, have you seen Renée Toulouse recently?"

Randy laughs as he pushes his chair under the table. "She has been in here almost every night for the last several months."

He leaves the table and walks to another table to greet some diners.

At a large table in the center of the restaurant, there is a party of some well-dressed Upper East Side diners drinking and eating. There is some lively conversation going on, but one man in particular has been watching Randy and Colrain talking. Colrain's ale arrives followed by his steak. He starts to eat when a lovely model stops by and says hello on the way to her table. Colrain is smiling and talking to her when Randy comes over and nods toward the bar area.

Renée Toulouse is truly stunning. Very slim, six feet tall, with pale skin, short black hair, and green eyes, she emanates the image of what a fashion model looks like. She is wearing a bright green dress that matches her eyes with an open, short, black embroidered jacket and pointed satin black stilettos. She takes a seat on one of the stools and summons the bartender.

The man at the large table is taking in everything. Colrain continues to eat and observe Renée. She orders a drink. A bar shark—a man in his fifties with a tan, light brown hair, wearing an open white-and-blue-striped shirt, khaki slacks, and Gucci loafers with no socks on—who is sitting at the end of the bar—moves over to the seat next to hers. When the bartender brings her a pale green gin gimlet straight up, he pays for the drink and tries to start a conversation. Renée does not pay much attention to the man but takes a big sip of her drink.

Colrain finishes his meal, summons the waiter, pays, and walks over to the bar and sits on the other side of Renée.

"Hello, Frenchie."

Renée turns and, upon seeing that it is Colrain, exclaims, "Johnee!" and throws her arms around him. He laughs at her and returns the hug. Colrain dated Renée briefly when Colrain started modeling. She really wasn't his type, but he was intrigued by her, and he liked her French style. They had parted as friends. Renée is drunk and starts to cry a little as Colrain looks over her shoulder at the sun-tanned man at the bar, who is staring at them. The man is obviously not happy with this development. Colrain gives him a hard look. Renée lets go and takes another sip of her drink.

"It has been too long, Johnee," she says with a sad smile.

"I know, Frenchie. It has. I need to talk to you," he replies.

Renée gives him a suspicious look but then shrugs, throws her arms around him again, and gives him a very hard hug. She lets go and gives him a nod. Johnny then helps Renée off the barstool and takes her out of the restaurant holding her waist.

The man watching from the large table gets up and goes to the pay phone. He gets his party.

"We may have a problem," he says.

"What?"

"I am in Macquilken's. A man who obviously is a male model was just talking with Randy, and he is now taking Renée out of the restaurant."

"See if you can find out his name."

Outside, Colrain has to help Renée walk properly. She is unsteady and leaning into him. It is comical to see him trying to escort her across the avenue and up the street to his bike. She is making a spectacle of herself. People on the street watch with amusement as only New Yorkers can. Colrain is a little embarrassed. Finally, with considerable effort, he reaches the bike and now has to get her on it. He pulls her skirt up so he can get her legs over the seat. She is sitting but wobbly. He quickly gets on before she falls. As soon as he is seated, she puts her arms around him and lays her head on his back. He starts the bike up and drives slowly as she holds on to him with her high heels on the passenger foot pegs. Colrain arrives at her apartment building and with less difficulty takes her off the bike and into the building. He does not notice the man in the car on the opposite side of the street watching them.

Once inside Renée's apartment, Colrain sits her down in the kitchen and makes some coffee. She is crying and sniffling. He manages to force her to drink some coffee and starts to question her. She is very upset and starts sobbing. Colrain coaxes and cajoles her into talking about Adrienne.

"Renée … it's me, Johnny. Talk to me! Do you know what happened to Adrienne?"

"No. I can't, Johnee! It's no good … no good!"

"I know Randy dated Adrienne. Can you at least tell me what happened to that?"

"I can't say, Johnee! Please! Don't ask me!"

Colrain shifts gears and tries asking about the marks on Adrienne's body.

"She had marks on her body, Renée. Was she into 'the rough trade'?"

This starts Renée crying again. Colrain pushes on.

"Was that her thing? She liked S and M?"

This makes Renée cry even harder. He gets her to drink more coffee and then takes her hand. He looks into her face and asks, "She did not commit suicide, Renée. Do you have any idea who could have killed her?"

Renée shakes her head. She is crying hard. She jumps when the phone rings.

Renée gets up and answers it. Johnny watches her freeze.

"I know someone is there with you, Renée. Remember what I told you. Don't say anything."

"I understand."

"Understand this. I am not kidding. You won't be pretty anymore, or worse, if you do." Dugan hangs up.

Renée walks back to the table. It is not hard to see how upset and afraid she is. Colrain tries to comfort her without success.

"Puleeze, Johnee! You have to leave. I don't know anything."

"You were her best friend, Renée. She must have talked about what was going on with her."

"Johnee, she didn't! I don't know anything other than she stopped seeing Randy, but I don't even know why. That is all! Please go. I want to be alone."

Colrain knows she is lying and gives her a funny look, but he gets up to leave. He looks back at her sitting with her head in her hands. She is obviously in distress. He wonders what is going on with her. He is sure that she knows something about what happened to Adrienne but is afraid to say anything about it. After he closes the door behind him, he can hear her sobbing.

———

Priscilla is sitting at Robespierre's with Simon Stone, a personal injury lawyer she met at the gallery. Simon is in his forties. He is divorced, a sharp dresser, and a smooth talker. He is five feet, ten inches tall, slender with brown hair. He has a narrow visage. Last week he went in the Robert Easton Gallery to kill some time before a deposition. He looked around and asked Priscilla about some of the paintings and chatted with her as they walked around the gallery looking at the art. Robert was busy talking on the phone. Priscilla found Simon interesting but a little slick. He asked her to dinner, and she decided to accept. He certainly had the gift of gab and could talk about a lot of subjects. She asked him if he really liked art. He said he did but did not know much about it. He just knows the art he likes, and then he purchases it if he can afford it and it fits with the décor of his apartment. Simon lives in a prewar building between Fifth Avenue and Madison on Eighty-Seventh Street.

———————

Dugan hangs up his phone. He rubs the gray stubble on his jowly pockmarked face with his chubby hand and fingers. He is sitting on his couch in his cheaply furnished apartment in Washington Heights. He looks as ratty as his furniture, dressed in a sleeveless undershirt and grubby long boxer shorts under his gut with the stub of a fat cigar in his mouth. He holds an open beer can in his hand, and there are several crushed empties on the cluttered coffee table. He is thinking. He doesn't like recent developments. His phone rings again, and he picks it up.

"Well?"

A voice replies, "I asked Randy. His name is Colrain. Johnny Colrain."

"Yeah, I know him."

Dugan thinks to himself, *Ashford must have asked for Colrain's help because Colrain did some modeling. That nigger and him are buddies.*

The voice interrupts his thoughts.

"Who is he?"

"An artist and part-time model who is a large pain in my butt. He took her home. I have Donnelly watching her building."

"Do you think she told him anything?"

"No way. She's scared shitless. I called while he was there and warned her.

He left right after I hung up. He couldn't have been with her more than ten minutes."

"We can't take any chances."

"I agree."

5

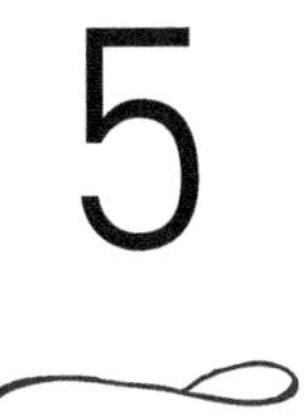

COLRAIN RIDES SLOWLY through Greenwich Village. When he turns west on Christopher Street, he doesn't realize that Donnelly, Dugan's man, who also has managed to capture that quality known as sleaziness, is following him in a black unmarked squad car. As he rides, Colrain takes in the leather boys, punkers, and other diverse denizens of the West Village. He approaches the Westside Highway and sees the crowd of men clustered in front of the S-and-M bars located there. Several of the men dressed in exotic leather gear notice him as he goes by, and then he guns the powerful bike through the light as he heads south toward Robespierre's.

––––––––––

Johnny enters the rustic restaurant and goes to an empty corner of the bar. Robespierre, working behind the bar, leaves the two customers he is talking to, draws a Bass Ale in a pint glass, sets it in front of Colrain, looks into his face, and waits. These two know each other well. Colrain takes a long hard swallow of the ale. He sighs and begins to tell Robespierre what he has learned about the case, which isn't much. He believes that the marks on Adrienne's body came from a kinky scene, which is probably a link to the murderer, but that is just a guess. He is not sure what his next move should be to help Ashford. He also has to get a painting to the gallery for his opening. Colrain smiles at Robespierre.

"You're pretty kinky, Robby. Any ideas?"

Robespierre laughs, exposing his gold bridgework.

"Let's take a ride and talk to a friend of mine. She might be able to help."

Colrain raises his eyebrow.

"Okay, let me go take a pee and finish this Bass."

He swings his body to the right off his barstool, takes a step, and runs into a woman returning to her table from the restroom who is passing by at the same moment. The woman starts to go to the ground as Colrain grabs both upper arms and helps her stand back up. He looks into her face, and it makes him pause for a second before apologizing to her. He sees her face full of freckles and likes it. *She is very cute*, he thinks.

"I'm so sorry. Are you okay?"

"Of course, I'm fine. It is not a problem."

She smiles at him.

"Nice leathers," she says, smiling more.

"Can I buy you a drink to make up for this?" Johnny asks, smiling broadly back.

Robespierre is watching with amusement.

"No thank you, really. I have to get back to my table."

Johnny looks out into the dining area and sees a man sitting by himself with two glasses and plates on the table.

"Now, I am sorry about that too," he says.

The woman doesn't say anything but holds his eyes a little longer than normal before turning and walking toward her table. Johnny looks at her as she leaves, noticing her strawberry-blond hair and brisk walk. He turns to Robespierre who laughs at Colrain.

"What was that, Johnny?" he says.

"I don't know. She's got something for sure," Colrain says with a grin.

Robespierre calls one of his employees over to the bar and asks him to cover for him as he takes off his apron. Colrain heads for the bathroom.

Colrain and Robespierre leave the restaurant. They climb onto Colrain's bike and head uptown. Donnelly follows them discretely. Robespierre directs Colrain to a unique little house in an enclosed courtyard in Murray Hill. Most New Yorkers don't know these little houses on a private street even exist. Robby rings the doorbell three times in quick succession. They hear footsteps, and a butler opens the door.

"*Bon soir, Monsieur Robespierre. Comment allez-vouz?*" he asks.

"*Tres bien, Yves. Et vouz?*"

"*Bien. Merci.*"

Johnny looks at Robespierre with surprise tinged with some mild disapproval. He figures that this is some kind of high-class cathouse. Robespierre gives him a sheepish grin and then asks for the lady of the house. Yves leads them into a beautiful sitting room furnished entirely with Louis XIV pieces and Aubusson rugs. The butler leaves, and Colrain examines the period art hanging in the room. He starts to tell Robespierre that the paintings are probably originals when a slim black woman with smooth café au lait colored skin, about five foot four, fifty-two years old, enters and greets Robespierre with a

Jamaican accent and a beautiful smile revealing gorgeous white teeth. She is wearing a softly flowing colorful silk tunic over black slubbed silk pants and gold slippers.

"*Monsieur Robespierre, comment vas-tu? Ça fait trop longtemps!*"

Robespierre smiles and replies, "*Bien, Miss Buttercup. Et tu?*"

"*Bien, aussi.*"

He turns to Johnny and says, "*Ceci est mon ami, Johnny Colrain.*"

Buttercup extends her hand and looks into Colrain's face. She directs her remark to Robespierre as she speaks, still looking at Colrain.

"*Il est beau.*"

Colrain understands but keeps his gaze on Buttercup. She switches to English and addresses him.

"It is a pleasure to meet you, Johnny. I have heard a lot about you."

Johnny looks at Robespierre with a quizzical look. He replies, "I hope it was favorable."

"Indeed. What brings you here?"

Robespierre chimes in, "I suggested that we come to see you. John is trying to get some important information for Detective Ashford."

"Ah ... Detective Ashford ... yes. Why would I want to help him?"

Robespierre explains to Johnny that Miss Buttercup Pierce runs the most high-class escort operation in the country. When government officials want beautiful escorts for foreign dignitaries, they call her. Because of her connections and the discreet service she provides, the police do not bother her, but she knows that Ashford does not like it.

Colrain speaks. "Ash is a friend of mine, and he is looking into the death of a model who was also a friend of mine. He asked me to make some inquiries because I modeled for a little while."

Buttercup looks at Johnny and assesses him carefully. There is a pause and then, "I believe you, Mr. Colrain. How can I help you?"

"My friend was thrown out of a window. Her autopsy revealed she was already dead, but based on her injuries I think she may have been involved in some kind of sadomasochistic scene. She was dating in wealthy circles. I was hoping that you might be able to tell me if any of your clients have sadistic tastes."

Buttercup looks at Robespierre, then Colrain and smiles.

"I am sorry about your friend. You have to understand that I cannot violate the confidence of my clients."

Johnny frowns.

"Can you tell me if you know anyone who has dated Adrienne Wyatt?"

"No. I don't," Miss Buttercup answers, looking straight into Colrain's dark blue eyes.

Colrain shoots Robespierre a look as if to say, *This is pointless.*

"Thank you, Miss Buttercup," he says to her.

"Before you go, I would like to show you something," she says and gestures to them. She leads them to another part of the house. It obviously is her special quarters. In a large living room furnished with modern pieces, there is a huge colorful painting. Buttercup looks at Colrain, who is astonished. Robespierre is dumbfounded.

"It's one of my favorites," she says.

"I wondered where that ended up," Johnny replies, smiling as he looks at the painting. He adds, "It looks good there."

Miss Buttercup, enjoying his surprise with a sparkle in her eyes, smiles and says, "I agree. I'd like to help. May I offer you a proposal?"

"Shoot," Johnny says with a quizzical look.

"If you have a suspect whom you think I might know, and you want to know if he or she has sadistic tastes, call me and give me the name. I will tell you yes or no or I don't know. I can't volunteer any names, but I can do that much."

"That would be a help," Johnny replies.

"Of course, I want something from you in exchange."

Colrain and Buttercup are looking at each other very intensely, and the communication is profound as they are sizing each other up. This does not escape Robespierre's notice, and he is quite amazed about what is happening.

"Of course," Colrain says.

"I would like you to allow me to purchase my choice of any painting at your next show for one half its listed price. Agreed?"

Johnny pauses, looking at her. A smile breaks out on his face.

"Agreed." Colrain sticks out his hand, and she shakes it. She asks him to wait a minute and goes to a small desk in the corner of the room. She comes back and hands him a card.

"This is my very private number. It is the number you should use to call me. Please do not share it with anyone." He nods his head.

Buttercup rings for Yves, the butler, who appears almost instantly, and she asks him to show the two men out.

"Gentlemen," she says, and they are led to the front door.

When they get outside, Colrain turns to Robespierre.

"Whew! Some friend you got there. I can see how she got that house."

"Yes," Robespierre replies, fascinated by what has just occurred.

"I am tempted to ask how you know her, but I'd better not. Let's get out of here."

They climb onto the bike and ride off.

———

As he holds on to the bike and Johnny, while Colrain drives across town on Twenty-Third Street, Robespierre thinks about Miss Buttercup.

Oh yes, that is a story that you don't need to know, John Colrain. It isn't a pretty one, he muses.

Buttercup Pierce was fifteen years old when her mother, fleeing an abusive husband who dealt ganja in Jamaica, came with her daughter to New York. Her mother got a job as a Merrill machine operator in the garment district. She and Buttercup lived in Brooklyn. Buttercup's mother worked long hours, and her daughter was a latchkey kid. One day a pimp lured Buttercup to his apartment and raped her. She fought hard and managed to scratch his face badly. He hit her and gave her two bad black eyes. She had no choice but to tell her mother, who was afraid to report the rape to the police in case she might lose her daughter. She moved the family to Mineola, Long Island.

Her mother became the housekeeper to a wealthy family. The family used to summer on Montauk. They would take Buttercup's mother and Buttercup with them. The family rented two cottages at Gurney's Inn. Several years went by. One summer, a lifeguard working at the inn became friendly with Buttercup. He was white, and she was leery at first, but he taught her to swim. She thought he was very handsome. He was in college and took her into town for ice cream sodas. They would take long walks on the beach and talk. They liked each other, and when the summer was over, he went back to Cornell. They wrote each other and spoke on the phone. She finally agreed to go to a football game at his school. She attended the City College of New York, and they became a couple. He was the first man from his family to go to college. His father was a cop in Brooklyn. When she met his father, she told him she had some information about crimes taking place in Brooklyn. She rode with him one night and pointed out the pimp who had assaulted her. The cops staked out the area and then arrested him.

Her boyfriend graduated and went into the Navy. He was shipped to Vietnam, commanded a patrol craft on the Mekong River, and never returned. This was very hard for her. She loved him and knew he loved her. During their time together she got to know many of his upper-class friends and observed that society.

Buttercup got a job as the administrative assistant to the head of research at a Madison Avenue advertising agency, eventually becoming the executive assistant to the president but did not find it very rewarding. Aware of the pressure of entertaining big clients when they came to town, she also realized that some of the girls she worked with would go out with wealthy older men because they liked the perks. She got the idea of forming an escort service. Slowly she built up a stable of girls and kept strict rules. No drugs or serious drinking, only educated women, and proper attire was required. Buttercup shared the profits with her girls and had a good reputation. Her business was spread by word of mouth. Because of her connections and her spotless record, not only was she called by the rich and powerful to provide escorts for special people who came into town, but also the police left her alone.

Before Robespierre had his restaurant, when he was bartending, he did a lot of running around after hours. One night he was drinking at a club with a young model who pointed Miss Buttercup out to him. He noted how striking she was with very smooth light brown skin and a face with small features. She was impeccably dressed. He thought she was extremely attractive and classy but somehow dangerous. She had a high forehead, and he thought she looked like some kind of Ethiopian princess. She was sitting at a table with a small, older pleasant-looking white man with white hair. They were talking and smiling a lot. Robespierre's model friend told him that the man was the editor of a fashion magazine, was French, and that

Buttercup was his girlfriend. He ran into them at several parties, and he became friendly with the editor, André, and Buttercup. They seemed to have a nice relationship. André introduced him to one particular Danish model he was interested in. That introduction did not amount to anything, but he remained friends with them.

André had a family in Paris and was wealthy. He bought Buttercup an apartment on Mercer Street where he would stay when he was in New York, which was often. Because of Buttercup's relationship with her French boyfriend, she met a lot of attractive women. When André died, he left Buttercup a sizable sum. Real estate prices began to plummet because of an oil crisis. Buttercup sold her apartment when she still could get a decent price, waited as prices went down, and then bought her house. Carefully, she developed her exclusive high-end escort service. Her girls were merely to escort the exclusive clientele. Despite the discretion Buttercup insisted on, relationships did develop on occasion. There was very little about her clientele that she did not know.

6

JOHNNY DROPS OFF ROBBY and makes for his loft. He opens the door, is greeted by his big polar bear of a dog, and grabs the leash. After a walk down the block with Johnny trying to piece together all that has happened, they go up the stairs to the loft. Colrain walks to the bedroom area, strips, jumps into the shower, finishes his toilet, and soon is in bed. He tries to read but falls asleep. There is some loud snoring going on. It's the dog. The wind is rattling the old windows of the loft, but there is another sound. The lock on the door is being picked. The door opens slowly. An intruder dressed in dark clothes enters gingerly, pocketing his lock pickers. There is some light in the loft from one small pharmacy lamp that sits by a large overstuffed beat-up chair in a corner. There is also some light from the streetlights coming in through the sides of the shades on the three windows facing the street. The man takes out a lead-weighted sap weapon wrapped with black electrical tape from the pocket of his coat and moves toward the sleeping area. He pauses, pulling out his gun when he sees the heavy bag but realizes what it is in time. He puts the gun away. He tries to get his bearings and continues moving toward the snoring.

All of a sudden, Baloo is up and barking. Colrain awakens and jumps out of bed shouting. Donnelly pulls his gun out again and starts firing. Colrain hits the floor. Baloo springs forward but catches a bullet and goes down with a cry. He manages to get up and struggles forward. Colrain reaches next to his bed for the ax handle that he keeps there in case of a break-in, throws it at the figure, and continues to shout. It strikes the intruder somewhere, and he cries out. He turns back, pulls open the metal door hard, and it bangs against the wall as he flees down the stairs. Colrain goes to his dog and looks at the wound on the side of his thick neck. He hears the screech of a car pulling away. The big dog whimpers as Colrain examines the wound and comforts the animal. He runs to the bathroom and comes back with peroxide and a roll of gauze. He pours the peroxide on the wound causing it to foam up over Baloo's thick coat. He dries it with a towel and wraps the gauze around the dog's neck. He manages to slow the bleeding. He gets dressed quickly to take the dog to the animal hospital emergency room. Johnny thinks of picking Baloo up to carry him, but luckily the dog can still walk. He manages to convince an early-morning cab driver to take them to the animal hospital.

The veterinarian examining Baloo shakes his head and speaks to Johnny who is watching him examine the wound.

"The bullet passed through the skin and some of the fat layer that Pyrenees have to protect their neck and tissue but did not hit any bone or vessels. He is a lucky guy. He should be fine once this heals."

Johnny is very relieved.

"Thanks, Doc. Does he get pain medication?"

"I don't think so. We will image him to see if there are any fragments or other damage that I could not detect. I think it best if we keep him here for a day to make sure he is okay."

Johnny leans down and looks into the big white dog's face, putting his hand carefully on his head. The dog looks back at him with his large dark eyes. He then gives Baloo a few gentle pats on the top of his flat head and says, "See you tomorrow, big guy." The dog on his side wags his tail, which thumps the stainless steel exam table.

Johnny thanks the vet and the person at the desk. He leaves the building and hails a cab. When he gets home, he gets back in bed. After several fits of thinking and sleep, the phone rings.

"John?"

"Ash?"

"I am sorry to call so early, but we have a bad development."

"What is it?"

"Renée Toulouse was killed last night. Throat cut. She must have put up a hell of a struggle. Your fingerprints have been identified, and her address book is missing. Dugan has an APB out on you. He's probably on his way to your place now."

"Someone broke in here last night. Whoever it was fired a gun and hit Baloo. I took him to the emergency vet, and the wound is superficial, so that's good, but he's spending the day there just to be safe."

"What?"

"Never mind that for now. Look, Ash, I took Renée home from Macquilken's. I tried to question her, but she got a phone call, and it scared her to death. I got nowhere. She did not have to be killed."

"Whoever it is, they are on to you. Maybe you should stop helping me."

"I can't do that. Now this is personal. I am in this, and I have some ideas. Talk to you soon."

Johnny looks around the sleeping area of his loft. He gets out of bed and puts on a pair of old pajama pants to join the old soft T-shirt he was sleeping in. After his visit to the bathroom, he heads to the area of the loft that he works out in. He looks at the colorful Turkish Azeri on the floor, the heavy bag hanging from a chain, the speed bag, also the chin-up bar, and decides on what workout he will do. He grabs two pillows on an old love seat next to the wall, lies down on the rug facing the TV screen with the pillows under his head, and starts exercising while watching the news. He finishes that calisthenic routine, lifts the dumbbells, hits the heavy bag extra hard, and thinks about Baloo, who would normally be right there watching him. He can't believe his dog was shot.

Johnny makes breakfast, his mind going over everything that has happened. He needs some help and has an idea. He showers and gets dressed. He then carefully wraps the painting he has just finished, puts a handle on it for carrying, and summons the elevator. He steps out in the bright sunlight carrying his large painting. There are no clouds, and the sky is a bright blue. It is a cool, almost crisp day in the Big Apple. He is dressed in his beat-up leather flight jacket, a plaid shirt, jeans, and sneakers. He walks up Walker Street to Spring Street. He enters the loft building near Broadway, takes the big elevator to the third floor, and walks into the Robert Easton Gallery. Robert Easton, the big robust man, spots him.

"It's about time! Where have you been? The show will open tonight."

"Sorry, Robert. Something came up."

"Is this the one you want to add?" Robert asks.

Johnny hands him the painting.

"It is."

"Well, we like the paintings and have left room for this one. Take a look how we placed them."

"Who is we?" Johnny asks, smiling.

At that moment a woman comes out of the back area carrying a painting. Johnny stares at her and then smiles at Priscilla Gans.

"Hey, I know you!"

"Hello there. You aren't going to knock into me, are you? I am carrying a valuable piece of art!"

Robert looks at the two of them and raises an eyebrow. Johnny has a big grin on his face and goes over to help Priscilla with the painting, which is one of his. Robert watches them with curiosity.

"Let me help you. Where do you want it?" Johnny says.

Priscilla points to a space on the far wall. Johnny takes it over to the wall, and they hang the painting. Robert goes in the back to his office where he unwraps the painting Johnny brought. He brings it out to Johnny and Priscilla to hang near the one that they just put up. They add the new addition, and the three of them look at the two paintings.

"This should be a good opening, Johnny!" Robert says.

Priscilla looks at Johnny with surprise.

"These are your works?" Priscilla says.

Johnny nods.

"I like them!"

"I'm glad," he replies with a big grin.

Robert goes back into the office and then comes out carrying a pot of coffee and three cups on a tray, which he places on a counter in the main space. Priscilla goes to get some half-and-half. As they stand drinking their coffees, a discussion ensues about Priscilla and how she came to work at the gallery. Robert puts down his empty cup and says, "Okay, you two. Priscilla, there is still plenty we have to do here to be ready."

Johnny fakes a scowl and finishes his coffee.

"I can take a hint. Thanks for the coffee. I will see you both tonight."

He waves goodbye and heads for the door. As he opens it, he looks back at the two of them. He smiles to himself. There is something refreshing about Priscilla that is very appealing to him. It is a rare feeling.

Johnny hustles down the stairs rather than wait for the elevator and makes for the subway. He takes the local 6 uptown Lexington Avenue train at Spring and gets out at the Sixty-Eighth Street stop and walks briskly up to Seventy-Second Street. He then goes over to Park Avenue and enters a beautiful old prewar building on the northeast corner of Park Avenue and Seventy-Second Street. The two doormen on duty greet him. They have seen him before but cannot understand his connection with Emilia Rusk, a socialite who lives in the building. One announces him, and the other takes him up to her gorgeous apartment.

Nina, a young, plump, blond British au pair opens the door.

"Hello, Johnny! How are you?"

"Fine, Nina. How is it going with you? Are the kids giving you trouble? Do I have to talk to them?"

Nina laughs.

"Oh no, Mr. Colrain. They are under control. But we have not seen you for a while, and they will be glad you're here when they get home from school."

"Well, I have been busy and won't have much time today, but we will have to take an excursion to the park soon!"

A thin attractive woman in her mid-forties, dressed in a neat ironed patterned shirt, black slacks, and black ballet flats, walks to the doorway and speaks.

"Who is going on an excursion with Nina and my kids?"

Johnny sees her and replies, "I am, Em, but don't worry. You can come."

Emilia smiles, walks up, and embraces him warmly.

"Hi, Johnny. To what do I owe this unexpected visit? I have a feeling it is not about an excursion to Central Park to throw a football around."

Johnny laughs. "There is a reason you have everyone figured out in this town." She leads him into the living room furnished with large overstuffed furniture.

Emilia Rusk is a wealthy divorcée who has known Johnny for about ten years. She met him at his first show, and they became friendly. She is very well connected and has had lots of boyfriends since her divorce—some of them well known in society circles or show business. She and Johnny had a brief fling during which he became friends with her children. He would take them to Central Park and throw a football around, and usually they would all have a picnic. Emilia became someone whom he could talk to about women and his art. He went through a period when he would stop by her house now and then just to hang out and chat. She asks Nina to make coffee and bring out some of her homemade cookies.

Johnny gets right to the point after Nina leaves the coffee and cookies, and they are alone. He tells her about Adrienne Wyatt. Emilia is shocked by what Johnny tells her, but interested.

"And you are telling me about this why?"

"Because you know a lot of important, well-to-do men, Em—the kind of men that Adrienne would date. I am trying to find out who she was seeing, probably secretly."

"Johnny, I know who she is, but that is it. I have no clue who she might have been seeing. There was a rumor that ex-mayor Burke Lambert had been seeing a gorgeous model on the sly. No one I know ever told me who it was. I am not sure you want me asking around after what has happened."

"Do you know if Lambert has any kinky tendencies?"

"Whoa, Johnny! I get gossip here and there, but I don't know the proclivities of everyone. I have heard he likes to have orgies with a few friends and beautiful girls, preferably models."

"You went out with him for a while, didn't you?" Johnny asks.

"The kinkiest thing we did was go swimming late at night in the pool of the Hotel des Artistes. Sorry, Johnny, but I don't know anyone who would be into hurting women."

"Thanks for talking to me about it," Johnny says with a little smile. He finishes his coffee, gets up, and grabs two of her homemade chocolate chip cookies from the plate on the table. Emilia stands and walks with him to the door.

"It's good to see you, Johnny. Don't be such a stranger."

"It has been a while. I have been busy trying to get everything ready for my show. Are you coming?"

Emilia smiles at him. "Wouldn't miss it."

They share a hug and say goodbye. Colrain, lost in thought, buzzes for the elevator.

Colrain steps out from the canopy of the building onto the sidewalk and adjusts his eyes to the bright sunlight. He walks down to Sixty-Seventh Street, munching on a cookie and takes the crosstown bus to Central Park West. Johnny approaches the doorman standing in front of the Hotel des Artistes and attempts to bribe him into giving up some information about Burke Lambert as smoothly as he can, but he gets nowhere. When he tries to offer the doorman some cash, the doorman is offended and asks him to leave. The doorman watches him walk away and then goes into the building to make a call.

———

A phone is ringing inside a desk. A well-manicured hand opens the drawer, extracts the phone, and brings it to a distinguished face. The man listens, thanks the caller, hangs up, and places a call.

"Can you talk?"

"Yes," responds Dugan.

"Colrain has been snooping around my apartment building."

"Did he get any information?"

"No. I take good care of the doormen."

"I wouldn't worry about it. Donnelly missed him last night, but I've got an APB out on him now for Renée's death. We'll get him, one way or another."

"The sooner the better. I want this mess ended."

"Don't worry."

"Worry is not what I do, Dugan. Do you understand?"

"Yes." Dugan sighs and hangs up the phone. He curses.

7

A DIFFERENT PHONE RINGS behind a bar. A slim brown hand picks it up. Robespierre listens and breaks into a grin. He speaks to one of his employees and then moves rapidly to his private quarters upstairs.

Colrain comes out of the subway in Tribeca. He walks carefully down the street and sees a dark gray sedan with a man in it parked across the street from the entrance to his building. He quickly enters a loft building located several buildings away from his on the same side of the street. He rings a buzzer and identifies himself. He is buzzed in and takes the elevator to the penthouse. He steps out into a fabulous loft beautifully furnished with antiques, wall hangings, and large Chinese rugs. Duncan Nagle, a bearded, portly man in his fifties who looks like Sebastian Cabot, greets him warmly.

Colrain explains his situation. Duncan reprimands him for getting involved in such things and not concentrating on his art. Duncan asks his friend if he would like coffee or something to eat, but Colrain declines, explaining he is in a bit of a hurry. They walk through a work area with various sculpture pieces of Nagle's to a stairway that leads to the gardened roof. Colrain thanks his friend and takes off across the roofs to his building. He opens the door to the stairs with his key and hustles down to his loft.

———

Priscilla Gans looks around the gallery and approves the installation. She says goodbye to Robert, who looks pleased with the show he has mounted with her.

"See you later, Priscilla. Come back a little early so we can set up the bar for the opening, okay?"

"I will. I am excited about this show."

"Me too. See you later," Robert agrees.

Priscilla grabs her bag and leaves.

———

It is late afternoon and quiet in front of Colrain's building. The gray unmarked car is still across the street. The freight elevator door opens, and Colrain roars out on his motorcycle. The light of the cycle hits the windows of the gray car, and then Johnny turns up the street as he guns the bike. The surveillance vehicle is started and begins to pursue him, but it is too slow. Johnny makes a few turns and loses the car. He stops at the little triangle at Christopher Street and Seventh Avenue. He waits near the exit from the uptown side of the Seventh Avenue IRT subway. Robespierre emerges looking very classy, dressed in a charcoal three-piece wool pin-striped suit, white dress shirt, and patterned maroon tie, matching handkerchief in his breast pocket, and natty, polished black wing-tipped shoes. He spots Colrain and flashes his magical grin. Colrain smiles back, amazed at his friend's appearance. Robespierre sticks out his hand, Colrain slaps it, and Robespierre climbs on the back of the motorcycle. Colrain heads uptown. When he gets to Columbus Circle, he shoots up Central Park West. Colrain lets Robespierre off after turning at Sixty-Sixth Street.

Robespierre approaches the black doorman of the Hotel des Artistes at Sixty-Seventh Street. He strikes up a conversation with him. Posing as a diplomat from Haiti, he explains that he is considering buying an apartment in the building, but he wants the apartment for a little fun away from his wife so he must be careful. He confides that he is worried that the building's personnel might not be sufficiently discrete.

"I cannot afford any bad gossip at all. My wife is related to the Duvalier family. You understand?" The doorman nods.

"I understand completely. You would not have any problem here. The personnel treat the residents' business as confidential."

Robespierre takes out his wallet and extracts some bills to give to the doorman, and while he has the wallet out, he asks the doorman if he would like to see a picture of his girlfriend. He proudly shows a photo of Adrienne cut from a magazine while praising her attributes. The doorman can't hide his shocked reaction. Robespierre notices.

"What is wrong?" he asks the doorman.

"Sir, the woman in that picture is dead, and the police are investigating her death. It has been in all the papers."

Robespierre becomes very agitated and explains that he has only been away one week.

"I have not been able to get her on the phone, but I assumed she was away on location, working. You must be mistaken."

The doorman shakes his head. "I am sorry, sir."

Robespierre becomes even more agitated and asks, "How can you be so sure?"

The doorman insists, "Because I know her from the building. She has come into the building on occasion with a resident."

Upon hearing this, Robespierre goes into high gear. Totally distraught, he begins to wail, "I don't believe it! Who? Who? I pay you!" He keeps going and is waving his money around, creating a scene.

"Sir, you have to quiet down and leave."

"I will leave if you tell me who. Who is the resident you say she comes into the building with?" Robespierre responds.

"I can't do that for exactly the same reason that you were asking me about earlier. I have to be discrete about such information."

Robespierre looks at him and quiets down, shaking his head.

"Okay, okay. I understand." He turns and starts to walk away. Suddenly he turns back and says excitedly, "Wait a minute! Burke lives here, doesn't he?"

The doorman is suspicious. "Who, sir?"

"Burke Lambert. Mayor Lambert!"

"Yes."

Robespierre makes a face. "Yes. I know they are good friends. She visited Burke, right?"

The doorman, concerned about this man and wanting to get rid of him, just nods. Robespierre keeps talking.

"Does he know?"

"Sir, the whole city knows. The six o'clock news covered her funeral."

Robespierre mutters, "Funeral ... It is true. She's really dead. I can't believe it."

Robespierre walks off, continuing to mutter to himself. He goes around the corner, smiles, and picks up his jaunty walk as he makes for Colrain waiting on his cycle. He is obviously proud of his performance. He quickly tells Colrain about what he has learned and sticks out his hand, and Colrain laughs as he slaps it. Robespierre loosens his tie and jumps on Colrain's cycle. They buzz up to Ruelle's on Columbus Avenue and go in.

Robespierre goes to the bar, and Colrain heads for the phone. He calls Miss Buttercup and asks her if she knows if Lambert has domineering sadistic tastes. She says yes. Colrain thanks her. Before he can hang up, she volunteers that Lambert has a certain male friend who shares that predilection. Colrain asks her who it is, but she reminds him of their deal, stating that she has already told him more than she should have.

Colrain sticks in another coin and calls Ashford at the station. Dugan is at his desk not far away. He pretends to be busy with some paperwork but watches Ashford. He clicks on to Ashford's line and listens as Colrain tells Ashford that Lambert had been seeing Adrienne on the sly before her death, and he suspects that they were into some kinky behavior that explains the marks on her body. Ashford tells him to keep in touch. Dugan hangs up after Ashford.

Colrain goes to the bar to find Robespierre, the charmer, talking to several attractive women. He is telling them a terrific story about Antigua. Johnny can't help but be amused as he watches Robespierre weave his spell.

8

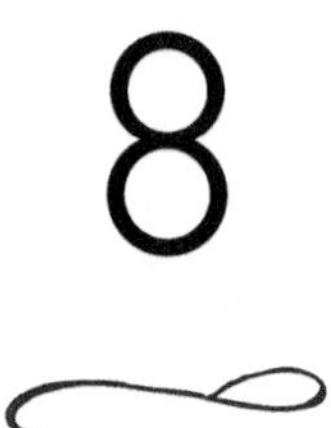

PRISCILLA COCKS HER HEAD to the left and looks at herself in the mirror. She is in her bra and panties holding a black dress up to her body. It is a simple sleeveless wool crepe sheath. She frowns. She calls out to Leighann, one of her roommates, who walks into Priscilla's bedroom.

"What do you think, Leigh?"

"It looks nice. You need the right necklace with it or, better yet, a string of pearls," she tells Priscilla.

"Ha ha! I don't have any pearls."

"I do. Put on the dress, and I will be right back!"

Leighann scoots out of the room. Priscilla slips on the dress, and she steps into plain black suede three-inch heels. Leighann returns with a red box. She helps Priscilla zip up the back of the dress and stands back to look at her friend, who looks lovely. She then opens the box revealing her string of lustrous Mikimoto pearls. She steps behind Priscilla and clasps them around her neck. The pearls fall three inches below the top of the dress.

"There! They look great!"

"They do, Leigh, but I can't wear these," Priscilla exclaims to her friend.

"Why not?"

"What if something happens to them?"

"Like what? You don't expect that lawyer Simon guy to grab them, do you?"

"Of course not, but I sort of feel funny borrowing them. They are so beautiful."

"That is why you should wear them, Priscilla," Leighann insists.

"Thanks, Leigh."

"Happy to help. Now put on your face and get going. Don't you have to be at the gallery before people start showing up?"

"Oh, damn, it is getting late," Priscilla says as she looks at her watch.

"Leigh, you are coming later, right?"

Leighann looks approvingly at her roommate.

"I'll be there. Now skedaddle!"

———

Priscilla enters the Robert Easton Gallery and immediately starts helping Robert set up the tables for the wine and hors d'oeuvres. Two caterers come in carrying garment bags and go into the back-office area to get dressed in their white coats. People begin to arrive and walk through the gallery looking at the paintings. Simon Stone walks in and goes immediately to say hello to Priscilla. He is wearing an impeccably tailored dark Italian blue suit, white shirt, bright blue solid tie with matching handkerchief in the pocket of his jacket, and highly polished black loafers.

"Hi, Priscilla."

"Hello there. You are early."

"Yes. I wanted to stop by now and make sure that we are on for dinner later. I can't stay. I have to go to a meeting at my club."

"Oh, I see." Something troubles her about this man, but she does not know what it is exactly. She smiles at him.

"I will come back later to pick you up, okay?"

"Sure," she replies. "See you later."

Simon Stone leaves, and she looks after him. Robert looks at her with a quizzical expression. She notices.

"Is this a new beau?" Robert asks.

"Not a beau. Just had dinner with him once," she says, embarrassed.

"Oh, okay. We better get this setup finished," Robert replies as he puts down a few more glasses and then leaves to make sure about the food that has arrived.

Burke Lambert is a tall, lanky, handsome man in his fifties. He is about six feet two, has thick salt-and-pepper hair that has decided to gray early, and a big smile that has served him well over the years in politics and his personal life. Women and men find him attractive and charming. He is sitting with his wife and the Gordons in the orchestra section at Lincoln Center watching *Swan Lake* and is wearing a tuxedo. At intermission they all go to the lobby with the crowd. Some of the patrons are dressed formally, and other younger patrons are dressed in casual clothes, even in jeans. As the crowd moves about talking and heading for the champagne that is served at a bar on one of the landings, Dugan is standing midway on the wide stairs leading to the Grand Tier looking for Lambert. He keeps his distance as the crowd swarms about but manages to make eye contact with him.

The two couples return to their seats. A few minutes after the ballet resumes, Lambert excuses himself. He leaves his seat and proceeds to the lobby and then the Grand Tier where Dugan had been. He sees Dugan waiting near an exit door that leads to an interior stairwell. He and Dugan go into the stairwell.

"We have a problem," Dugan says quietly.

"What is it now?"

"Colrain knows that you were seeing Adrienne, and about your sexual tastes."

"How?"

Dugan frowns, "I don't know, but that is not the point."

"What is the point?"

"The point is that if Colrain knows that much, he'll eventually connect me to you, and you might sell me out. I can't take that chance."

As Dugan finishes the last sentence, he pulls out a gravity knife and buries it into Lambert several times. The tall ex-mayor crumples to the ground. Dugan wipes the blade on Lambert's tuxedo jacket, pockets it, and then goes down the stairs.

The door to Ruelle's swings open. Robespierre and Johnny exit with two pretty young women. Robespierre hails a cab and jumps in with one. Colrain leads the other to his bike. She grabs his face and kisses him on the mouth as he reaches to help her onto the back of the bike. Donnelly watches ominously from his car nearby. Colrain takes off with Donnelly following closely behind with his lights off. Donnelly tries to force Colrain into a parked car, but Colrain notices and just manages to avoid a collision by gunning his bike at the last moment. Colrain looks over his shoulder as Donnelly puts on his lights and speeds after him. Colrain realizes that the action is deliberate, and he yells for his terrified passenger to hang on as he speeds up even further. The chase is on.

Colrain peels off suddenly, turns west, and then north on Amsterdam Avenue. Donnelly makes the turn bouncing off one car, causing all kinds of pandemonium with people and traffic. The chase continues through a red light at Seventy-Ninth Street as Colrain manages to swerve around the front end of a truck pulling into the intersection. Donnelly goes around the other end of the truck and partially into the left lane, just avoiding the cars stopped there. Colrain turns east on Eighty-First Street. Donnelly follows. They both move rapidly toward the intersection of Columbus Avenue and Eighty-First Street. Colrain must slow down because of the Columbus Avenue bus in the intersection, and Donnelly bears down on him. The bus finally moves out of the way, and Colrain does a wheelie through the intersection, mounting the sidewalk and roaring into the corner pedestrian entrance to the park behind the Museum of Natural History with people scattering and yelling. Donnelly is right behind him and ends up mounting the sidewalk and crashing into one of the stone sides of the entrance, which can't accommodate a car. He flies into the windshield. Colrain shoots through the park and back out to Columbus Avenue on Eightieth Street. His passenger is frozen with fear on the back.

Colrain continues down Columbus Avenue, and as he crosses the intersection at Broadway and Columbus, he notices ambulances and police vehicles with their lights flashing. He approaches Lincoln Center. He stops to get a better look at what is going on and sees a body being taken to a waiting ambulance. He is surprised to see the Gordons comforting a woman. He drives his bike to West Sixty-Second Street, parks, and gets off, telling his frightened passenger on the seat behind him that he will only be a minute. He approaches the ambulance and asks a uniformed policeman what happened. The cop is reluctant to talk even after Colrain mentions that he is a friend of Lieutenant Ashford. At that moment, Dugan and Ashford pull up in separate cars and get out rapidly. Colrain sees them and walks away quickly through the crowd to his cycle. His passenger is gone. He smiles, shakes his head, gets back on his bike, fires it up, and proceeds down Columbus Avenue as the ambulance starts its siren.

———

The opening at Robert Easton Gallery is going well. People are walking around with wine in plastic cups, chatting, looking at the exhibit. There is a good turnout, and people are coming in and out of the gallery. Priscilla is talking with some patrons who are looking at Colrain's work. The front door opens and Robespierre comes in with the woman he met at Ruelle's. She is in her twenties and smiling at something he said on entering. Priscilla notices him, excuses herself, and walks over to greet him.

"Hello there. Welcome to the gallery."

Robespierre realizes he has seen her before and breaks into a big smile. "Hello. Is this where someone who almost knocked you over in my restaurant has a few paintings as part of this show?"

Priscilla laughs. "Indeed it is. Do you know where he is?"

"Actually, I don't, but I'm sure he will be here soon."

"Well, please get something to drink and look around. I think you will like these new pieces of his."

Robespierre smiles again. "Thank you, we will."

Ashford finishes interviewing the uniformed policeman at Lincoln Center. He puts his memo book away. He watches Dugan talking to the other uniformed cop. He can't say what it is, but something bothers him about this murder. Burke Lambert was popular and not known to have any enemies. It appears that he was not robbed; nothing was taken from his wallet. Dugan was supposed to be off duty but for some reason showed up. He decides he will hold off talking to Dugan for now.

———————

Simon Stone is at the bar at the University Club. He is sipping a Tanqueray martini and talking to two men. One is Judge Harold Katz, a Civil Court judge who seems to have a permanent sneer on his face because his upper lip curls upward on the left side. The judge is dressed in a plain light gray suit with a nondescript print tie and white shirt. His clothes are not worn out, but they do not seem clean, pressed, or neat. He appears shabby. He is wearing dull thick-soled black nondescript shoes. He is a short man with very thin gray hair in his early sixties but looks older. In addition to his sneer, there is something about this man that makes you not like him on sight. The other person is another attorney, Stuart Schlussel. He is dressed in a dark tan glen plaid suit, dark brown silk tie over a light blue shirt, and shined brown plain-toe shoes. He has black, curly, thick hair and a long thin face. He is five feet eleven and very lean. The two attorneys, Stone and Schlussel, are in their mid-forties, both listening intently to Judge Katz.

"I don't know what to do about this guy Fredericks," Judge Katz says to them. He continues, "He doesn't understand how it works. He advocates for his client hammer and tong. No wavering. He does not negotiate if he thinks he shouldn't, and he won't be intimidated. I held him in contempt, but I am sure he will bring an Article 78 proceeding, the contempt will be overturned, and I will end up looking like a jackass."

"What happened?" asks Schlussel.

"I ruled that Fredericks could not use a microfiche reader to show the jury the hospital record that his opponent, Ivan Sanders, had not used in the plaintiff's case. He asked for the basis of the ruling. I had no basis, so I said it was because the plaintiff's attorney did not use one. He was incredulous, strongly objected, stating that my reason was not a legal basis, and he was entitled to use it to show the jury what the record said about the plaintiff's condition. I was stuck because he was right about that, and the hospital record would show that Ivan's case was bull, and Frederick's defense was accurate. I had tried earlier to pressure Fredericks to settle the case, but he refused, saying he could not see what his client did wrong. I went ahead and ordered the court officer to stop the hospital's staff member from setting the microfiche reader up in the courtroom. Fredericks got angry and stood by the reader. Fredericks is a big guy, in shape, and looks like an athlete, so the court officer hesitated. He stopped and didn't know what to do. It was a standoff. I ordered Fredericks to sit down. He shot me daggers and refused unless he could make a statement on the record. I had to let him, so I sent the jury out, and he put on the record what happened, why he wanted to use the microfiche reader, and my order not to let him use the microfiche reader, including the reason I gave. I held him in contempt. That was it for the day. I sent the jury home. The next day Sanders made a motion for a mistrial, which I granted."

"Harold, this will not be good for you. I know Fredericks. He is principled, has no fear, and will take you on," Stuart Schlussel says and looks to Simon Stone.

"I know him too, and I agree, Harold," Stone volunteers.

9

COLRAIN HEADS BACK to his loft. He parks the bike, enters his building, and runs up the stairs. He opens the door and yells out, "B! Big B!" before he remembers that his dog is still at the vet.

He goes into the sleeping area of the loft with a big old pine armoire and a large pine chest with curved drawers. He strips and heads for the shower. After showering, he puts on an ironed denim shirt, clean jeans, a gray tweed sport coat, and a polished pair of brown leather boots.

Back on the bike, Colrain looks around to see if anyone is watching. He doesn't see anyone suspicious. He fires it up and heads uptown to Robert Easton's gallery.

George Fredericks closes the deposition, or, as trial lawyers call it, EBT (examination before trial). He has decided to stop preparing for a trial coming up. He has been working late, sitting at his desk in the office of the law firm where he works at 355 Lexington Avenue between Fortieth and Forty-First Street, with his long yellow legal pads full of writing. He is in his shirtsleeves with his tie undone. It is evening, and he is restless and has no plans. He is thirty-eight with thick brown hair, a dark complexion with a few freckles, a mustache, dark blue eyes, six feet, three inches tall, in very good shape physically, and tough as nails. He brokers neither stupidity nor prejudice. He grew up in a garden apartment complex in Eastchester, New York, in Westchester County outside Manhattan, but you would have thought he grew up on the Lower East Side. He was a late bloomer and was small until puberty kicked in. Perhaps this, plus being the son of immigrants, put a chip on his shoulder; he was always getting into fights growing up.

He is a first-generation American, his parents having emigrated from Hungary right before World War II. They believed in America and the ideals it stood for. His sophisticated parents were hardworking upper-middle class. His father was tall, elegant, and European in his parenting. He was a strict disciplinarian when it came to adhering to the rules of the house. He had been the national pentathlon champion of Hungary when he was seventeen years old and was physically very strong despite not working out anymore. The punishment for a violation of those rules was certainly not pleasant but always just. Being stubborn, George got a lot of spankings. His mother was very beautiful and a wonderful cook, so he developed a palate for fine food. His parents were principled and instilled those principles in him and his sister. Prejudice was not countenanced, and both he and his sister learned that it was wrong. He wanted to make his parents proud of him and was ambitious. He grew up near a lake and was an excellent swimmer, but he played varsity football and basketball in high school because there was no swim team. He worked hard at his studies in high school and was admitted on scholarship to Yale where he was on the swim team and played water polo, becoming captain of the team his senior year. He then went on to Columbia Law School. He did not like law school much, but his interest was to be a trial lawyer, and he pursued it. He wanted to prosecute criminals, but he did not have the political connections to get a recommendation to the Manhattan district attorney's office, so being an assistant DA did not happen. He ended up in a personal injury defense firm with a specialty in medical malpractice after six months in the Navy Reserves. He worked his way up in his firm. His brain and aggressive personality, along with his thorough preparation plus dramatic talent in court, led to many trial successes early, giving him a reputation in personal injury trial attorney circles in the city.

George leaves 355 Lexington carrying a briefcase with a shoulder strap and walks toward Grand Central Station where he enters the subway at Forty-Second Street and Lexington Avenue. He jumps on the Lexington Avenue 6 local downtown. He stays on until the Bleecker Street station and exits. He has decided to just wander around and look for a good place to have a beer and maybe dinner. He is wearing a charcoal suit, a white point collar shirt, a bright blue Hermès tie with little skiers on it, and shined black cap-toe Oxford Allen Edmond shoes. He has a prescient feeling that something good is going to happen and is looking for adventure. He walks past some bars and restaurants but nothing beckons him. He continues toward Broadway and Spring Street. A man on a black motorcycle comes roaring up Spring and stops between two cars right as George is walking by. George pauses, looks at the Honda V4 as the man driving it walks it back to park it in the space, puts down the kickstand, turns it off, and starts to dismount.

"Nice bike," George says with a smile.

Johnny looks at him and is amused.

"You like bikes?" he says as he stands and takes off his helmet.

"I tried riding a Montesa in Europe one summer and almost killed myself twice," answers George with a laugh.

"Yeah. They can be dangerous. I almost had a problem earlier this evening."

"Hey, do you know a good place around here where I can grab a beer and maybe a good dinner?" George asks.

"I have a few ideas, but if you like art and want a free glass of wine, you should come to the opening that I am going to."

"That sounds good, but don't I need an invitation?"

"I am inviting you," Johnny says, smiling.

"Oh, is it your gallery?"

"No. But I am showing there."

George looks surprised.

"That's impressive. I would love to see your work."

"Great! Follow me."

Johnny locks his helmet on the bike seat. He then enters the building, and George follows. They head up the stairs as they talk.

"Law or business?"

"Trial law."

"Criminal?"

"No. Personal injury."

"Okay. What is your taste in art?"

George laughs.

"All over the place. Whatever appeals to me I like."

Now Johnny laughs.

"That actually sounds like a good way to look at it."

They enter the gallery, and Johnny scans the room for Priscilla as the two men head for the table set up for serving wine with two guys in white jackets filling plastic cups for patrons. George looks around as they order one red and one white. It is a big airy space with beautiful maple floors and lots of large paintings on the walls. Most of them are abstract; some are by aboriginal artists. There is a great deal of color.

Robert Easton is feeling good. His gallery is full of people, and he has already sold three paintings. He is holding a plastic cup full of white wine and talking to several friends who are admiring a painting by an aboriginal artist. Priscilla joins the group. She picks up on Robert's mood and is chatting with a man and a woman who are discussing the painting. She spots Johnny and George getting their wine. Johnny looks over in her direction, and they lock eyes. She smiles at him. He and George walk toward her.

Johnny introduces George to Robert and Priscilla. They begin chatting, and George asks which paintings are Johnny's. Priscilla walks with Johnny and George to where they are hanging. Several people are admiring Johnny's paintings. Robespierre and his date are looking at some paintings on an adjacent wall. Robespierre is talking rapidly, pointing out something, when he looks over and sees his friend Johnny with George. He calls out.

"Fredericks! Is that you?"

Johnny and his group look over at Robespierre who immediately walks to them with his date in tow. George starts laughing.

"Robespierre! You crazy man!" George shouts at him, and the two men embrace.

"How have you been?" asks Robespierre.

"Fine. Practicing law. What about you? Have you opened the restaurant that you always talked about?"

"Indeed I have, and you have to come and have dinner and meet my moms!"

Johnny and Priscilla watch this with amazement, smiling. Someone else is watching also. Donnelly has entered the gallery and is standing unobtrusively with a group of people opposite where Johnny, George, and that group are.

"I'd love to!" George responds.

"Are you free later?" asks Robespierre.

"I can't make it a late night, Robby. I have to be in court tomorrow morning."

"Okay, we'll make it an early one. Let's exchange telephone numbers."

As the two of them are exchanging their cards, Johnny notices a man in a dark raincoat, who somehow looks out of place, taking an unusual interest in what is going on. He leaves Priscilla and hustles over in the direction of the man, who immediately walks rapidly to the door and exits. Johnny walks slowly back to the group.

"What was that about, John?" asks Robespierre.

"I think that was the guy who broke into my loft, Robby."

"Someone broke into your loft?" George asks.

"Yeah. I have been helping a friend of mine who is working on the deaths of two models."

George looks at Johnny with curiosity and interest.

"Are you a detective when you are not painting?"

Johnny laughs.

"No, but I used to model, and he wanted me to ask around about the first model who was killed, Adrienne Wyatt, and then the second one got killed after I talked to her."

George raises an eyebrow. "Damn! Can I help in any way?"

"I can't see how, but thanks."

Robespierre looks at the two of them with affection.

"How do you know Robby anyhow?" asks Johnny.

"It's a long story, but I met him when I was in college," George answers.

Johnny looks at Robespierre, who just grins. George continues, "He got me out of a jam."

"How?" asks Johnny, adding, "He did something similar for me."

"He was visiting the campus with a friend one weekend to go to a Yale-Columbia football game in New Haven my freshman year. I was introduced briefly to him. I had a big war going on with some prep school guys in one of the rooms on my floor as a result of a prank that went bad. This guy put tacks on the floor in front of the bathroom, and I stepped on them leaving the shower to go to my room. I did not find it funny. I went into their room to call the preppy prankster out. He gave me some lip, and I grabbed him. His roommates then attacked me, but I fought my way out of their room. Anyway, one of my assigned roommates on Old Campus where all the freshman live sided with the guys who had fought with me. I was in my room and a friend of mine came running in and told me that this roommate was supposedly coming for me with two of his friends. When I learned about this, I got really angry and went outside with this friend of mine to meet them. As they approached the arched entrance to the quadrangle, I didn't wait. I attacked immediately. I slugged him and then pulled his face down into my raised knee. All of a sudden, I was grabbed forcefully and pulled swiftly away by someone. Somehow Robespierre figured or knew that any student could be expelled for fighting no matter the reason. He got me away from there really fast even though he didn't know me well. I was fortunate that he was there. I escaped without getting thrown out, and I have been forever grateful."

He looks over at Robespierre and continues, "If I recall, he reprimanded me also," George says with a grin.

"I know about that too," Johnny says with a chuckle.

Both men look at Robespierre, who just smiles.

"We spent some time the rest of the weekend talking about life and our plans over some beers. I visited him at Columbia once, but then we lost track of each other somehow. That was a long time ago."

Johnny and Priscilla are listening and taking everything in. She excuses herself to talk to Leighann, who has arrived. Johnny's eyes follow her as she walks away, and George notices.

"She is lovely. Is she your lady?" George asks.

"That would be nice, but no. I just met her the other day."

Leighann looks over toward Johnny, George, and Robespierre with his date. George and Johnny notice, and they both smile at her. Priscilla comes over with Leighann and introduces her to Johnny as the artist she has mentioned. Johnny introduces George and Robespierre, who introduces the woman with him.

"Do I get to see these Johnny Colrain paintings that I have heard so much about?" Leighann asks.

Priscilla points to the walls where the Colrain paintings are being displayed, and the talking stops as they move around looking at them. After discussing which ones they like the best, the discussion turns to going to Robespierre's restaurant. Johnny, George, and Robespierre ask Leighann if she would like to come with them. She agrees. They say goodbye to Robert and Priscilla. Johnny invites the two of them to join the group later. Robert says that he cannot; he wants to supervise the cleaning up of the gallery. Priscilla explains that she has plans. Johnny then asks Robert if he can use the phone in the office before they leave. He goes in the back and calls Ashford at home.

———

Ashford is stumped. He now has three unexplained deaths, but he is pretty sure they are linked. He is home sitting at the dinner table with his wife but is obviously distracted.

The phone rings. Ashford answers it and listens as Johnny tells him about being chased, how he ended up at Lincoln Center where he saw someone being put into an ambulance, and Ashford and Dugan's arrival on the scene, and then a suspicious guy who showed up at the gallery opening. Ashford tells Johnny, "That someone you saw being put into the ambulance was Burke Lambert. He was stabbed to death in a stairwell. The assailant got away." Johnny is shocked. Ashford tells him to be careful and watch out for Dugan.

When he comes out of the office, Johnny spots Emilia Rusk and goes to her. "Hi, Em. I'm glad you could come."

"I told you I would."

They walk over to the area of his paintings, and Emilia looks at them carefully.

"I like them, Johnny. I like them a lot. They should sell."

"Thanks. I am going to Robespierre's with some friends. Would you like to join us?"

"I am sure that would be fun, but I have to meet someone for dinner. By the way, any luck on your research that we discussed the other day?"

"No. Have you thought of someone who could be a candidate?"

"No. I was just curious. Go ahead with your friends. I am going to look at a few other paintings and then take off. Stay in touch."

"I will."

Johnny goes over to George, Leighann, Robespierre, and his date, who are chatting, and tells them he is ready to leave. As they are going down the stairs, Simon Stone is heading for the elevator to take him to the gallery. Colrain recognizes him as they emerge from the stairwell into the lobby. It makes sense. Priscilla has plans with this same man he saw her with at Robespierre's when he bumped into her. George recognizes him also from seeing him in the various courts where he practices law. They leave the building. Johnny checks the feeling he is having. He is surprised that he is a little unhappy that Priscilla is going out with the man he has just seen.

————

Robespierre opens the door to his restaurant. His maître d' Thomas greets him. He tells Thomas that he will be taking the table next to the kitchen when it empties. He goes behind the bar, and Johnny, Leighann, and George take seats in front of him. Johnny rode his bike to the restaurant, but George, Leighann, and Robespierre took a cab after Robespierre put his date in a separate cab to go home.

Robespierre, standing behind the bar, asks Johnny, Leighann, and George what they would like to drink. The two men both opt for a beer. Leighann asks for a Manhattan. Johnny asks Leighann about the man that Priscilla has a date with. Leighann does not know much other than he is a lawyer. When they tell George it was the guy coming in when they were leaving, he confirms this and adds that he does personal injury work. George then asks Johnny more questions about his helping a detective to solve the deaths of the two models, which he had mentioned. This rivets Leighann since she read about the deaths. Johnny does not elaborate on what he knows in regard to Adrienne and Renée but tells them about what he saw earlier in the evening.

"Burke Lambert! Who would want to kill him and why?" asks George, shaking his head.

"My questions exactly. And is it connected to the deaths of Adrienne and Renée?" Johnny says.

"Do you think it is?" asks Leighann.

Johnny just shrugs.

Robespierre watches these friends talking and smiles. Thomas comes over to him to tell him the table is ready. He signals to everyone to go to the table, and he goes into the kitchen. He and Lucienne come out, and he introduces her to George and Leighann.

"I am so glad to finally meet you, Lucienne," George says as he gets up. Lucienne gives him a hug.

"*Moi aussi*," she says.

"Robespierre has told me a lot about you."

Lucienne laughs and asks, "Are you going to stay and have something to eat?"

"I sure am."

"Are you good with spicy?"

George grins and shakes his head in the affirmative.

"Okay, then. I will fix something special I have in mind."

"Hey, you never say that to me, Lucienne. What am I, chopped liver?" chimes in Johnny.

Lucienne winks at Leighann and retorts, "John, you will be sent to purgatory for lying. You know that, don't you?"

They all laugh and settle in to talk as Lucienne gives Johnny a hug and then heads back to the kitchen.

10

IT IS A CLOUDY MORNING, rather cool. Johnny thanks the vet and grabs Baloo's leash. He bends over to pat his flat polar bear head and his side. Baloo wags his tail and tries to jump up on his master, but Johnny restrains him, and they walk out of the building. At that moment a squad car pulls up. Two cops get out.

"John Colrain?" the older one asks.

"Yes."

"We have to take you down to the station."

"Why?"

"There is an all-points bulletin for your arrest," the other policeman chimes in.

"You're kidding."

"We aren't. Now, are you going to make this easy or hard?"

"I have no problem, but what about my dog?"

The older policeman looks at Baloo who is looking back at him wondering what is going on.

"Why don't we drop him off at your place?"

"Can we walk him a little before we do?" Johnny asks.

The older cop smiles and says, "Okay. We can do that."

———

Ashford is reading the autopsy of Burke Lambert when the desk clerk calls him.

"Detective, John Colrain has been brought in," the desk sergeant says.

"What? I'll be right out there."

When he gets out to the booking desk, he sees Johnny.

"Sergeant, I will take it from here."

"You have to sign for him, Detective."

Ashford signs the document and takes Johnny's arm. He leads him to a secure interrogation room, and they sit across from each other. They go over everything that has happened.

"How do you figure the Burke Lambert murder, Ash?" Johnny asks.

"I am not sure, but it may have something to do with the deaths of Adrienne and Renée."

"Where is Dugan?" Johnny asks.

"I haven't seen him much. He's been working with a detective named Donnelly."

"What does Donnelly look like?"

"About forty-three years old, five feet nine, and stout. Dark black hair. He is always a bit unshaven, likes black shirts, and wears a black baseball cap."

"I think that is the guy who broke into my loft and shot Baloo. Then he was at the gallery. He probably was tailing me."

"What?"

"Yeah. He chased me with an unmarked car yesterday, but I lost him. When he broke into my loft the other night to do whatever, Baloo started barking. He shot at him. Luckily, it only grazed the big guy. I threw my club at him, and he fled. I never saw the intruder, but he was all in black. It could easily have been him. I picked Baloo up from the vet this morning right before the uniforms picked me up."

"Damn!"

"Yes. I owe that guy a little something."

"John, don't get into trouble. Let's keep this as simple as possible. It is already more complicated than we know. Dugan must be involved somehow."

Priscilla and Leighann are in their robes having coffee.

"Well? Spill the beans!" Leigh says, smiling at her roommate.

"He's okay, I guess."

"Geez, such a resounding endorsement. You don't seem very excited about him."

"He is very nice and took me to a lovely restaurant, but, honestly, I am not that attracted to him. He is too smooth. I am not used to it."

"It sounds like he is well off."

"I would say so. He lives in an apartment off Fifth Avenue. I tried to contribute to the dinner again, but he would not let me."

"Did he try anything?"

"He kissed me good night, but nothing more than that."

"Is there someone else you like, Priscilla?"

A shy smile creeps across Priscilla's face.

"Maybe ... not sure. Now, what about you? Tell me about George."

"Well ... very interesting guy. First generation, and someone who has worked hard for everything he has. Also a lawyer, but my guess is a lot different in style from your Mr. Stone. I think he is tough and a straight shooter. He has class, not slick at all. I would bet he is a hammer in court as opposed to a knife."

They both laugh.

———————

It is 11:00 a.m. George Fredericks is sitting on the marble bench in the hallway outside a courtroom at 111 Centre Street. He is not happy. He usually is not in this courthouse, but Judge Harold Katz's courtroom is in this Civil Court building. George is normally in the Supreme Court building at 60 Centre Street where most New York County civil cases involving large amounts of damages are tried. He is dressed in a gray flannel suit, a blue point collar shirt, and a bright multicolored red pattern tie, with brown suede wing tips. He has his briefcase with him. He is distracted and angry. This is the third time he has been ordered to come back to Judge Katz's courtroom in regard to the contempt citation that Judge Katz levied against him during a trial three weeks ago. The judge makes him wait for hours each time and then orders him to come back in a week. It is keeping him from his work on other cases. It is a colossal waste of time, which he understands the judge is doing on purpose, and it angers him. He is prepared to start an Article 78 proceeding to have a hearing in regard to the contempt order and have the judge testify about the justification for holding him in contempt. He would love to have the judge on the stand in front of a real judge and cross-examine him. He would call the hospital tech, the plaintiff's lawyer, and the court officer to testify, and he himself would testify. The contempt citation against him can't be upheld in his estimation. It is all such nonsense.

As George is thinking about it and fuming, Stuart Schlussel walks down the corridor, stops, and sits next to George.

"Hi, George," Schlussel says.

George looks over Schlussel's face and is suspicious.

"Hello, Stuart."

"I heard about what happened with Judge Katz, George," Schlussel volunteers.

George looks at him and says nothing.

Schlussel continues, "I can help. Judge Katz knows me. I will go into the courtroom with you, and I will say I am representing you. He will vacate the contempt, I am sure, but you have to promise me that no matter what he says, you will hold your tongue. No matter what he says about you, don't say anything. Do I have your assurance?"

This befuddles George.

"Why are you getting involved, Stuart?"

"I think the judge doesn't really want to pursue it but needs a way to save face, and I want to help you."

George isn't sure about this but figures he can always bail out if things go south, and he agrees.

George goes into the courtroom with Schlussel. It is packed with lawyers there to conference cases and argue motions. Judge Katz sees Schlussel and George. He finishes talking to the two attorneys who are in front of the bench and gestures to Schlussel and George to come to the well where the counsel tables are. They approach, and Schlussel states that he is representing George. George notices that the judge does not seem surprised or say anything about this. At that point Judge Katz, with his sneering lip, launches into an excoriating speech about George in front of the room full of attorneys. George does not like what he hears this judge saying about him. He is looking daggers at the judge thinking, *I could leap up to the bench, rip that sneer off his face, or tear the bastard's throat out with my bare hands, but, of course, I would end up in prison. So, should I just listen to his nasty slandering rant and see what happens? I guess I'll wait until the end of it and see.*

Sure enough, the judge winds down and then vacates his contempt order. George glares at the judge and Stuart grabs his arm.

"Let's go, George." He guides him out of the courtroom.

When they get outside, Schlussel adds, "I told you."

George hasn't quite figured out why Schlussel has interceded, but he thanks him, and they leave the building.

———

Colrain is released from the precinct. Ashford has taken care of the APB. Johnny takes a cab back home to his loft. He opens the door and calls out to his dog. Baloo comes running to meet him, wagging his tail.

"Hello, big guy. How are you?" he says as he pets and pats the big white Pyrenees. He looks at the dog's wound. The bandage is not leaking any blood.

"Let's go for a real walk."

———

Priscilla is in the office at the Robert Easton Gallery. She is checking the invoices of the paintings that have been sold so far as a result of the opening. Robert is on the phone. No one else is in the gallery. The bell rings indicating someone has come in. Priscilla goes out to see who is there. Johnny Colrain walks over to her with Baloo.

"Hello there. Who have we here?" Priscilla says.

"Hi. This is my roommate, Baloo."

"The name of the bear from *The Jungle Book*?"

"Yup! Not everyone knows that," Johnny says, smiling.

Priscilla bends over and scratches Baloo behind the ears, which he responds to happily.

"Handsome dog," Priscilla says as she straightens up.

"Thanks. I didn't get a chance to talk to you much last night. I thought the opening went pretty well."

"It did. Robert was pleased."

"Good." Johnny is feeling awkward, which is unusual for him.

"You have some interesting friends," Priscilla says with a big smile.

"Yes. I guess so. One I just met, and he turned out to be an old friend of my friend Robespierre. Small world sometimes."

"I agree."

Robert comes out from the office and comes over.

"Hey, Johnny! Did your friends like the opening?"

"They did. Not just my paintings but some others also. Those by aboriginal artists are really interesting," Johnny responds.

The phone rings and Priscilla goes back into the office to get it. She is gone for a few minutes. Robert and Johnny discuss the sales of two of his works. They will stay up until the show closes, but they both think it bodes well for more sales. Priscilla comes out with a concerned look on her face. Robert asks her if everything is all right. She responds that one of her roommates is ill. She excuses herself saying that she wants to go back to her work in the office so she can get home early.

Giambone's Italian restaurant on Mulberry Street is right behind the New York State Supreme Court building at 60 Centre Street and the federal courthouse on Foley Square next to it. Its clientele consists mostly of attorneys and courtroom staff. It does the majority of its business at lunchtime. At 3:00 p.m., well past lunch, the restaurant is empty except for Judge Katz, Stuart Schlussel, and Simon Stone sitting at a table in a corner. Judge Katz is smoking a cigar. His lip still curls up. They have finished lunch and are having espresso.

"What are we going to do about Judge Franco demanding so much money?" Simon Stone asks.

"He will listen to reason, I am sure," Schlussel responds.

"I am not so sure," Katz offers, blowing out some smoke.

"But why wouldn't he?" asks Stone.

"He has a new girlfriend," offers Schlussel.

Stuart Schlussel pays the bill, and they get up and leave the restaurant. They walk up the street between the two courthouses.

―――――――

George Fredericks leaves his conference with Judge Swift in her courtroom on the third floor of the Supreme Court building at 60 Centre Street. He catches an elevator and gets out at the distinctive ground-floor hexagonal rotunda designed by architect Guy Lowell with its pieced-together beautiful marble floor, columns, brightly colored murals on the curved ceilings, and pendulum hanging light. He walks through the rotunda down the hallway leading to the main doors and exits the Supreme Court building onto the large terrace with columns that lead to the broad stairs down to the street. As he approaches the stairs, he sees Jimmy Ryan, a well-known plaintiff's attorney, sitting on the edge of the base of one of the columns. He looks a little distraught and frazzled. George approaches him.

"Jimmy, what's up? You all right?"

Jimmy looks at George with an odd expression.

"Hi, George. Yes, I am okay. I always get this way after finishing a summation."

"I know that feeling. I always have a letdown but feel good as long as I know I did everything I could to win for my client."

"That's not it for me, George. I feel a little sad that the trial is now going to be over. The only time I really feel alive is when I am on trial."

George is astonished by this remark. He always feels somewhat spent at the end of a trial and glad he has done right by his client, especially if the summation has gone well. He addresses Jimmy.

"Well, good luck with the case, Jimmy."

George thinks about Jimmy Ryan, a whipsaw-thin Irish guy who likes to run around the reservoir in Central Park. He is very successful and rich from his cases. For some reason, Jimmy has always been very polite and friendly to George, and this surprises George a little. They have never been opponents or worked together, but there is mutual respect. Jimmy has known George for some time. He worked for an insurance company before becoming a trial attorney and was aware of George and his success with his trials. George turns and is about to start down the steps in front of the building when he sees Schlussel, Katz, and Stone walking together. It makes him wonder even more about what happened to him with Katz and Schlussel's involvement. He waits for them to pass, goes quickly down the stairs, and makes for the subway.

11

JOHNNY GETS AN IDEA sitting at the side of Ashford's desk. No one but Ashford is around. He asks to use the phone. He dials and then speaks, "Hi, Mary. Is Christine there? Thanks."

He waits. Ashford gives him a quizzical look, but Johnny speaks into the phone again, and Ashford listens, trying to figure out what he is up to.

"Hi, Chris. This is Johnny Colrain. How are you doing?"

"I am good, Johnny. Why are you asking for me? I don't book male models."

"I know. You're still the booker for Aarika, aren't you?"

"Yes. And I am not supposed to disclose booking info."

"I know. I know you aren't, but I am her friend, and I need to speak with her ASAP. It's important."

"Let me see, Johnny. I will check."

A few minutes go by, and she gets back on the phone. She starts to give him the address on East Twenty-Fifth Street.

"Hold on," Johnny says as he grabs a pad and pen from the desk and writes down the address.

"Thanks, Chris. I owe you." He hangs up the phone and hands it over to Ashford.

"I have an idea, Ash. I'll call you later."

"You want to tell me about it, John?"

"I want to speak to a model who knew Renée."

"Okay. Call me if you learn anything. I am still trying to do some research on Lambert and the models."

Johnny arrives at a building on East Twenty-Fifth Street between Fifth and Sixth Avenues. He is buzzed in, takes the elevator, and enters a busy photographer's loft studio. There are clients, assistants, and various other production people around. Colrain asks for Aarika and is sent to the makeup-changing room at the far side of the studio.

Aarika and another model are in lingerie getting makeup and hair done. Colrain sticks his head in.

"Aarika?"

Both the models yell, "Hold on!" They both put on dressing gowns and then give the okay. Colrain enters. Aarika recognizes Colrain.

"Hey! What are you doing here, Johnny?"

The punk-looking makeup artist with rings in his nose and ears and tattoos on his arms looks at Johnny for a second and then resumes applying makeup. The plain female hairdresser is busy working on the other model. Aarika is still in curlers.

"I am helping a friend investigate the deaths of Adrienne and Renée, and I would like to speak with you."

"Johnny, it's so horrible and shocking. How can I help you?"

"I need to ask you a few questions about Renée mostly."

"Can you wait for a few minutes? Helmut will be finished soon."

The makeup artist smiles at Colrain.

"Sure," Johnny says.

He leaves the room and moves across the loft toward the windows on the other side of the space where there are some couches, chairs, and magazines. He sits in a chair, picks up an old *Elle* magazine, and thumbs through it, reflecting on the fact that he knows this scene from doing some modeling. He watches two assistants pull down a huge roll of white paper in front of the back brick wall of the studio and emergency exit to be the backdrop for the photos. He thinks about Adrienne and muses that, contrary to what many think, not all models are vacuous.

He watches Aarika walk across the loft and take a seat on an ugly green chair next to him. He is glad to see her. She is a beautiful woman with a brilliant smile and auburn hair. Johnny thought about trying to date her at one point, but somehow that never came to pass. She was not always single. They did a couple of shoots together, and she was fun to work with, a little kooky, which he liked. She looks at him with concern. She has huge blue eyes, pale flawless skin with a few very small freckles, and proportioned curves that many models don't have. He can't help but appreciate her beauty.

"What do you want to know?" Aarika asks with seriousness.

"What happened to your friendship with Renée?"

Aarika takes a big sigh as if she were about to dive into a pool that she knows will be too cold. She explains that Renée started seeing Burke Lambert, and he made her heavily dependent on coke. He got her into S and M. There were group scenes. Burke grew tired of her and started to fix her up with some of his friends who were rich and also had a plentiful supply. Burke eventually asked Renée to fix him up with one of her model friends. Renée asked her. She knew he was married and apparently had an arrangement with his wife but did not know anything about his predilections. Renée did not share that information with her. She was on the rebound so she agreed.

Lambert was very charming and nice at first but eventually got around to a midnight swim in the basement pool in his apartment building. When he suggested that they go to the exercise room, she assumed that it was for some normal fun, but he wanted to tie her to a weight-lifting bench for some spanking, and, she assumed, sex. She refused, and Lambert tried plying her with some coke, but it did not work because she does not do coke. He took her out a few more times without trying anything unusual. He then tried to persuade her to go with him to a huge Southampton estate on Long Island for a party. She just didn't trust him and said no. He lost interest after that. She never saw him again. She got mad at Renée for fixing her up with him without warning her about his proclivities. They had a big argument that ended their friendship.

"Did she ever tell you about who Adrienne was seeing?"

"No. I don't think she was seeing anyone special at that time. I know she went out with Randy Macquilken a few times, but that is all I know."

"Thanks, Aarika," Johnny says with a smile.

"No problem, Johnny. I am glad to help if I can."

They both get up. Aarika gives him a hug, then takes a step toward the hair and makeup area when there is a commotion in the front part of the studio just as Johnny turns to walk to the entrance of the loft where the commotion is coming from. One of the assistants to the photographer is trying to stop Dugan, who is showing his badge and telling him to get out of the way in a loud gruff voice. He then sees Johnny, who sees him. Johnny tells Aarika to go to the makeup room fast. She does, and he starts to run for the back of the studio. Dugan yells for him to stop and pulls out his weapon. People start screaming and hiding behind tables and hitting the floor.

There is pandemonium as Dugan, who really can't run, walks fast after Colrain, pushing people out of the way and knocking over a strobe light. He sees Colrain go behind the huge roll of paper that was unrolled to be the backdrop for the shoot. Dugan fires. The bullets tear holes in the paper in a line where he guesses Colrain must be. When his gun is empty, he walks with caution toward the paper, reloading the service revolver as he moves. He quickly grabs the edge of the paper and looks behind it only to find that Johnny has gone out the emergency fire door behind the roll of paper and down the stairs. Dugan hustles out the same door and down the stairs. He emerges in the back of the building, looks up and down, then quickly walks up the alley between the buildings with his gun drawn. He looks around at the front of the building, but Johnny is gone. Dugan hears a motorcycle and curses. He goes to his car and gets in.

Colrain speeds uptown on his cycle. He is yelling out his anger over the sound of the bike and street noise. When he calms himself after a few minutes, he thinks about what just happened. *How did Dugan know where he was and show up there? He must have been followed! He didn't spot anyone. He has to be more careful.*

12

IT IS LUNCHTIME the next day at Harry's Restaurant in the basement of the Woolworth Building at 233 Broadway, and the restaurant is busy. Waiters are bustling about in white shirts with white aprons wrapped around their waists carrying large thick silver aluminum trays full of dishes. Six trial lawyers who represent plaintiffs are sitting around the table finishing their lunch. One of them is Simon Stone. He speaks.

"I am okay with helping to get a judge nominated and elected, but I am not okay with kickbacks. It's dangerous."

Stuart Schlussel just listens and says nothing. Jimmy Ryan looks at Schlussel and Ivan Sanders sitting with him, and then responds to Simon Stone.

"I agree. Kickbacks are not a good idea for a lot of reasons."

Joseph DeFeo, a corpulent attorney with dark-rimmed glasses, a black mustache and beard, in his shirtsleeves with a loosened tie, tears off a piece of Italian bread, starts to butter it, and comments,

"Does the defense bar know which judges are taking kickbacks?"

Stone replies that he is not sure, but he expresses his concern that this has gotten out of hand and will lead to a scandal that is going to be bad for all plaintiff attorneys.

"We know which judges are taking them. We have to stop any scandal from happening," he says.

Bart Ashby, thin, fifty-five, dressed in a beautiful tan herringbone suit and bright red tie, agrees.

"We don't want the defense bar or any district attorney to pursue this," he says.

Frank Santangelo, a silver-haired sixty-year-old from the Bronx in a shiny gray sharkskin suit, says, "Can we agree, then, that kickbacks are forbidden, and we will report to the group any lawyer who is trying to do it from now on? Win or settle your cases without that kind of help from your judge. Everyone, get the word out." There is a general murmuring of agreement. They start getting up to leave the restaurant.

———

Harold Katz is in his chambers talking on the phone with Judge Anthony Franco, a Supreme Court judge in the Bronx.

"I got a call from Stuart, and our friends are not going to do it anymore, Tony."

Judge Franco, a small, slight, very pale man with thin gray hair in his mid-sixties, is not pleased. He purses his lips and then speaks, "Really? I don't think they will like it when they come before me. I have helped some of them make some big bucks."

"Take it easy, Tony. They might reconsider at some point, but don't do anything rash for now, okay?"

"Okay, Harold."

Judge Franco hangs up the phone. He takes the elevator down from his chambers to the floor his courtroom is on and enters the office behind the courtroom through a passageway. He speaks to his law secretary. The law secretary enters the courtroom. It is filled with attorneys. He speaks to the clerk sitting at a small desk to the side of the bench near the door to the inner office and then returns to the inner office. The clerk calls out the name of a case, and two attorneys approach the desk. The clerk tells them to go in. One of the attorneys is George Fredericks, and the other, Frank Santangelo. They enter the office, and Judge Franco indicates for them to sit down.

"What is your demand, Mr. Santangelo?"

"Three hundred and seventy-five thousand if we settle before trial," Frank responds.

"Are you prepared to settle this case, Mr. Fredericks."

"I have $15,000 on this file, Judge," responds George.

The judge is exasperated. He makes a sour face. He turns to the plaintiff's attorney.

"Frank, please step out for a minute."

Mr. Santangelo gets up and goes back out into the courtroom. Judge Franco speaks, looking hard at George.

"Are you trying to be a hero, Mr. Fredericks? You could get hit for a lot of money in this case."

"I don't agree, Judge."

"You have exposure here, and if Mr. Santangelo wins, the jury could give a big number. Would you like me to speak to your carrier?"

George doesn't appreciate the judge's remarks or his coercion. This kind of inappropriate judicial behavior angers him. He can't believe this judge is trying to bully him, but he stays calm, cold, and firm.

"No. I have discussed the case with the adjuster, and he has given me full authority to offer what I have offered; otherwise defend the case."

Judge Franco is furious and tells George to go out and get Mr. Santangelo. George steps out into the courtroom where Mr. Santangelo is standing talking to the clerk sitting at his desk. He motions for Santangelo to come back into the judge's antechamber office. When they walk back in, Judge Franco addresses them.

"Okay, I can do nothing with Mr. Fredericks, Frank, so I am sending you out to pick a jury."

The judge looks at George. He expects George to protest and say he is not ready, but George says nothing and just looks at the judge stone-faced. He *is* ready. Frank Santangelo is not happy with this development. He understands that it is an effort to force an offer of settlement from George, but he is not ready to select a jury, and he speaks.

"Your Honor, I am not prepared to pick today. Can we put this over?"

This is not what the judge wanted, and he is annoyed.

"When do you want to select, Frank?"

"Can we make it next Tuesday?"

Judge Franco, exasperated, looks at his calendar and responds.

"I expect to be on trial in another matter then, but you come in and pick, and then we will see when we can start the trial. The other case should be short."

In his chambers in Manhattan, Harold Katz turns to Stuart Schlussel.

"Franco could be a problem, Stuart."

"I know. I have to go. Talk later."

Stuart Schlussel leaves the judge's chambers and takes the elevator to the ground floor. He exits the building and walks toward Broadway. A young woman is watching him from a van parked near the corner of the New York Family Court building as he crosses Lafayette Street. When he starts to walk up Leonard Street toward Broadway, she follows him at a discrete distance. She watches him go into 377 Broadway and then goes to a telephone booth at the corner.

David Morgan at One Hogan Place picks up the phone. He has been waiting for this call. He is a former college football player and marine but now is a senior assistant DA. He is five feet, ten inches tall and solid-looking. He is in his fifties but looks younger and works out religiously. He keeps his gray hair in a crew cut and is clean-shaven. Sitting in his shirtsleeves and tie, you can see his pectorals and biceps pushing against his tight-fitting shirt.

"Morgan here."

"Hi, Dave."

"What have you got, Jenny?"

"I think that Schlussel is spooked. He was at a lunch with a lot of other plaintiff attorneys, and then he went to see Katz. Katz called Franco."

"And ... ?"

"He told him that kickbacks were going to stop, and Franco was not happy about it. He has a reputation as a revengeful prick."

"Such language, Jenny. I am surprised," Morgan says, feigning shock but stiffing a chuckle. He continues, "Come into the office. I want to get a court order to tap Schlussel based on what we learned from the tap on Katz."

"Okay, boss."

Dave is pleased. The decision to tap Katz based on the interviews with the two court officers is yielding some helpful information. He wants to see the bank account information on both of these judges.

———

George Fredericks is suspicious. He knocks on the door of one of the senior partners at his firm, Robert Campanella.

"Come on in," Campanella yells. He is sitting at a large cherry desk with stacks of doctor and hospital records upon it that he has been reading next to several yellow legal pads with his notes, smoking a cigarette. He is a legendary medical malpractice defense trial attorney who has been around for a long time and is suffering health-wise from drinking and smoking too much. He is a thin man. You can easily see his entire collarbone outlined underneath his blue Oxford button-down shirt. His skin is pale and mottled. He has fine gray hair, showing scalp with flakes of dandruff, and large light blue eyes. He wears dark thick horn-rimmed glasses that magnify his eyes, and he speaks with a raspy voice. Somehow there is always dandruff on his shoulders. He is George's favorite. He has a knack for reducing the issues in any case to one or two essential questions that must be answered. One of his cross-examinations of a medical expert is considered classic. Campanella has mentored George and, without saying much, it is obvious that he likes him. George marvels at how Campanella always gets to the kernel of a case, which ultimately will determine the outcome.

George sits down in one of the two brown leather studded chairs in front of the desk. Robert puts out his cigarette in a big glass ashtray sitting in a leather container. The ashtray is full of cigarette butts.

"What is on your mind, George?"

"Something is fishy, Mr. C," he begins.

George then relates what happened with both Judge Katz and Judge Franco. He is particularly miffed about what Judge Katz did.

"I have been before several judges who are obviously biased and have an axe to grind, but these two are beyond that," George says.

Mr. Campanella, who already knew about the episode with Judge Katz, looks at him with seriousness.

"You think they are on the take?"

"I am wondering."

"That is a serious allegation."

"I know. What do you think I should do?"

"I have run into judges who played favorites to some degree, but I never suspected kickbacks. I think you have to get more proof and then report them."

George looks at him and asks, "Getting evidence will not be easy. Do you have any ideas?"

"I do. I know a detective who might be able to help. Let me call him. I will let you know if he can help look into this. In the meantime, you better get ready for your trial before Franco in the Bronx."

He smiles at George and George smiles back as he gets up from his chair.

"I'm ready, but I do want to talk to our examining physician again."

George turns and leaves. Robert watches him and looks at the closed door, lost in thought. He then sighs as he reaches for the phone and lights up another cigarette.

"Hello."

"Ash?"

"Is this that famous attorney, Robert Campanella, calling me?"

"I don't know how famous ... maybe infamous. How are you?"

"I am fine, Bob, are you still smoking like a chimney?"

"I plead the Fifth. I need a little help. Could you look into something for me?"

"That is a silly question to ask me. Of course. I have hit a stone wall on three killings I am trying to solve anyway. How can I help you?"

"I read about those killings. Awful. I hate to trouble you, but I was wondering if you heard anything about some civil judges taking kickbacks?"

"No, I haven't, but I would not be the guy looking into that. Let me make a few calls and get back to you."

"Thanks, Jim. How is Amy?"

"She's good. She has a new job at the *Times* and is happy."

"Glad to hear it. I'll wait to hear from you ... and thanks!"

———

Ashford hangs up the phone. Robert Campanella was the attorney that successfully defended his father from a medical malpractice claim that was not true. It caused his dad to be very upset. He was very worried because his insurance coverage was not adequate and the family's asset were in jeopardy. It was a difficult time for the family, and Ashford went to court to see the trial on several days. He was in awe of Mr. Campanella's detailed knowledge of the medicine of the case and his manner of cross-examining the plaintiff's physician expert. The case collapsed against his dad when it became clear that the codefendant doctor had falsified his records to implicate his dad. When it was over, they all went out for drinks to celebrate. He has been friends with Robert Campanella since then and has helped him on a few occasions in researching the background of certain people. Ashford dials the phone.

"Morgan."

"David, it's Jim. How are you?"

"Pretty good. What's up?"

"I need a favor."

"How can I help?"

"An old friend of mine, an attorney, just asked me if there is an investigation into kickbacks or bribes of judges handling civil cases. I told him I would try to find out."

"You called the right guy, old friend. We are investigating just that, and I have a question for you. Do you think this attorney could help us get an attorney handling a case to wear a wire, whether it is himself or someone else?"

Ashford smiles at the request and retorts, "I will ask and get back to you. Thanks for the info." He hangs up.

———

It is late afternoon, but the sun is still high in the sky. Priscilla leaves the gallery and walks to the uptown subway. She exits the station at Fifty-First Street and Lexington Avenue and walks down to the east side of Third Avenue and heads uptown. She crosses Fifty-Fifth Street. Priscilla opens the door to the big dark bar at P.J. Clarke's. Her eyes adjust to the darkness from the sunny street, and she sees Simon Stone sitting at the bar. He smiles at her and waves. She goes to him as he rises to give her a peck on the cheek hello. She sits next to him. They order drinks.

———

Joseph DeFeo is sitting in his very dark corner office in the Woolworth Building. He likes it dark. He is dark. He has black hair. His black mustache walks around his mouth into his black beard. He is corpulent. The spare tire around his waist is obvious. He is thinking about the lunch that he attended at Harry's.

Those guys don't really understand how many payoffs have been happening. Not just to judges but to witnesses and investigators to rig accident scenes and testify falsely. There is a lot at risk and at stake.

Joe picks up the phone, dials, and asks the receptionist to get his party.

"Stuart, I think we need to meet."

"I was thinking the same thing."

"Why don't you come to my office?"

"I don't want other people in your office to see me there. Let's meet at Sloppy Louie's. When can you meet?"

"How about five thirty tomorrow?

"See you there."

Jenny takes her headphones off. She smiles. *We can learn from this meeting,* she thinks. She calls Dave to tell him about the call.

————

Robert Campanella picks up the phone.

"Yes?"

"Bob, it's me, Ash. Do you have a minute?"

"Of course, Jim. Is this about the judge question?"

"Yes. You are right about kickbacks. I spoke to the senior DA in Manhattan who is investigating the players and what is going on, but he asks for help of his own. He wants to find an attorney who will wear a wire. I am assuming that would not be you, but do you know someone who would be willing to do that or who knows someone who would?"

"I am not sure. Let me work on that and get back to you. And, Jim?"

"Yes?"

"Thanks."

"We're not there yet, but you know I am always happy to help if I can."

Robert Campanella thinks about what Ashford has asked and decides he will talk this over with George when he returns from court.

———

Priscilla is standing on the sidewalk outside P.J.'s. Simon steps onto Third Avenue and hails a cab. Yellow cabs are going by with their roof lights dark, showing they are occupied. He has to wait, and finally one with its vacancy light on pulls over quickly. Simon goes over to Priscilla and kisses her on the mouth. She lets him and when they disengage, she thanks him for lunch. He smiles at her and opens the cab door.

"It was fun. Let's do it again," Simon says as he closes the door.

He watches her cab leave and go to Fifty-Sixth Street where it turns to go over to Second Avenue and proceed downtown. He notes that Priscilla does not turn around to wave from the back seat. He is not sure about how interested in him she is. The conversation was okay. He ended up telling her some war stories from his cases. Simon finishes his thoughts and puts his arm up to hail another cab. He gives the address of his office on East Seventy-Sixth Street as the cab pulls out and then continues uptown.

After Simon finishes his day, he calls Stuart Schlussel at home. When he hangs up, he grabs his jacket and briefcase and walks to Schlussel's brownstone on East Eightieth Street near Lexington Avenue.

Simon Stone climbs the stairs of the brownstone and rings the bell. Stuart Schlussel opens the door to let him in. Simon follows Stuart through the foyer into the living room. Stuart motions Simon toward a comfortable club chair and heads to the bar and makes both of them a double Scotch over ice in low-ball crystal glasses. Stuart hands Simon his drink and walks across the room to sit in a chair facing him.

"Can we talk?" Simon asks in a low voice.

"Yes, Rita is out."

"I'm concerned, Stuart," Simon says after taking a sip of his drink.

"What about?"

"Dugan knows about the kickbacks."

"How did Dugan find out about the kickbacks?"

"You know he attended a few of Burke's secret get-togethers, right?" Schlussel nods somberly. Simon makes a face and continues, "I don't know if he learned about the kickbacks at one of the parties or extorted his way into the parties because he already knew about them."

"Will he keep quiet?" Schlussel asks.

"He will until he needs something, and then he will use it as blackmail, is my guess."

"Yes. That worries me. What do you think we can do?"

"I don't know. I haven't thought of anything at this point."

13

CAROLE LANSDORF sips her Negroni. She is sitting at a table in the Plaza Hotel's Oak Bar with Aarika West, who is nursing a Campari and soda. Carole's face is striking, not exotic like a fashion model's but with a loveliness that attracts both men and women. She is five feet, six and one-half inches tall, slender with a full chest, bright blue eyes, narrow waist, and beautiful long slim legs. She is wearing her shoulder-length blond hair down with curls in a 1940s hairdo. She has smooth skin and only a little makeup on. She is twenty-nine years old and is wearing an elegant beige dress with a small fitted brown brocade jacket and metallic copper heels. Her only jewelry is a gold watch and small gold stud earrings. She has been studying acting with several different teachers for the past three years. She started with Warren Robertson, moved on to HB Studio with Steven Strimpell, and then Uta Hagen. She is now studying with Wynn Handman, the avant-garde artistic director of the American Place Theatre, but her focus has changed to singing.

Carole grew up in Virginia, Minnesota, in the iron-rich Mesabi Range. Her home life was not good. Her mother made poor choices in men. Her father, a first-generation Norwegian, left shortly after she was born. Her stepfather drank and was abusive to her mother and her. Despite an offer of marriage from her high school boyfriend, she wanted to leave town and decided to expand her world by becoming an airline hostess after attending the local community college where she acted and sang in some college and local productions. She settled in New York City and started taking singing and acting classes when she was not flying. She became friendly with Aarika West, a well-known successful model who took acting classes at Warren Robertson's workshop, which was popular with models. After a while, Aarika convinced her to go on a few go-sees for modeling jobs, and she got some of them. She was not high fashion or editorial, as she was on the short side for that type of modeling, but certain clients found her just right for their magazine ads. She was signed by the Gordon Agency and stopped flying.

She addresses Aarika, "I don't want to model anymore, Riki. I like the acting classes, but what I really want is to sing."

"I understand but can you afford to give up the money?" asks Aarika.

"I have some put away. Taking modeling jobs prevents me from going on auditions."

"Have you told the agency?"

"Not yet."

"Have you gotten any gigs lined up?"

"Nothing definite, but my agent sent my tape to some clubs in the Village."

"Wow! That is great, Carole."

"Thanks. Now, tell me what happened at your booking that I heard about."

Aarika proceeds to tell her what happened at her shoot with the visit of Johnny Colrain and the pandemonium caused by the gunfire of a detective going after Johnny.

"Holy crap, Aarika! Were you scared?"

"I was, but it happened fast and then was over."

"Is Johnny okay?"

"He escaped, if that is what you mean."

"I don't know him, but I have heard a lot about him," Carole says.

"He's cute all right, and talented. He is very into his art and has given up on modeling now that he is selling some of his paintings. You have something in common," Aarika says, smiling.

"Do you have any idea what happened to Adrienne and Renée?" Carole asks.

"No. But I think it could have involved Burke Lambert somehow."

When Dugan lumbers to his desk, Ashford meets him right there and tells him that he needs to talk to him in private. Dugan looks at Ashford with a blank look on his face, but he knows what it is about, and inside he is leery. He actually is a little fearful but is managing to show nothing on his face. He doesn't know what Ashford is going to say or do. Ashford gestures for them to go into an interview room. He opens the door and Dugan enters followed by Ashford who closes the door. They sit opposite each other across the metal table. Ashford's face is cold and impassive. He is really angry but staying in control and calm. His eyes are riveted on Dugan's pockmarked face. Dugan is not used to being under someone else's heat. He shuffles his butt in the metal chair and puts his thick arms out on the metal table. Ashford is just looking daggers at Dugan and then finally speaks.

"What the fuck are you doing?"

"What do you mean?" Dugan replies.

"You know exactly what I mean," Ashford says coldly and waits.

Dugan remains silent. He is not sure how much of what he has done or arranged Ashford knows. He wants Ashford to spell it out. The two of them have interrogated witnesses, and Ashford knows the game Dugan is playing.

"Okay, I will just go to the captain and IAB to report what I know." Ashford pushes his chair back and starts to stand.

"Hold on," Dugan says.

Ashford, who is standing at this point, looks down at Dugan.

"You mean what happened at the fashion shoot?" Dugan says.

"That, the APB, and putting a tail on Johnny Colrain."

"I wanted to talk to Colrain about the murder of the second model," Dugan says.

"That is nonsense, Dugan. You shot at him!"

"His prints were in her apartment!"

"I am not buying, Dugan. You had him dragged in and could get ahold of him anytime you wanted. You know he is my friend."

"Yes, but I wanted to talk to him without you being present."

"So you shoot at him in a photography studio full of people?"

"He took off. I shot to scare him into stopping."

Ashford looks at Dugan hard. He doesn't believe him for a minute.

"That is crap, Dugan. The department is dealing with a complaint about your escapade. You are lucky that you did not cause any serious damage or hit anyone. You have it in for him. I know you had Donnelly tail him. So, what is your beef? Is it still about that CO controversy?"

"Naaa. I know you have asked him to get some info for you, but I think you might have blinders on in terms of his possible involvement with the murders of the models."

"Did you send Donnelly to break into his loft and hurt him?"

There is a pause. The two detectives look at each other intently. Dugan takes a chance thinking that Colrain and Ashford don't really know it was Donnelly.

"I don't know anything about anyone breaking into Colrain's loft."

"Dugan, I am going to say this just once. I don't know what you are up to, but if you fuck around with Johnny Colrain anymore, I will see to it that you pay. And I mean pay."

"Are you threatening me?"

"Whatever you want to call it."

Ashford walks out of the room, slamming the door.

———

It is a bright day with only a few wispy clouds, a very blue sky with a slight breeze. Manhattan is starting its daily bustle. Fall is not far off. Ashford and Johnny are having breakfast in Johnny's loft. Johnny has made his signature omelet and French roast coffee in his big maganette coffee pot. As they sit at the round center pedestal oak table talking, Ashford reaches down to pet the head of Baloo, who is sitting by his chair. He is telling Johnny about what Dave Morgan asked.

"Do you know any lawyers?"

"What does this have to do with solving the murders, Ash?"

"Nothing, John, but it's important to help a DA when you can because they can help you sometimes when you need it, you know?"

"Okay. I get it. I do know a lawyer who does PI. I just met him recently and like him. He is an old friend of Robby's. Based on what I know from Robby, he is a straight shooter."

"Would you ask him if he will meet with Dave for me? Maybe he will have an idea that can help with his investigation."

"I will. I don't have his number, but Robby does. They are planning to get together, and I need to call Robby to find out when so I can join them."

"Great. Now, I have to go. Watch out for Dugan. I warned him, but he's got it in for you," Ashford says as he heads for the door. Then he adds, "And, John … thanks for the breakfast. You are going to be a good catch for some woman," Ashford says with a grin.

"Yeah, yeah … very funny," Johnny replies as he turns to take the plates to the sink.

———————

George is on the phone at his office. He is talking with his examining physician for the case coming up before Judge Franco in Bronx Supreme Court. The doctor has confirmed his opinion and is set. George has told him that he will let him know when he needs him to come to court and testify. He will call him with updates about what is being testified to by the plaintiff's expert. He gets off the phone and decides to go out to get a sandwich and an apple juice from the deli on Lexington Avenue. He returns with a salami and provolone sandwich and is unwrapping it at his desk when Bob Campanella enters the doorway of his office. George looks up.

"Hi, George. Sorry, I did not mean to disturb you, but I have some info on that matter we discussed."

"No problem. Please come in. I have to go on a conference this afternoon, so I hope you won't mind my eating lunch while we talk."

Bob takes a few steps into George's office.

"Of course not, go ahead. I spoke with a friend of mine who is a detective sergeant. He called a senior DA he knows who, it turns out, is investigating kickbacks to civil judges. He wants to know if I can help in terms of getting a lawyer to wear a wire when dealing with such a judge. I know you would do it, but that probably would not prove actual kickbacks. What are your thoughts?"

"I would do it, but, as you say, the most that would reveal is the biased rulings and behavior, not the reason for the behavior. Let me think about who should be the target. I don't know any staff of a judge who would be willing, so that's out. A defense lawyer getting help for a payoff is unlikely. It has to be someone who will profit from the bribe. We somehow need to get a plaintiff's lawyer who actually is involved in the kickbacks. Unless the lawyer is just pissed about paying the judge a kickback, the DA will probably have to get the goods on someone and then leverage him or her to wear the wire talking with the judge and giving the judge the payoff."

"That sounds right, George. I will leave you to think about it, but be circumspect, okay?"

"I will. Thanks for making the call."

Robert Campanella leaves George's office. George takes another bite of his sandwich and a swig of his apple juice, thinking about who would be a candidate for a wire. He finishes his sandwich and opens his desk to take a piece of dark chocolate, which he always keeps on hand as his dessert. The phone rings, and he picks it up.

"Hello."

"George Fredericks?"

"That's me. How can I help you?"

"I am looking for a guy who used to ride a Montesa in Spain and appreciates fine art."

George laughs. It is obvious who it is.

"Is this the famous artist Mr. Johnny Colrain?"

"Ah hah, I figured I wouldn't stump you. It is."

"What's up, John?"

"When are you going to Robby's for another dinner?"

"I don't know. Robby has not called about it, but I would love to have more of his mom's cooking and see him and you again."

"Great. Can you meet me there tonight at around seven? I want to talk to you about something. It's Friday so no court tomorrow."

"I can do that. See you there."

George hangs up and wonders what Johnny has on his mind. He slips on his suit jacket, grabs his briefcase, and leaves his office to go to court.

14

STUART SCHLUSSEL HUSTLES down Fulton Street, crosses Water Street, and enters Sloppy Louie's. It is still light out. He looks around, searching for Joe DeFeo. He doesn't see him so he takes a table near the bar. Don Wilkins is sitting at the bar in Sloppy Louie's having a Budweiser. He is dressed in a worn gray Henley shirt and jeans with work boots on. He has a two-day stubble on his face. He looks like he could be a worker on the docks or at the Fulton Fish Market. Schlussel looks around and gestures to a waiter for a menu. When the waiter comes over with the menu, Schlussel tells him that he is waiting for someone, and they will order then. He is thinking about some of the tactics used by Joe and the risk to himself. A few minutes later Joe DeFeo comes in and looks around. He sees Schlussel and joins him. Schlussel waves to the waiter, who goes to the table with another menu, and the two men look them over. After a few minutes, DeFeo motions for the waiter to come back and orders Manhattan clam chowder and steamers. Schlussel orders the skate.

They both order Miller Lite beers, and when the waiter leaves, DeFeo speaks angrily.

"I think someone had loose lips about the fake potholes and it got back to Dugan. He snooped around and probably learned about the kickbacks but not the extent of them."

"Shit, Joe. That is bad. He will make trouble for us at some point."

"I know. We have to get something on him to keep his mouth shut."

"What about the parties?" Schlussel offers.

"Yeah. That gives him something else against us. We have wives and families. It does not prove anything against him. He would deny supplying drugs, and we would not want all that being brought up."

"Do you think he would try to blackmail us?"

"That is what worries me."

"Do you know anyone in the DA's office or in the police department who might know him?" Schlussel asks.

"No. I have to involve him as a witness in one of our phony cases, and then he will be careful not to say anything. It will mean giving him a payoff."

"How can you do that? He is a detective. He doesn't testify in auto cases."

"He's greedy. There has to be a way. Let me work on it," DeFeo says as he finishes his chowder.

The two attorneys start in on their main courses. They fall silent, each thinking about his own jeopardy. Then they start talking about the judges who have been given kickbacks. As they finish the lunch, DeFeo says, "Stuart, have you had any dealings with Franco recently?"

"Yes and he has let his power up there in the Bronx go to his head."

"I'll say. I was up there last week, and he had fifteen lawyers sitting in the hallway outside his courtroom waiting for their cases to be called. He keeps them waiting for a long time. He then calls them in and, if the case doesn't settle, he will have them come back every day for weeks or send the case out for jury selection right then to pressure them unless he knows one or more of the attorneys. He has compiled a record of disposing of a lot of cases that way. It's his little fiefdom. He also steers any case that needs an annuity to be purchased to a specific company that he has ties to—namely, the company his girlfriend works for."

"That is probably not too smart," Schlussel muses.

"No. But let's face it. He has a Napoleon complex or something. He likes pushing attorneys around if he can get away with it. I heard George Fredericks has defeated his pressure tactics by being ready to pick a jury and then going to trial and winning his cases. He is not afraid of Franco, who begrudgingly respects him as a result."

"I heard the same from Frank Santangelo, who has a case with him. Have you had cases with Franco, Joe?"

"Yes. He can be a real dick, and he is greedy."

Stuart laughs. "You have him pegged."

"How much do you think Dugan knows?"

"Hard to say. That really does not matter much. He knows enough to be dangerous."

The two lawyers finish up their meals. DeFeo orders an espresso and Schlussel a regular coffee. Schlussel pays with his credit card, and DeFeo hands him some cash. They have their coffees, leave the restaurant, and walk back toward Broadway.

Don Wilkens gets off his barstool. He stretches, reaches into his jeans, and pays cash for his beer. He then goes to the phone and calls DA Morgan.

"Dave, Schlussel and DeFeo met and had a big talk over lunch. I heard some of it. They are worried about someone named Dugan, and they definitely are involved in both fraud and kickbacks to judges."

"Dugan ... huh? Okay. I think I know who that is. Good work. Come in."

———

Dave hangs up and dials Jim Ashford.

"Ashford."

"Jim?"

"Yes. What's up, Dave?"

"There is an attorney I am focused on who might be persuaded to wear a wire, but we have to get to him first. I just want you to know."

"What's his name?"

"Stuart Schlussel. He just had lunch with another lawyer we have been watching because we suspect he is involved in kickbacks and fraud. They are worried about someone named Dugan."

"Dugan?"

"Correct. Your partner is named Dugan, right?"

"Yes. I thought he might be involved in something but not with attorneys paying kickbacks to civil judges for favors or fraud in civil cases."

"Well, I am assuming it is your Dugan so keep alert and call me if you find out something you think I should know."

"Definitely. Same for you."

"Right. Talk soon."

"Later."

The two men hang up.

Ashford tries to think how Dugan got involved with these civil attorneys and paybacks to civil judges. Dugan has nothing to do with that end of the legal system. Ashford taps his pencil against his metal desktop. He looks over to Dugan's desk. Dugan is not there. Supposedly he is running down a lead on the three murders. Ashford ponders if there is a connection between the murders, Dugan, and the kickbacks. People kill for money and to protect themselves from being exposed. He can't imagine how Dugan would be involved with models unless it involves drugs. He has tried to figure out the connection with Burke Lambert, but he has come up empty. *Lambert was mayor and then went back to being a successful attorney. He might have strayed from his marriage, but that does not make him involved with the murders of two models. What could that have to do with kickbacks to judges?*

George Fredericks finishes showering in his third-floor one bedroom apartment on East Seventy-Eighth Street between Madison and Park. It is in a five-story brick apartment house with an elevator. Each floor has two one-bedroom apartments. His apartment is comfortable but not large. He leased it after moving out of the San Remo where he lived with a fashion model for six months. She was very pretty and nice but crazy. This apartment has a great location and is rent stabilized. He got it by being assertive when he saw it advertised in the *New York Times*. He had been living for some weeks in his sister's apartment with her and her husband and was desperate to get his own place. He called the tenants moving out at 7:30 a.m. That upset the husband of the couple, but then George called again at 9:00 a.m., spoke to the man's wife, and talked her into letting him come to the apartment to look at it. He liked it, went directly to the managing agent's office, and rented it.

The main complaint he has is that the apartment faces north so there is not much sun or bright outside light. It does not help that the large wraparound casement window in the living room facing north and east looks out mainly on the brick wall of the adjoining apartment house, and the apartment is surrounded by much taller buildings. Nevertheless, the apartment has charm. It has herringbone parquet floors, a working fireplace, and a curved archway to the hall leading to the bedroom, which is spacious. He likes that it is near Central Park and the Lexington Avenue subway. He originally decorated it mostly with hand-me-downs, including a flokati rug, but recently he purchased some new furniture and a red Bokhara rug, making it much nicer. It obviously is a bachelor pad.

He dresses in gray pinwale corduroy slacks, a light blue polo shirt, and a navy-blue blazer. He is wearing Allen Edmonds brown-and-black loafers with blue-and-black argyle socks. He grabs his wallet and keys from his antique oak dresser, which his parents bought from a dealer on Second Avenue for two dollars when they came to New York City from London. He had it restored. It is beautiful with serpentine drawers. He takes a quick check of himself in the mirror, runs his fingers through his thick hair, and proceeds to the front door. He opens the Segal door lock and exits the apartment, double-locking the door behind him. He passes on the elevator and sprints down the stairs.

It is still light out, and George decides to walk over to the West Side. He enters Central Park through the Seventy-Ninth Street entrance at Fifth Avenue and walks up the hill past the Metropolitan Museum through the Great Lawn of the park to take the Eighth Avenue subway at Eighty-First Street and Central Park West. He takes the C train to Forty-Second Street, switches to the A Express to Canal Street. He walks to Beach Street and then west to North

Moore to Pier 25. The weather is mild and has turned partly cloudy as evening is approaching. George is feeling good. He likes Johnny Colrain and wants to know more about him. He is looking forward to seeing Robby and his mom again, not to mention her savory cooking.

George enters Robespierre's and looks around. He sees Johnny at the bar talking with Robespierre. He waves and approaches the bar. He sits next to Johnny, who pats him on the shoulder. Robby smiles at him.

"Hi, George. How are you?"

"I am good, Johnny. How are you doing?"

"I am okay but still stumped by the murders of the two models that I want to help my detective friend solve. He asked for some help in regard to something else that I want to ask you about."

"I am all ears," George says.

"As am I," chimes in Robby. He then asks, "What can I get you guys?"

"I'll have a dry Tanqueray martini, stirred, straight up with a twist."

Robespierre raises his eyebrows and comments, "Excellent choice, John."

"Sounds good to me, I'll have one too," George says.

Robespierre grabs the Tanqueray bottle from behind the bar and starts to make the martinis. George then focuses on Johnny.

"What can I help with, Johnny?"

Johnny tells George about his conversation with Ashford and his request.

"I told him that I do know a lawyer whom I just met and would ask."

George laughs out loud.

"That is interesting. Let me tell you why."

George explains that by definition a judge is supposed to be a neutral player in a case. But sometimes there are judges who are biased, or just not that bright, or tend to favor lawyers they like or who contribute to their elections, but it is subtle. They don't usually go overboard trying to force a settlement of a case or interfere directly with the trying of the case to make the outcome go a certain way, that is, blatantly favor a certain lawyer or side. But lately there has been some funny stuff happening with judges on two of his cases. He tells the two men about his experience with Judge Katz as an example of going over the line. Robespierre manages to listen despite stirring the martinis. He pours the two drinks carefully through a strainer into the martini glasses he has set on the bar. He rubs each glass with a lemon twist, which he then floats on top of the drink. He places the full glasses on napkins in front of his two friends and speaks.

"That sucks, George, for lots of reasons, but it certainly isn't fair to the litigant on the other side of the favoritism in play. I know bad stuff happens in the criminal system, especially for minorities, but I am surprised that it happens on the civil side also. I guess I shouldn't be, especially where money is involved."

"That's right, Robby. It is not what I signed up for when I went to law school to be a trial lawyer. It is unfair and subverts the whole system. It really pisses me off."

Johnny, taking a sip of his drink, says, "Very smooth."

George takes a sip of his drink, smiles at Johnny, nods his yes, and then explains, "I spoke to the senior partner in my firm about my suspicions, and he made a call to see if someone knew anything about kickbacks to judges. He obviously must have spoken to your friend Ashford, who wanted you to talk to a lawyer about who could wear a wire ... small world."

Johnny smiles. "I guess so. Do you have any ideas?"

"I do. I have to think about how to handle it."

"Would you be willing to meet with a senior DA after I talk to Jim Ashford?"

"Sure. I would be glad to get this unraveled."

Robby addresses the two of them.

"Okay, you two. How about something to eat?"

Both George and Johnny say yes at the same time and laugh together.

"Okay … I will go tell my mom and see what she can come up with."

———————

Dugan and Donnelly are sitting at the bar at the Emerald Inn on West Seventy-Second Street, drinking beer. Dugan is not happy.

"I missed getting that meddling turd, but I will get him."

"What do you plan to do?"

"I am not exactly sure, but I need him out of the way."

"Why do you hate him so much?"

"He cost me a promotion to second-grade detective."

"Does it have anything to do with the murders of the models?"

Dugan looks hard at Donnelly and says, "I just don't like the guy or to be interfered with."

"You thought he killed one of them, right?"

"Well, his prints were all over her apartment, but apparently they were friends, and he took her home that one time, as you know. He may still be involved somehow."

"Anyway, I don't think that is why you asked me to meet you. What is on your mind?"

"How would you like to make some serious extra money?"

Dugan then proceeds to tell him about his plan.

15

CAROLE LANSDORF LOOKS in her closet. She is in a robe trying to decide what to wear for her gig at the Village Vanguard. She has managed to put together a nice wardrobe. Some of the clothes she bought at modeling jobs when she liked them, and the stylist and client agreed to sell them to her, but most she just shopped for at good stores. She has excellent taste despite her background of growing up in a little mining town. She lives in a prewar building on East Eighty-Fifth Street on the fifth floor with only a view of Eighty-Fifth Street, but it is just off Madison Avenue and is a very spacious nice one-bedroom apartment with a dining room. She likes to cook and occasionally entertain her friends. She had been living with a photographer boyfriend in his big apartment in the Parc Cameron on West Eighty-Sixth Street. It had a big kitchen that she loved, but she caught him cheating on her with one of the models he was photographing. She suspected that it wasn't the first time, and she did not like some of his friends who she knew did drugs so she ended the relationship and found this apartment, which she really likes.

———————

Johnny, George, and Robby are finishing up a spicy meal of jerk pork with curried peach relish, fungee, and callaloo. They are telling stories about each other.

Lucienne has come out to check how they liked the food. They all are very happy and full. She doesn't ask if they want dessert but brings them a classic dessert from Antigua called ducana made with yams. They have had some rum drinks with the meal, and everyone is pretty loose. They dig into the dessert.

"Delicious!" exclaims George.

Johnny and Robby grin.

"Is anyone up for going to the Village Vanguard and listening to some music?" Johnny asks.

They all say yes as they finish up their ducana. Robespierre calls his maître d' over to the table and gives him instructions. They all go into the kitchen to thank Lucienne for the wonderful meal and prepare to leave. When the three men get outside, Johnny climbs on his bike. George and Robespierre walk to North Moore and Greenwich and hail a cab.

Johnny arrives first and parks his bike on Perry Street. He walks to the entrance on Seventh Avenue and waits for his two friends. He sees the sign on the outside about the program but decides not to go in. While he is wondering about the name of a singer on the bill, Aarika gets out of a cab and taps him on the shoulder. She laughs when he turns to face her and shows his surprise.

"Hi, Johnny."

"Well, hello!" he exclaims, recovering.

"That was a dramatic departure from my shoot the other day."

"Yes. Sorry about that. Everyone was okay afterward, right?"

"A little rattled, of course, but yes. Did that have something to do with Adrienne's and Renée's deaths?"

"I don't know but thanks for your information. It helps a lot."

"I am glad. It's pretty terrible thinking about two people you knew and worked with on occasion being killed."

"It is. I hope I can help find out who killed them," Johnny says with seriousness.

There is an awkward pause.

"Are you here to listen to Carole?" she says, nodding toward the sign and picture.

"Did she used to model also? She looks familiar," Johnny says.

"She did—a lot of print. I met her at Warren Robertson's studio, and we are friends. This is her first big gig."

At that point, the cab with Robespierre and George shows up. They pay and get out of the cab. Robby smiles, seeing Johnny with a beautiful woman, and says hello to Aarika. She smiles at him.

"Hello," Aarika says back to him.

George looks at them, surprised that Johnny is there talking with a woman he obviously knows. Johnny smiles. "These are my friends, Robespierre and George, Aarika," Johnny says.

"Nice to meet you," George and Robby say to her. She smiles and says the same.

They are about to go in when a tall lean guy calls out to Aarika. Everyone turns around. The man in his thirties is dressed in a black turtleneck and black slacks. He has very black wavy hair, thick eyebrows, dark eyes, and a closely trimmed mustache and beard. He is handsome in a forbidding way. He is slim, not athletic looking. He does not project friendliness.

"Riki, can I speak with you a minute?"

Aarika turns to Johnny and his friends. "Excuse me, please. I hope I see you all later."

"Same here," George replies as he, Johnny, and Robby watch her turn and approach the man, and the two start to speak. George looks at Johnny.

"You know some lovely women, Johnny."

Robespierre grins. "Indeed, he does."

The three men open the door, go down the stairs, enter the club, pay the cover, and get a booth facing the stage. The waitress comes over, and they order drinks as the first act takes the stage. They listen and talk as the room fills up more. After two acts finish, the band strikes up "I Love Being Here with You," and Carole Lansdorf walks out and takes the microphone. She is stunning in her gold lamé sheath dress. The band stops playing, and the audience gets quiet. She looks out at the crowd.

"Good evening, I would like to sing some classic songs for you."

The band starts up. After "I Love Being Here with You," she goes right into "My Baby Just Cares for Me." She has the attention of everyone in the room, especially the men. Johnny, George, and Robby are watching intently. George is especially affected.

"Who is that?" George asks. "She is beautiful! And talented."

Johnny looks at him and laughs. Robby's eyebrow goes up. He looks at Johnny.

"Uh oh, John. I don't know if George should get this distracted."

"You know him better than I do, Robby!"

They laugh, and George hears them but has a hard time taking his eyes off Carole and not concentrating on her. He has a feeling of excitement. His heart flips over. They listen without talking. She finishes "Cry Me a River" and starts "The Nearness of You." They are all mesmerized. They don't notice that Aarika and the man she was speaking with have also entered the club and are sitting at a table in the center of the room. A little while later two other men join them. Johnny notices them and looks over for a minute but thinks nothing of it.

———

Priscilla and Simon Stone come out of the Broadhurst Theatre west of Broadway at Forty-Fourth Street.

"Well?" asks Simon.

"It was great, Simon. Kind of sad, but I thought the acting was superb."

"*Death of a Salesman* is a classic. Poor Willie."

They are holding hands but don't really seem to go together. Priscilla is wondering about whether it is a mistake to keep seeing this attorney. She is enjoying being wined and dined and now going to the theater, but her feelings for Simon have not grown much.

"Let's go for drinks to a little French place I know, Demarchelier, on East Eighty-Sixth Street. It is small and quite charming."

"Okay. That sounds nice."

Priscilla is letting herself slip into something that may not be what she bargained for but is feeling that she cannot turn him down at this point. They get a cab uptown and then enter the charming red façade at 50 East Eighty-Sixth Street, a stone's throw from Simon's apartment.

"Hello, Mr. Stone," the bartender says as they sit at the bar at the front of the restaurant. Priscilla notes this. Simon must be a regular here. They sit catty-corner at the end of the bar closest to the window next to the entrance. The bartender brings them their drinks, and Simon offers a toast.

"To many more lovely evenings like this, Priscilla."

Priscilla blushes and smiles.

"Yes. It has been lovely," she answers.

———

Carole sings "The Look of Love" and then finishes the set with "Let's Fall in Love." George can't believe his reaction to her; he really is taken. Robby and Johnny notice but don't disturb his reverie while she is singing. There is a lot of applause after her last song. She thanks everyone—there is more applause, so she sings "Deed I Do" and then walks off the stage during more applause and some whistling. She comes back and sings "There's a Lull in My Life" and, despite the loud applause and more whistling, she leaves the stage for good. The spell is broken. George looks at Johnny and Robby, who are looking back at him, amused. They say nothing. George makes a sheepish face.

"Sorry, guys. She is fantastic."

"We agree," Johnny says as Robby nods and smiles.

"Do you know her, Johnny?" George asks.

"No, I don't, I have never met her, but my friend Aarika who you met outside knows her."

"Oh," George says, the wheels turning in the obvious direction. "I wonder if she is involved."

"I don't know, George, but I can find out."

"Nice," is all George can muster in response.

Robby just listens and then gestures with his head toward the stage. Carole has just come out of a door and proceeds through the audience. Aarika waves to her, and she heads for Aarika's table but makes a face when she sees whom Aarika is sitting with.

"Let's get the bill and leave."

They try to get a waiter's attention. Robby makes the motion of writing on a bill. The waiter sees him and acknowledges the message and walks toward the bar to write it up. They all take a glance over at the table where Carole has gone and can see there is some intense discussion going on. Carole is not sitting, and the tall dark man stands up as he is talking. Aarika grabs the man's arm and is obviously asking him to sit down. Carole walks off toward the cloakroom. She emerges with a little black jacket over her dress.

The waiter brings the bill, and they all throw down enough cash to cover it and get up. George looks over at Aarika's table, but it is empty. They follow some other people leaving and slowly make their way up the stairs to the door. Finally, they get outside.

George looks around when he hears loud voices and arguing. There is a group of people about thirty feet up the avenue from the entrance where they have emerged. He sees that Carole is protesting about something, and the tall dark man is grabbing her arm. Aarika is trying to get him to stop, and the other two men are just standing there. One is small with a pointy face and dressed in gray slacks and an open-collared Hawaiian shirt. The other is of medium height but stocky with a short-sleeve blue print shirt and black jeans. He is muscular and looks fit. He has brown close-cropped hair and a nondescript face whose main feature is a nose that turns up at the end. George looks at Johnny and Robby. Johnny can tell he is concerned and, frankly, Johnny also doesn't like what is going on.

Robby speaks, "Guys, I don't know if it is a good idea for us to get involved. They look like they all know each other, and it is just a dispute of some kind."

They continue to watch what is going on. Carole is trying to pull her arm away, and finally manages to do so. Aarika is talking. It looks like she is trying to calm the waters. She takes Carole's arm, and they start to walk away. The man Carole pulled away from and his two friends follow the two women, and George starts walking in the same direction. Johnny and Robby go with him. Somehow, George, Johnny, and Robby all smell trouble.

Carole suddenly moves away from Aarika and lifts her other arm to hail a cab as one approaches with its vacancy light on. When the cab pulls over, Carole steps into the street to open the door, and the tall dark man moves quickly forward, reaches past her, opens the door, pushes her in, and jumps in after her, slamming the door shut. Aarika protests and yells at the cabbie to wait as she steps into the street toward the cab with her arm out. The short man stops her, and the other man holds her arm. The dark man is inside the cab yelling at the cabbie to drive away, and Carole is yelling at him to stay put. The cabbie is confused, and the cab does not move.

George runs to the back door of the cab on the street side and opens the door. He ducks his head in the cab, ignoring the man's angry face, looking straight into Carole's beautiful eyes, round with shock. Johnny and Robby arrive next to Aarika and tell the two men to let her go. The two men look at Johnny and Robby and decide to do just that.

"Do you want to go with this man, Miss Lansdorf?" George asks.

She looks up at him with a surprised look and says no. He reaches out his hand, which she grabs, and exits the cab. Carole is standing by the cab in the street totally flummoxed. George continues to hold on to her hand, very aware of its warmth and smoothness. He starts guiding her toward the sidewalk. At that point, the dark man furiously exits the cab on the sidewalk side, runs around the back of the cab, and takes a swing at George. Johnny yells to George, but George has already sensed the blow and moves enough that it only glances off his cheek as he lets go of Carole's hand. The man swings again, and this time George moves his head outside the punch, which misses. He then steps forward, throws a quick left jab, followed by a short quick right, and is about to follow that with a left hook, but the tall dark man has already gone down from the right. He is lying on the street on his back and not getting up. There is some blood coming from his mouth. George looks at him with disdain for a minute, unclenches his fists, and then walks to Carole who is stunned standing by the curb. Aarika runs to Carole as the cab takes off.

"Are you okay?" asks George.

The two men who were standing close to Aarika stay put for a beat and then go to help their friend up. George watches them, alert in case something develops.

"Yes. Are you?" replies Carole, reaching up to touch his cheekbone, which is already getting red. He turns to look at her then reaches up and gently puts his hand on her hand touching his cheek, never taking his eyes from her face, and smiles. He marvels at the blueness and sparkle of her eyes. He likes her face.

"I am better than fine."

Carole laughs at him, a little embarrassed, but does not take her eyes off his face as she slowly takes her hand away, very cognizant of the good way his feels on hers. Aarika is also staring at George. Johnny and Robby approach as the two men help their friend get up, look around, and the three of them slowly walk away. As they do, the dark man wipes his bloody mouth with his sleeve. The small man turns his head and looks back. Johnny records his nasty look and watches him carefully until the man turns his head back facing forward.

"Thank you, Mr. uh ..." Carole turns to Aarika for help.

"I don't know it either, Carole," Aarika says as she turns to Johnny.

Johnny and Robby are standing there looking at George with amusement.

"We don't know him either, Riki!" asserts Johnny with a chuckle. There is a pregnant pause, and then he adds, "At least this side of him."

Then Robby says, "Speak for yourself, John. I have seen it before a long time ago."

This breaks the spell between Carole and George.

"Meet my friend, George Fredericks, Ms. Lansdorf," Robby continues.

"Thank you, Mr. Fredericks," Carole says slowly, looking intently at George.

She registers his high cheekbones, very dark blue eyes, tanned skin with some freckles, aquiline nose, and thick brown hair.

"George, please, Ms. Lansdorf," George says, looking just as intently back at her.

"Carole, please, George."

Everyone laughs, and the mood has totally shifted. Robby is relieved. He is happy this did not turn out to be a real fight with cops getting involved.

"It is getting late, but how about we all go to my place for a few drinks before the night is gone," Robby suggests.

Everyone agrees.

"I will take you on my bike, Riki, if you are game," Johnny offers.

"I would love to, Johnny," Aarika answers, and they walk to his bike.

Robby, George, and Carole hail a cab.

Dugan is riding in his unmarked patrol car with Donnelly. They cross the Brooklyn Bridge and go into Brooklyn Heights. He finds the brownstone building he is looking for and parks. The two of them walk up the stairs, and Dugan rings the bell. A woman opens the door. She is dressed simply and is dark and quite thin with glasses.

"Hello, Ms. Morton, I am sorry to disturb you. I want to introduce you to my friend Donnelly here. He would like to avail himself of your service."

———

Priscilla is lying in bed in Simon Stone's bedroom. She is trying to go to sleep, but she can't. She is reviewing in her head what happened this evening. They had some drinks at Demarchelier, and then it was a short walk to his apartment. She now realizes that was part of the plan. She finds him interesting and thought she would like to see his apartment, but she wasn't planning on sleeping with him. He opened a bottle of champagne and poured it into two thin flutes. She could not handle it after the drinks she had already consumed and got a little tipsy. It is not an excuse, but she succumbed. He obviously is experienced, but she did not climax. She did not feel comfortable despite the drinks. He tried hard, but she just could not relax enough. Now she really wants to go home, but it is very late. He is asleep next to her. She really has no desire to be there with him or wake up with him. She slides to the edge of the bed, slowly pulls back the cover, and gets out. She picks up her clothes, takes them into the next room, and puts them on. She quietly lets herself out, summons the elevator, and leaves the building.

———

Robespierre, George, and Carole find Johnny and Aarika waiting for them at the door to the restaurant when they arrive after the cab drops them off. Carole sat between George and Robby during the ride. George felt like a schoolboy. He is amazed how attracted he is to her. Her nearness, the touch of her leg next to his, her scent, her energy and smile made his heart flip over again. The conversation flowed easily during the ride. He asked her where she grew up and when she came to the city. Carole asked him a little about his background and how he knew Robespierre and Johnny Colrain. She asked Robespierre to confirm his story in jest. Robby told her a little bit about himself, George, and Johnny during the ride.

The restaurant is closed. Robespierre takes out his key, opens the door, and turns on the lights. They go in and sit at the bar. Robespierre goes behind the bar and asks everyone what they would like to have. Aarika asks him if he knows how to make a Martinez. He laughs at her and tells her of course he does. Johnny, George, and Carole don't know the drink but decide to try it. Robespierre gets to work making them.

"Who was the man who tried to get you in the cab?" George asks Carole once they get settled. They are sitting next to each other.

"He is my ex. We broke up about six months ago," Carole says, looking at him with seriousness. "You were brave doing what you did."

George looks back with concern in his eyes. "Has he tried anything like that before?"

"No. That surprised me. He wants to get back together, but I have moved on."

Aarika and Johnny are sitting at the bar next to each other to the right of Carole, who has turned to talk to George. Aarika is turned toward Johnny and they are involved in their own discussion.

"Riki, did you know who those guys were?" Johnny asks.

"I knew the tall dark guy was Carole's ex, Andrjez. I met him a few times. I could never understand what she saw in him. He is a photographer and gets a lot of magazine work. That's how Carole met him."

"Did he ever date Reneé or Adrienne?"

"Not that I know of. He lived with Carole for a while, or rather Carole lived with him. Have you made any progress in helping your detective friend solve their deaths?"

"I can't say that I have been much help."

"I wish I could help more."

"Thanks, Riki. What you told me did help."

Robby sets all the drinks down in front of everyone, and he has one for himself. He proposes a toast. He lifts his glass.

"Here is to new and old friends."

They all smile and raise their glasses. They clink and take a sip. Carole then addresses Robespierre.

"Robespierre, are you unattached?"

"Yes," he says with a raised eyebrow.

"Do you know who Felicia Bailey is?"

"The singer?"

"Yes."

"She sings the blues. She is good. I believe she is from North Carolina. I know she is very beautiful. Why?"

"Well, I just met her recently at an exercise class, and we have become friends. She is a very sweet person. She helped me get the gig at the Vanguard. I think she would like you based on the little that I know about you."

Robespierre breaks into a huge grin and replies, "Are you suggesting that you could introduce me to her?"

Carole smiles back at him. George is watching her. Her smile is warm and magnetic.

"Precisely. She is not seeing anyone. She is quiet, smart, and very particular."

Johnny breaks in here.

"Do his friends have anything to say about this? Would Felicia like to talk to George and me before she agrees to meet this rogue?"

Everyone laughs, and Carole says, "I will talk to her and give her a rundown."

The five of them talk and drink into the wee hours, and then it is time to go home. Johnny offers to take Aarika home on the bike. She agrees. George and Carole walk over to Greenwich Street to find a cab. Carole holds on to George's arm. He likes feeling her next to him, holding his arm. She likes feeling the muscle of his arm. He gets serious for a minute.

"Carole, who were those other guys with your ex?"

"I don't know. I think they are new friends that he has met drinking. He has called me up a few times late at night, obviously drunk."

"I don't like the look of them. You should be careful."

"Yes, sir." She smiles at him and gives his arm a squeeze. She actually likes his concern about her. This is a bit of a surprise since she has always been independent and able to take care of herself from the time she was young.

"I don't mean to be presumptuous, but I am serious."

"I am getting that. I will be careful."

They find a cab and give the cabbie the address of her apartment house on East Eighty-Fifth Street. They are holding hands. Again, George marvels at the warmth and feel of her hand. Her presence fills the cab for him. Their fingers intertwine and then let go to hold the entire hand, and then they intertwine their fingers again. They both look down at their hands clasped together, then at each other. She is amazed how excited she is by this man she has just met. She wonders what is going on with her but then tells herself to just go with it. He wants to lean in and kiss her, but he doesn't. He smiles at her, and she smiles back. He is trying to control himself and not be too forward. He pays the cabbie despite her protests, and he helps her out of the cab. He stands with her outside her building for a minute. He is sorry to have the night end despite the fact it is really early morning. They have exchanged telephone numbers. They face each other. He holds both her hands. It is awkward but not. She does not want the night to end either. They look at each other's faces in silence, exploring, for a little while. There is some kind of silent communication going on. Finally, she lets go of his hands and gives him a hug and a quick kiss on the mouth.

"Good night, you."

"Good night, Carole."

She turns and walks toward the entrance to her building. He watches her. She turns as the doorman opens the door to the lobby, and she sees George watching her. She quickly waves and disappears into the building. Once Carole is in the lobby, she does a little skip and laughs at herself. She feels a special kind of excitement. George walks to Madison Avenue and then south toward Seventy-Eighth Street, full of all kinds of thoughts that surprise him. He is a goal-oriented man who has constantly been fighting to achieve his ambitions since he was young. He has had a few crushes and infatuations, but he has never felt the way he does about this woman even though he has only just met her. It is disconcerting in a good way. He wants to know her better. He smiles at himself.

16

JOHNNY COLRAIN TAKES BALOO for a walk in his neighborhood. It is early, and the weather is cloudy and cool. He is trying to process everything that happened last night and also what information he has concerning the murders of Adrienne and Renée. He reflects for a minute about Aarika. They kissed good night, but he does not think he will be calling her. She is very beautiful and truly nice, but he is not sure they have anything in common other than modeling. He isn't feeling it, and he is intrigued by a very different woman, Priscilla. He decides to call Robert Easton and ask a few questions about her.

George wakes up late for him. He makes some oatmeal for himself, topping it off with berries, a tiny amount of dark brown sugar, and some heavy cream. He demolishes the cereal and has half a grapefruit. Looking at the *New York Times* as he is drinking some dark French roast coffee, he decides to take a run around the reservoir in Central Park before tackling his work. He finishes a second cup of coffee, dumps his dishes in the dishwasher, and changes into some shorts and an old T-shirt with the Sun Valley ski resort name on it. He puts on his running shoes, grabs his keys, locks the door, and heads down the stairs.

He runs down East Seventy-Eighth Street, crosses Fifth Avenue there, and then up to the Seventy-Ninth Street entrance to the park. He makes his way up behind the Metropolitan Museum on the sidewalk that leads to the bridge over the bridal path to the running track around the reservoir. He jogs twice around the reservoir thinking about the previous night. George is not crazy about jogging. He always hated it, but when he stopped playing volleyball because of a shoulder injury, he started jogging. It took some getting used to because he couldn't help being competitive with some of the guys jogging around the track fast, not to mention a few fast women. This was not the point of jogging, he realized, plus some were real runners, and he isn't. Finally, he stopped trying to keep up with them.

At the end of his jog, George walks past the north end of the museum down the hill to Eighty-Fourth Street and Fifth Avenue. He crosses the avenue and goes up to Eighty-Fifth Street and then continues over to Madison Avenue. He laughs at himself. He knows he is hoping he will run into Carole. *What are you, a kid?* he thinks to himself with a smile. *Maybe,* is the inner response. He does not see her and walks down Madison toward his apartment. George has plenty of work to do but would love a beautiful distraction named Carole. He hums that old jazz standard "I've Got You Under My Skin" as he walks, turns the corner at Seventy-Eighth Street, and enters his building. He has to buckle down and get some work done.

Robespierre is in a dressing gown having a latte with his mother. He is recounting the previous evening, and she is listening carefully.

"This friend of yours, George, is handy with his fists," Lucienne says.

"He is. That is how I originally met him."

"I remember the story. I am glad no cops showed up last night."

"*Moi aussi.*"

The phone rings, and Robby goes to answer it.

"Robespierre's, can I help you?"

"Hi, this is Carole. We met last night."

Robby laughs. "Yes. The evening is burned into my mind."

She laughs also. "I know what you mean. Thank you for your help. Anyway, I was thinking that I would have a dinner party at my apartment and invite Johnny, George, you, and Felicia. I don't know if Johnny has someone he would like to bring, but, if so, we could add her also. What do you think?"

"That sounds wonderful. I will bring the wine and, by the way, Johnny doesn't have a girlfriend—yet."

"Deal. I will let you know when. Is there any evening that will not work that you know of?"

"I know George is starting a trial, and it would be hard for him on a weeknight if he is on trial. Let me get back to you. May I have your telephone number?"

"Of course."

Dugan, Donnelly, and Joe DeFeo are having coffee at the Moonstruck Diner on West Twenty-Third Street.

"Donnelly here can be an investigator for you, Joe."

"I already have one, Dugan. You know that," responds DeFeo, looking at Dugan and trying to figure out what he really wants.

"You need more than one. You can't just have one guy testify all the time. It will look suspicious. I told Donnelly that he could pick up some extra money working for you."

"Okay. When I have an auto or slip-and-fall case coming in, how do I reach him?"

"Just call me," Dugan says.

"What about you? Are you interested in looking into some cases for me?" Dugan snorts.

"No. I am an active detective. It would not look good," Dugan says with a smile. *I am not doing your dirty work for you*, Dugan thinks to himself.

Johnny hears his phone ringing as he opens his door coming in from walking his dog. He runs for the phone.

"Hello?"

"Hey, John. Did you talk to your lawyer friend?" Ashford asks.

"I did. He will meet with the senior DA, Morgan. I gave him the telephone number."

"Any new information on the model murders?"

"I think there is a connection to Blake Lambert, Ash, but I don't know exactly what it is yet."

"We really don't have much. I spoke to all the models' neighbors but came up empty. There was nothing unusual that they could tell me about a boyfriend or ex. I also can't figure out about Lambert's murder. There was no robbery. He had political enemies but not the kind that would murder him. I am going to talk with his wife on Monday."

"Ash, how about a little hoops? Maybe we can get a two-on-two game on the Village courts and let off some steam."

"I'd like to, John, but I promised the wife I would go out to the Island with her to see her folks."

"Okay. Rain check. Talk soon."

———

Johnny calls Robert Easton.

"Hello. Robert Easton."

"Hi, Robert. It's Johnny."

"Hi, Johnny. I have sold another of your paintings to a friend of Emilia Rusk."

"Great! Can I talk to you about something else?"

"Sure. What's up?"

"I am wondering about Priscilla. Do you know if she is serious about that lawyer?"

Robert Easton smiles to himself. He likes both of these people, but he does not want to get involved.

"Johnny, I know she has seen him a couple of times, but that is really it. I don't know how involved she is or what her feelings about him are, nor is it any of my business."

"Right. I can see that. Is she there?"

"No. She is off today."

"Okay, thanks."

Johnny is frustrated. He does not have Priscilla's number and really does not want to ask Robert for it and put him in an awkward position. He is not sure he would call her cold if he had it. He takes out a new canvas.

———————

Robespierre is in the living quarters above the restaurant. He is reclining on a flowered chaise with his feet up. There is a round brass table next to it with a cup and saucer on it. He is reading and also listening to Felicia Bailey sing the blues. He loves the smooth sound of her voice. She has a tremendous range including a very low register that is extremely sexy. The idea of meeting her is intriguing, and the prospect does excite him, but he is trying to keep his expectations under control. He wonders what it would be like to have her as a love interest. It is definitely an enticing thought, but he allows that it is not an easy thing to be involved with a singer. *Who knows what she is like as a person? Pretty, yes, but maybe she is single because she is difficult.* Also, he has a unique living situation with the restaurant and his mom. Maybe this would not be of interest to her. He realizes he is in fantasyland. This makes him think of George's being smitten with Carole, and he wonders if George, the lawyer, his friend, has thought about what it might mean to get involved with a singer. Robespierre smiles. *It was interesting to see George move so fast and take action to rescue Carole. He did not hesitate.* Robespierre's mind then drifts to another intense friend. *Johnny Colrain's investigating the murders of the two models is dangerous. Johnny got shot at. His dog took a bullet. It's no joke.* Lucienne, calling to him, interrupts his musings. Robespierre goes downstairs.

———————

George is having trouble concentrating for long stretches of time. His mind drifts to Carole. He is angry at himself for not trying to arrange a date before saying good night, but at the same time he is hesitant about calling her. He doesn't want to rush anything. He can't help but feel that something special could happen between them. He is also about to start a trial. He turns back to the preparation of his questioning of the plaintiff in the case he is about to start. He has catalogued the page numbers of important testimony on his yellow pad so he can access them if necessary to cross-examine the plaintiff about any discrepancy between his deposition and testimony at trial. George also has mapped out his plan of attack in questioning the plaintiff to expose his false claims. He turns to the plaintiff's work records. He then goes back to checking the doctor and hospital records, highlighting key portions. He also has to plan his cross-examination of the plaintiff's expert. He feels he is very prepared, but he knows that there will be fireworks when he gets in front of Judge Franco.

Muriel Lambert gets up and answers the intercom. She is a small woman in her mid-sixties—very slim and about five feet, three inches tall. Her face is quite wrinkled but you can see the intelligence in it. She has short gray hair, wears no discernible makeup, and her glasses have silver metal frames, which accentuate her very blue eyes. Her only jewelry is a man's Cartier Tank watch on her left wrist and a thin gold chain around her neck. She is wearing a crisp white shirt, black gabardine slacks with a narrow Hermès belt accentuating her small waist. On her feet are gray suede Belgian Shoes with black leather trim. She tells the doorman to send the detective up to her apartment. Jim Ashford gets off the elevator and goes to the door of the duplex apartment. Muriel opens the door and asks him in. They go into the living room. Originally built to be an artist's studio, it has huge double-height windows and is impeccably furnished.

She beckons him to sit on one of two slip-covered love seats. She sits on the other one, facing him, and speaks, "Detective Ashford, how can I help you?"

"I would like to know if you have any idea who would want to kill your husband."

She gives him a hard stare. She can't believe she is having this discussion.

"I don't. I really don't."

Muriel is very upset but tries not to show it. She was married for a long time to Burke Lambert, and they weathered a lot of storms together. She does not seem like the kind of woman who puts up with too much nonsense. He was the glamorous half of the couple, and she was the backbone.

"Did he have any enemies?"

"He certainly had some political enemies but not the kind that would want to actually kill you."

"Was he involved in drugs in any way?"

"Frankly, Detective, I think he did do some recreational drugs, but it never was excessive, and I never saw him have a problem."

"Where did he get these recreational drugs?"

"I think from friends that he used to go out with on occasion."

"When you say recreational drugs, what are you referring to?"

"Pot. I think he may have done some cocaine also, but I am not sure about that."

"Did you use these drugs with him?"

"No. I was never was interested. Yes to a dry martini or glass of wine, but I never was into drugs of any kind."

"Did he do them with you or in front of you?"

"No. Neither. As I said, I suspect he might have done them occasionally with friends."

"Which friends?"

"I don't know specifically. He had lots of friends. You can go to the New York society pages for a list of all our friends."

"What makes you believe that he did these drugs?"

"He has come home on occasion, after being out without me, rather high. Not drunk, just buzzed."

"Did you ever hear him arguing on the phone with anyone about drugs?"

"Absolutely not!"

"Did your husband ever go out with Adrienne Wyatt?"

Muriel gives Ashford a steely look.

"Not to my knowledge," she says with annoyance.

"How about Renée Toulouse?"

"Same answer."

"Do you know who they are?"

"Of course, Detective. I read the papers."

"Did your husband know either of those two women?"

"Not to my knowledge."

"Did your husband have any trouble at work?"

"Just the normal kind. He was mostly a rainmaker, and I think his firm liked it that way."

"No difficulties with any partners, secretaries, support staff, or clients that you are aware of?"

"No."

Ashford closes his notebook and stands up.

"Thank you, Mrs. Lambert. I am sorry to have disturbed you. Please call me if you think of anything that might be relevant to his death."

"I find it hard to believe he is really dead, Detective."

Ashford hands her his card. They walk to the door, and she opens it.

"Yes. I understand. Thank you for talking with me."

"I don't understand why he is dead, Detective, and I want you to catch his murderer."

Ashford calls for the elevator and turns to Muriel.

"That is what I intend to do, Mrs. Lambert."

Once outside, Ashford finds a telephone and calls Dugan at the precinct.

"How did you make out with his law partners, Dugan?"

"Nothing. They all know nothing."

"What about his former political opponents?"

"They say that they disagreed with him politically and his policies, but they actually liked him. They all had no problems with him once he got out of politics."

Ashford shakes his head.

"How did you do with Muriel Lambert?" Dugan asks.

"No better."

"Did she know of anyone who might have a reason to kill him?"

"Nope."

"Anything new with the deaths of the models?" Dugan asks.

"Nothing that you don't know. I may go and talk with Randy Macquilken. Did you run the bank accounts?"

"Nothing unusual."

"I'll see you back at the precinct."

Rita Schlussel is thinking about her husband. He has seemed strange recently. Something is wrong. She walks into the study and opens a drawer in the desk. She looks at his phone book. She has never done that before. She doesn't know what she is looking for. She wonders if her husband is having an affair. She thumbs through the phone book and sees a number for *BL*. She dials the phone number, and a woman answers.

"Hello?"

"Hello. I am sorry to call like this. My name is Rita Schlussel, and I found this number in my husband's phone book with just the initials *BL* by it, and I wondered who that could be."

"That would be the initials of my husband, Burke Lambert."

"Oh." Rita pauses. "Sorry to trouble you at this time, but I have never heard my husband mention him. Do you have any idea why he would have his home number?"

"I don't. Maybe there is a political connection. My husband was in politics for a long time. It also could have something to do with his law practice."

"I see. My husband is a personal injury attorney. Did your husband ever mention him, Stuart Schlussel?"

"Not to me, but he did not bring his work home and rarely discussed business. He also did not do personal injury. His practice was confined to corporate finance."

"Do you know if they socialized in any way with mutual friends?"

"I don't."

"Thank you. I am sorry for your loss."

Muriel hangs up the phone and thinks about this strange call. She wonders if it could have anything to do with her husband's murder. She reaches for the phone.

She calls Detective Jim Ashford and tells him about the call. He thanks her. He thinks about what could be the connection between Stuart Schlussel and Burke Lambert. He calls Dave Morgan.

"Dave, do you know of an attorney named Stuart Schlussel?"

"I sure do. How do you know of him?"

"I just got a call from Muriel Lambert, Burke Lambert's wife.

Schlussel's wife called her because she found the number next to the initials *BL* but did not know who that could refer to."

"We are tapping Schlussel's office phone because he is a suspect in regard to the kickbacks to certain judges."

"Do you think there is a connection between the kickbacks and the murders of the models and Burke Lambert?"

"I don't know. I can't think about what it would be right now."

"Okay. Do me a favor. Keep me posted on the kickback investigation."

"I will, Ash. And you keep me posted about the murders, okay?"

"Of course."

Ashford puts down the phone and calls Johnny Colrain. He gets the machine and leaves a message to call him.

17

GEORGE WALKS WITH Frank Santangelo from the jury selection rooms in the Bronx Supreme Court on the Grand Concourse. Some lawyers do not like to go to the Bronx courthouse, he assumes because of the ethnicity of the surrounding neighborhood with African Americans, Puerto Ricans, and West Africans living there, which caused white middle-class flight to the suburbs. George always appreciates the big square limestone fortress with a large terrace. The courthouse, built in the early 1930s, is renowned for the quality of the sculpture flanking its four sides. George likes taking the subway to Yankee Stadium and walking up the hill with all the attorneys streaming up the large flight of steps leading to the portico in front of the building on 161st Street.

Having completed jury selection, the two lawyers walk back to Judge Franco's courtroom. Frank is representing a thirty-four-year-old Con Ed worker, Ed Flanagan, who fractured his ankle and claims it was misdiagnosed in the ER at Mount Herman Hospital. As a result of that, he claims that he suffered for three days at home before he went to an orthopedist, was diagnosed, and had the fractured bones in his ankle reset. He claims that he has permanent injury as a result of the missed diagnosis and that he lost a great deal of work. He is married with two children. George is representing the hospital. They report to Judge Franco's clerk and are ushered into the office behind the courtroom. They both sit in chairs in front of the judge's desk. The judge addresses Frank.

"What is your demand, Frank?"

"Five hundred thousand."

"What is your offer, Mr. Fredericks?"

"Fifteen thousand dollars."

Judge Franco becomes angry. He addresses George.

"Are you sure you understand this case, Mr. Fredericks? This man has been seriously injured and is claiming permanent damage."

"I understand the case, Your Honor," George replies dryly.

"As I have told you, there is significant exposure here, and your client could get hit for a large sum. Do you want me to call the claims adjuster and speak with him?"

"I have gone over the case with the adjuster, and he agrees with my position in terms of the offer," George replies firmly.

"Please step out, Mr. Fredericks," Judge Franco directs, barely able to keep his anger under control.

George gets up and leaves the office.

Judge Franco addresses Frank.

"If I help you win or get this case settled for you, I want you to pay me that $15,000, Frank, and depending on what the final recovery is, I may want more."

Frank is rattled by this.

"Judge, I don't think I can do that."

"You can, and you will if you want to recover any money on this case. Now go out and send in Fredericks."

Frank goes out and tells George to go in. He waits outside the door to the office near the clerk's desk. George enters the office.

"Mr. Fredericks, I want you to go back to your office and speak to the senior lawyers in your firm and come back tomorrow with a more substantial offer." George resents this pressure but keeps his cool as he locks eyes with Franco looking up at him from behind the desk. He says nothing. He doesn't want to argue with this judge. There is an awkward pause. Judge Franco then adds, "I will see you here tomorrow at 10:00 a.m."

George turns and leaves the office. He wonders why some judges are just so craven. It always is refreshing to be before a decent, smart, and honest judge who will let you try your case.

———

Frank Santangelo calls Stuart Schlussel after getting back to his office. He explains what Judge Franco said to him. He adds, "If I don't agree to pay him off, he will make the trial tough on me. I am up against Fredericks, and he doesn't play games."

Stuart Schlussel does not understand why, but Judge Franco is not going along with what the plaintiff lawyers had agreed to in regard to not paying off judges.

"I know Judge Katz told him that there would be no payoffs for the present time, and the greedy dick did not like it. I still was under the impression that he was accepting it for now. Maybe he is in debt. I would stall him."

"I will try, but you know how he is."

"Yes, I do. Keep me posted."

———————

George Fredericks enters One Hogan Place and proceeds to Dave Morgan's office. Several male assistant DAs in their shirtsleeves walk by him carrying papers or files. A secretary sitting outside of Morgan's office asks who he is, buzzes Dave Morgan, and announces that Mr. Fredericks is there to see him. Morgan responds, and the secretary ushers him into Morgan's office. Dave comes out from behind his big desk and sticks out his hand. George notices Morgan's physique, crew cut, and military bearing. George steps forward and shakes it. Dave indicates that he should sit down in one of the leather chairs with brass studs in front of the desk, and he does. Dave goes back behind his desk. He looks at George sizing him up as an athlete and smiles.

"How do you know Jim Ashford?"

"I don't. I know a friend of his, Johnny Colrain, the artist."

"Oh yes. I have heard of him from Jim."

"How can I help you?" George asks.

"As you know, and I believe you are interested in this investigation, I am looking into a few judges on the civil side taking kickbacks."

"Yes. I told one of the senior attorneys at my firm that something fishy was going on with a few judges. I think he called your friend Jim Ashford. Detective Ashford spoke to Johnny, and Johnny spoke to me. That about covers it."

"Do you have the name of any attorneys or judges who may be involved?"

"I have some suspicions but nothing definite."

"Can you give me names?"

"Well, there is an attorney named Stuart Schlussel that I am suspicious of. There are two others whom I am not completely sure about. I suspect Judges Franco in the Bronx and Katz in Manhattan."

"Interesting. We have a tap on Schlussel's office phone, and I think you are probably correct. You are on trial in front of Judge Franco now, I believe."

"I am."

"Well, it seems that Judge Franco wants a payoff on your case from your opponent, Frank Santangelo."

"That doesn't surprise me that much."

"This might give us an opportunity to catch Judge Franco in the act."

"How?"

"We have to work out a plan so that Santangelo or one of his pals wears a wire when the judge asks for the payoff."

"He's not going to do it in front of me. That's for sure."

"I get that, but maybe we will get an opening if we can get Schlussel to wear the wire during the trial. I will let you know."

"Okay. I think my trial is going to be a big fight so it will go for a while."

"Good luck with it."

"Thanks."

George leaves the office thinking about what he has just heard. He heads for the Brooklyn Bridge subway station to take the Lexington Avenue subway to the Upper East Side. He exits at the Seventy-Seventh Street stop and decides to call his writer friend, Roy Nance. He is going to stop at the Mad Hatter on Seventy-Eighth Street and Second Avenue for a burger so he doesn't have to cook at his apartment before settling in to work. Roy is a screenplay writer and is usually happy to join him. He lives on Third Avenue and Seventh-Seventh so it is an easy haunt of his.

"Roy! It's George. You up for a burger at the Hatter?"

"Hey, George! That sounds great. I am bogged down on the project that I am working on, and that will work for me."

"I just got off the subway at Seventy-seventh Street."

"Okay. I will meet you there."

George and Roy were introduced by a mutual friend whom George met when he took some acting classes. He thought it would be fun and interesting to do, and it was. Roy is heavyset, with wild, thick black hair. His usual outfit involves wearing sweats and sneakers. He is a very funny guy who is mentally quick and usually writes comedy. He is wry, witty, often sarcastic, and he makes George laugh. They talk about all kinds of things including Hollywood gossip and the various girls that George has dated. Roy's dating life is a mystery that he does not talk about. George does not pursue that part of his life. Roy knows most of what is going on in show business and usually comments on it for George's amusement. George knows he will tell Roy about Carole. He also knows he wants to.

18

JOHNNY COLRAIN IS SLOPPY with paint on his clothes. He is standing in front of an easel, making broad strokes on a big canvas. He is intense and into what he is doing. The phone rings. He puts his brush down on the table next to the easel and scoots over to the phone, pushing past his big white dog.

"Hello."

"Johnny?"

"Yes. Riki?"

"Yes."

"What's the matter? You don't sound too good."

"I know it's early in the morning but can I come to your place?"

"Sure. Do you know where I live?"

"No."

Johnny gives her the address and looks around his loft. He straightens up his kitchen, putting two dishes in the dishwasher, and makes his bed. Baloo moves over to the sleeping area and then plops down on the rug with a big sigh. He puts his head between his paws. When the buzzer goes off, the big dog stands up and starts walking toward the door. Johnny hits the intercom, confirms that it is Aarika, and pushes the buzzer for the street door. In a few moments he hears the knock and goes to open the door to his loft. Baloo is behind him. Aarika is there in jeans, a white T-shirt, and a faded jean jacket. She looks somewhat disheveled. Johnny knows her as always being meticulous about her appearance. She has a concerned look on her face. He holds the door open, looking at her. She walks in and gives him a hug. She takes a look at Baloo and smiles. They go into the kitchen. Johnny puts on the kettle to make some coffee. They sit at his counter as he prepares the coffee. As usual, Baloo lies down nearby with a big harrumph.

"What's happened, Riki?"

She grabs her cup with both hands and starts to tell her story.

"I attended a party last night. It was held at a brownstone in Brooklyn. I went with a couple of new younger models you don't know. There were a lot of people there. You know, me, Johnny. I am not a big drinker, but I had a couple of glasses of white wine. I started to get very sleepy. I remember talking with one of the men there. He was a lawyer, well dressed but kind of slimy, if you know what I mean. He tried to get me to do some lines of coke with him, which I declined. He then asked me some lurid questions about whether I was into being spanked and stuff like that. I walked away from him. Later on, I saw one of the girls kind of out of it coming out of a bedroom with the same guy, and then I saw him go and talk with a man I recognized. It was the police officer who shot at you."

Johnny pours coffee into her mug and points to the half and half. "You're kidding."

"No. He was talking to the man who came out of the bedroom. That freaked me out, and I left the brownstone. I managed to get a cab right away. I gave the guy my address and then actually passed out in the cab. The cabbie woke me up when we got there and with the help of the doorman assisted me into my building. I fell into bed, and I awoke this morning hungover. I think there was something in the wine. Anyway, Chris from the agency called me to ask me if I knew where Susie Griffin, one of the new girls, was. She found out that Susie had been at a big party in Brooklyn that some of the other girls had attended. I said no, that I did not know her, but I was at a party in Brooklyn last night with a lot of models too.

"I took a shower and then got another call that the agency had to cancel Susie's go-sees because she wasn't well and asking if I could go over and check on her. Of course, I said yes, got her address, and went to her apartment. It was the girl I saw coming out of the bedroom. She was a mess. She let me in and started crying. She took off her pajamas and turned around to show me her backside and legs. She was black and blue. It looked like she had been beaten. Her face was not touched, but she had definitely been beaten on her back, buttocks, and legs. She had no marks on her wrists and ankles. I guess she was not tied up, but I imagine that she didn't have to be. I asked her what happened, and she was not sure. She said she had done some coke, had some wine, and then she was out of it and thinks she eventually passed out."

"Did she report this to the police?"

"I asked her, but she said no. She is pretty sure she was not raped, but she did have dried semen on her. She has a boyfriend back home and did not want to report it. She also is afraid about what might happen at the agency if she did that since she is new and just starting out."

"How did she get home?"

"One of the men put her in a cab, she thinks. I thought you should know about this in case it might have a connection to the murders of Adrienne and Renée."

"It is good you told me. It might, but I am not sure."

"Johnny, that detective gives me the creeps."

"Yes. He gives me the creeps too."

"I have to go, but I was wondering if you would like to come for dinner sometime."

"That would be nice."

"Good. I will call you."

Aarika finishes her coffee and gets up to walk to the door. Johnny walks with her and grabs Baloo's leash.

"We'll go out with you."

Baloo wags his tail as Johnny leans down to put the lead on him. They exit the building together, and Aarika gives him a quick hug and kiss on the cheek. She pets the dog and then hails a cab.

Johnny finishes his walk with the dog and hangs up the leash. He gets on the phone and calls Jim Ashford. Jim's phone rings, but he is not at his desk. Dugan picks it up.

"Hello, Ash?" Johnny asks.

"He is not here, Colrain. What are you calling about?"

"Ask him to call me."

"Listen, Colrain. We don't need you interfering with our investigations. You could get in trouble, and that would be a shame."

Colrain's skin prickles hearing Dugan, but he manages to control himself.

"I'll bear that in mind, Dugan," he says, keeping his dislike in check.

"Be sure that you do."

Johnny does not take the bait and hangs up. He then redials the precinct. He asks for the front desk. He then leaves a message with the sergeant to have Ashford call him.

———

Priscilla is doing office work at the gallery, but she's distracted. She is not sure about her relationship with Simon Stone and is thinking about breaking it off. He is a nice guy and obviously wealthy, but her feelings have not progressed. There is something that makes her feel uncomfortable. They don't laugh together. He is not silly or much fun. She does not think they have a lot in common, and now she knows that they don't have much chemistry.

As she is winding down her work, her roommate Leighann comes into the gallery. The two friends are going out for drinks and dinner. They say goodbye to Robert Easton and walk down the stairs.

"Where shall we go?" Leighann asks.

"How about Robespierre's. It's a nice walk, and we can talk our way there."

"Good idea. You told me the food is really good."

It is a nice walk, and they are gabbing the whole way. Priscilla starts to tell Leighann about her feelings in regard to Simon Stone. They arrive at Pier 25 twenty minutes later. They walk down the pier to the restaurant and open the door. When they enter, it is not crowded, and the bar is empty. Robespierre, behind the bar, greets them. They wave and wait to be seated at a table. A waiter tells them to sit anywhere, and they take a table not far from the front of the restaurant. The waiter comes over, and they order Manhattans.

Ten minutes later the door to the restaurant opens. Johnny Colrain and Jim Ashford come in. Robespierre is happily surprised. The two men take seats at the bar. They order two Bass Ales from Robby who turns to get them. He puts an open bottle and glass in front of Johnny, catches his eye, and nods towards the dining area. Johnny looks out into the room and spots Priscilla. She notices him and gives a short little wave. Leighann looks over at the direction of the wave and smiles at Johnny. He gets up and goes over to their table.

"Hello."

"Hi, Johnny. You remember Leighann, my roommate?"

"Of course."

"I think Robert would like you to come to the gallery before the exhibit closes," Priscilla tells him.

"I have to do that."

"Where is your buddy with the mustache?" asks Leighann.

"Probably working, if I know him. He is on trial."

"Oh. That makes sense. He told me he was a trial lawyer."

"I think he knows your lawyer friend, Priscilla," John says, probing. Priscilla blushes. "He probably does."

Leighann interjects. "We were just discussing him."

The conversation becomes awkward.

"Well, I just wanted to say hello. I will let you get back to your discussion."

Johnny walks back to the bar.

"I think he likes you," Leighann says.

"I work at the gallery that is showing his paintings, Leigh."

"Just sayin' ..." Leigh says with a big smile.

Robby was watching and asks, "How did that go?"

Johnny smiles wanly. "Not well. Not well."

Ash raises an eyebrow and then the three men then start talking about what Johnny heard from Aarika. They are not sure if it means anything, but there might be a connection in view of the marks on Adrienne's body. Ashford wonders about interviewing the young model. He doubts that she remembers much because of her state either from alcohol or from being drugged. Maybe he can get a name. He also would like the address of the brownstone so he can research the owner or renter. Ashford is very concerned about Dugan's presence there. It doesn't mean he did anything wrong, but it is very curious. Some other customers come in and sit at the other end of the bar. Robespierre leaves to take their orders and make their drinks before returning to Johnny and Ashford. The three of them discuss whether there is a relationship not only between the party events but also whether there is any connection to Burke Lambert's death. Ashford relates the conversation with Muriel Lambert and the call from Schlussel's wife. He mentions that Schlussel is under investigation for kickbacks to judges. "What is the connection there?" they wonder out loud. Ashford brings up that Dugan was at the party where the model was beaten, and his name came up in the discussion overheard at Sloppy Louie's. They discuss what the connection could be. Johnny reminds Ashford about what happened at the photo shoot. Ashford explains that Dugan says Johnny was a suspect because of his fingerprints at Renée's apartment, and he ran.

"Do you believe that, Ash?" Robby asks.

"No. I called Dugan out about it. That is his justification, and he is sticking to it. He is involved somehow, but I can't believe he would risk his career."

The conversation is interrupted by a ringing phone. Robespierre picks it up, and his face changes its expression, becoming concerned and serious. Johnny and Ash watch him listening and then saying thank you and hanging up. He comes back to the group.

"That is very unusual."

Johnny and Ash just look at him and wait for him to continue.

"Miss Buttercup said a friend of one of her girls was drugged and beaten at a party in Brooklyn. The name was Susie Griffin. She thought we should know based on Johnny's questions."

"That must be the same party that Aarika told me about!" says Johnny.

"It's the same model," Ashford says.

———

Simon Stone and Stuart Schlussel are sitting in the sauna at the Russian and Turkish Baths on Tenth Street in the East Village with towels around their waists.

"You missed a great party last night, Simon," says Stuart.

"Really? What made it so great?"

"Lot's of pretty girls, models, and high-quality coke."

"How do you get out, Stuart? Doesn't Rita get suspicious?"

"I told her that I had a lawyer dinner in Brooklyn."

"Where did the coke come from?"

"Dugan."

"He was there?"

"Yes. And he got a little rambunctious."

"Meaning?"

"You know."

"Did anyone get hurt?"

"One girl got pretty bruised up, but she is okay."

"Where was it?"

"A brownstone that I rented for the party."

"Where does Dugan get the coke?"

"I am not sure. I think either it's confiscated, or he knows a dealer. Anyway, he seems to have a big supply."

"Are you seeing someone now?" Stuart asks.

"Yes. A nice girl, but I am not sure it's going anywhere."

———————

Johnny Colrain and Jim Ashford ring the bell outside a walk-up apartment building on East Twelfth Street. The buzzer rings them in. They walk up three flights and knock on the door. The door opens a little, and they see a young woman through the space past the chain lock.

"Hello, I am Detective Ashford, and I am here with Johnny Colrain, a friend of Aarika West, to speak with Susie Griffin."

"Come in, please. I am Susie."

She closes the door, removes the chain lock, and reopens it. The two men enter. The tall, thin, disheveled young woman is dressed in a pink robe. She has flannel pajamas on underneath her robe and is barefoot. She is attractive in a raw unsophisticated way. Johnny notices her large gray eyes and dark eyebrows. Her nose is just a little too big for her face, but somehow it just makes her look exotic. She looks very young, not more than nineteen, about six feet tall, and lanky. She tells them she shares the apartment with two other girls who are not home. She asks the men if she can get them something, like coffee or tea, and they decline. She beckons for them to sit in the kitchen at a Formica table that has chrome legs with matching chairs. Susie gets herself a bottle of Evian water from the fridge and sits down.

Ashford asks her about how it was she went to the party, and what she remembers about what happened. She is embarrassed but not intimidated. She removes the cap of the water bottle and takes a sip. She tells them she went to a go-see where there were tons of girls. She was just chatting with a girl she did not know, who said she was going to a party in Brooklyn and invited Susie to go with her. The girl said lots of models were going. Susie agreed, and they went together. After they entered, they went into the crowded living room and saw several people sitting around a coffee table snorting coke. The other model spotted someone she knew and walked away to see her friend.

Susie had never done anything stronger than pot before. An older guy beckoned her to sit down. He showed her what to do, and then the two of them did some lines. She got high, and the man got up and came back with two glasses of wine. They drank the wine and talked a little, but it was hard to talk because the music was so loud. He asked her to dance with him. She saw some girls and guys going up the stairs to other rooms. She recalls not feeling well and being escorted out to a cab. The next thing she remembers is the cab driver's helping her to her building, buzzing her apartment, and one of her roommates coming downstairs to get her. Her roommate brought her upstairs, and both roommates undressed her and put her to bed. When she woke up, she was really hurting and smelled of urine. She looked at her back, backside and legs in the mirror and was freaked out when she saw all the bruising. After she took a shower, she called the agency to tell them she was not feeling well and could not go on any of the go-sees that were scheduled.

Ashford asks Susie if she can tell him the name or telephone number of the model who invited her to the party. She explains she can't. She doesn't even remember her first name. The girl is not from her agency, and they did not exchange numbers. She also doesn't know the address of the brownstone. She met the girl at Union Square and the girl told the cabbie the address, which was written down on a piece of paper. Susie knows that it was in Brooklyn, and that they did not drive for a long time after they crossed the Brooklyn Bridge. It was a nice neighborhood with well-maintained brown-stones on the block. She doesn't know who gave the party.

Johnny asks her what she remembers about the guy who did the blow with her. She said he was average height, was dark, and wore a suit and tie. He was older and sort of slick. Not the kind of guy she ordinarily would be hanging out with. Ashford asks how old. She guesses around forty. She remembers that the suit he had on was shiny and that it looked almost purple. She thought that was unusual. He also wore a purple tie. He had a narrow face and dark hair and eyebrows. He was clean-shaven. She does not remember any name other than a first name he gave, which was Stan. Johnny followed up with a question about whether there was any other person there that she could describe. The only other person she remembers was a fat unattractive older guy walking around talking to a few men. He was partly bald and had bad skin.

Ashford asks her if she is sure that she was not violated. She replies that she knows her body, and she does not believe so. She had a tampon in and was in the middle of her period. Everything was in place. She did volunteer that she thinks there was ejaculate on her back and left leg when she stood up and looked at herself with her back facing the bathroom mirror. She smelled of urine. She took the hottest shower she could stand and scrubbed her body. Jim Ashford then asks her if she wants to be taken to a hospital for an examination, but she declines.

They thank her, and Ashford gives her his card. He asks her to call him if she runs into the model that went to the party with her or if she remembers anything else.

19

CAROLE CLOSES HER MUSIC and walks away from the piano in a rehearsal studio near Carnegie Hall. She is happy. The session with her accompanist has gone very well. She looks over to the woman sitting in one of the chairs along the wall looking back at her with a serious look on her face. Carole is wearing a white shirt and jeans with bright blue flat shoes. She walks to the woman in the chair holding her sheet music.

"What do you think, Felicia?"

"I think you have it, girl," Felicia says, breaking out into a big grin.

"Oh, Felicia. Did it really sound good to you?"

"It really did, Carole."

"I loved your session, Felicia. You have such range."

"How about a coffee?"

"That sounds great."

Felicia gets up. She is wearing a creamy yellow sweater set and charcoal gray skirt with black low heels. She is thirty-five years old.

Her brown hair is curly and medium short. She has flawless smooth dark skin. Her face is small and proportioned with large dark eyes and nice lips. She is very pretty. Her figure is slim with gentle curves that make her extremely feminine and attractive. Men find her sexy. She does not dress to accentuate that characteristic. Her smile is sweet and magnetic. It produces two small dimples in her cheeks. When she laughs, she lets out a funny high-pitched sound and shows perfect white teeth. She has a good sense of humor, and when you get her laughing with her sounds, it is infectious. You laugh and it makes you want to make her laugh more.

The two women walk to the Carnegie Deli and sit down. They decide to go crazy and order pastrami sandwiches. The waiter hustles over with his white apron wrapped around his waist to take their order. The place is bustling, and the men behind the counter are calling out when an order is ready. The smell is classic deli from the garlic pickles on the table to the meats behind the counter and the sauerkraut.

"The sandwiches here are huge, Felicia. Shall we order one to split? Maybe an extra potato salad?"

"Sounds right to me. I don't like eating a big lunch," she says.

They order one pastrami on rye for two and two coffees. It comes with coleslaw and they decide to order a second coleslaw and not a potato salad.

"Are you going to come to my dinner, Felicia?"

"Are you sure about this guy Robespierre, Carole? I sing the blues, but I am not interested in experiencing them again anytime soon."

"I wouldn't invite you to meet him unless I thought he was a quality individual. I don't know any of them very well, but they stood up for me, and I like them all."

"You aren't fooling me, Missy. I know one of them has you a little over the moon, right?" Felicia says with a laugh.

"Now, what do you mean, Miss Cool Breeze? Where did you get that from?"

"I don't have to be a detective to figure that out based on what you told me about your evening after the Village Vanguard performance. George is his name, I believe."

Carole smiles at her friend, a twinkle in her eyes.

"To tell you the truth, Felicia, it worries me a little. I have never had such a big reaction to a man. He really is something special. You'll see. That is another reason why you have to come to my dinner!"

The waiter brings over their order.

"Wow! This is a huge sandwich. They do overstuff them. I am glad you suggested we split one. If we finish all this, we will have to take an extra exercise class. But more importantly, tell me about Robespierre. Is he cute?" Felicia asks.

"He is, and very charming with an incredible smile that makes you smile back at him. He is from the Caribbean. He came to New York City as a kid with his mom. He got himself educated, was an English teacher for some years, and then, after working at The Raunchy Brit as a bartender at night for a while, he decided to open his own restaurant, Robespierre's over on Pier 25 with his mom, who does the cooking. They live in a big apartment above the restaurant. That is what I know, but I have a feeling he would like to have a real love in his life. That is just my assessment based on instinct and from some remarks he made. I will tell you he loves his two friends. That impresses me."

"He sounds interesting. Honestly, you know me a little, Carole. I am pretty quiet and more of a homebody than people would guess. Do you think I will like him?"

"I don't know for sure, but I am thinking yes. He is dedicated to his mom, the restaurant, and his friends. He is smart, charming with a big smile, and, as I mentioned, pretty darn cute even though I know, despite the fact that you asked, you aren't into that superficial stuff." Felicia breaks out in her patented high-pitched laugh that makes Carole laugh too.

"Okay. You have me convinced. I will definitely be there. Can I help?"

"I think I have it, but if you could come over early and just talk me down, that would be great."

"You are so silly. Of course I will."

20

GEORGE SITS QUIETLY LISTENING to Frank Santangelo tell the jury about the horrible malpractice in failing to diagnose the plaintiff's ankle fracture and all the damages that occurred as a result of this failure. You can tell nothing from the serious look on his face. He glances up at Judge Franco and wonders what makes a guy like that tick. Frank finishes telling the jury that after listening to all the evidence, they will find malpractice against the hospital, and he will be asking them to award a substantial amount to his client at the end of the case. Santangelo sits down, and Judge Franco nods to George. He says, "Mr. Fredericks."

"Thank you, Your Honor," George replies and rises. He walks in front of the jury box and holds the banister in front of the jury with both hands, looks at the forelady, then the rest of the jurors. He pauses, then lets go of the banister and begins his opening by carefully addressing them.

"May it please the court, Madam Forelady, and ladies and gentlemen of the jury ..."

He speaks quietly and effectively. He explains to the jurors that he will show through the evidence and testimony how the ankle fracture was missed and that what happened after that was not what Mr. Santangelo has told them so that by the end of the case they will render a verdict consistent with the true facts and with the law.

Judge Franco breaks the jurors for lunch. He instructs the attorneys to go into his office behind the courtroom. They enter. He goes behind his desk and addresses George, who is standing.

"Mr. Fredericks, have you done what I instructed yesterday afternoon?"

"I have, Your Honor," George replies.

"Well?"

"Nothing has changed, Your Honor. Our offer is $15,000."

"You are going to be sorry. Please step out."

George leaves the office and goes out into the courtroom. He gets his briefcase and leaves. Frank Santangelo remains with the judge.

"Well, Frank, what about our prior discussion?"

"I am not prepared to do anything about that today, Judge."

Judge Franco is steamed. He slams down his pen. "Well, Frank, we will see how your trial goes. I'll see you after lunch. Be back at 2:00 p.m."

———

George grabs the elevator and walks out of the building past the columns and down the steps to 161st Street. He heads for the Court Deli down the hill from the courthouse. It is a little early so the lunch crowd is not fully there, and he can get a table. He sits down in the glass-enclosed elevated area and places an order with the heavyset woman who comes and asks him if he needs a menu or knows what he wants. He has ordered from her before. She is always in a rush, and you have to know what you want or she becomes exasperated. He orders a ham and Swiss cheese sandwich on rye and a ginger ale. He opens his briefcase and takes out some notes to look over. The deli starts to fill up. Eventually, lawyers are looking around for a place to sit. His head is down as he eats and looks at his notes when he hears a familiar voice.

"Can I sit with you, George?"

George looks up to see Stuart Schlussel looking at him.

"Sure," George replies.

"Are you on trial?" asks Stuart.

"Yup," answers George, turning back to his notes.

The waitress hustles over and Stuart orders a cup of matzo ball soup and a corned beef sandwich. George asks her for a coffee and the check. He keeps studying. Stuart takes out his copy of the *Daily News* and looks at it. The waitress comes with Stuart's food and George's coffee. She can carry multiple dishes. When she returns with another table's order, she drops George's check on the table. Stuart eats and reads his paper. George gets up, picks up the check, and puts a few bills on the table as a tip.

"See you, Stuart."

"Good luck, George," responds Stuart.

"Thanks."

George goes to the cashier, pays, and leaves the restaurant. He walks up the hill toward the courthouse. Stuart Schlussel looks out the window and watches him for a moment before turning back to his lunch. George's mind is full of his cross-examination of Frank's first witness, whom he expects to be his medical expert. He has about an hour before court will start so he heads for the lawyers' library where he can study more.

———

Stuart finishes his meal, leaves his tip, and pays the cashier. He strides up the street and into the courthouse. He takes the elevator to Judge Franco's chambers. He has two cases scheduled for conferences on the judge's calendar. He enters the outer office and says hello to the secretary. He asks if he can see the judge. He waits a minute as the secretary goes inside and talks to the judge. She comes out and waves him in. Stuart enters. Judge Franco looks at him from behind his desk.

"Hello, Stuart. You should have come up before I broke for lunch. I would have taken you to Arthur Avenue to eat with me."

"Thanks, Judge, that would have been great, but I had some matters that had to be taken care of," Stuart replies, smiling and knowing full well that being taken to Arthur Avenue to Judge Franco's favorite Italian lunch spot there would mean the judge would invite one or two other attorneys or pals, and he or another plaintiff's attorney would be picking up the tab.

"What can I do for you? I don't think you have any cases before me until later this week."

"That's right, Judge. You have a great memory."

"Well?"

"You remember the infant Randolph case that I settled in front of you two weeks ago?"

"Yes. I remember it."

"Well, you recommended that we use a certain company for the structured payout to the plaintiffs."

"Yes. What is the problem?"

"My client and the referring attorney want a different company."

"Why?"

"I don't know, but they insist."

"I am not happy to hear this, Stuart."

"Look, Judge. I did not object to your referral to the company that you recommended, but I can't really argue with this attorney who sends me cases and the client whom he controls."

Judge Franco frowns and looks at Stuart.

"You know that I signed the compromise order with the understanding that Consolidated would be used for the structure, right?"

"I do."

Stuart and the judge look at each other. It is awkward. The judge breaks the silence.

"You can't change their minds, Stuart?"

"I tried, Judge."

"Okay. I guess we have to go with it."

Stuart stands up and looks at the disgruntled judge. He is unaware that the ethics committee of the Bar Association of New York has been looking into the referral of such structures from Judge Franco to one company where his girlfriend works.

He leaves Judge Franco's chambers.

Frank Santangelo puts on his expert witness who proceeds to explain to the jury using the X-ray that the ankle fracture was missed. He then testifies what can happen when the fracture is missed and what pain is endured when you step down with such a fracture. He concludes that the doctors on duty in the emergency department departed from good and accepted medical practice in failing to diagnose the fracture and that this departure caused pain and suffering to the plaintiff. He is vague on how long that initial pain would last. The expert also opines that the missed fracture could lead to arthritis, which could mean some pain and possibly stiffness for the rest of the plaintiff's life.

George gets up to cross-examine. He is very conscious of every detail of what went on with this patient. He initially attacks the expert, getting his admissions that he has testified multiple times for plaintiffs and does not testify for the defense. George takes him through what he charges for a fee and what percentage of his income comes from testifying for plaintiff attorneys.

He then goes after him on his medical conclusions. The expert admits that the fracture is subtle on the X-ray and not clearly evident. George then gets the expert to explain that in this case the fracture was repaired by being stabilized without the necessity of a surgical incision, what a patient might refer to has having the bones reset. This type of repair is called a closed reduction.

The expert then is forced to admit that *any* traumatic fracture can lead to arthritis without any diagnostic miss of the fracture initially. In fact, George asks him directly if it is true in general that it is the trauma of the break that causes arthritis if it develops. The expert hems and haws but finally when confronted with major orthopedic texts he recognizes as authoritative is forced to agree. George then pushes the expert to begrudgingly admit that he does not even know if the plaintiff will have arthritis in the future. In fact, George pushes him further to reluctantly admit the most likely probability would be that if arthritis develops, it would come as a consequence of the plaintiff's fall causing the initial traumatic fracture of the ankle or the necessary repair as opposed to a three-day delay in setting the fractured ankle. The expert tries to deny this, but George will not let him get away from admitting that it probably is the most likely scenario.

The expert concedes that he has not treated the plaintiff or examined him so he cannot say anything about any atrophy of the leg that the plaintiff has suffered as a result of the injured ankle. George takes him through the fact that the repair took place three days after the initial missed diagnosis and that even if the broken ankle had been diagnosed in the ER, the plaintiff still would have required the same treatment with the same recovery requirements of physical therapy and the same possibility of arthritis in the future. The doctor admits that he does not know what the level of the plaintiff's pain was initially or has been after the corrective reduction. He has no physical findings that he can report to the court or jury. George concludes his cross examination by pushing the expert to agree that the X-ray of the plaintiff's ankle after the reduction shows all the bones of the ankle in perfect alignment. Stuart Schlussel watches the entire testimony before slipping out of the courtroom.

The judge adjourns for the day and calls for Mr. Santangelo to come into his office behind the courtroom without George, the opposing counsel. This is not considered ethical. The judge sits at his desk and looks hard at Frank.

"Frank, you understand that you need help with this case."

Frank Santangelo says nothing. He is very uncomfortable. Judge Franco makes a scowling face.

"You heard what I told you the other day, right?"

"I did. I can't do that, Judge."

21

JOHNNY COLRAIN AND Jim Ashford are sitting in Johnny's kitchen talking.

"I am not sure this party in Brooklyn has anything to do with our two model murders, John," Ashford offers.

"There might be some model connection, I think, but I'm not sure. What is our next move?"

"We need a little help. Maybe my friend Dave might be able to be of assistance."

"How?"

"I know he has a tap on Stuart Schlussel. He is trying to get a handle on the payoffs to judges, but what if Schlussel knows something about what happened to Adrienne or Burke Lambert since his wife found the home number of Burke Lambert in his personal private phone book? We know Lambert went out with models including Adrienne. Have any more coffee?"

"Yup."

Johnny fills his mug. He takes a swig and grabs Johnny's phone. He dials.

"Dave?"

"Hi, Jim."

"I am calling to see if you heard any discussion about a party where a woman was beat up or about the murders of the two models in your tap on Schlussel."

"No. But I will let you know if we hear anything like that. Are you thinking about an S-and-M scene?"

"We think there is a something like that involved. There were marks on the first model's body."

"Okay. Will do. Later."

Dave Morgan hangs up the phone and turns to his senior investigator, Jenny.

"I want to know if you hear Schlussel discuss anything about hurting any women or a party where that is or was going on or anything about either of the murdered models or Burke Lambert."

"Got it. What about if Dugan's name comes up again?"

"Yes. Anything about him."

———————

Dugan answers the phone at his desk.

"Dugan."

"This is Joe DeFeo. I have a job for Donnelly."

"What is it?"

"I need him to talk to ... interview a witness."

Dugan smiles. He knows what that means.

"I will have him call you. Are you in the office?"

"Yes."

"Okay."

Simon Stone is in his office. He is working later than normal considering he is not on trial. His secretary left at 5:00 p.m. His paralegal now says good night, and he looks up and answers her, wishing her a good night. He reaches for the phone.

"Priscilla?"

"Hello, Simon."

"Would you like to grab dinner?"

There is a pause.

"Simon, I want to take a break."

"What happened?"

"I just don't feel comfortable moving forward."

"I am sorry to hear that. Is it something I've done?"

"No. I just am not feeling right about it, and I have to pay attention to that feeling."

"Okay. I get it. Uh, will you promise to call me if you change your mind?"

"Yes. I promise. I am really sorry."

Simon hangs up. He is disappointed but not surprised somehow. He thinks he may have slept with her too soon. She didn't stay the night, which was definitely not a good sign. He decides to walk to Mortimer's to have a great steak dinner and a big glass of red wine. He gets up from his desk and takes his suit jacket off the hook on the back of the door. He puts it on and leaves the office.

Stuart Schlussel sits down at his dining room table to have dinner with his wife. She looks at her husband and ponders whether she should start a conversation with him about what she found in his phone book. He starts to taste the soup when she asks, "How did you know Burke Lambert?"

Stuart stares at her. He is shocked and knocked off balance.

"Uh, why do you think that I knew Burke Lambert?"

"Never mind answering my question with a question. Please answer me."

"He is a friend of a friend."

"What friend?"

"Someone you don't know."

"Try me."

"Judge Harold Katz."

"What is your connection with Mr. Lambert?"

"Just networking. I thought he could refer me some cases."

"Really?"

"Yes."

"So, it was business?"

"Yes. Now what prompted this inquiry?"

Rita decides to lie rather than admit that she went through his phone book.

"Mrs. Lambert called me. She wanted to know who you were."

"What did you tell her?"

"That you are a personal injury attorney."

"What did she say after that?"

"Not much. She found a number in her husband's papers and wasn't sure who it was." She looks at her husband carefully. "Is there something else you want to tell me?"

"No."

"Why would he have your home number?"

"I don't know. Can we drop it now?" He starts to eat his soup.

Rita looks at him for a long moment and then picks up her spoon.

George does not go to the office but directly home carrying his trial bag, which is a rectangular leather brief case about the size of an overnight suitcase. He takes the elevator up to the third floor. He is pleased with the day but wants to make sure he is prepared for tomorrow. Notwithstanding that feeling, he would like to have a drink and some dinner before he goes over some notes for tomorrow. He drops the bag in the dining foyer and goes to the bathroom to wash his face. He comes out to the dining area and thinks for a moment. Even though he has to work, he needs to eat dinner, so he makes a call.

"Hello?"

"Hi, Carole. This is George."

"George, George … Do I know a George?"

"Uh oh, I am calling the fabulous jazz chanteuse. Do I have the wrong number?"

"I hope not. Hi, George. How are you?"

"Well, I am on trial and trying to stay focused, but I do have to eat and would love some great company, so I thought I would call and invite you for a quick informal dinner somewhere in the neighborhood."

"That's sounds wonderful. Where are you thinking?"

"Do you like Japanese?"

"I do."

"Do you know East on Third Avenue?"

"Yes. I know where it is but I have never been there."

"Can you meet me there in twenty minutes?"

"You don't give a girl much time to get ready," Carole says, laughing. "I'll see you there."

George goes into his bedroom and changes into jeans and a comfortable soft light blue shirt. He slips on a pair of brown loafers, checks himself in the mirror, dabs a little Eau Sauvage on his face, grabs a gray wool sport coat, and heads for the door. He is excited about seeing Carole again. He has thought about her a lot during downtime, but he has forced himself to concentrate on his trial.

When George gets to East Japanese Restaurant, he takes off his shoes and heads into the dining room. Each rectangular table is in its own sunken area so that when you step down into the pit, the floor around the table forms the bench where you sit so the tables are very low in traditional Japanese style. He finds an empty table, steps down and slips onto the seat. A waitress in a kimono comes over and kneels down to take his order. He tells her that he is waiting for someone and asks for a Kirin beer. The waitress brings it over, and he thanks her, takes a sip, then looks toward the door. He is very excited and wonders about that. Usually calm and certainly disciplined, he ponders, *What is going on?* Whatever it is, he likes it.

Carole had come home from an audition. She thought it went well but the owners of the club were noncommittal. She wondered about the two songs she chose to sing. She washed her face, changed into jeans and a T-shirt and was about to start cooking dinner for herself when George called. She is glad he did. She has been musing about him and thinking all kinds of crazy thoughts, like: *What would it be like to be with a trial lawyer? Has he thought about what it would be like to be with a singer? What does he like to do in his spare time? What does he read when he is not on a case? Does he like good food? Does he like to dance? Does he like to travel and explore? Does he like to hike? Swim? Does he like to ski? Does he like the ocean?* She likes all those things and wants a partner to share them with her. There is so much she is curious about and wants to know about him. She is excited to see him again but also a little scared. It's unusual for her to have these feeling about someone she has just met. Carole puts on a little blush, checks her hair, then puts on a spritz of cologne. She slips on a pair of red Capezio flats and a smart cashmere navy V-neck sweater. She is happy, and she knows why.

When Carole walks in, George is looking at the menu, thinking about what sushi he will order. She looks down into the restaurant, sees him, and stops just to take him in. The way the restaurant is set up, he is below her. He has put his sport coat on the seat next to him. Even though he is dressed casually, he looks sophisticated. He doesn't see her at first but then looks up, sees her, and his heart skips a beat. He smiles. He cannot believe how lovely she looks. She smiles at him. George points to her shoes. She looks around and notices the shoes lined up. She takes off her flats, puts them next to a pair of loafers she thinks are probably his, and walks to the table and steps down. He stands up and gives her a hug and kisses her cheek as she does the same, the two of them standing without shoes. They laugh and say hello and look at each other for a moment, hearts racing. He gestures to the seat across from him. She slides onto it.

———

Dugan comes out of the Emerald Inn with Donnelly.

"Okay, Donnelly. Call Joe tomorrow and make sure you let me know what he wants you to do. I know it has to do with talking to a witness to an accident. Whatever he offers, double it. Remember, you share that fee with me."

"Got it. I will call you tomorrow."

They separate. Donnelly goes to his car and heads to Mrs. Merton's in Brooklyn.

————

Johnny Colrain is in the studio part of his loft. He is painting and listening to Stevie Wonder's *Songs in the Key of Life*. He has it turned up loud and is singing along. He hears the phone and curses. He puts his brush down and goes to answer it.

"Hello," he says, making it sound like *yellow* loud enough over the music.

"Johnny?"

"That's me. Riki?"

"Yes. I told you I would call you for a dinner. Have you already eaten?"

"No. I have been painting, and the time has slipped by."

"Would you like to come over? I am making tacos."

"Sounds good. What time?"

"As soon as you can make it. I have started getting things ready. Do you know where I live?"

"I remember from the other night. Listen, it will be at least an hour. I have to clean up, and I want to walk Baloo before I leave."

"Okay. See you in about an hour. Don't rush."

They hang up. Johnny goes to the big easel and cleans his brushes. He then hustles to shower. He jumps out, shaves, brushes his hair, puts on some black jeans, a blue checked shirt, and short black boots. He throws on his old leather jacket and calls to his dog. Baloo is happy to go out, and the two of them hustle down the stairs and outside. When they return, Johnny feeds the big Pyrenees and grabs the key to his motorcycle. The phone rings as he is walking to the door.

"Riki, just leaving."

"Oops. Not Riki. It's Priscilla. Sounds like this is a bad time."

"Oh ... hi, Priscilla. I was just going out. Are you okay?"

"Yes. I am fine, Johnny. I just thought I would take you up on your offer to buy me a drink a long time ago, and we might talk about your paintings. Maybe another time."

"Yes. I really would like that, Priscilla."

"Okay. Rain check. Bye."

"Bye." Johnny slowly hangs up the phone. He is surprised in two ways. One—that she had the gumption to call and ask him to go for a drink. Two—that he is so happy about it. He smiles. He takes a look at Baloo, who is busy eating, and he goes out the door.

Robespierre's is quite busy, and Robespierre has a bar full of people. He and a bartender are making drinks for the patrons at the bar and for waiters. Three men come in and move to the bar standing behind patrons who are sitting. They stand there, and then the tall dark man in the group gets Robespierre's attention. When Robby looks over at the man with his friends, he recognizes all of them. It is the trio who were outside the Village Vanguard. The tall dark one pushed Carole into the cab and tried to take off with her. The tall dark man smiles and orders three Heinekens. Robespierre opens three bottles and puts them on the bar. The man asks for glasses and pays with a large bill. Robby gets out the glasses and makes the change. As the man picks up the change, he speaks.

"Excuse me. Don't I know you?"

"I don't think so," Robby says, looking hard at him. He does not like these guys.

"I believe you were at the Village Vanguard the other night when I was talking with Carole Lansdorf."

"Is that what you call what you tried to do? Talking?" Robby says.

"I am not going to argue with you. I want to ask you a question. Who was that guy who pulled her out of the cab and hit me?"

"Why would you want to know that?"

"I have my reasons."

"Well, I am sorry that I can't help you. You'll have to excuse me. I have to get back to my customers." He moves away.

A little while later Robespierre looks in the direction of the three men who are still standing near the bar drinking their beers. The little guy, who reminds him of a weasel, is talking to the tall one, and the other is just listening. He definitely has a bad feeling about them. He reminds himself to warn George about the tall one's asking about him.

Johnny stops at a Korean deli for some cut flowers and then cruises uptown to Aarika's apartment building on his motorcycle. He parks his bike and walks to the building. The doorman knows he's coming and sends him right up as he calls Aarika to let her know her guest is on the way. She is waiting for Johnny at the door when he gets off the elevator. She takes the flowers and thanks him with a kiss on the cheek. She ushers him into the nice large two-bedroom apartment in the El Dorado on the Upper West Side at Ninetieth Street and Central Park West.

"Come into the kitchen, Johnny," she says, looking for a vase for the flowers.

He is amazed at the size of the kitchen. It has stainless steel counters, which he has never seen before, and a huge white porcelain sink. It is a large old-fashioned kitchen with a doorway to a maid's room on the back wall.

"It smells good, Riki, and I am hungry," Johnny says as she puts the flowers in a vase that she places on the counter.

"Good. What would you like to drink. I have beer, which I think goes with tacos."

"That sounds great to me."

She goes and opens the refrigerator. "Take your pick." Johnny takes out a Carta Blanca, and she takes a Corona.

Riki walks over to the counter next to the stove. She has seasoned chopped beef in a skillet on a very low flame to keep it warm and all the fixings for the tacos out on the counter: lettuce, tomatoes, salsa, guacamole, sour cream, and a bottle of hot sauce. She unfolds a kitchen towel to reveal soft corn tortillas.

"Give me a second, Johnny, while I warm these, and then we can eat."

Johnny leans against the counter drinking his beer, watching her. She heats the tortillas in a second skillet and puts them on a plate.

When they are all done, Riki says, "Take a plate and make yourself a few tacos with all the fixings." Johnny takes a plate and makes himself three tacos. Riki makes herself two. She grabs several cloth napkins and leads them past the large dining room into a little alcove where there is a love seat, a coffee table, and a TV. It is a lot cozier. They put their plates and beers on the coffee table, sit, and then place the plates on their laps.

"Johnny, have you learned anything about the deaths of Adrienne and Renée?"

"Not much, I'm afraid. I think that there may be a connection to some kind of S-and-M scene."

"Wow. Is that why you were asking about Burke Lambert?"

"Yes," he manages to get out with a mouthful of taco.

"And why you were so interested about what happened to Susie?"

Johnny nods and holds up his hand gesturing for her to wait as he finishes chewing and swallowing. He wipes his mouth with a napkin and then speaks.

"This is delicious, Riki."

"Thanks."

"Why you are asking?"

"I am really upset about what has happened, and I don't like that someone took advantage of Susie. Maybe there is a connection."

"I would say that we have run into a dead end for now. It was good that you told me about Susie, and if you hear anything more about a model's getting beaten like that, obviously, I would like to know."

"Of course."

Johnny and Aarika eat and reminisce about some of the modeling jobs they did together and the other people that were there. The two of them posed for a print ad for rums of Puerto Rico. They used his dog Baloo in one of the shots. They have more beers, and both are enjoying themselves. As the evening wears on, it is obvious that they get along.

"It's getting late, Riki. I better get going."

She looks at him with affection. She is a little tipsy, and her inhibitions are at a low ebb.

"Do you have to, Johnny?"

Johnny smiles at her and leans over to give her a sweet kiss on the mouth. She kisses him back and pulls him in for a hug. She breaks the hug and starts kissing him passionately. He touches her face but then does not carry on with the kissing. He gently separates from her and holds her by the shoulders.

"I really can't."

"Okay," she says, obviously disappointed.

"I have Baloo, who was shot, and I should get back, check on him, and walk him again before I get to bed."

"I understand."

Riki gives him a little kiss on the mouth and walks with him to the door. He gives her a hug, and he leaves.

———————

Carole and George are talking, smiling, and laughing. They both are asking questions about each other. Many of the questions have led to long stories, and the time has been going by fast. George looks at his watch.

"Uh oh. Look what time it is, Carole. I said a quick dinner. This is a school night for me. I have to be in court in the Bronx in the morning."

Carole looks intently at him and smiles.

"I am sorry, George. I admit to having a good time, though."

George looks at her and puts on a serious face.

"I am glad you have because this has been really rough for me. So many questions—now I know what witnesses feel on the stand when I am cross-examining them."

She looks at him quizzically, not completely sure he is joking. He can't keep a straight face and breaks out laughing.

"Oh ... you! You are in trouble!" Carole says, laughing and pointing at him. "But we better go," she adds.

The bill comes. George takes out his wallet, and Carole takes out hers.

"Let me contribute," she says.

"No. Thanks, Carole. I appreciate your offer. I asked you out for dinner."

"Well, guess what? I was going to ask you to my house for dinner on Saturday night with your friends. Kind of a thank-you dinner for rescuing me and a way to introduce Felicia to Robby."

George pays and can't stop smiling.

"That sounds fantastic. You were going to? And now you have second thoughts?"

She gets his teasing, and she gives it back to him.

"Well, you know, actually after tonight, I *am* having second thoughts ..." she says in mock seriousness.

George picks up the mantle.

"Yes. I certainly can understand that after tonight. It has been quite stilted and awkward ..." he says, his eyes laughing. He is having a hard time keeping a straight face.

"My sentiments exactly," Carole says, watching his struggle and trying to keep her own serious face on, but she can't, and she breaks out in laughter joined by him. He points at her, laughing. Finally, he stops and speaks.

"You have to tell me what you are cooking so I can bring some wine."

"Sorry, big boy. Robespierre insists on bringing the wine."

"Hmmmm ... Maybe I should bring some too."

"Well, you can talk that over with him. I think bringing yourself will cover it. But we better get going so you can get a good rest to be ready tomorrow."

They walk out of the restaurant toward her apartment. At first they are holding hands, but then she decides to hold his arm and be closer to him, which she loves. He is tall and muscular. He loves feeling her body close to his. They talk about his work a little, and he mentions that if she is free sometime, she could come up to the Bronx and observe his trial. He mentions the name of the judge. They then just walk, and he hears her humming very quietly. Unbeknownst to him, it is an old song called "There Is Something in the Air." When they get to her building, they stop, and she turns to face him. They look at each other for a while, eyes searching the other's, saying nothing. She smiles and moves toward him, gives him a hug and a kiss on the cheek.

"Be awesome tomorrow," she says, then she turns and starts walking toward the door to her building.

George is stunned and speechless. He was thinking they would share a real kiss. He just stands there looking at her walking away purposefully. All of a sudden, she turns, looks at him, laughs, runs back to him, and wraps her arms around him in a full embrace. He does the same. He feels the soft fullness of her breasts against his body and the firmness of the rest of her. Her face is very close to his, and their lips slowly approach each other's. He stops and her mouth slightly open proceeds slowly toward his. He looks at her beautiful face. She places a soft kiss on his lips and pulls her mouth away gently. It is a teasing. He takes a deep breath. He smells her scent. Not her perfume, her wonderful scent. Her mouth is luscious. He is very aroused. She is examining his face, then she moves her mouth quickly on his, and they kiss, deeply, fully with tongues exploring, for a long time. They pull apart and gasp, then they both share some quick short but deep kisses. They look at each other's face in between the kisses, trying to read the unspoken communication of feelings. He strokes her hair once. She gives him one last deep kiss that lasts a little longer before she breaks free. She looks at his face intently, and then speaks.

"I wasn't kidding about tomorrow."

She turns and walks into the building without looking back. George is rocked. So much to take in; she is an amazing kisser, and he loves the way she tastes and smells.

Carole goes into her building. She is in a good daze. She goes to the elevator and up to her apartment. She unlocks the door and goes right to the kitchen. She puts on a kettle and takes down a mug from a cupboard for some chamomile tea. She stands leaning against the counter. She is going over everything that happened tonight. The dinner was great fun. He is very interesting and expressed a lot of interest in her. He wanted to know about her childhood but did not pry. She loved asking him about his, an interesting intense family with principles and goals, very different from hers.

She cannot believe how wonderful it was to run, embrace, be in his arms, and to kiss. She loves his soft lips, his mouth, and the way he kisses, his taste, his musky smell, and feeling him close. His body is hard. She felt his excitement, and it made her feel good. She was excited too. She can't believe it. She has never felt so much. It is especially crazy because it happened so quickly out of nowhere. She feels the desire to be cautious, but it is being outmatched by her other desires and feelings about this man. So much is racing through her mind. She tells herself to slow down as the kettle whistles, and she grabs a teabag. She drops it in and lets it steep as she continues her musings standing by the counter for a few more minutes. She then removes the bag, goes to the kitchen table, and sits down. She tells herself to be careful, but she has to admit that this is unlike anything she has ever experienced, and she wants to let it happen. It's big. She has had a few serious relationships, but she never really gave her heart away. She had feelings, but if she were honest, she had to admit that she never really has let anyone in, really in, where she is completely vulnerable. She starts singing the song she had been humming on their walk: "There Is Something in the Air." She gets up and dances around the kitchen as she sings.

22

DONNELLY WALKS to the offices of Joseph DeFeo, LLC, at 233 Broadway. He knows that he is going to be interviewing a witness to an accident. He figures this should be a piece of cake, an easy way to pick up some extra money. He gets off the elevator, finds the right door, and enters. He goes to the plexiglass window at the end of the waiting room behind which there is a secretary who is also the receptionist. He asks for DeFeo, and she tells him to take a seat. There are some smudged tan and green Naugahyde chairs and an end table with some magazines on it. It is a shabby waiting room. He picks up an old *Time* magazine just as the receptionist calls to him. She opens the door into the inner office. There are several secretaries typing away, and he follows her past a large Xerox copier to the corner office. Joe DeFeo's office is dark even though the fluorescent lights are on. The blinds are shut, and he is behind a big desk, which is mostly covered with papers. Many of these papers have blue or gray backs, and he is reading one, which he puts down when he sees Donnelly.

"Hello, Mr. Donnelly, I need you to talk to a witness."

"So I understand from Dugan."

"Sit down. Let me explain the accident case."

Donnelly listens as DeFeo explains that there was a serious accident in Brooklyn at the intersection of Atlantic and Utica Avenues. A young woman had multiple fractures to her hip and leg in addition to hitting the windshield with her face, which was badly lacerated. The question is who had the light.

"Your job is to refresh the witness's memory about who had the light. He doesn't seem to understand the situation."

"I see."

"Yes. There is a lot at stake, and your absolute discretion is a must. Do you understand what I am saying?"

"I do. And without being too blunt, what is in it for me?"

"I am prepared to pay you $2,500 now and $2,500 after he testifies, assuming he testifies the way we want him to."

Donnelly smiles.

"You'll have to do better than that, Mr. DeFeo. The damages in the case will be substantial if you prevail. I have expenses."

DeFeo is not happy about this development. He thought the amount would be immediately accepted.

"What are you thinking, Mr. Donnelly?"

"Doubling those amounts will suffice."

DeFeo looks hard at Donnelly. He is stuck because of the connection to Dugan.

"Is Dugan getting a cut?"

Donnelly laughs.

"You know him. What do you think?"

DeFeo pauses for a minute. He does not want to get into a hassle with this man or with Dugan. He can afford this fee but hates to be pressured. He decides to close the negotiation.

"Okay. We have a deal."

DeFeo opens a drawer and takes out the cash. He puts the $5,000 in an envelope, closes the drawer, and gives the envelope to Donnelly.

"Also, here is the information you need," he says, as he hands Donnelly a sheet of paper on which are written the facts of the accident as he wants them to be, as well as witness information, including personal details.

"Call me after you have talked to the witness. I want to know how it went."

DeFeo gets up, and Donnelly rises, nods, and pockets the envelope. He folds the piece of paper and puts it in his other pocket, turns, and leaves. DeFeo watches him go. He does not feel completely comfortable with Dugan's man and even less comfortable with Dugan.

———

Stuart Schlussel is having trouble working. He has the young model that he met at the party in Brooklyn on his mind. She was beautiful, and he was able to indulge himself with her when she was out of it. He did everything short of entering her and having intercourse. He did not want to do that. He was afraid that she would know that she had been violated that way, and a criminal investigation would happen if she made a complaint. Even if he used a condom, she might know she had been raped. What he hated was that Dugan came in and did his thing—he hit her and masturbated at the same time. He then peed on her. Schlussel is wondering how he is going to be able to see her again. Maybe he could make a regular thing happen. Give her money. She was very young, from out of town, obviously new to New York, and trying to make it as a model. He tries to shake his thoughts. He will get back to it. He tells himself that he has to be careful. His wife asked some questions about how he knew Burke Lambert. He turns his mind back to work.

———

Dugan is sitting at his desk. He is wondering about Donnelly's meeting with DeFeo. He is thinking about how corrupt some of these civil lawyers are. *They pay off judges to help them win. They hire investigators to fake evidence and intimidate witnesses. They are no better than other white-collar criminals who steal and cheat in the corporate world. I would like to get in that world where the money is really big. Of course, you have to make sure you don't get caught, but those corporate crooks usually don't. A lot of them are Jewish and smart. It is usually the poor guy who holds up a liquor store or sells some dope that gets nailed in the criminal system. Of course, most of those criminals are black so they deserve what they get. Sometimes it is a jilted man or woman in some crime of passion, which is just plain dumb. You should always be able to get another lover, wife, or whatever you need.* He snorts. He has seen some doozies. His phone rings.

"Dugan."

"Dugan, it's Donnelly. I saw DeFeo. I am on my way to talk to a witness."

"Good. Did you do what I told you?"

"I did, and I'll have some cash for you tonight."

———

George is on the Lexington Avenue local. He is standing against the door with his trial bag and trying to keep his mind on the day he has ahead. It is difficult. He cannot believe what happened last night and what a terrific woman Carole is. He could not believe that she walked away but then came running back to him, the embrace, and the amazing kisses. It makes him laugh to think about his delighted shock. He is smitten, but he has to focus on his trial. He switches to the 4 Express at 125th Street and looks at the notes on his yellow pad.

———

Frank Santangelo is on the phone with Stuart Schlussel.

"Stuart, the judge is really pissed at me. He wants to be paid. He may even try to sabotage my case. Believe me, Fredericks doesn't need any help from the judge. I am not sure what to do."

"How much does the judge want?"

"Fifteen thousand."

"He is greedy. Frank, do you think you can hold him off until tomorrow? I have to be up there for a conference and will talk to him."

"I think so. The plaintiff goes on today. I am hoping the jury will like him."

"Okay. I will see you soon."

"Good. I have to go."

"Good luck, Frank."

———

Jim Ashford finishes his interview with another friend of Burke Lambert. He has gotten nowhere. Lambert's friends have no clue why he would be killed. He was very well liked, even by his political opponents. He decides to stop for lunch before heading back to his office. He goes to Giambone's and is eating at the bar when a large group, he assumes lawyers, comes in. It is noisy, and he cannot hear their conversations, but something about one of them attracts his attention. He has a purplish-colored suit on. Jim waits for them to sit down and asks a waiter hustling by who that man is. The waiter does not know but says he will try to find out. Jim tells the waiter he is a detective, gives him his card, a folded ten-dollar bill, and asks the waiter to call him with the information if he gets it but not tell anyone. The waiter agrees. Jim finishes his eggplant parm, pays, and leaves. He heads to his friend Dave's office. He is neatly dressed as usual and walks with purpose. He is a professional, and even though he is frustrated, he believes he will crack the three murders he is working on.

———————

Dave Morgan is talking to his investigators about what they heard on Stuart Schlussel's office phone. He feels the case may very well be breaking, and he wants to get Schlussel to wear a wire. They are brainstorming about a strategy. Jim Ashford comes into the reception area. Dave's secretary tells him that Dave is in his office talking to two of the senior investigators. Jim asks her not to announce him. She knows he is a friend of Dave's and nods at him with a smile. He approaches the door to Dave's office and knocks on the doorjamb since the door is open. Dave is standing and talking animatedly to Don and Jenny, who are sitting. He stops and looks toward the door, as do his investigators. When he sees Jim Ashford, he smiles and tells the two investigators that they should think about what he was saying, and they will resume the conversation later. The two investigators get up and start to leave. Dave stops them and introduces them to Jim Ashford.

"Jim, these are two of my best investigators, Jenny and Don."

Jim extends his hand to shake theirs.

"Pleased to meet you. You have to be good to be working for Dave Morgan."

They smile and say they are glad to meet him as well. They leave, and Dave goes behind his desk and sits down. Jim sits down in front of Dave's desk.

"To what do I owe a personal visit from Jim Ashford?"

"I have been interviewing friends of Burke Lambert and getting nowhere so I decided to grab a quick lunch at Giambone's. Then I thought since I was close to your office, I would come over and talk to you about your investigation and pick your brain."

"Well, first of all, I should be mad at you for not calling to see if I was free for lunch," Dave says with a smile. "That being said, we are getting close. We know Judge Franco asked a plaintiff's attorney for $15,000, but we want to get the judge on tape. We know that from the wiretap on Schlussel."

"It sounds like you will. Any ideas in regard to my three murders?"

"No. I haven't heard anything."

"I am struggling in regard to the reason for the killings. You know that I think it has something to do with the party where a girl was beaten. I was also thinking that maybe there is some connection with kickbacks or some of the lawyers involved."

"It's possible, but I have nothing in that regard so far," Dave says.

"Okay. Stay in touch, and I will do the same, and, I agree, we have to do lunch soon," Jim replies.

Bronx Supreme Court, Room 534, is in full session with Judge Franco on the bench and Frank Santangelo taking the plaintiff through his direct testimony. Mr. Flanagan describes the breaking of his ankle, his trip to the Mount Herman ER, his discharge without a fracture diagnosis, then spending three days at home limping around to the bathroom with his wife helping him but laying on the couch most of the time. Frank Santangelo asks him about his pain, and he testifies that his ankle hurt him a lot and that he could not put any weight on it. He then goes on to testify about seeing an orthopedist, the diagnosis being made of his fractured ankle, and the need for repair. He then went through having the reduction, a cast, and using crutches for several weeks, with physical therapy after the cast came off, and using a cane for a while after that. He claims that it interfered with his relationship with his wife. He testifies he was able to get back to work two weeks after the cast came off, but his hours were limited, and he lost a lot of overtime, which meant that his earnings suffered.

Judge Franco breaks for lunch. George stays in the courtroom and goes over the subpoenaed records that have been brought to the courtroom from the record room. He finds what he is looking for and stays in the courtroom preparing his cross-examination. He munches on a sandwich he brought with him. He goes out to the fountain to drink some water before going back into the courtroom.

When court resumes, Frank asks a few more questions and sits down. Judge Franco nods toward George for him to start his cross. At that moment, a lawyer comes into the courtroom in a rush through the side door that the judges use. He goes up to Judge Franco, who is on the bench. He mumbles something about excusing his entrance. He says something to the judge. He thanks him and then takes the judge's left hand, kisses the judge's ring, and hurries back out of the courtroom. George is amazed. He has never seen anything like that. Obviously, this Napoleon of a judge who has the Bronx Supreme Court as his little kingdom did some favor for that attorney.

George rises slowly, looks at the jury, then the witness, and starts his cross-examination as he paces the courtroom. He establishes a few initial things for the jury. Mr. Flanagan had a fall at work, and he is not blaming anyone for the fall. He was taken to the ER, and his ankle hurt. He could not walk or put weight on it. He was X-rayed, and he was told there was no fracture, but he should try to keep his weight off the ankle and stay home from work for a few days. He was given crutches. George then asks him about the three days at home. Did he take any pain medication? Did it help? Did he spend the days mostly on the couch watching TV? Did he keep his weight off the ankle? Did his wife help him to the bathroom even though he had crutches? The answers were all in the affirmative. George then summarizes what has already been testified to concerning the corrective reduction and the post-op physical therapy. George goes over what Mr. Flanagan had said in responding to Frank Santangelo about his employment. He then puts Mr. Flanagan's employment record in evidence. Upon cross-examination, when confronted with his work records, Mr. Flanagan has to admit that despite his fractured ankle, once he recovered, he was working more overtime hours than before the fracture. In fact, he made more money the year following the fracture than he had the year before. He also had to admit that he was able to work and has had no problems in terms of his mobility once his fracture healed.

George asks point-blank if his ankle has interfered with his marital relations with his wife after his ankle was repaired. Mr. Flanagan admits the pain bothered him for a short time, which briefly interfered, but the answer overall was no. George thanks him and takes a seat.

Judge Franco glares at Frank Santangelo. He asks him if he has any further witnesses. Frank says no. The judge then asks if he is resting his case. He says yes. Judge Franco then adjourns for the day and asks Mr. Santangelo to step into his office behind the courtroom.

Frank leaves his papers on his counsel table, and George starts gathering up his papers. The court officer follows Frank into the back office, and George goes to the subpoena records table and looks at the X-rays there. He selects four X-rays and confirms that they are the same as the ones he has in his file. He then leaves.

Frank follows Judge Franco into his office. The judge sits down behind his desk and shakes his head looking at Frank Santangelo, who is standing on the other side of his desk.

"What do you think, Frank? It seems you might need a little help in this trial."

"I think we made out a case, Judge."

"You made out a case barely, Frank. But I don't think it impresses this jury much. I might be able to help you out if you do what I asked you."

"I will see what I can do, Judge."

"I would advise that you do so before this case slips away from you."

Frank nods and then turns and leaves.

ASHFORD IS AT HIS DESK, and the phone rings.

"Ashford."

"Detective Ashford, this is Tom, the waiter at Giambone's. The man you asked about is named Stuart Schlussel."

"Thanks. You have been a big help."

"Okay, think nothing of it. I am happy to help."

Jim Ashford hangs up, writes the name down on a pad, and taps a pencil on his desk as he thinks about this. *A purplish suit doesn't mean that Schlussel was at that party, but it is kind of an unusual suit. Susie Griffin did mention that she did coke and had wine with a man in a purplish suit. This is also the guy whose phone is being tapped by Dave Morgan.*

Stuart Schlussel is in court at 60 Centre Street in courtroom 312. The room is packed with lawyers who have conferences in front of

Judge Brenda Swift in the medical malpractice part where all the cases are some type of medical malpractice case. Lawyers are not only sitting in the gallery but also sitting in the jury box talking to each other, waiting for their cases to be called. Other lawyers are walking in and walking around the wooden partition that separates the gallery from the well where the counsel tables are to stand in line to check in with the law clerk sitting at his desk to the side of the judge's elevated bench. Every so often the clerk shouts out to the room to keep the talking down and then calls out the name of a case. The lawyers on both sides of the case called get up and approach the bench if the judge is sitting there, but if not, they wait with the clerk for the lawyers on the prior case to leave the inner office behind the courtroom. They then are ushered into the office where they sit in front of the judge's desk. At that point, the judge examines the court's file on the case and, after introductions, asks for argument on a motion or will try to settle the case.

Schlussel is sitting in the jury box talking with Simon Stone.

"Simon, I would like to have another party."

"Stuart, are you sure? You said you got pretty wasted last time."

"I did, but I had a great time."

"And you met a very pretty young model-type girl."

"Uh huh. I plead guilty."

"What happened to her? You said Dugan went upstairs after you took her up there."

"He did. He is a weird bastard. I couldn't say too much since he supplies the drugs."

"Would you invite him again?"

"I have no other source. I wish I could exclude him; he has some strange sexual proclivities."

The clerk calls out a case, and Simon gets up.

"That's me. To be continued, Stuart."

Dugan is in the precinct talking with Donnelly in an empty office.

"So what did you do to convince him to see it your way?"

"I ran his name and told him that his boss probably would not like learning about his DUI."

"How did you know that would do it?"

"I just figured it was worth a try. He actually had two DUIs in the last five years, and I figured this could be a problem for him."

"Good thinking. Did he know you were a cop?"

"No. I don't see how."

"Did he fold right away?"

"Yes. He said he remembered that the other car went through the red light."

"Was Joe happy?"

"Extremely."

"Good. We can milk him."

Jim Ashford, standing outside the door, is listening. He walks away to his desk, figuring out what the best thing to do is. Then he calls Dave Morgan. He relates the conversation he has just heard.

"It's not about payoffs to judges, but I figured you would be interested in it."

"I am, Ash. It sounds corrupt, all right. I am good with nailing him and the lawyer who put him up to it. I should be able to get a tap on DeFeo's phone."

George takes the subway to his garage and drives into Westchester County. He finds the doctor's office that he is looking for on Mill Road in Eastchester, New York. He rings the bell and is buzzed in. Dr. Vincent Fritz is in his office making some notes in a patient's chart.

"Hello, Counselor. I was wondering when you would arrive. I have to get home shortly."

"Hi, Dr. Fritz, sorry. I got a little delayed driving here, but this should not take long. Here are the pre-op films and the post-op films after your reduction," he says as he takes the four films out of his briefcase and hands them to the doctor.

Dr. Fritz takes the X-rays and turns on the view box mounted on the wall next to his desk. He pushes the pre-op films up onto the box first and then the post-reduction films next to them. He examines them carefully for a few moments and then turns to George and smiles.

"I think the bones have knit together perfectly. Look here."

He shows George the original fracture and then the bones after his reduction.

"I did a good job," he says, smiling at George.

"Would you be willing to come to court and testify as to the result you just showed me?"

"Yes, I would."

"That is great. Can you come tomorrow after lunch?"

"I will have to juggle a few patients, but I can manage it. Where do I go?"

George tells him the number of the courtroom and the address of the Bronx courthouse on the Grand Concourse. Dr. Fritz takes down the X-rays and hands them to George.

"I will see you tomorrow. Just come into the courtroom and sit down. I will come and talk to you during a break if I can and then call you to the stand. Oh, and by the way, I will ask you about traumatic arthritis. Am I correct that if it occurs, it is as a result of the trauma of the original break?"

"Yes. That is the thinking."

"Do you think the delay in diagnosis would be a cause?"

"No. If he gets it, and that is not certain at all, it would be from the trauma of the initial break that affects the joint as he uses it. By the way, in this case, the repair would have been the same if he had been diagnosed immediately."

"Yes. That makes sense. Thanks, Dr. Fritz. I appreciate your help," George says. Dr. Fritz smiles and waves him off as he packs up to leave. George grabs his trial bag and waves goodbye to the doctor. He thinks to himself that there are some good guys around. It feels great when you find one.

———

Dr. Peter Maggiore is driving to the Bronx. George Fredericks has told him where to find a parking garage near the courthouse. He met George a few years ago when George represented him in a medical malpractice suit. He showed up at George's apartment after office hours as requested to be prepared for trial. George opened the door barefoot, dressed in jeans ripped at the knee and an old Yale Water Polo T-shirt. Dr. Maggiore was taken aback. He immediately had reservations about being represented by George, seeing how young George was and how he was dressed, but after sitting down, being grilled about the patient's care and what his role was, he forgot his reservations. George cross-examined him as to what happened, and he was impressed with George's knowledge of the records, the details of the treatment, and the insightful questions that he posed.

Dr. Maggiore had been only tangentially involved in the patient's care but was named as a defendant. George took him through what he would be asked in court and what the cross-examination by the plaintiff's attorney most likely would be. He actually cross-examined him as if he were in court, not allowing any stop for questions or concerns by the doctor. When Dr. Maggiore answered in a way that was not clear or as strong as it could be, George explained why after the questioning was finished. Dr. Maggiore left feeling very prepared. George got the case against him dismissed after he testified. He liked testifying and told George to call him if he wanted some help about orthopedic medical issues. Since then, they have been friendly, and George would, on occasion, call him to give an opinion about whether a case involving orthopedics had any merit or review the medical records as an expert. He also would sometimes examine plaintiffs who were claiming orthopedic injuries, make a report, and come to court to testify about his findings. Dr. Maggiore was very interested in the orthopedic medicine involved in George's cases. He and George have gone over the findings of his physical exam of Mr. Flanagan, and he is ready to testify.

George makes the usual motion to dismiss made at the end of the plaintiff's case, which Judge Franco denies from the bench. Frank asks for a concession or stipulation of liability from George because he orally has conceded that the fracture was missed in his questioning of the plaintiff's expert, but George refuses. Judge Franco argues with him and tries to pressure him to stipulate to the liability, but George still refuses. Judge Franco is obviously trying to assist Frank, but it does not work. He cannot force George to stipulate.

George calls Dr. Maggiore to the stand. George takes him through his qualifications, how much he is being compensated for his time and all his findings. Dr. Maggiore testifies that Mr. Flanagan made a good recovery and that he cannot find any residual injury. On cross-examination by Frank, he is asked if he measured Mr. Flanagan's calf to see if there was any atrophy of the muscles from lack of use of the leg that sustained the ankle fracture. Dr. Maggiore says he did not, but he can now right in court. This throws Frank, and he does not agree right away. George gets to his feet and asks Judge Franco to allow it. Judge Franco is curious, and now that it has been proposed out loud in front of the jury, he figures he better allow it. Maybe it will show atrophy and help Frank's case. He orders Dr. Maggiore to do the exam.

George is not exactly sure what Dr. Maggiore is going to do, but he has faith in him. Dr. Maggiore gets off the stand and asks Mr. Flanagan to take the witness chair. He then pulls out a piece of string from his pocket and measures Mr. Flanagan's left leg, which had no ankle fracture, by wrapping the string around the middle of his calf. He marks the string. He then does the same with the leg that suffered the ankle fracture. He thanks Mr. Flanagan, who then leaves the witness chair. Dr. Maggiore retakes the stand, and the judge asks him what his findings are. Dr. Maggiore testifies that the measurements are basically the same. The judge asks what that means. Dr. Maggiore explains that it means there was not any significant period of diminished use of the leg due to the fracture of his ankle. Diminished use—lack of use of the leg—would have caused some muscle wasting. There is no muscle wasting or atrophy of the leg. In other words, Mr. Flanagan has been able to use the leg that had sustained the ankle fracture and obviously has done so. Judge Franco asks Frank if he has any further questions on cross, and Frank says no. He then turns to George who says, "No questions, Judge." Judge Franco then directs the court officer to take the jury out and breaks for lunch, instructing George to have his witness ready to testify at 2:00 p.m.

George packs up his briefcase. Frank goes into the office behind the courtroom with the judge. George walks through the gallery. He sees Dr. Fritz sitting there. He has been watching the proceedings. Dr. Fritz gets up as George approaches. George stops.

"Hi, Dr. Fritz, thanks for coming. "I will put you on at 2:00 p.m. Let me buy you a sandwich."

"Sure. "

They leave the courtroom.

————————

Dugan leaves the precinct and goes to a bodega and uses the phone. He places a call and listens.

"I can do that," he says.

He hangs up the phone. He looks around for Donnelly but doesn't see him. He dials again and calls Stuart Schlussel. He sets up a meeting. Jenny is listening to the call and notes down when and where they are going to meet. Stuart also gets a call from Frank. He is not happy about Judge Franco and the way the trial is going. He has decided to pay the judge the money and hope that he can help him win the case and get a good number from the jury.

————————

Ashford is at his desk doing some research on Stuart Schlussel. He calls Johnny.

"Hello?"

"John, I need a favor."

"What's up, Ash?"

"I need your friend George to fill me in on Stuart Schlussel."

"What is the angle?"

"I think he was at the party where the young model Susie was hit."

"Okay. I should be seeing him soon."

"Good. I am looking for anything about his personal habits, whether he is married and the status of his marriage, who he pals around with ... that kind of stuff."

"Right."

Ashford hangs up.

Priscilla is in the gallery. She is cataloguing the new art that will be coming in for the next show. Robert is in the back office with her. They are both busy and not talking. Johnny Colrain comes into the gallery. A bell rings, indicating someone has entered, and Robert goes out to see who it is. Johnny is carrying a big paper bag. He greets Robert.

"Hi. I know you guys have been working hard with the show, and I thought it would be nice to have lunch together, so I brought some sandwiches from a nice place in my neighborhood."

Robert is obviously pleased.

"That is awfully nice of you. Priscilla is in the back. Why don't you take them in there? I will be right in."

Robert heads for the bathroom. Johnny goes into the back where the office is. He leans his head in.

"Hi."

Priscilla looks up.

"Hello. I am surprised to see you."

I thought I would come by with some lunch and then maybe we could talk.

"What have you got there?" Priscilla asks.

"Just some sandwiches, but they are really good."

"Great idea!"

She clears the small table that they use to eat in the gallery office next to a small kitchen area. Robert comes in and finds some plates. Priscilla pulls up chairs and sets the table with paper napkins. Johnny opens the package and takes out three nicely wrapped sandwiches—turkey on rye with lettuce and Russian dressing. Robert gets some seltzer water and cups. They all start to eat and laugh when Priscilla squirts Russian dressing out on her chin. Priscilla and Robert exclaim that the sandwiches are delicious, and Johnny tells them the place he got them from doesn't use deli meat. They roast the turkey breast themselves and because of that have quite a following in his neighborhood.

The show was quite successful, and Robert tells Johnny he will have a nice check for him at the end of the week. They discuss leaving some of the unsold paintings up until Robert might need the space for another show.

They finish lunch, and Johnny asks Priscilla if she has time to take a walk with him. She looks at Robert, who laughs and says, "I was going to suggest that myself. Thanks for bringing lunch, Johnny."

Priscilla starts to clean up, and Robert tells her to take off. She and Johnny leave the gallery.

Priscilla and Johnny walk down the street.

"That was nice of you, Johnny. I really enjoyed that sandwich."

They walk along in silence for a bit, and Johnny speaks.

"I was wondering about that drink I owe you."

Priscilla stops and looks at him.

"Yeah ... I probably shouldn't have called you, but, frankly, I thought it would be fun."

"Does that mean you are not in an exclusive relationship with the attorney I saw you with?"

"Yup. I am not."

"Okay, then. When are you free?"

"How about tonight after work? I want to get back to the gallery now and do a few things."

"Sounds good. Ever been to McSorley's on Seventh Street?"

"No, I haven't."

"If you're okay with drinking ale, I think you would enjoy seeing the place. It's one of a kind."

"Great."

"Okay. See you there at seven."

Dr. Fritz takes the stand at 2:00 p.m. in Judge Franco's courtroom. Frank Santangelo is in shock and angry when the doctor gives his name, and George takes him through his qualifications. Frank objects strenuously and starts making a scene in front of the jury. He does not want the subsequent treating orthopedic surgeon testifying.

"It's not proper, Your Honor. Not allowed under the law."

George cannot believe that Frank is saying such things, especially in front of the jury.

"That is not true, Judge," he says back firmly.

"It is. He is not allowed to put this witness on, Judge!" Frank argues.

The judge starts to agree with him.

"Well, Mr. Fredericks, Mr. Santangelo may have a point."

George is furious that this is happening in front of the jury with the implication that he is doing something underhanded or improper. He protests to Judge Franco.

"That is totally not true, Your Honor. This is the subsequent treating physician who has every right to testify about his treatment and how the patient's ankle is. I object to what Mr. Santangelo is saying and Your Honor's remarks."

This pisses off the judge, who now is about to rule that Dr. Fritz cannot testify. Frank sees this and reasserts his claim that George's calling this witness is not allowed under the law.

"He can't call this doctor, Your Honor."

The judge looks at George and again sides against him.

"I am inclined to agree with Mr. Santangelo."

George is extremely angry and cannot abide what these two are trying to do. He jumps up and rushes to the elevated bench where Judge Franco is sitting above him. George shocks the judge by thrusting both his arms out in front of him, putting his wrists and closed hands together directly in front of the judge. He exclaims loudly, "Judge, if I have done anything illegal or improper by calling this witness, I demand that you call the court officer to cuff me and take me to jail! I am totally within my rights to call this doctor, and I insist that you tell that to the jury!"

The jury has not only been present for the entire exchange but is riveted by what is going on. Judge Franco looks at the jury, then Frank Santangelo. He knows George is right, and he has his back to the wall. He does not want to look like an ass and be embarrassed if he calls for the court officer. There would be a mistrial, and George most likely would make a complaint to the Office of Court Administration and the chief administrative judge. He could get sanctioned or lose his position.

"On second thought, I agree with Mr. Fredericks. Mr. Santangelo, your objection is overruled. Please proceed, Mr. Fredericks," he finally states with chagrin.

George takes his hands and wrists down, turns, and returns to the well and the podium in front of the witness. He calls for the shadow box to put the X-rays of Mr. Flanagan's ankle on it. Dr. Fritz then explains what he was faced with after looking at the fracture on X-ray and what his treatment consisted of in aligning the bones carefully. He determined that because the bone was not shattered or displaced, the fracture did not need plates, screws, or pins, but just casting. He was able to set the bones in alignment without making an incision. He then casted the ankle to go up the leg to mid-calf. George then asks him what was to be done after that. Dr. Fritz testifies that he instructed the patient to use crutches and return after six weeks and have the cast removed. He then prescribed physical therapy.

At this point, Dr. Fritz shows the X-rays of the ankle.

"You see here," he says to the jurors, pointing to the fracture on the pre-op X-ray. Then, pointing to the post-op film, he says, "It is now in perfect alignment. I would opine that there was no damage from the delay, and there are no residuals."

George then asks Dr. Fritz if this is the same repair Mr. Flanagan would have needed if he had been diagnosed with an ankle fracture when he first went to the emergency room. The doctor answers with an emphatic "Yes."

"Assuming that he would have been treated and his fracture aligned as you aligned it, would the result in terms of any effect from the fracture be the same?"

"Yes. He could possibly have some arthritis when he is older from the trauma of the fracture. To be explicit, if arthritis does develop, it would be from the effect of the trauma on the joint from the fracture, not the delay of three days before it was repaired."

"Thank you, Dr. Fritz," George says, sitting down and smiling internally.

Judge Franco turns to Frank Santangelo.

"Your witness, Mr. Santangelo."

Frank is flummoxed. He doesn't even ask if Dr. Fritz is being compensated for coming to court. He pulls out a medical article from some journal that has general language about the effects of delay on certain types of fractures and the development of arthritis. He starts reading from a paragraph without asking Dr. Fritz whether he recognizes the author of the article or the journal the article is in as an authority in the field of orthopedics. George immediately jumps up and objects.

"Your Honor, counsel cannot read from a journal for the purpose of cross-examination without asking if the material is recognized by the witness as authoritative."

Judge Franco hesitates. He rules that Frank should ask those questions to the witness. When Santangelo asks those questions, Dr. Fritz answers that he's never heard of the journal or its author and does not recognize either as an authority.

Frank Santangelo is not deterred, and he starts reading again from the journal article. George stands and objects. Judge Franco overrules him and tells him to sit down. He reluctantly and slowly lowers himself into his seat. He cannot believe what the judge just did and the slimy tactic this lawyer is trying to pull. Santangelo continues to read, at which point George cannot contain himself and slams his hand down on his counsel table, making a loud bang, and jumps up, interrupting Frank.

"Your Honor, this is not proper. No expert witness can ever be cross-examined with a text that he or she does not recognize as an authority. That is long-established law. Mr. Santangelo must be directed by the court to stop reading and put the journal away!"

Judge Franco looks at him with cold eyes. He cannot believe

what this attorney has just done, but he knows George is right. There is a long pause. He looks over to Frank Santangelo.

"On reflection, Mr. Fredericks is correct. Please stop reading and put away the medical journal, Mr. Santangelo. Proceed."

Frank is at his wit's end. He has nothing.

"No further questions, Judge," he says.

Franco turns to George.

"No questions," George says quietly.

"Okay, thank you, Doctor, you are excused," says Judge Franco.

Dr. Fritz gets off the stand and walks past George, who signals him to wait. He walks up the aisle and sits in the gallery. Judge Franco then turns to both the attorneys.

"Mr. Fredericks, do you rest?"

George rises. "The defense rests, Your Honor," George states.

"Okay, I am adjourning for the day. Will the clerk escort the jurors out of the room."

When the last juror exits, the judge continues, "I want all motions and any requests to charge in the morning, after which we will do summations and then I will charge the jury."

George starts gathering his papers and puts them in his trial bag. He turns and walks up the aisle halfway through the gallery to the row where Dr. Fritz took a seat by the aisle. Dr. Fritz rises, and George thanks him profusely.

"Thanks, Doc. You were great!"

Dr. Fritz smiles.

"I am happy to help, George. I don't know how you do it. The tension is greater than when we are losing someone on the operating table."

George takes that in, and making sure that there are no jurors around, shakes the doctor's hand and thanks the doctor again.

"Make sure you tell me what the jury does, George," Dr. Fritz says.

"I definitely will," George replies.

Dr. Fritz says goodbye, turns, and starts walking up the aisle and out of the courtroom with George following him.

George then notices the beautiful blonde sitting on the aisle several rows beyond where the doctor had been sitting. The seats in the gallery are like theater seats. She has slid down slightly in her seat and has one knee up on the back of the seat in front of her. She is smiling at George. George walks up to the blonde and looks down at her with a big grin.

"How long have you been here?"

"All afternoon. You are very dramatic, Counselor."

"I don't like it when someone is trying to cheat, especially with the help of a biased judge."

"I see that."

Carole takes her knee off the seat, sits up, and then stands, straightening her light blue suit skirt. She is wearing a white blouse under a matching jacket and dark blue low heels. She has taken care to dress conservatively, and she has her hair up. George is taking her in with his eyes.

"By the way, I heard the doctor's comment and agree with him." She leans up and gives George a kiss on the cheek. She then grabs his arm, and they walk up the aisle and out of the courtroom.

Susie Griffin picks up the heavy thick white plates of food to take to her customers. She has not gotten any modeling jobs and is waitressing. J.G. Melon on Seventy-Fourth Street on the Upper East Side is busy. She thinks to herself that she would be okay if she never smelled another cheeseburger or cottage fries for the rest of her life. It is Melon's signature dish.

Susie came to New York City from Compton, California, two months ago. She is the youngest of six kids in a family that struggled financially. Her father, an auto mechanic, died when she was eleven years old. Her mother works part time cleaning schools. Susie grew tall, thin, and rangy but big boned. She has a slightly large nose, a nice smile, and a big laugh. As a young girl she read fashion magazines and thought she looked like some of the exotic models she saw on those pages, not like an all-American girl. Looking at those pictures and clothes, she knew she wanted to get out of Compton and to model. As soon as she finished high school, she left for New York City. She went directly to several agencies, including Wilhelmina, Ford, Elite, and the Gordon Agency. The first three were not interested because she did not have a portfolio.

Gordon thought she had potential. The agency did not sign her to a contract but said they would help her get a portfolio together and then send her on some interviews—called go-sees—to see the reactions. She has gone on some go-sees for jobs with her limited portfolio, but she has not secured any modeling work. She needs to earn money for living expenses and to hire a fashion photographer to take some photos to fill out her portfolio.

She found her roommates by luck. Two girls had posted a note at the agency office saying they needed a roommate. Her high school boyfriend, a tall blond basketball player, went away to school at Fullerton College in Fullerton, California, and has not visited her in New York City yet.

She is struggling to get over what happened to her at the party. It haunts her at night, and she has had difficulty sleeping. She brings three plates of cheeseburgers with tomato, lettuce, red onion, and pickles as well as three plates of cottage fries to a table. She then goes to the bar to pick up three draft beers for the same customers. As she walks to the table, she notices two men sitting at a table at the rear of the restaurant. One of them is wearing a shiny purplish sharkskin suit and has dark hair. The hairs on the back of her neck stand up. She shivers like she had put her finger in an electric socket. There is something about his looks she recognizes. She is not certain, but she thinks he could be the guy she met at the party who got her drugged out and did things to her.

Simon Stone and Stuart Schlussel are eating and talking intently.

"Santangelo told me that Franco asked him for $15,000," says Stuart.

"Really? What did Frank do?"

"He told him no, but Judge Franco kept after him. He told him that he was losing his trial."

"Is he?"

"Well, it is an unusual case, and he is up against Fredericks."

"That probably means no settlement offer."

"Minimal. Fredericks is tough. I think Frank is going to pay the judge."

"That is not what we all agreed," Simon Stone says.

"I know, but you know how Franco is. Anyway, changing the subject, I am going to have another party and thought you might want to come. I expect some lovely ladies to attend," Stuart says, taking a swig of his beer and smiling at Stone.

"What about Dugan?"

"I am not sure. I need him to supply the models and the drugs that these models seem to love."

"Where are you going to do this?"

"I have access to a brownstone in Brooklyn."

"Well, let me know when you have it set. I assume you will want a contribution."

"That would be appreciated. I will give you the details when it is all arranged."

———

Priscilla leaves the Easton Gallery and takes the fifteen-minute walk to McSorley's. She is wondering if this is a date or a just-getting-to-know-your-art-dealer kind of thing. She is attracted to Johnny. He is not like anyone she has ever dated in the past. She is a little excited but uncertain about him. He definitely has charm. She knows he has dated models, and she does not have those kind of looks. She loves art and New York City but has not forgotten her small-town roots. She is dressed in a thin butter-yellow sweater, a straight skirt in a tartan-like plaid just above the knee, a short boxy navy-blue wool jacket with gold buttons, and red leather Mary Jane flats. She is wearing her strawberry-blond hair in a French braid. She walks in and looks around the dark old drinking establishment. It has sawdust on the floor and memorabilia from many years of being around as a watering hole. It is a New York institution. When her eyes adjust, she sees Johnny waving to her from the corner of the bar. It is pretty crowded. She goes to him.

"Hello," she says. Johnny smiles.

He likes the way she looks. Her outfit suits her.

"Hi. Ready for some ale?"

"I sure am."

"What's your pleasure, light or dark?"

"What are you drinking?"

"I like the dark."

"Okay. I'll have that too."

He gets the bartender's attention and asks for two orders of dark ale. The bartender brings over four smallish mugs of ale and puts them on the bar. He asks Johnny if he wants to run a tab, to which Johnny says yes. He takes one glass mug of brown ale and gives it to Priscilla. He then takes one and clinks hers.

"So, are you going to tell me how you ended up working for Robert Easton?"

Priscilla then proceeds to tell her story about being interested in art, studying at Barnard, and deciding after college that she would try to work at a gallery.

"How did you get started painting?"

"It's a long story," Johnny tells her.

"I am not in a rush," she replies, smiling at him.

Johnny explains that he majored in political science at NYU, thinking maybe he would become a diplomat, but decided after one year that he would never fit into the Foreign Service. While he finished the major, he took as much art history as possible. During college he started modeling and saved all the money he could. He also got to travel for a few of the jobs. After graduation he decided to take some time for himself and bummed around Europe for a year. He originally took trains and hitched rides from people who posted on the bulletin boards of the hostels where he stayed. At one point he rented a small 250cc Spanish Bultaco motorcycle, which he used to teach himself how to ride and took it around Spain and Portugal. After that he decided it would be the best way to travel and bought a used 75/5 BMW cycle in Hanover, Germany. He visited as many museums as he could. He spent all his savings and returned home to New York. At that time, it looked like he could be drafted, so he decided to join the US Coast Guard Reserves. Without telling the story he explained that was where he met his friend Jim Ashford.

"How about Robespierre?" Priscilla asks.

"I met him at The Raunchy Brit where he used to tend bar."

Priscilla laughs.

"That figures. He is a real character, isn't he?"

"He is. He and his mom are like family to me," Johnny says, looking at her.

The bar is getting more crowded.

"Shall we get out of here and grab a bite?" he asks her.

"I would like that," Priscilla answers.

Johnny gets the bill, which the bartender runs on his card, and they leave.

"There is an interesting French-Vietnamese restaurant that recently opened on Lafayette Street not too far from here. I haven't been there but have been looking forward to going. Would you like to try it?"

"I don't know Vietnamese food, but I am game."

"I am not familiar with it either, but I hear that it is quite unusual and good."

The two of them take the short walk to Indochine on Lafayette Street. It's not on the second floor of the building, but it is up a short flight of steps. Johnny takes Priscilla's arm as they ascend and enter a lovely dimly lit room decorated to approximate the tropical climate of Vietnam. They are shown to a table, and after looking at the menu, they decide not to order entrees but to share appetizers of fried spring rolls, crispy rock shrimps, and grilled baby back ribs, which are all spicy and tasty. At the recommendation of the waiter, they have a bottle of Gewürztraminer, which goes well with the food. They both wind down from the day and start discussing art. The talk flows, and Johnny finds Priscilla has a sense of humor and laughs a lot. She is fun.

———

Susie Griffin is working hard, but her heart is beating fast with nerves, and her mind is going a mile a minute. She has an idea. She walks up to Nate, the waiter who is serving the two men in the back, when he goes to the bar to pick up some drinks. She says to him that if the man in the purplish-maroonish suit pays with a credit card, she would like to see the payment receipt. Later, as she is standing at the end of the bar waiting for drinks to take to one of her tables, Nate comes and stands next to her. He takes the signed credit card receipt off his tray and shows it to her. She asks the bartender for a piece of paper and writes down *Stuart Schlussel,* puts it in her pocket, and thanks Nate.

———

Dugan hangs up the phone. He has arranged for Schlussel to rent the same brownstone in Brooklyn he leased before. He goes to his locker and pulls out an old gym bag that he keeps there and checks his stash. He makes a mental note that he has to get more from his sources. Usually that means from some cops who keep some of the drugs that are seized. Dugan has actually planted drugs on a suspect to justify an arrest in the past. He gets up and goes to his car.

———

It is a nice evening. The sky is clear. There is some wind, but it is just cool, not chilly. There are a few leaves on the sidewalk and street blowing about. The moon is full. Carole and George approach his apartment building. He wants to drop off his trial bag before they go out to dinner.

"Carole, why don't you wait here, and I will run up and drop the bag."

Carole gives him a funny suspicious look.

"George, why do I have the feeling that you don't want me to see your apartment?"

George is chagrined.

"Carole, my apartment is a mess. I am on trial, and I have not straightened it up in a while. I don't want you to get the wrong impression."

She laughs at him.

"You are pretty cute. You know that? I want to see it. I don't care if it is a mess."

"Are you sure?" George says, feeling uncomfortable.

"I am sure," Carole says, grinning at him. She is getting a kick out of seeing this big, tough, handsome trial lawyer nervous. She is very curious about his apartment. It will tell her more about him. "You are supposed to want to get me up to your apartment," she adds with a chuckle.

George gives her a faux scowl and pulls out his keys. They enter his building and walk down the short hallway to the elevator. He is tempted to dash up the stairs and drop the bag, but he knows that is foolish. He opens the elevator door for her. It stops at the third floor, and he opens the door to his apartment. They enter the foyer and are greeted by George's small table next to the kitchen, which is loaded with yellow pads, pencils, and various legal papers, with a half-full coffee mug on it. Carole smiles and is very interested in seeing everything.

George puts down the trial bag by the table as Carole looks around. She peeks into the small galley kitchen to the right of the table. George has put in a long rectangular butcher block counter along one wall next to the refrigerator opposite the sink, cabinets, dishwasher, and small stove. George watches her. She moves into his living room and sees his art on the walls, the big bookcase that houses his stereo, albums, and lots of books, the light beige sofa and black leather chair opposite each other on the red Bokhara rug and the fireplace. She then walks down the short hallway with the curved ceiling, past the bathroom, toward the bedroom. George follows her and says nothing. She looks in, noticing more art and the antique dressers but does not step in. George is glad he straightened his bed this morning. She turns and looks up at him standing behind her.

"George, it is charming."

"Well, it was a good find for me."

She leans up and gives him a kiss.

"I like it! Shall we go?"

"Yes," he says, somewhat relieved.

They walk east on Seventy-Eighth Street. Carole is holding his arm, and they are quiet, both thinking. George points east. The two of them look and are a bit amazed by what they see. As they look down the street, the moon is absolutely huge and seems like it is right there at the end of the street.

"I can't believe how big the moon is," George exclaims.

"I know. It's amazing. I feel like we are walking right into it!" Carole replies and squeezes his arm.

He has never seen the moon so big in the city and wonders if it is some kind of special good omen for them. He hopes so. He sure feels bewitched. He pulls himself out of that thought and speaks.

"Okay, what will it be? Fancy and delicious Italian or not-so-fancy, very tasty Indian?"

"Hmmm ... that is not fair! I like both. What strikes you?" she says.

"Either is good for me. I really like the food at both of the restaurants I have in mind." He smiles at her. He can't believe how strong the urge is to kiss her and tell her it doesn't matter about the food as long as he is there with her.

"You still have to get ready for court tomorrow, right?"

"I do."

"Okay. So, this should be an early evening. I think we'll try the casual Indian tonight. Let's save the fancy Italian when we can linger," she says, looking up at him with a smile and sparkle in her eyes.

"Good. Let's go! I am hungry."

George steers them up Third Avenue toward Eighty-Third Street and the Tandoor Oven. They walk in, and the owner standing behind a bar on the right side of the restaurant comes out to greet them. He asks George where he has been and remarks that he has not seen him in a while. A waiter walking by says hello to George with a big smile. He asks George where he would like to sit, and they get seated. The staff obviously knows him, and the other waiters also greet him. Carole takes this all in and smiles.

"I think they like you."

"This is one of my favorite restaurants. It's my neighborhood go-to."

The waiter hands them menus and asks George if he would like a Kingfisher beer or the larger Taj Mahal. George looks at Carole.

"Would you like to have a beer or something else?"

"I am in your hands for this meal," she says.

"Well, Indian beer goes well with this food, so I recommend we share a Taj Mahal," he replies.

He tells the waiter, who nods and leaves to get the big bottle of beer. Carole looks at the menu, and George looks at her looking at the menu. She glances up and catches him.

"What?" she says with a curious look.

"Nothing. You just surprise me."

"Really? How?"

"I will tell you someday," he replies with a big smile.

He thinks about how attracted to her he is, which truly does surprise him. It's not just her looks but her manner and the way she engages with him. He has never felt this way before. *Not even close.*

The waiter comes back with the beer and two glasses. He puts them down and pours half a glass of beer in each. He then asks, "Chicken tikka masala, saag bhaji, aloo gobi, poori, raita, mango chutney?"

George laughs. He looks at Carole, who has put down the menu, and says, "I have to ask Carole if there is something else she would like." He addresses her: "Is there something on the menu that catches your fancy?"

Now she chuckles.

"Like I said, I am in your hands for this meal. It sounds like you have certain dishes you like."

"Well, there are lots of good dishes on the menu, but the sauce with the chicken tikka masala is really wonderful, and I'd like you to try it. The servings are large, so with a couple of vegetable dishes, the rice, and condiments, there will be plenty of food for the two of us."

"It sounds good to me, but I am interested in what the vegetable dishes and other things are," she says, reaching for a spicy papadam that is in a little basket on the table.

George explains that the saag bhaji is sautéed spinach, aloo gobi is a cauliflower and potato dish, and poori is fluffy fried bread. The condiments are mango chutney and raita, which is yogurt laced with cucumber.

"It sounds very delicious. I am excited to try it all."

George orders the food and asks for some plain papadams, which he prefers to the spicy ones that are in the basket. The waiter smiles at him and says, "Of course, Mr. George," before rushing off to place the order.

George raises his glass, and then Carole raises hers. They clink, and George speaks, "Thanks for coming to court today. It was a really nice surprise."

"It was great to see you in action, Counselor."

———

Priscilla and Johnny have finished their meal. Priscilla tried to contribute to the bill, which Johnny refused. Now they are walking, holding hands, around the East Village. As they walk down St. Mark's Place, they look at the variety of places, pausing here and there. They walk past the building that used to house the Polish National Home, a dance venue called The Dom, and The Electric Circus nightclub. Johnny feels comfortable and is enjoying himself. Priscilla is excited about this man who is striking and is an artist. She is trying not to project, but she feels they have a lot in common. They swing their hands a little. They see the moon and comment on how big it looks.

———

Susie finishes her shift and heads for her apartment. She gets home, takes a shower, and goes to the phone. She makes a call.

"Hello? Aarika?"

"Susie?"

"Hi. I think I saw the guy from the party who took me upstairs. I have his name."

"Are you sure?"

"Pretty sure. He was eating at Melon's with another guy and wearing the same purplish suit."

"What's his name?"

"Stuart Schlussel."

"I will call Johnny so he can tell his detective friend who talked to you."

"Okay. I don't think this guy should get away with what he did."

"Right. I will be back to you. Take care and do not tell anyone about this, okay?"

"I won't. Thanks, Aarika."

———

George walks Carole home.

"That was yum, and I am stuffed!" Carole says, holding his hand as they walk up Eighty-Third Street.

"It was especially good tonight," George replies, smiling.

They walk to the front of her building. She turns to look at him.

"Thanks for dinner. It was grand."

"My pleasure."

George is staring at her.

"What?" she says with a quizzical look, one eyebrow going up.

He keeps staring for a few beats, not believing how much he likes her and what he is feeling, and then says, "I really enjoyed it. It *was* grand," he repeats.

"Okay, you. Don't get me crazy. You are coming for dinner at my house on Saturday night."

George rubs his chin. "Gee, I don't remember being invited."

"Oh my, I thought I invited you. I invited two of your friends and one of mine. Gee, I must have forgotten to ask you," she says with a grin.

George laughs.

"Oh really! I am afraid to ask which friends you invited, but I will just let it be a surprise." He pauses, then says, "That reminds me to talk with Robby about the wine."

Carole smiles. She likes the cut of this man's jib. She feels like a teenager, but she likes the feeling. The two of them are now in front of her apartment house. He leans down and gives her a very soft kiss. She kisses him back, and the kiss lasts a long time. He gently holds her face. When the kiss ends, she speaks: "You are in trouble, Counselor. Good trouble. Knock 'em dead tomorrow with your summation."

They just look at each other for a few moments, neither wanting the evening to end, and Carole speaks again.

"Now go and prepare."

She turns and heads for the door. As she gets to the doorman, she turns back to look at him and waves. He smiles and returns the wave.

———

Priscilla and Johnny decide to forego the little crêperie on Ninth Street and head to Veselka, an old Ukrainian restaurant and late-night hangout on the corner of Second Avenue and Ninth Street for some dessert. Priscilla orders cheesecake but Johnny goes for the apple crumb cake à la mode. They chatter away and taste each other's dessert. They decide they should go to the Museum of Modern Art together and see what the exhibit is. Johnny asks if Saturday would work for her, but she cannot commit because of her hours at the gallery. She is thinking that Sunday might work better. They finish their dessert and walk outside. They stand talking. Priscilla finally says to him, "Johnny, this had been great. I probably should get home."

Johnny smiles at her.

"It's been fun. Don't forget to let me know about going to MoMA."

"I will."

She gives Johnny a hug. He can feel her soft chest. She feels nice to him. He returns it and then looks into her freckled face. She looks back inquiringly. He smiles and kisses her on the mouth. She returns the kiss. He likes the fresh taste of her. They break, and Priscilla laughs a little nervously and turns to hail a cab. Johnny takes over that job, and a cab pulls over. Johnny pulls open the door, and she hops in.

"Good night, Johnny."

"Good night, Priscilla."

He closes the cab door, and it pulls away. She looks back at him and waves, and he waves back. The cab disappears, and he stands there wondering about her and the evening. She is different—something very sweet and straightforward about her that he likes. She basically is a country girl with brains who is interested in and knowledgeable about art. He is fine with that.

24

JIM ASHFORD answers the phone.

"Ashford."

"Jim, this is Dave."

"Hey, Dave. What's up?"

"Schlussel has been talking with Dugan."

"Do you know what it's about?"

"Schlussel is setting up a party, and he wants Dugan to get some drugs for the players."

"Oh, great," he says sarcastically. "Anything happening with your investigation into kickbacks or payoffs to civil judges?"

"Yup. It looks like Schlussel knows an attorney who is giving a payoff to a judge in the Bronx. I am working with DA Torres. We are figuring out how to get him to wear a wire."

"That sounds like it could work. It also might help me."

They end the call.

———

Johnny Colrain has finished his workout and is making breakfast. The phone rings, and he grabs it.

"Hello?"

"Hi, Johnny, it's Riki."

"Oh, hi. How are you?"

"I'm good. Susie called me last night. She told me she thinks she knows the name of the guy who was with her at the party and took her upstairs. I told her I would tell you."

"What's the name?"

"Stuart Schlussel. She got it from a credit card receipt when he paid at Melon's where she is working."

"Thanks, Riki, that could be helpful. I will pass it on to Ash."

"Good. What should I tell her?"

"Tell her we will check him out and to be patient."

"How are you, Johnny?"

"I am good. I would like to help Ashford solve the murders."

"Yeah."

Aarika hesitates. She cannot read Johnny. She likes him but can sense that he might not be interested in her. She is not used to this kind of reaction from men, and it makes her that much more interested in him.

"That would be great," she says. She hesitates and then adds, "Call me and let me know how it is going, okay?"

"I will, Riki. Thanks for your help."

"And be careful, okay?"

"I will. Talk soon," Johnny says, wanting to get off the phone.

"Good," Aarika says, and she hangs up somewhat frustrated.

Johnny thinks about Aarika for a moment and wonders why he

is not more attracted to her. He was once, but now Priscilla is some-one he would like to get to know better. He does not want to see two women. He does not dwell on it and picks up the phone to call Ashford.

———

Jim Ashford and Johnny enter Dave Morgan's office.

"Dave, this is Johnny Colrain who has been helping me investi-gate the two model murders I am working on."

"So I understand," Dave says, extending his hand and saying, "Good to meet you." Johnny shakes it.

"Same. I've heard a lot about you," Johnny replies, and the two men look at each other doing the normal male thing, sizing each other up. Jim smiles at these two macho guys, and then the three of them sit down to contemplate their strategy to confront Schlus-sel and convince him to wear a wire. Dave calls his secretary on the intercom and asks her to come into his office.

"Donna, would you please take coffee orders from these two gentlemen and call them into the deli with my normal order and anything that you want. Oh, and you better ask Jenny and Don if they want anything, and then ask them to join us."

He reaches into his coat hanging on the back of the door, takes out some cash, and hands it to her.

She says, "Sure," takes the cash, and leaves.

When Donna returns carrying coffees, there is a vigorous discus-sion going on about using the knowledge they have of Schlussel's being at the party where Susie was beaten. They are pretty sure he is the one who did it and believe they can use that fact to pressure him to wear a wire with Judge Franco. They all take their coffees and keep talking. Since Dave has been investigating the kickbacks involving Manhattan attorneys, Reuben Torres, the Bronx DA, has agreed that this task should be handled by Dave Morgan's office in Manhattan, not in the Bronx. The consensus is that Don and Jenny will confront Schlussel and explain the facts of life to him. They are going to leave Dugan out of the equation for now. Ashford does not want Dugan knowing that he is on to him for more than going after Johnny.

———

Stuart Schlussel is hustling down Mott Street. He turns at number 17 and goes down the stairs to Wo Hop Restaurant. He enters the very plain interior with bright lights and Formica tables. A waiter bustles by carrying some plates and gestures toward the tables, telling him in a thickly accented voice to take any table. Stuart sits at an empty table on a chair against the wall where he can see everyone coming in. The waiter comes over with some tea, and he orders cold sesame noodles. A few minutes later he sees Dugan at the bottom of the stairs opening the door. Dugan steps in and looks around the restaurant. He spots Schlussel and walks over to his table. He sits down opposite him.

"I have just ordered, if you want something to eat," Schlussel says to him.

"Nah. Not hungry. What is on your mind?"

"I want to make sure you will be able to bring coke and Quaaludes to the party next week."

Dugan eyes him suspiciously. There is a pause with Dugan's small blue eyes staring at Schlussel's face. Dugan thinks to himself that he really doesn't like this presumptive, spoiled, Jewish asshole.

"That shouldn't be a problem," he replies.

"I also want to discuss something else," Schlussel starts but then pauses, trying to figure out how to say what he wants to say without provoking Dugan. He decides to just forge ahead.

"Remember at the last party I met a very young model wannabe, and you came into the room?"

"Yeah, why?" Dugan says with a scowl.

"Well, if I manage to entice someone to a room, I would appreciate privacy and not being interrupted," Schlussel says, keeping his voice steady. There is a long pause. Dugan is not happy with this and is mulling it over.

"I'll keep that in mind but can't guarantee anything," Dugan replies seriously.

This annoys Schlussel, and he gets his dander up.

"Look, Dugan. I am financing the party. I want to be able to enjoy myself privately without you in the room."

"Look, Stuart, I found the brownstone you use, and I am providing drugs and models so you can have your way with anyone you can snare at your little party. That is my contribution. If I happen onto your scene, I can't promise that I won't want to partake in the activity depending on my mood. I have to be blunt with you. If that doesn't work for you, I can just pass on the whole thing," Dugan says matter-of- factly.

Dugan knows Schlussel is married and hooked on smacking pretty young models around. He needs someone to provide drugs to get the models under the influence because he can't rely on just alcohol, and he won't be giving up the gig.

There is another long pause as the two look at each other. The waiter comes over with the plate of food and asks Dugan if he wants to order. Dugan declines, and the waiter leaves. Schlussel stirs the noodles as he thinks about that answer. He lifts the fork and takes a mouthful. After he swallows, he says to Dugan, "Delicious. Are you sure that you don't want to order?"

Dugan smiles. He knows he has the upper hand and has won this discussion.

"Yes. I am not hungry," he replies.

Dugan slides his chair away from the table and stands up.

"Same time on Tuesday night?" Dugan says.

"Yes," Stuart replies, looking up at Dugan.

"Okay. See you there."

Dugan turns and leaves the restaurant. Stuart takes another forkful of his noodles and thinks to himself that he has to figure out a way to eliminate Dugan from the picture. He hates the officious fat bastard.

———

Frank Santangelo finishes up his summation. He has outlined the missed fracture in the ER and tried to paint a very painful time for his client as well as permanent consequences of arthritis in the future as a result of missing the ankle fracture, which requires an award of substantial monetary damages. He tries to suggest that not only did Mr. Flanagan lose some time immediately from work, but he will lose more time in the future as a result of the arthritis that will develop. George stands and objects to the statements about arthritis as not proven by the testimony and actually contradicted by the testimony, but his objections are overruled by Judge Franco. Frank concludes by asking the jury to award $500,000. He sits down.

Judge Franco nods to George, who then rises and slowly walks to the railing in front of the jurors. He rests both hands on the railing and looks at them for a moment. He then begins in classic fashion: "May it please the court, Madam Forelady Askew, ladies and gentlemen of the jury."

It is an unusual summation in that he is not arguing against the liability for missing the fracture. He is arguing against what the plaintiff is claiming he suffered and the amount of financial damages he is entitled to as a result of the three-day delay caused by missing the diagnosis of the ankle fracture. George carefully goes over the testimony of all the doctors. He tells the jurors that this young Con Ed worker's ankle fracture certainly was missed, and he had to stay home for three days with his wife helping him to the bathroom. And, yes, he certainly was in some pain during that time, especially if he inadvertently put weight on that ankle. He then points out it is undisputed that after that time he received the same corrective reduction of the fracture he would have had if the fracture had been diagnosed three days earlier. He reminds the jurors of the orthopedic surgeon Dr. Fritz's assessment of the success of setting the fracture and his opinion that there was no additional damage to the ankle caused by the delay and that whatever arthritis might develop, which is not a sure thing, would be from the trauma of the fracture, not from any delay in setting the bones. George then goes over the fact that based on the work records he subpoenaed, Mr. Flanagan actually worked more overtime hours after the fracture healed than before it happened, so he was not disabled, no matter what was argued by Mr. Santangelo. He did not lose income beyond the normal recovery for a treatment he had to have. Assuming he might lose some income in the future beyond that, it would be from the fracture not from the three-day delay in diagnosis. He reminds them of Dr. Maggiore's physical exam that showed both legs equally developed, which means he used both equally. He then tells the jury that Mr. Flanagan is indeed entitled to compensation for those three days he spent home in pain, which was uncomfortable and required the assistance of his wife. He suggests to the jury that $5,000 a day for those three days would certainly be fair and reasonable compensation for those three days, and the jury should award $15,000 to Mr. Flanagan in order to render civil justice. George stops and looks the panel of jurors over carefully. He then thanks them for listening to the case and sits down.

Judge Franco quickly dismisses the jurors for lunch after telling them that he will charge them at two o'clock when court resumes, and then they will get the case to decide.

———

Schlussel is walking up Broadway. He approaches the Woolworth Building heading north. The brow of his thin face is furrowed as he thinks about the conversation with Dugan. He is about to enter when Jenny and Don approach him.

"Mr. Schlussel?" Jenny says.

"Yes," Schlussel says, looking at her quizzically.

"Our boss would like to have a talk with you at the office."

"Who is your boss?"

"District Attorney David Morgan."

"What is this about?"

"We are not at a liberty to discuss it," Don says.

"Can you come with us now?" Jenny asks, ignoring his surprise.

"Now? No. I have to go to a deposition."

"When will it be over?" Jenny inquires.

"I have no idea. It will go until five, I am sure," Schlussel says, visibly upset.

"Is it taking place in this building?"

"Yes."

"That's perfect. Please come to the office as soon as it concludes," Jenny says, handing him her card. Schlussel looks at the card. He realizes that Dave Morgan's office is not far away.

"We will see you at around 5:30 p.m.," Jenny says.

Jenny and Don walk away. Schlussel is stunned, and his mind is running wild.

He is wondering what it could be about. He doesn't think it could be about the murders. *Did they pick up Dugan? The model from the party?* He has no clue.

He rushes into the building holding the card.

George returns to the courtroom. He sits at the defense counsel table. Frank is at the other table in front of the bench to his left. Judge Franco tells the court officer to bring in the jury. They file in. Both attorneys look at the jurors' faces. They look serious but not too serious. It is hard to read what they will do. Judge Franco gives them his charge, which are his instructions as to what the law is that the jurors have to consider and how to apply it to this case in order to render a verdict. George is listening carefully. It is the standard medical malpractice charge. The judge is not pulling any tricks. George is glad he is playing this part of the trial straight. The judge finishes the charge and sends the jury out to deliberate. There are no exceptions to the charge or requests by either attorney.

George heads for the phones down the hall. He calls into his office to tell them the jury is out. Francine, the receptionist, tells him that Mr. Campanella wants to speak with him. She says that she will put him through, but first she asks, "So? Did you win?"

"The jury just got the case, Francine."

"Okay, good luck. I will put you through now."

"George?" Robert Campanella asks.

"Hi, Mr. Campanella. The jury is out."

"How did it go?"

"I thought pretty well. You know I never stipulated to liability, but I conceded it in my summation."

"How much did Frank ask for?"

"Five hundred thousand."

"That probably wasn't a good idea. What did you advise them to give?"

"The fifteen thousand we offered from the start. Five thousand for each of the three days that surgery was delayed."

"Smart. Look, I got a call from Dave Morgan. Can you go down to his office directly from court when it ends?"

"Of course. What is up?"

"I think the DA wants you to help convince someone to wear a wire in regard to payoffs."

"Wow! Okay! I will be there."

George is a bit fidgety. It is always like this for him as he waits while the jury deliberates. It used to be that once the case went to the jury, the judge would keep the jurors deliberating into the night until they came to a verdict unless the judge decided it was too late. Many trial lawyers would go to dinner or a bar and come back drunk. It also pressured the jury as the hours progressed into the night. This practice was finally stopped.

George has that feeling that keeps him so focused and diligent. He knows he did everything he could do for his client to, in his way of thinking, achieve civil justice. It is a good feeling, but it does not allay nerves about what the jury will do.

Two and a half hours go by, and the court officer indicates that the jury has buzzed. He goes into the jury room and comes back to announce that they have reached a verdict. Reaching a verdict that fast George knows is usually not a good sign for the plaintiff, but you can't ever be sure, especially in this case. Both lawyers take their places at the large counsel tables. Judge Franco enters and tells the court officer to bring the jurors in. George looks at them carefully. They seem calm and easygoing. They have not been fighting. This is a good sign. After they are seated, the clerk asks the foreman of the jury, a heavyset black woman, who is a bus driver, to rise. She does. At that point Judge Franco addresses her, "Madam Forelady, has the jury reached a verdict in the case of Flanagan against Mount Herman Hospital?"

"We have, Your Honor."

Judge Franco turns to the clerk and asks the clerk to read the questions on the verdict sheet.

The clerk begins.

"Did the Mt. Herman Hospital depart from good and accepted medical practice in failing to diagnose and treat the plaintiff's fractured ankle?"

The forelady responds, "Yes."

"By what number of jurors?"

"It is unanimous. All six jurors."

The clerk continues, "Was the departure a substantial factor in causing the injuries sustained by the plaintiff?"

"Yes."

"By what number of jurors?"

"Again, unanimous. All six jurors."

"State separately the amount awarded for the following items of damages, if any, up to the date of your verdict.

Medical expenses."

The forelady responds, "None."

"By what number?"

"Unanimous."

"Pain and suffering, including loss of enjoyment of life, up to the date of your verdict."

The forelady says, "$15,000."

"By what number?"

"Unanimous. All six jurors."

"Loss of earnings."

"None," says the forelady.

"By what number?"

"Unanimous. All six jurors."

"The judge says "Thank you, Madam Forelady. Please be seated."

George keeps a straight face but is smiling inside. He is extremely pleased that the jury agreed with his summation. Frank also keeps a straight face but is upset. This case is a big loser for him. Not only did he pay off the judge that amount, but now he will only recover 30 percent of that verdict after his office's out-of- pocket disbursements have been deducted, not to mention the time he has spent prosecuting the case.

Judge Franco turns to the attorneys. "Mr. Fredericks, do you wish the jury to be polled?"

"No, Your Honor."

"Mr. Santangelo?"

"Yes, Your Honor," Frank says, looking at the judge who has locked eyes with him. The judge then instructs the clerk to poll the jury. The clerk asks each individual juror if what the forelady has said is his or her verdict both on liability and the amount of damages awarded. They all confirm what the forelady has said. Judge Franco then thanks them all for their service and, after telling them they can now talk to the attorneys if they wish, but that they do not have to, dismisses them. The jurors get up and file out with several of them looking at George and smiling.

Judge Franco then asks for motions. George has none. Frank makes the usual pro forma post-verdict motions usually made by the losing side. In this case, he moves to set aside the verdict as inadequate and not consistent with the evidence or in the alternative for an increase in the award or a new trial. Judge Franco denies his motions from the bench.

George gets up and starts packing up his trial bag. He always likes to get out of the courtroom quickly after a verdict comes in. No sense sticking around, he figures. The postmortem can come later. As he is packing up, Frank Santangelo comes over to him and congratulates him. Much to his surprise, Judge Franco comes down from the bench and joins Frank. Judge Franco looks at George, and a wry smile breaks out on his pale face. He addresses George, "Congratulations, George. No one else could have gotten that result."

"I agree, George," Frank adds.

George is stunned, totally shocked, considering how hard the two of them fought against him, especially Judge Franco trying to force a settlement and railroad the case in favor of Frank.

"Thank you," he says, looking at both of them nonplussed.

Frank and the judge then go into the judge's office behind the courtroom, and George finishes packing up his trial bag. The court officer looks at him almost expressionless but not quite. George exits the courtroom. He then stops at the phones in the hall. He calls the office. Francine answers for the firm.

"Hi, Francine, I need to speak with Mr. Campanella."

"Has the jury come back?"

"Yup!" George says with a little chuckle.

"Okay, let me have it."

"The jury did what we wanted."

"Yay! I'll put you through to Mr. Campanella who has been waiting to hear from you."

George tells Robert Campanella about the verdict, the comments from Frank and the judge, and that he is leaving to go to Dave Morgan's office. He laughs at Mr. Campanella's happy reaction to what the jury did and his shock about what Frank and Judge Franco said after the trial. Robert Campanella is thrilled about the result.

"George, you know this is a great win. It is very hard to admit liability and convince the jury to award what you suggest would be the right amount of damages."

"Thanks, Mr. Campanella."

"The comments by the judge and your opponent after the verdict are extraordinary. I have been congratulated on winning but nothing ever said like that. Congratulations, George."

"Thanks again, Mr. Campanella."

"You better get going. Please let me know what happens at Morgan's office."

"Will do. Bye."

George hangs up and savors the words of his mentor, a great trial lawyer. They were meaningful coming from him and very special. He heads for the elevator.

In Dave Morgan's office the heat is being turned up on Stuart Schlussel. He is sitting opposite Dave in one of the two chairs, and Don is in the other. Jenny is on the light brown couch behind the chairs, listening.

"Mr. Schlussel, I am giving you your Miranda rights." He does and then goes on, "Do you understand what I have just told you?" Stuart gives him a dirty look like, *I am an attorney, you know!*

"Mr. Schlussel, you have been identified as the man who physically and sexually assaulted a young model at a party after drugging her. We have witnesses, in addition to the model, who place you at the party with the model," Dave says to him.

"I am not saying anything without a lawyer."

"We happen to know that you are aware of a certain judge in the Bronx asking for a payoff and receiving it. He has been under investigation for some time. We know that you have cases in front of this judge. Do you know who I am talking about?" Schlussel is taken aback but tries not to show it. He wants to be careful.

"I might," Schlussel replies.

"Let's not beat around the bush. You know it is Judge Franco." Dave is staring at Schlussel, who is not saying anything. Jenny shifts her position on the couch. Don is looking at Schlussel from his chair. Dave continues, "You can do yourself a favor if you cooperate with us. We haven't filed any charges in regard to the assault on the model yet."

Stuart does not like the way this is going. There is another long pause. He is extremely nervous, which he hates. *I am a trial lawyer, for crying out loud,* he thinks to himself. *Get a grip*! He is not sure what he should do at this point. He speaks.

"Without admitting anything, what do you mean cooperate with you?"

"We want you to wear a wire."

Schlussel is shocked.

"Are you crazy? Why would I do that?"

Dave Morgan looks at him and makes a face that can only be labeled a scowl.

"You don't seem to get it, Mr. Schlussel. You are in serious criminal jeopardy. Cooperate with us, and we will take that into consideration. Please go out to the chairs outside by the secretary's desk and think about what I have said while we confer about what we are going to do."

Schlussel gets up and walks out, carrying a light overcoat.

Dave Morgan closes the door looks at his two investigators and raises his eyebrows.

"What do you think? Will he bite?"

They both shrug, but then Jenny speaks.

"I have an idea. George Fredericks has been asked to come here now because he knows Schlussel. He is coming from Bronx Supreme and is in transit. Maybe he can help turn this guy. Why don't I go downstairs and intercept him before he gets to the office, fill him in, and see if he will talk to Schlussel—maybe persuade him to wear the wire?"

Turning to Dave, Don says, "I think that is a good idea, boss. He can act like he has been questioned or is part of the investigation we are conducting."

"Okay, Jenny. Get going. Fill Fredericks in and tell him that he should use that tactic with Schlussel. He knows that we are doing this and has been concerned about the abnormal actions of some of the judges. That made him suspicious."

Jenny gets up and leaves the office. She walks by Schlussel quickly, goes out the door, and down the stairs. She gets to the first floor, looks toward security, and sees George walking by the officer at the desk. She immediately goes to him.

"Mr. Fredericks, remember me?"

"Yes, you work for Mr. Morgan," George says as she pulls him aside.

"Right. We have Mr. Schlussel upstairs. He is sitting outside Dave's office. We explained to him that we believe that he assaulted a young woman, and we are using that to leverage him into wearing a wire. He is thinking it over. Our thought is that you could come in and go into Dave's office, stay in the office for ten minutes, and then go out, sit down next to Schlussel, and talk to him as if you do not know anything about his situation but have been called in to talk about kickbacks and payoffs. You would then volunteer that it appears we have a lot of evidence concerning your case in the Bronx and kickbacks in general. You then would ask him why he is there. He won't say anything. Then you suggest that if he needs any help with DA Morgan, you have a friend that has some influence with Mr. Morgan and leave. When you get downstairs, go to the phone and call Dave, and we will call Schlussel in."

"That would be ironic. He volunteered to help me in a situation with Judge Katz, whom I think takes kickbacks or payoffs, and held me in contempt. Yeah. Okay. I can do that."

"Great. You go up, and I will call up and tell them the plan. You will be able to go right in. I will wait a while and then go up."

Jenny heads for the phones, and George goes to the elevators.

Stuart is sitting in the chair, thinking. He wonders if the DA is bluffing, but he can't fit that with the fact that Morgan is alleging an assault on a drugged woman associated with him. At that moment the outer door opens, and he hears a voice he knows and then Morgan's secretary speaking.

"Oh yes, Mr. Fredericks. DA Morgan is expecting you. Go right in."

"Thanks," George replies.

George approaches the office carrying his trial bag and acts surprised to see Schlussel there.

"Stuart!"

"Hello, George," Stuart says, chagrined.

"Talk to you later," George says, indicting with a nod of his head that he has to go into Morgan's office. He opens the door and goes in. Stuart hears talking but cannot make out what is being said. Ten minutes passes, and Jenny walks by Stuart carrying a bag with coffees from the deli and brings it into Morgan's office. He hears more talking. He wants to leave but does not dare. He doesn't want to be arrested, especially at his office or home. He waits nervously despite his efforts to be calm. So many thoughts run through his head: *Have they talked to Dugan? Have they learned about the party he has arranged for next week? Do they know about the parties in the Hotel des Artistes? What has George told them?* He is lost in his thoughts when the DA's door opens, and George comes hustling out. He stops and sits down next to Stuart, putting his trial bag down.

"Are they talking to you about kickbacks and payoffs to judges?" George asks innocently. Stuart gives him a curious look like, *How would you know that?*

"Yeah."

"Yeah. They sure seem to know a lot about Judge Franco. I couldn't help them much. Anyway, I've got to run. See you."

"Okay, see you," Stuart gets out in a low voice.

George gets up and grabs his trial bag. Looking down at Stuart, he adds, "By the way, Stuart, I have a friend who is tight with DA Morgan. If you need me to talk to him, let me know," George adds casually and then leaves. After he gets outside, he smiles to himself. He knows that Stuart has ties to Judge Katz that most likely involve payoffs, which is why Stuart represented him before Judge Katz after he was held in contempt. It was not to help George but to help the judge out of a sticky situation that could expose him.

25

CAROLE IS WALKING ACROSS Central Park to Zabar's on Eightieth and Broadway. The Park is pretty full with people sitting on benches around the Great Lawn and on the grass. Some guys are playing softball on one of the baseball diamonds. Carole is in a good mood. She thinks about the dinner she is making for George and his friends on Saturday night. She wants it to be special so she is trying to decide between her delicious Swedish meatballs or her favorite—chicken paprikash with *nockerli*, the Hungarian version of spaetzle, which she feels is always good; however, she knows George's mother is Hungarian and a great cook. She doesn't want the first meal she cooks for him to be a disappointment. She smiles to herself and decides to go for it.

Carole exits the Park at Eighty-First and Central Park West and walks past the Museum of Natural History. The sun is out with high cumulus clouds. It is brisk but not cold. She is dressed in jeans, brown leather boots, and a cream-colored cable-knit sweater over a blue blouse. Her blond hair comes out to her shoulders from her cream-colored knit cap. When she gets to Broadway, she looks toward the front door of Zabar's and smiles as she sees Felicia waiting for her. Stylish as usual, Felicia is wearing a black velvet beret, black-and-white houndstooth double-breasted blazer over a thin black cashmere turtleneck with a black wool skirt just below the knee, black tights, and black ballet flats.

"Hey there," Carole says as she approaches.

"Hi. How are you?"

"Good. And you?"

"I am kind of excited."

"Really?" Carole says with a laugh, raising her eyebrow.

"About the dinner, not Robespierre, silly!" Felicia says, making a face.

"Oh sure," Carole teases.

"Come on, let's do this," responds Felicia, smiling and grabbing her arm.

They go into Zabar's and head upstairs to the mezzanine to check out the cookware and cooking utensils. They browse around picking up items and talking about them. As they are looking at box graters, a voice says hello. They look around and see the tall dark man who tried to get Carole to go with him in the taxi, her ex.

"Hello," Carole responds.

Felicia just looks at him, wondering who he is and not feeling good about him.

"Can we talk privately for a minute," he says.

"I really have nothing to discuss with you, Andrzej."

"It will only take a minute. Please."

Carole looks at Felicia. She is uncertain. Finally, she decides to agree. Felicia, who is holding two mixing bowls, has not taken her eyes off this man but finally looks over at Carole.

"I will go to the counter and pay for these mixing bowls and be right back," Felicia says.

Carole watches her and then turns to her ex.

"Okay, talk."

"First of all, I am sorry about the other night."

Carole says nothing and just looks at him. He continues, "I got carried away seeing you again."

Carole still says nothing and keeps on looking at him.

"I would like to take you to dinner, Carole, and make amends."

She smiles sardonically and then responds, "It's too late for that."

He reaches out to touch her arm, but she steps away.

"You are making this hard, Carole."

"Say what you want to say, Andrzej."

"I really miss you and want to get back together," he says.

"Look, I am sorry, but that is not anything I want."

"Are you seeing someone else?"

"That is not any of your business."

"That guy who hit me?"

Felicia returns with a Zabar's bag containing the bowls. Carole smiles at her and then turns to Andrzej. "I have to go now. Goodbye."

The two women walk away toward the stairs and then head down to the first floor.

"Who was that?" Felicia asks as they make the turn in the stairs.

"My ex. It is a long story," Carole responds.

"The one who tried to get you in the cab?"

"Yes." Then Carole laughs. Felicia looks at her quizzically, not understanding what she is laughing about.

"The way you asked me that, Felicia. How many exes do you think I have floating around?"

There is a pause, and then both of them laugh.

"By the way, Missy, I was getting ready to clobber the guy with a bowl. I saw him reach out for you," Felicia says.

"I am sure he wouldn't want to tangle with you, Felicia."

"I didn't like him," Felicia says seriously.

"I could tell."

"I know the type," Felicia adds. "I could tell you some stories."

"I bet you could," says Carole, looking at her friend. "Let's get what I need and get out of here."

Since Carole has decided to risk having her cooking compared to George's mother's, she buys sweet paprika imported from Hungary, chicken, and sour cream. The two women exit with their purchases and then walk down Broadway to Fairway Market where Carole carefully picks out the best green beans and cucumbers. She also picks out some purple Italian plums. She has everything else she needs. They walk out with their shopping bags and hail a cab. On the other side of Broadway, Andrzej watches them.

26

SMOKE IS CURLING UP from the cigar in the portly detective's pudgy hand. Dugan and Donnelly are sitting in Bryant Park behind the Fifth Avenue library. Dugan's beady blue rheumy eyes are scanning in front of him as he puts the wet somewhat flattened end of a fat Churchill cigar that has been smoked down to about three inches into his mouth. He takes a puff on it, removes it with his index finger and thumb, and speaks.

"I still want to get that bastard Colrain."

"I know you do," Donnelly replies with a nasty smile. He continues, "What do you want to do now that Ashford is on to you about him?"

"I'll think of something. Meantime, are you coming to the party on Tuesday?"

"I am. Do you have the drugs you need?"

"Don't worry about it, my friend," responds Dugan without looking at Donnelly.

"Do you do any?"

"Naaaa … Do you?"

"Sometimes," Donnelly says, looking at the side of Dugan's pockmarked face.

"Look," Dugan interrupts with a nod of his head.

They have been staking out a drug dealer's spot. A young man in his late twenties with a three-day growth on his face and dreads, wearing an old army fatigue jacket and jeans, who looks like an unkempt Bob Marley, arrives. He stands next to a trash basket a few feet from a bench. They continue to watch him. All of a sudden, a skinny young woman in her twenties with badly dyed blond hair showing her roots, in torn bleached jeans, a blouse, jeans jacket, and red Reebok Freestyle Hi sneakers comes up to him and says something. He says something back. She hands him a folded wad of bills. He takes out a small envelope and hands it to her. She leaves quickly. Dugan tells Donnelly to walk by the dealer, and once Donnelly gets by him, Dugan walks toward the perp.

The dealer looks up as Dugan approaches and turns to run but is grabbed by Donnelly who stopped walking and doubled back. Donnelly puts the dealer's hands behind his back and cuffs him. Dugan frisks him. As he goes through his pockets, he removes envelopes of cocaine, Quaaludes, and about $900 in cash. They hustle him away to their car and take him to the precinct. Dugan confiscates seven envelopes of coke and two with Quaaludes. He keeps four of the cocaine, all the Quaaludes and half the cash. He turns in three bags of cocaine and the remaining half of the cash.

———

Muriel Lambert bursts awake thinking she has to swim to her husband. She has been having horrible nightmares. In this one, he is drowning, his face contorted in a silent scream underwater with his arms outstretched to her, but she can't get to him. It makes her wake up in a cold sweat. It is about 4:30 a.m. She knows that she will not be able to get back to sleep. She throws back the covers, grabs her robe, puts her feet in her slippers, and shuffles off to the kitchen. She snaps on the lights, fills the kettle, puts it on the stove, and turns on the flame. She takes down one of her Royal Copenhagen blue-and-white mugs and drops a Lady Grey tea bag into it. She sits at the kitchen table and puts her head in her hands for a minute. She is not only grieving but struggling to understand. *Who would want to kill Burke? What was going on that she did not know, did not pick up on? He did not seem upset or worried about anything before his death.*

The whistle of the kettle interrupts her thoughts, and she gets up to pour the boiling water into the mug. She sets her timer for four minutes and sits back down again. She tries to just clear her mind while the tea brews, to concentrate on her breathing and meditate. It doesn't work very well as thoughts stream through her head. She starts reconstructing the last few days before his death. *Damn!* She knows that she is supposed to clear her mind, breathe deeply, let any thoughts just float through. She begins to chant, and then the timer goes off. She gets up, removes the teabag, goes to the refrigerator, grabs the milk, pours in the amount she likes into the mug, takes a teaspoon from a drawer, and stirs the tea.

Her brain takes over again.

What did I miss? she thinks to herself. She racks her brain and sips the tea. She decides that she should try to find out but acknowledges that she doesn't have a clue where to begin. The one tickle in her brain is her conversation with Rita Schlussel. She never heard her husband mention Stuart Schlussel's name ever. She never met him or his wife. She thinks it strange. *Why would this attorney have Burke's home number?* She decides that it is time for her to go through all her husband's papers carefully.

———————

Johnny, George, and Robespierre walk up the long pathway next to the Metropolitan Museum from Fifth Avenue by the Eighty-Fourth Street exit of the Eighty-Sixth Street Transverse. Families and couples are walking up with them and coming down from Central Park. They let a young guy going too fast down the hill on a skateboard go by, snaking his way through everybody. Johnny and George are wearing shorts, T-shirts, and regular basketball sneakers. Robby has on sweatpants, not shorts, and Converse All Stars. Johnny has Baloo on his lead. The big dog pulls to examine a smell, but Johnny does not let him get off the path. The men are talking quietly about the upcoming dinner at Carole's. Robespierre remarks that he was told that red wine would be the preferred color to go with the meal but not what the meal was. George laughs.

"That is like Carole. I will bring some red wine also, Robby," he says.

"Okay. Sounds good," Robespierre responds, then he addresses Johnny.

"Are you bringing someone, John?"

"I am," he says.

"Are we allowed to know who?" says George.

"Nope. I will surprise you," Johnny says with a grin.

They follow the path to the basketball courts on the right just before the Great Lawn. Pickup basketball games are always being played there. George and Robby sit down on the bench on the southern side of the first court and watch the action. Johnny walks

Baloo around the perimeter of the two basketball courts and a volleyball court so the big white dog can relieve himself and then joins his two friends. Baloo lies down at his feet, and Johnny ties his lead to the bench.

A fast-paced game is going on. There are black, Hispanic, and white players— city guys playing hard. Some are pretty good. There is a lot of talking between teammates, trash-talking to opponents, and complaints when someone gets fouled. Johnny definitely gets the feeling that many of these players know each other. A give-and-go play creates the winning basket for one team, and the game ends.

The winning team waits for the next opposing team to form. Everyone waiting to play drifts out on the court and shoots baskets to warm up. After a little while, the winning team leader says they are ready to play the next team. The other players on the court line up to shoot from the foul line. Whoever makes the shot goes to one side, and those who don't are eliminated.

George, Johnny, and Robespierre all make the shot along with a few other guys for a total of eight. Most of the players from the losing team are still around. Johnny was watching that game carefully, and two of the young players on that team had game. He goes over and asks the two guys if they would play with them to form a team. They look at Johnny, George, and Robby skeptically but want to play again without waiting, so they say yes. Johnny then goes to the five other players who remain from the shoot-off and says he has formed a team, and they should flip for who plays the winners next. They do. Johnny wins the toss, and his team of George, Robby, himself, and the two players from the losing team take the court with him. The team that lost the coin toss sits down to wait to play in the next game. As the team challenging the winners, Johnny's team gets the ball first. The winning team matches up their players with Johnny's team in terms of who they want to cover, and the game starts.

Johnny starts dribbling up the court and passes to Robby, who takes the ball to midcourt. George immediately cuts to the basket without the ball from the left side of the court, and Robby lobs the ball high to him. He grabs the ball in the air and lays it softly off the backboard. It goes cleanly into the basket.

"Okay, George!" yells Johnny as he backpedals and gets back on defense. The teams are well matched. The team they are playing consists of regulars on this court, and they know each other pretty well. However, they are all about offense, not so much about defense, and several of their players are ball hogs so they don't always mesh. They have egos and clash when one or the other heaves up a shot from too far out that misses, does not pass to the open man and shoots, or fails to cover one of Johnny's team on defense, allowing an easy basket. As the game proceeds, Johnny, Robby, and George take advantage of the skills of the two younger players Johnny picked and pass to them when they are open. They are fast and like getting the ball so they keep cutting, getting away from the man covering them, and receiving a pass as they get free, which either allows them to shoot an easy shot or pass it to someone else who is free and has a better shot. George is matched up against a guy who is taller than he is but is holding his own guarding him and making some good shots under the basket when the player's defense falters, and he gets a nice pass. George has some underhanded moves and an old-fashioned hook shot, which makes the guy who is guarding him crazy, and Johnny and Robby yell and clap.

The player guarding Johnny is tough and a real street player. He is all over Johnny, guarding him closely. He also tends to foul when Johnny gets away from him. Johnny calls the obvious fouls, and the guy complains loudly, but the fouls are so obvious no one backs his complaints and denials. The game is close, but Johnny makes a few nice jump shots and layups. Slowly his team pulls ahead. He also closely guards the player matched with him, and the player tends to force bad shots. The killer for the other team is Robespierre. His old street-playing days spring to life. As soon as he gets the ball, before he can be defended, he starts shooting long push shots from all over the court that more often than not fall beautifully through the hoop. Johnny and George howl their delight and compliments. This takes the life out of the other team as they work hard for their shots but can't keep pace. One last long shot by Robby gets nothing but net and seals the win. He accepts the high fives from Johnny and George and the two young guys that they picked up to form their team.

The other team who had been waiting on the bench to play next lost one player but picked up one who had arrived and had been waiting alone. They come onto the court to take on the winners. John looks at Robby and George and asks if they are up for another game. They are, and the two young guys are delighted because the team plays more like a good college team rather than five street players. The team has now jelled quite a bit. They all know what to expect from each other, and they polish off their new opponents pretty easily. George even gets in a dunk, which causes all his teammates to yell their approval. At the end of the game, Johnny doesn't have to ask his friends about playing another. Part of them would like to do that, but they are sweaty and tired and ready to stop. They shake hands with the two young guys and the opposing team players and leave the court. The players who were watching come onto the court and start shooting some baskets before the shoot-off for new teams will start again. Johnny unties Baloo and leads him away.

As they are walking down the path toward Fifth Avenue, the three men agree to meet at Carole's apartment at 7:00 p.m. George has given all of them her address. They split up. Johnny and Robby look for a cabbie on Fifth who will take them downtown with the big dog.

George starts walking home to Seventy-Eighth Street. As he walks down Madison Avenue, the late-afternoon sun creates shadows across the road, and people pass him on their way home. The buses flow up the avenue like a herd of elephants, in bunches. It has been a nice afternoon. He is sweaty, but the exercise has made him feel good. He smiles about the fact that New Yorkers don't even give him a second look as a result of his appearance. He can't remember when he last had so much fun playing hoops. He is looking forward to the dinner at Carole's.

Stuart has spent the day with his wife and is very itchy. His thoughts run the gamut from the young model to what occurred in Morgan's office. She has picked up on his mood. They have gone through their regular Saturday routine. Today, however, they decided to drive up to the big Fairway on 130th Street and Twelfth Avenue to do their weekly big shop for groceries. As they are putting the groceries away, Rita asks him what is wrong. He says that he is worried about a case. She doesn't buy it but remains silent. He goes into the living room and turns on the TV. She starts making dinner. She tries to figure out what is troubling her husband but comes up empty.

Johnny Colrain comes out of the shower, grabs a towel, and is starting to dry his hair with it. He goes out into his loft when the phone rings. He picks it up.

"Hello?"

"Johnny, it's Priscilla. I am in a state. I had to work a little late at the gallery. Can you pick me up a little later than we scheduled? Maybe give me an extra fifteen or twenty minutes?"

"Sure. Not a problem. We will just have to go a little faster on the cycle."

"I am ignoring that. I will see you around 6:40 outside my building, okay?"

"Yup," he says, drying his hair with the towel.

"By the way, I'm looking forward to it," she says with a smile in her voice.

"Me too," Johnny replies.

———

There is music softly playing in the living room, and it wafts gently into the kitchen where Carole and Felicia stand talking and humming along with some of the tunes. The table is set in the dining room. Felicia has placed the ironed light blue and white checked cloth napkins carefully by each setting. It looks festive.

Carole has taken out her favorite kitchen pot and put it on the right front burner of the stove. It is a wide copper braiser, which she bought with her first significant modeling fee. Polishing it always delights her, but cooking for one, she doesn't get to use it much. A model she worked with learned how to make what has become one of Carole's favorite dishes from her Hungarian grandmother and gave the recipe to Carole.

There is a pot filled with water on the left back burner of the stove in which green beans will be blanched. On the left front burner is another pot filled with water to cook the *nockerli* in.

Carole has already chopped one and a half large yellow onions and cut two green peppers into half-inch slices. Trimmed raw green beans are on the counter in a small colander. Ten chicken thighs sit on a blue-and-white platter next to a cream-colored bowl. The bowl holds the batter for *nockerli*, which Carole has already prepared by first breaking an egg into the bowl, adding a little kosher salt, and beating it with a fork until it was frothy. Next, she added one cup of all-purpose unbleached flour followed by half a cup of room-temperature tap water, stirring with the same fork, making a thick batter, which will go through the holes on her spaetzle maker into a pot of boiling salted water when she slides the hopper across the perforated base.

Felicia is watching Carole in her full apron as she picks up a paper towel to grab the chicken skin and pull it off the chicken thighs. She uses kitchen scissors to trim some, but not all, of the fat from the now naked chicken. Next, Carole covers the bottom of the copper pot with a little oil, then stirs in the chopped onions, turns the heat on, and cooks the onions until they turn pale gold. She adds two tablespoons of sweet Hungarian paprika and stirs it into the onions for about a minute. Then she adds two eight-ounce cans of tomato sauce to the pot, followed by an equal amount of chicken stock, which she measures by pouring it into the tomato sauce cans in order to get all of the sauce out. She tastes it to see if the sauce needs salt, which will depend on how salty the tomato sauce and the chicken stock are. She tells Felicia if she needs to add salt, she will do so sparingly, and that is what she does, putting a little salt into her palm from the sugar shaker that holds salt on the kitchen counter. She stirs everything, lets it come to a soft boil, then turns the heat down and lets it simmer for five minutes. Next, she slips the pieces of chicken into the simmering sauce, strews the slices of green pepper over the top, puts the lid on the pot askew, and lets it continue to simmer until it is done, which will take about forty-five minutes.

As Carole cooks, Felicia asks her questions about the preparation of the meal. She also asks about the plate full of dumplings sitting on one side of the kitchen table. Carole tells her it will be a surprise dessert.

She then gives Felicia an apron and shows her how to make the cucumber salad. Carole puts a little cider vinegar in a bowl, and then adds a little kosher salt. She waits a bit then adds a heaping tablespoon of sugar and briskly stirs in a little more than a quarter of a cup of sour cream. Carole tells Felicia to taste it to see if it is well balanced, or if she needs to add a little more salt or sugar to smooth the taste out. Felicia says that it is delicious. She instructs Felicia to take the two cucumbers on the counter and slice a little bit off each end, then, taking the Swedish peeler sitting next to the cucumbers, peel them and then slice them lengthwise and use a teaspoon to scoop out the seeds. Next, she tells Felicia to cut the cucumber halves into quarter moons a quarter of an inch thick and stir them into the bowl with the dressing. Carole then asks her to put the bowl in the refrigerator.

The kitchen smells delicious. Carole is singing "There Is Something in the Air" as she works.

"What is that song, Carole?" Felicia asks.

"It is a tune from 1940 that I really like."

"Hmmm ... I think it has something to do with your mood, Carole," Felicia says with a chuckle.

Carole laughs.

"Maybe," Carole says.

Felicia looks at her with amusement. She likes this woman.

————————

Robespierre looks at himself in the mirror. He likes what he sees. He has put on black slacks, a black belt with a small silver buckle engraved with his initials, black highly shined monk strap shoes, a crisp light blue shirt, and a light gray crew-neck cashmere sweater. He checks his hair and thin mustache. He puts a small amount of Drakkar Noir on one hand, rubs his hands together, then pats them gently on his face. He takes the stairs and goes to his mother in the kitchen. Lucienne looks up from the shrimp stock that she is stirring on one of the burners on a big stove and smiles.

"You look nice. Why do I get the idea that this is an important dinner?" she says.

Robespierre looks at her and grins.

"Because it is. Remember when I told you about Felicia Bailey, the blues singer?"

Lucienne nods.

"I know that you have been playing her music too."

"Right. Well, she is going to be at this dinner."

"With all your friends?"

"Yes. It should be fun. Carole, the singer who George rescued, is a friend of Felicia's and wants to introduce us. She is cooking the dinner at her apartment. I am bringing a few bottles of red wine. I have spoken to everyone in the restaurant, and everything should be under control."

"It sounds nice. Have a good time," Lucienne says and turns the stock.

"Thanks, Ma. I might not get back until late."

Lucienne gives him a look like, *Son, I know that.*

Robespierre goes to a counter where there are three bottles of

Cabernet Sauvignon and a shopping bag. He grabs a cardboard box from the storeroom and tears it in strips, puts the bottles in the bag, and puts the cardboard between the bottles. He goes over to his mom, gives her a hug with his other arm and a kiss on the cheek. They say goodbye, and he walks out the side door.

———

Dugan is sitting at home looking at the TV holding a beer can. He is in long boxer shorts and a sweat-stained T-shirt. His feet are on the coffee table. His phone rings.

"Dugan, can you talk?"

"Kristin. Good to hear from you. I was going to call you."

"I am about out and need more."

Dugan smiles. He knows how to play this game.

"I need you to get some models to come to another party."

"Really? How many and when is the party?"

"At least six, but more is good. It is at the same address in Brooklyn on Tuesday night starting around seven."

"I will do what I can."

"Try hard, Kristin. I'm sure you can do it. Let me know, and I will have a package for you."

Dugan hangs up with a smirk. He can't believe how easily he can manipulate certain people. It helps if they are hooked on something, of course. He is very sure that Kristin will come through.

———

George can't decide what he's going to wear to Carole's dinner party. He is trying on different clothes like a teenager on his first date. He laughs at himself. This is not like him at all. He finally decides on a pair of gray pinwale corduroys, English brown suede plain-toe shoes, argyle socks, and a blue-and-black-checked shirt. He grabs his blue blazer and leaves his apartment.

———

Johnny is trying to hurry Baloo back to the loft from a walk. The big dog is being recalcitrant. He has discovered a very intriguing smell and is circling before he decides he will pee on it. Johnny looks at the sky exasperated.

"Come on, B!" he urges loudly.

Baloo finally finishes his business, and Johnny urges him along. They go up the stairs and into the loft. Johnny puts down food for Baloo and then checks himself out in the mirror. He is wearing black jeans with an R.M. Williams Drover belt, a blue-and-white-striped dress shirt, a blue cable-knit alpaca vest, and polished black half boots. He leans down and gives his dog a pat on his side.

"Okay, big guy. Be a good boy. See you later."

He grabs his leather jacket and two helmets and heads out the door to his motorcycle.

———

Leighann looks at her friend who is checking herself out in the full-length mirror. Priscilla knows she will be riding on Johnny's motorcycle so she has decided to wear a white silk shirt and slim black slacks with a two-inch belt, which she knows accentuates her small waist. She has a long thin gold necklace around her neck and short black ankle boots on her feet. Her long hair is loose to her shoulders. She looks at herself and cocks her head to the side.

"You look great, Pris," says Leighann.

"You think so? Is it too casual?"

"Absolutely not. It's perfect. Will you be warm enough?"

"I thought about that too. I'll wear the short black leather jacket I got when I was at Barnard. It is still in good shape and is exactly what I need for tonight," Priscilla says with a chuckle.

"Sounds good—and you'll look cool, kiddo."

The buzzer rings.

"Uh oh, time to fly," Priscilla says, turns, and pulls her hair into a pony tail.

"Have fun," Leighann yells after her as Priscilla puts on the jacket and heads out the door.

Johnny is on his bike and watches Priscilla walking rapidly toward him. As she gets close, he gets off the bike, unclips her helmet, and smiles.

"Looks like you're ready for the bike," handing the helmet to her.

She winks, puts the helmet on, jumps on the back, and off they go.

George reaches the apartment house and tells the doorman his name; the doorman buzzes Carole's apartment. She tells the doorman that he can send George up and the names of the other people she is expecting so he can send them right up.

George comes out of the elevator holding a bag made for carrying wine, and Carole is right there in her apron. She puts her arms around his neck, raise up on her toes, and gives him a big kiss on the mouth. He holds on to the bag but puts his other arm around her waist.

"Hello," he says with a big grin after their kiss.

"Hello back to you," Carole says, grinning also.

"You are the first of the guys to arrive. Come in and meet Felicia."

She leads him into a short hallway that opens to the living room with the entrance to the kitchen on the left.

"Hmmmm ... I smell something delicious—and familiar." George exclaims happily as they walk into the kitchen where Felicia is standing by the counter. He puts the wine package down on the small kitchen table.

"George, this is Felicia."

"Happy to meet you, Felicia. I have heard a lot about you," George says as he leans forward to air kiss her near each cheek, *a la bise*, in the French style.

"Oh my!" Felicia says, smiling, somewhat surprised, and then adds, "I have heard a lot about you as well."

"George, I confess, it's chicken paprikash you smell," Carole says.

"Great! In that case I think I should open one of these right away," George offers, taking one of the wine bottles out of the sack. "It will definitely go with paprikash. It's a Hungarian red called Bull's Blood. I thought you might like it, but it turns out it was better than a good guess."

"Yes! Perfect! I will get some glasses."

They hear a knock on the door, and Carole on the way to get the glasses calls out to come in. Robby walks into the foyer carrying his bag of wine, and Carole greets him.

"Hi, Robespierre."

"Hello!"

"Come into the kitchen."

As he walks in, Robespierre's eyes see George holding a bottle of wine, but then they find Felicia looking at him. He smiles, and she does the same. *She is prettier in person than her pictures,* he thinks. He puts his bag with the wine down on the kitchen table and smiles at George.

"Greetings, everyone," he says.

Carole says, "Felicia, this is Robespierre."

"Delighted to meet you," Felicia says, putting forward her hand.

Robby smiles and says, "Call me Robby. I am delighted to meet you, Ms. Bailey," and he kisses her hand.

"Wow, this is a continental group," Felicia says to Carole and then adds, "Please call me Felicia," and everyone laughs.

Carole gets George a wine opener and another glass. George opens the bottle. Robby and Felicia begin to chat, and there is another knock on the door. Carole answers the door, and Johnny and Priscilla are there.

"Hey, Johnny!" Carole says.

"Hi, Carole." He is carrying some flowers, which he hands to Carole who thanks him.

"This is Priscilla."

"Great to meet you. Please come in."

"Nice to meet you," Priscilla says.

"Come in. Everyone is here."

They enter the kitchen, and George and Robby say hello. Carole introduces Priscilla and Johnny to Felicia. George has opened the bottle, and he pours wine for everyone. Carole quickly finds a vase to put the flowers in and places it on the table. She then raises her glass to make a toast.

"To my brave rescuers, thank you!"

Johnny and Robby look at each other and point to George. He just makes a sheepish grin like it was nothing. Priscilla is puzzled. She turns to Johnny, but Carole notices and proceeds to tell her what happened outside the Village Vanguard.

Everyone starts putting his or her two cents in, and the discussion becomes lively. Carole is thrilled to have the group there drinking and kidding each other. It is a sharp contrast from the gatherings when she lived with her ex. After some minutes, she checks her pot, stirs it, and asks, "Is everyone hungry?"

She gets a chorus of affirmatives, so she starts to finish the meal while the others keep talking.

Carole turns the heat on under the two pots of water. As soon as they come to a boil, she puts salt in both pots and asks Felicia to put the green beans in the pot on the left back burner. She sets a timer for seven minutes. She is going to make the *nockerli* in the pot of boiling water on the left front burner. When the seven minutes is up, she turns off the back burner and drains the green beans, adds a generous pat of butter to the pot, puts the green beans back in, covers the pot, and puts it back on the unlit burner. Now she is going to make the *nockerli*, which will be done quickly.

George comes over to Carole to watch her. He stands close, and he is feeling a combination of emotions, which all feel good. He remembers countless times being in the kitchen when his mother was making this dish and the *nockerli*. He feels touched that this lovely woman is now doing it for him and his friends. George's mother uses a very small cutting board and knife to cut and drop small pieces of dough into the boiling water with a flick of her wrist, but Carole has a spaetzle maker, a metal sliding device with a hopper on it that she puts the dough in, then moves back and forth over what looks like a grater with wide holes that does the same thing in a very uniform way. As soon as the *nockerli* rise to the surface, Carole stirs the pot, then drains it. She puts the *nockerli* back into the pot, adds a little butter, and covers the pot.

Carole asks everyone to go to the dining room table and says she and Felicia will bring out plates if that is okay. Everyone says yes except Priscilla who says she would like to help. Carole smiles at her and agrees. She asks her to get the container of sour cream out of the refrigerator and put some in each of two small navy-blue bowls sitting on the counter and bring them to the dining table. Then she gets out a stack of her blue-and-white Furnivals Denmark dinner plates, which she got at Conran's from a cupboard and puts them on the kitchen table. Felicia takes one, and Carole puts the chicken paprikash, *nockerli*, and some green beans on the plate.

"Felicia! I almost forgot your cucumber salad!"

Felicia laughs, puts down the plate, and goes to the refrigerator to take out the bowl of cucumbers. She serves a portion onto the plate. Carole asks her to take it to Robby and tell everyone not to wait but start eating when the food comes out so it does not get cold and to mix in a dollop of sour cream on the paprikash before starting. Felicia takes the full dish to the dining room and goes to Robby. He looks up at Felicia as she puts the plate down in front of him and repeats the instructions from Carole.

"Looks delicious," Robby says loudly enough for Carole to hear.

"I hope so," she replies.

Priscilla then comes in with a plate for Johnny. Carole follows with a plate for George and puts it down before him. Before she can leave, he touches her arm, looks up at her, and says something to her in Hungarian.

"*Csókolom a kezed.*"

Carole stops and looks inquiringly at his face, into his eyes. He looks back into hers. There is a pause.

"Will you translate for me?"

"I kiss your hand. It is a way to thank you for preparing and serving this wonderful meal."

Carole blushes. Johnny and Robby look at the two of them as do Felicia and Priscilla, who have entered carrying dishes for themselves. They all smile at these two people. Carole breaks the spell by looking around, a bit embarrassed, and saying, "Everyone, please, start eating! I don't want it to get cold."

She then rushes out to the kitchen to make a plate for herself as everyone starts digging in. The conversation starts flowing again. Carole returns with her plate and sits next to George, who is at one head of the table.

"It is delicious, Carole," Robby says.

"Absolutely!" Johnny adds.

Felicia and Priscilla also agree and start questioning Carole about what the little dumplings are called and what cookbook did she find it in. She answers that she got the recipe from a model friend of Hungarian descent, who told her to serve the sour cream separately rather than stirring it into the sauce at the end of cooking so it does not make the sauce grainy, and if you are lucky enough to have leftovers, the sauce won't curdle during reheating. Carole turns to George who has just finished a big mouthful of *nockerli* covered with the rich paprika sauce.

"Well?" she says nervously, knowing that he has had this dish many times.

He finishes his mouthful.

"You have nailed it. The sauce is wonderful. It all goes together beautifully."

"Really?"

George reaches out for her hand.

"Yes. I wouldn't just say that if I didn't mean it. I figure if I am not honest then you won't know what I really like."

Carole gives his hand a squeeze.

"I like that," she replies.

The conversation turns to Johnny and his art, then Priscilla and her history and when she started seeing Johnny. The stories flow about Robby and his mom, about how he met George and then ran into him at the gallery after Johnny invited George up to see his paintings, about how Robby and Johnny got friendly in an abbreviated way. The talk then turns to Carole and Felicia and their singing. Everyone wants to know about Felicia's career—when she started singing, how she got her start, what she is doing currently, and how she met Carole. They then turn to Carole—when she began modeling, singing, and then decided to try to make singing a career.

All the men go into the kitchen individually to help themselves to seconds after asking if they can get more for anyone, returning to jump into the conversation circulating at the table. George opens more wine and fills everyone's glasses. No one mentions the three murders and Johnny's helping Ashford. There is no talk about kickbacks or George's role in helping that investigation. Carole is tempted to bring up George's trial and how amazing he was but decides not to unless she is asked directly if she has seen him in court.

As everyone finishes eating, Carole gets up to start clearing the table. Priscilla and Felicia join her, and Carole pointedly asks the men to stay seated.

Carole turns the flame on under a big pot of water to bring it to a boil. She asks Priscilla to go to the refrigerator and get the big square of sweet butter. She takes out a big cast-iron skillet. She scoops a large amount of the butter and puts it into the skillet. Carole goes to another cupboard and takes out a jar labeled with writing on green tape, "Cinnamon Sugar." The water boils, and Carole carefully drops the big dumplings from the plate that had been on the table into the water. Felicia and Priscilla have been watching her move around the kitchen wondering what she is making. Carole asks Felicia to go to another cabinet and take out the canister of plain breadcrumbs. Felicia takes the breadcrumbs to her as Carole puts the flame under the skillet with the butter in it. As soon as the butter melts, she tips some breadcrumbs into the skillet and stirs them. She then starts extracting the round dumplings from the boiling water using a round perforated spatula, placing them in the skillet. She stirs the dumplings around in the browning breadcrumbs. She then directs Priscilla to grab the dessert plates. She hands Felicia the cinnamon sugar, and she takes out the doughballs that have sautéed in the browned butter with the breadcrumbs and puts three on a plate. She asks Felicia to shake the cinnamon sugar on the dumplings. Felicia and Priscilla remark on how good this dessert smells.

"Okay. I think we have this down. Let's see how we like them! Felicia, please serve that dish," Carole says.

Felicia takes out the dish. Carole hears George speaking loudly. "Oh my God! *Gombócs!*"

Carole laughs hearing him. Priscilla takes Felicia's place with the cinnamon sugar, sprinkles it on, and takes out another plate. Felicia returns for another plate. The women complete the plating and go out with the last two plates. They sit. No one has started, and Carole laughs at them.

"Okay. Let's see how these are," she says as she takes the side of a fork and pushes down on a doughball with it. George is smiling because he knows about this classic Hungarian dessert. He does the same. Out squirts the juice of the Italian plum inside as its dark skin is revealed. Everyone follows suit. George is ecstatic as he tastes it.

"So good! I haven't had these since forever!" he exclaims.

Everyone joins in remarking about the unique dessert that combines the dough covered with browned breadcrumbs and cinnamon sugar with the juice and fruit of the dark Italian plums inside.

"An explosion of taste in your mouth," says Felicia.

"Yummy," adds Priscilla.

"I am so full, but I have to have another one," Johnny says.

"I am with you, brother," Robby replies.

"Me too! Anyone else want another *gombócz*?" George says, smiling at Carole as he gets up with Robby and Johnny. The women demur; they are stuffed.

The men come back with another *gombócz* each and polish them off as the dinner conversation continues. Carole heads into the kitchen, and Felicia and Priscilla follow her. Felicia and Priscilla come back with small glasses, and Carole follows with a beautiful pear-shaped bottle of Belle de Brillet.

"This isn't plum, but it is pear and delicious. I think we should all have a glass," Carole offers.

Everyone wants to try it. It is delicious, and the group slides into pleasant contentment and toasts Carole for a wonderful dinner.

––––––––––

Andrzej is eating at Macquilken's with his two buddies, Petr and Dominik, from the Village Vanguard scene. He has had a little too much to drink. He and his friends are finishing up a bottle of wine when Randy Macquilken walks by and asks them if everything was to their satisfaction. He knows that Andrzej is Carole's ex but does not let on. He smells trouble and wants them out of the restaurant. Andrzej recognizes Randy. He asks for the bill. Randy goes to the bar and has it tabulated. He asks the waiter to bring the bill to the table. Andrzej pulls out his wallet and throws down a credit card. The waiter takes it to the bar. He returns after running the card for the signature. Andrzej signs it, and the three of them get up to leave. At the cloakroom on the way out, he goes back into the restaurant to find Randy over the objections of his two friends.

Randy sees Andrzej weaving through the tables toward him. He moves to the bar so that Andrzej meets him there.

"I recognize you," Andrjez says to him, tilting a bit.

"How can I help you?" Randy says.

"You went out with Adrienne Wyatt, right?"

Randy's hackles go up, and he is not comfortable with this guy asking about her.

"Why are you asking?" he replies.

"Some people are saying she was killed."

"I heard that. I was shocked to hear it."

"I photographed her a few times and liked her."

"Yes, I liked her too."

"Okay. One last question. Do you know I used to be with Carole Lansdorf?"

"Yes," Randy answers.

"Have you seen her in here with a new boyfriend?"

Randy gets his dander up at that question.

"Look, I wouldn't answer that question if I had. Now leave, please."

Andrjez gives him a hostile look and weaves his way back to the front door where his friends are waiting holding his jacket. He takes it roughly and speaks to them.

"I want to walk by Carole's building."

His two friends frown.

"Probably not a good idea," Petr says.

"You don't have to go," Andrzej spits out, turning on him.

Petr just looks at him with expressionless eyes in his wizened face. Dominik shakes his head at the two of them but says nothing. The three of them leave the restaurant and head west toward Carole's building.

———

The group at Carole's table are laughing at a joke told by Robespierre.

"Robby, you are too much!" Johnny says, laughing hard.

"Well, boys and girls, maybe we should help Carole clean up," Robby says.

"Absolutely not," Carole says.

"I think we should help. It will make it go faster," Felicia adds.

"I agree," Johnny chimes in.

"I appreciate that, but really I have a system and I will do it," Carole responds.

"I can wash glasses and pots," Priscilla offers.

"No, really, guys. I have this. I might ask one person to help me a little," Carole says, looking at George.

"Whooaaaaa!" the whole group whoops, laughing.

"Okay. We get it," Johnny says, getting up, smiling at George.

"Yeah, probably time to go," Robby adds.

"Are you sure I can't help?" Felicia says.

"Really, Felicia. I'm good," Carole says.

"I feel funny not helping with the cleanup," Priscilla says.

"Thanks, Priscilla, and everyone, but I am fine with the cleanup, and I am sure George will pitch in."

"I am a great cleaner-upper. Don't worry, everyone," George says with a big smile.

"Yeah, yeah ..." they all say back at him.

Everyone pushes back from the table and gets up. They get whatever jackets they brought and congregate in the hall. Priscilla and Johnny each hug Carole.

"It was scrumptious, Carole. Thanks. I need that recipe!" Priscilla says as Johnny helps her with her jacket.

"I will get it to you, Priscilla."

"Totally delicious, Carole. Thanks for a wonderful meal and getting us all together," Johnny says.

"I am glad I could," Carole responds.

"Yummy, Carole. You are such a good cook. I learned a new dish tonight. Talk soon," Felicia tells her and gives her a hug.

"I loved it, Carole. You will have to come and taste some of Lucienne's fare," Robby says as he gives her a kiss on the cheek.

"I would love to, Robby. I have heard her food is delicious," Carole says, giving him a hug.

The elevator is called. It arrives, and the two couples get in. As they reach the lobby, they see the doorman having a heated argument with Andrzej, who wants him to call up to Carole's apartment despite her instructions not to. He is threatening to just go up. Johnny looks at Robby as the two couples get out of the elevator and start walking toward the two men arguing. They see Petr and Dominik standing nearby and recognize all three men from the Vanguard. Johnny immediately goes to the doorman. Robby asks Priscilla and Felicia to wait and hang back from the conflict. He then walks and stands next to Johnny.

"What is the problem here?" Johnny says.

"None of your business!" Andrjez says loudly, turning and facing Johnny.

"I think it is," Johnny says calmly, returning Andrjez's stare.

"What are you saying?" Andrjez says with a snarl.

"I have a friend who lives in this building. You cannot just come in without consent of a tenant and abuse the doorman."

Andrjez recognizes Johnny, and this agitates him further.

"You are a friend of the guy who slugged me!"

"You mean the guy you swung at who returned the favor?"

Andrjez's brain is putting some things together. He takes a step toward Johnny.

"Is he here? Upstairs with Carole?"

"That is none of your business," Johnny says.

"I want to know!"

"I don't care what you want. You have to leave."

Johnny looks at him coldly, trying to keep his anger under control. He is preparing to deck this guy but does not want to make a scene.

"I am going up to see her. I need to talk to her!" Andrjez yells and starts to bull his way forward past the doorman, who grabs his arm. Johnny steps in front of him. Andrjez's two friends are uncomfortable, but they move slightly forward in support of their friend. They are hesitant since neither of them is looking to get into a brawl in the lobby of this Upper East Side building. Robby gives them a look and puts one hand in his pocket—and they stop. There is something about his cool demeanor and gaze that evokes danger despite his small size—maybe it is his history of street fights in Harlem. He could have a weapon in that pocket, and he looks all business shooting an icy dagger warning with his eyes. Johnny and Robby have women watching, which heightens the tension. It is a tense standoff, and the doorman is not sure what to do. He doesn't want to let go of Andrjez to call the police. He is afraid of what Johnny will do if he does, and Andrjez tries to go forward. He is aware of the menace of Robby glaring at the two guys with Andrjez.

A yellow cab pulls up in front of the building. A moment later the outer door opens and two women, one late-fifties and one in her thirties, apparently a mother and daughter coming back from a trip, open the door noisily. They are dressed beautifully, pulling rolling suitcases, and each one is carrying a large shopping bag. They come into the lobby, their shopping bags rustling.

"Bobby, can you help us with these shopping bags, please?" the older of them says to the doorman, not noticing the scene with Andrjez. The younger woman is trying to fish her keys out from her purse while not dropping her shopping bag. Andrjez looks at them, and the wind goes out of his sails. He pulls out of the grasp of the doorman but does not walk farther. The doorman stands there frozen for a moment, looking at Andrjez and then Johnny, who is in front of Andrjez. The women who came in stop and stare as they now comprehend that there is a potentially violent situation going on. After a long pause, Johnny speaks.

"Go help the women, Bobby. I believe these gentlemen are just leaving."

There is another pause, and then Bobby walks rapidly over to the two women, takes their shopping bags, and starts to walk with them toward the mailboxes and elevator. As they approach Andrjez and Johnny standing together, Andrjez turns abruptly and walks toward the front door. His two buddies follow him. Johnny and Robby watch them leave. Johnny turns to Robby.

"Carole may have a problem there," he says.

"I sure hope not. George will not like it," Robby replies, staring after the three men.

"No. He won't. Let's go."

The two men go to Priscilla and Felicia. The women ask about what happened, and Johnny explains that the guy is Carole's ex who George rescued her from in front of the Vanguard.

"It was good that you were here to stop him," Priscilla says.

"Shall we go somewhere for a nightcap or call it a night?" Johnny asks.

"It's late," Felicia says, looking at Robby and taking his hand.

"I think we'll pass," Robby says, looking back at Felicia.

"Okay," Johnny says with a smile.

The two couples exit the building. Johnny and Robby instinctively look up and down the street to see if Andrjez and his friends are waiting for them, but the street is empty. Everyone says good night to each other. Johnny and Priscilla walk down toward Park Avenue on Eighty-Fifth Street to where he has parked his motorcycle. Felicia and Robby walk to Madison Avenue where he hails a cab.

———

Once in the cab, the driver asks them where they want to go.

"I don't know where you live, Felicia," Robby says.

"I am subletting an apartment in the Beresford on Eighty-First and Central Park West, 211."

Robby tells the driver to go to Felicia's building. They sit close together in the back seat. He reaches out for her hand, and she takes it.

"You have wonderful friends, Robespierre," Felicia says, looking at him.

"They are special guys. I think your friend Carole is also," he responds.

"She is. We just hit it off. I think she is talented too."

"I would agree. She was great at the Vanguard."

"What a story that is. It was good you all were there."

"George doesn't fool around," Robby says with a chuckle.

"I guess not," Felicia agrees, looking at the expression on Robby's face with amusement. There is a pause, the two just reflecting on events.

"I think they are good together," Felicia offers.

"I agree," he answers and then adds, "I am glad she invited me to meet you."

Felicia laughs her little laugh that ends in a high pitch.

"I think she invited me to meet you!"

They both laugh. Robby leans in closer to her face.

"Either way, I am happy about it," he says.

He gives her a soft kiss on the mouth.

"Me too," she murmurs after the kiss and cuddles closer to him.

When they arrive, Robby asks the driver to wait, gets out of the cab, goes around it, and opens the door for Felicia. They stand together on the sidewalk and look at each other.

"I would like to see you again, Felicia," Robby says.

"I would like that," she responds, moving closer to him.

He leans in to kiss her, and she wraps her arms around him, and they softly kiss again.

"I will call you," Robby says huskily.

"You better," Felicia responds.

Robby opens the door to the cab and gets in. She stands and watches him. He gives her a wave as the cab pulls away. She waves back and walks to the entrance of her building.

———————

Johnny and Priscilla are cruising down Second Avenue. Priscilla is holding on to his waist and leaning into him, her face against his back. Her ponytail is flying behind her, but it is all good. She likes holding on to him. He feels hard and strong. He finds his way to her building. She gets off the bike slowly. She takes off her helmet and attaches it to the strap across the seat.

"Johnny, that was fabulous!"

She looks at him with a big grin, and he grins back.

"Are you talking about the ride home or the dinner?"

"Both! Carole's meal was wonderful, as was the company."

"I am glad you came."

"Me too."

Johnny turns off the engine, puts the kickstand down, and gets off the bike. He takes off his helmet and puts it on the seat. He moves close to her and puts his arms around her. She leans back against his arms to look at him and then moves close to him, and they kiss. After they break, he takes his hand and brushes away some hair from her forehead, kisses her face all over, and then her mouth again. She looks at him with earnestness.

"Johnny, I can't invite you up. I have roommates."

"I know."

They just look at each other. The idea of going to his loft with him is laying over them like a low cloud. They are silent. Johnny breaks the silence.

"This might sound a little unusual to you, but we don't know each other all that well. I like you, and I want our first time together to be special."

"I do too, Johnny. I really do, and as much as a part of me would love to go to your place with you, I don't feel ready to do that."

He smiles at that answer. He actually likes it.

"Okay, then. I will say good night but first ..." He leans in and gives her another big kiss that she returns just as passionately. After a little while they pull back. She looks into his face intently, and he smiles. Then she gives him a big hug, which he returns. When they break apart, he grabs his helmet.

"I will call you about going to MoMA."

"Great! Hey, by the way, take care going home."

Johnny gives her a look like, *Are you saying that you care?* and laughs.

"Will do. Good night."

"Good night, Johnny."

Priscilla turns and heads down the walk to her building. Johnny cranks up his Honda and speeds off. She turns and watches him for a moment and then goes in.

———

Carole is drying a wine glass and looking at George, who is standing over the sink cleaning the cast-iron frying pan that she finished the *gombócz* in. He uses a sponge and some dish soap but is not scrubbing hard.

"I don't want you to lose the seasoning in this pan," George says when he catches her looking at him. He finishes it and puts it on the stove. He turns on the flame and watches it.

"It's dangerous if you walk off and forget you have it on a flame, but it is a good way to dry a cast-iron pan," he says, watching the wetness disappear.

He turns to Carole, who is grinning at him.

"What?" George says.

"You are pretty cute, you know that?"

George frowns.

"You must have me mixed up with someone else," he says.

"Nope. I don't."

George turns off the flame under the pan and turns to her. She walks over to him and puts her arms around his neck. He wraps his around her waist.

"Would you like to have another glass of Belle de Brillet?" Carole asks.

"Are you kidding? I am perfect."

"You are," Carole says, smiling.

"I mean perfectly content after that wonderful meal," he says.

"Are you trying to butter me up?"

"Absolutely," he says as he leans down and kisses her neck gently, moving eventually to her ears and then to her mouth. They kiss softly.

When they finally part, she says, "Oh, I get it. Just melt me."

He takes her face in his hands and kisses her eyes and her entire face. She makes little mewing sounds, and then he gets back to her mouth. Another long kiss as they explore each other's mouths with their tongues. Finally, they pull apart, and she takes his hand and leads him into her bedroom.

They stand next to the bed and help each other take off their clothes except for her bra and panties and his trim boxer shorts. Then Carole goes to the bed and pulls back her down comforter and the top sheet and gets in bed. He lies down next to her. They turn to each other and kiss. He reaches back and undoes her bra. She throws it aside and lies back. He takes in the beauty of her full breasts and body. He wants to remember this moment. She smiles at him, and he moves over to kiss one breast while caressing the other. He slowly makes love to them as she becomes more and more aroused. He is happy to discover that her breasts that are so erotic to him are also sensitive and erotic to her. He sucks on her nipples and bites them gently, which causes her to moan. He kisses his way down her body, moving slowly. It is slim and firm. Her natural scent only excites him more. When he finally moves past her stomach and between her legs, he kisses her inner thighs, smoothes her pubic hair before separating her wet lips gently with his fingers, and then inserts his tongue. She gasps as his tongue gently searches her. He finds her clitoris and strokes it with his tongue slowly at first and then more and more rapidly. He feels her body react and her moans increase in rhythm to the reactions. All of a sudden she arches up and lets out a louder moan as her body shakes and she climaxes. He stays there slowing his tongue but not stopping. She reaches for his head with both hands and says, "No. No. I want you."

He pulls his head up, and she leans forward and takes it in her hands and then he gets up over her. He moves up, and she grabs his erect penis. He moves up farther to her chest, wets his penis, and puts himself between her breasts. He tells her to push them up with her hands, and his glands are lost within the full softness of them. The feeling is wonderful to him. He moves back and forth between them and is aroused more, if that is possible. She is looking at his face, exploring how he looks in passion. She takes her hands away from her breasts and takes him in one hand and starts to kiss his penis. She then puts him in her mouth. Now it is his turn to moan. He moves in her mouth as she manipulates him with her hand and moves her head. Seeing her do this and feeling what she is doing excites him further.

He starts feeling his excitement rise to what he considers a dangerous level. He does not want to climax now. It is his turn now to say no, and he gently withdraws himself. He slides his body down hers and inserts himself into her, and they both gasp. He moves very slowly and carefully, savoring the feel of her. After a short time, he begins to thrust harder and faster. They are kissing deeply at the same time as the movement increases. They are now in sync. All of a sudden their bodies tense, and they both let out a yell as they climax together. She can feel his penis pulse as he climaxes. When he finishes climaxing, he stays in her and, still hard, slowly starts moving again. She has a few little shudders, little climaxes, and she cries out "oh" each time. He keeps moving slowly, and she says, "No, no, really. I am so sensitive." He feels her squeeze his penis. His face is in her neck, but then he lifts it. He is not sure she means it. She looks at his face. She cannot believe this man. It appears that he might want to keep going, but he stops and just stays in her, continuing to revel in the feel of her until he finally withdraws. He wants her more but doesn't want to disturb what he is feeling now and hopes she is feeling. He kisses her face and lets his feelings wash over him. She is feeling very complete, very happy. He rolls off her, and they lie next to each other looking at the ceiling. She reaches for his hand, and they hold hands, both contemplating what has just happened. After a few minutes he takes her hand and puts it on his penis, which is still aroused.

"See what you do to me," he says.

"I do," she responds and scootches down and kisses it, then takes it in her mouth, moving up and down its length, which makes him moan, then returns to his side.

"And I like that I do."

She puts her head on his chest, and he slides his arm around her, pulling her close. She has never really been able to feel comfortable enough next to a man to go to sleep in his arms, but she feels very comfortable this way. He loves having her right there on his chest. The two of them drift off to sleep.

27

STUART SCHLUSSEL IS VERY NERVOUS. He is sitting in his kitchen in his pajamas having coffee. His wife is out buying lox and bagels. He has agreed to wear a wire when he goes before Judge Franco. He figures he has no choice. He wants to avoid being charged with sexual assault if possible or at least have the charge reduced. He knows he has to be careful, but he still intends to have the party on Tuesday. He thinks, *This might be it for a long time. What if he has to go to jail?* He picks up the phone and makes a call.

"Dugan, is everything set? You have arranged for models, right?"

"Yes. Do you have the cash?"

"Yes. Are you planning to go?"

"Of course. Is your friend Stone coming?"

"I don't know. Maybe. Are you sure you want to come?"

"Yes. Is there a problem?"

Stuart thinks. He does not want to mention what Dave Morgan told him about the last party and what happened with the model. He decides to blow it off.

"No. No problem. I will see you there and give the cash to you then."

He hangs up and wonders whether the girl who was at the last party will be there. She was so young. He liked her and would like to maybe get something going with her. Maybe help her out financially. She might not press any charges. He just needs someone other than his wife. He goes back to his coffee. After a few minutes the door to the brownstone opens, and his wife returns. She calls out to him as she enters.

"Stuart, I am back! I have beautiful lox!"

———

Jim Ashford is not sure what to do. He knows Dugan was involved in the party where the model, Susie Griffin, was beaten, and he suspects that there is more to it than meets the eye. *But what?* He can't believe that Dugan would be involved in a sexual assault. He wonders about the drug angle and what the best course of action for him is. He has checked with the property clerk about drugs that were removed and has gotten nowhere. If he is going to catch Dugan, it has to be airtight. He would like to put a tail on him, but he does not think this is the right time for that. He decides he will bide his time.

———

Aarika is surprised. She just got a call from Shelley, a girlfriend of hers, to go to another party in Brooklyn. The girl works through a different agency. She is not inclined to go but wonders if she should call Johnny and tell him. She is not happy about Johnny. It is obvious he is not interested in her, and this bugs her. Still, maybe she can change his mind. In any case, she wants to help solve the murders if she can.

———————

Priscilla and Leighann are sitting in their living room, dressed in pajamas, with their coffee mugs. The Sunday *New York Times* is scattered about, and "Heartbreak City" by The Cars is playing on the stereo. It is a dreary day and good to be inside.

"Tell me more about Johnny," Leighann says, turning down the volume.

"He is fun and has a lot going on right now."

"What do you mean?"

"Well, he is painting, but he is also helping his detective friend solve the murders of two models."

"He mentioned that after his opening. I read about one model killing herself, not murder, and the murder of another. What can he do?"

"Well, he used to model, and his detective friend wanted him to make some inquiries about who the models were hanging out with and any other info about them from the inside."

"Okay. Well, that sounds interesting in a scary way. Do you like him?"

"I do. We have a lot of interests in common. We talk about art, and he is very down to earth, which I like."

"Not bad on the eyes either," Leighann says, laughing.

"That too. You know I always figured I would end up with someone tall, dark, and handsome," Priscilla says with a chuckle.

"Gee, who wouldn't?" Leighann replies smiling.

———————

"Yummmm ... that was delicious. I could get used to Sunday breakfast like that," George says, sitting across from Carole in his

T-shirt and boxer shorts. She is wearing pale-blue pajamas. She smiles at him.

"Well, if you play your cards right, that could happen," she replies and takes a sip of coffee. The little table in the kitchen has their plates with the remnants from fried eggs and sausage. There is a plate with two English muffins on it and two open jars of jam, one apricot, the other raspberry.

"Oh yeah?" he says with a little challenge in his tone and gets up. He moves his chair and sits next to her. He then leans over and starts kissing her ear. She gets goose bumps.

"Hey, you better cut that out, Mister."

"Or what?"

"You will be in trouble."

"Hmmm ... that doesn't sound bad," he says and keeps doing it. She leans her ear into his face as he keeps kissing and blowing into it. More goose bumps ...

"No fair," she murmurs. All of a sudden, she feigns anger and turns her head and grabs his face in both hands and kisses him hard on the mouth. He kisses her back just as hard. As they come up for air, she stands. He looks up at her, smiling with a quizzical look. She reaches for his arm and hand.

"You will have to come with me," she says with a stern face.

"I do?"

"Yes. You have to face your punishment," she says, still being stern with a twinkle in her eyes.

"Oh no," George protests innocently.

"Yes," she says, pulling him up.

"Come with me," she adds and starts pulling him toward the bedroom. He pretends to protest and be a bit recalcitrant for a few seconds, then he scoops her in his arms and starts to rush the two of them into the bedroom. In they go as she screams, and they fall onto the bed, laughing. After a few moments, they are on their sides facing each other. George takes his hand and brushes back her hair. He looks intently at her face, into her eyes that are now looking inquisitively at him, and gently moves his hand to the side of her face. She puts her hand over his.

"Maybe you are in trouble, Miss," he says. Her reply is to just keep looking into his eyes. Inquiring. There is a pause, and then he adds, "Because I really could get used to this with you."

She smiles mischievously.

"That is my plan," she says, then she leans in to kiss him.

———

Felicia finishes putting on some light makeup. She looks at herself in the mirror as she hums "At Last," the classic sung by Etta James. She is fine with what she sees and is excited. She is going to Robespierre's restaurant for lunch with him and will meet his mother, Lucienne. She is wearing a gray skirt with wide pleats, a crisp cotton lavender blouse, and a single-breasted, three-quarter, plum Harris Tweed jacket. She again has on her little black velvet beret and black ballet flats. The look is complete. She grabs her small black handbag and heads out the door, which she double locks. The doorman hails a cab for her.

Robespierre is uncharacteristically nervous. This morning at breakfast he told his mother how much he enjoyed last evening and especially meeting Felicia and that he has, in fact, invited her for Sunday lunch. He finishes dressing in carefully pressed tan slacks, a bright white shirt, and polished brown loafers. He heads downstairs and walks into the kitchen. Lucienne whistles.

"Son, you look very handsome," she says.

"Seriously, Mom. I am a grown man, and I can't remember the last time I was nervous meeting a woman for lunch."

"It is understandable. You like her. You had a good time with her, and you feel potential, which you have not felt in a long time."

"I think you will like her too. She is special."

Lucienne smiles and goes back to her cooking as a waiter comes in to pick up the fried snapper she has plated and set on one of the kitchen tables. Robby heads out to the bar and talks with the bartender on duty. As he is explaining an order that he has made for more liquor and that he will not be working that afternoon, the door opens, and Felicia walks in. She looks around and spots Robespierre talking with the bartender. She watches him, notices his impeccable clothes and the manner in which he is talking to his employee. She takes in how well-groomed and together he is about his person. She likes it. He is talking with authority but with respect for his employee. Robby turns and sees her. A huge smile breaks out on his face. He finishes what he was saying, and he walks over to her. It is obvious he is happy to see her. She smiles back and feels the same way. She can't help but like how warm and welcoming his smile is. He gives her a small hug and then says, "You look lovely, Felicia."

"Thanks, Robby."

He leads her over to a table in a corner that has been held for him. He pulls out a chair for her and then takes the seat on the corner next to her. He asks what she would like to drink, and the waiter comes over. When she orders a Dubonnet cocktail, his eyebrow goes up and he orders a Scotch and soda. They fall into an easy conversation about the dinner at Carole's and his friends. Robby reaches for her hand during the conversation. They hold hands until the drinks arrive.

Muriel is going through her husband's desk. It is an old roll top that she has gone through before, but she is going through it again now that it has been mostly emptied. She opens the little drawers and taps on the wood. She hits a space between two of the drawers by accident and hears a click. She pulls at the molding there, and a little hidden cubby is revealed. She takes out a small address book. She opens it and sees initials and phone numbers. She dials the number under *AW*, and she gets a recording that the number is no longer in service. She immediately turns to the *R* listings. She dials the number under *RT* and gets the same recording. Her heart is pounding. *What was Burke doing with these numbers? Did he have something to do with the murders of those two models? Was that why he was killed?* The thought shoots chills through her. She finds Jim Ashford's card and calls him.

28

STUART SCHLUSSEL is entering Bronx Supreme Court on the Grand Concourse. Simon Stone sees him and hustles after him.

"Stuart!"

Schlussel turns to see who it is. When he sees Stone, he slows down.

"Hello, Simon."

"Are you going to Franco's courtroom?" Simon asks.

"Yes. I have a conference. You?"

"No, I have to go to McMann. Is the party on for Tuesday?"

"Yes." Schlussel stops. I will call you later with the address. It will start at around seven," he says.

The two of them go to the elevator bank where there is a crowd of lawyers, jurors, litigants, and witnesses waiting for elevators. After two elevators come up from the basement full, they manage to squeeze on the next one. Schlussel gets off at three, and Stone stays on and gets off at five. Schlussel hustles down the corridor past lawyers and clients sitting on benches talking and others standing looking at posted lists outside courtrooms trying to find their cases. He finds the courtroom that he is looking for at the end of the hall and goes in. He goes past the seats and past the wood railing separating the gallery from the well with counsel tables and the judge's bench. He walks to the desk in front of the entrance to the judge's office.

"Hi, Richie."

The secretary looks up.

"Hi, Stuart."

"I am here on Schwartz and Robbins."

The secretary looks at his book and speaks.

"Defense counsels have not checked in yet."

"Can I see the judge?"

"Let me check." He picks up his phone and dials. "Judge, I have Stuart out here. He wants to see you." There is a pause as the clerk listens.

"Okay, Stuart, go in."

Schlussel opens the heavy door and walks in. Judge Franco is behind his desk with stacks of pleadings and motions with blue and gray backs in front of him.

"Sit down, Stuart," Franco says, looking at him with a wry smile. He continues, "Do you have something for me?"

"I can only pay you on the Schwartz case."

"You have the $10,000?"

"Yes. Here it is."

Stuart hands the envelope to the judge.

"That is smart, Stuart. You could use some help on that case. You have a motion pending, I believe. My ruling on the motion should help. When will you have the ten on Robbins?"

"Next conference."

"Has defense counsel offered a settlement on either case?"

"No."

"Well, we shall see what I can squeeze out of them today. Now you better leave. I want to start calling attorneys in." Stuart gets up and leaves.

He cannot believe what he has just done. The judge is on tape. He has accepted marked bills. Stuart leaves and goes out through the gallery of seats. He sees the investigator, Jenny, sitting in the back of the room. He walks out the door. She gets up and follows him. He stops in the hall for a second before going to the men's room. He enters and goes into a stall. He removes the microphone from under his shirt, the wires going to the tape recorder taped to his side, and the recorder. He puts it all in his briefcase. He then leaves. Jenny is waiting outside for him. He heads for the stairs, and she follows him. Once in the stairwell he hands her all the recording gear and the tape. She takes it and puts it her briefcase.

"DA Morgan will be in touch, Mr. Schlussel."

He just looks at her. She opens the heavy metal door to the hallway and leaves. He waits a few moments then goes back out into the hallway and into the courtroom.

———

Dave Morgan dials Jim Ashford.

"Ashford."

"Jim, it's Dave. Can you talk?"

"Yes."

"Dugan isn't there or listening in?"

"No. What's up?"

"I've been thinking. Dugan obviously was at the party where the model was beaten because he is supplying the drugs. Maybe he knows something about the model murders that he is not revealing because model parties are connected to the deaths."

"Yes. Maybe. I am trying to figure out what that could be. He is supposed to be investigating those murders. I am pretty sure he is stealing or keeping confiscated drugs, but I don't want to bust him only for that. I want the other information that he might know."

"Okay. I get that, but do you know about his friend Donnelly?"

"I know they are friends and occasionally are assigned together."

"Well, Don and Jenny have been watching him. Apparently, he is intimidating witnesses for a Manhattan attorney named Joe DeFeo. We assume he is getting paid for this, and there is a connection to Dugan."

"Why doesn't that surprise me? Are you going to arrest Donnelly?"

"We want to get more evidence in regard to some other stuff we think he is doing like making false photos and other evidence for personal injury cases. Do you know of this Joseph DeFeo?"

"No. Johnny Colrain's friend, George Fredericks, probably does."

"Yes. Well, let's see how things go. We are on him."

"Okay. Keep me posted."

"Right. You do the same. Bye."

"Bye."

———

Aarika West is putting on her street clothes in the changing room of a large studio on lower Broadway. It has been a good shoot for Aarika. She is going to be in a big ad campaign for Smirnoff Vodka in major magazines, and she is being paid for the day at a considerable rate. She feels especially good because the ad campaign will involve multiple shoots over the next six months. The male model has left, and the two other girls in the ad that features her are also changing. One of the girls is Susie Griffin. She and Susie have had a chance to talk during the day, and she likes this young girl trying to break into the business. Aarika approaches Susie as they are about to leave.

"Susie, would you like to go for a drink somewhere?"

"That sounds like a good idea. Anywhere except Melon's," she says with a laugh.

"What about Macquilken's?"

"I have never been there but have heard about it."

"Randy, the owner, is an old friend. It's a nice place, and I haven't been there in forever. The food is pretty good too if we end up eating something."

"Sounds good," Susie says as she slips on her jacket.

————

"That was delicious, Robespierre. And I am so full," Felicia says.

Robby puts down his knife and fork.

"I am too. How about a special dessert?" he asks with a smile.

"That is not fair, Robby. I am full, but it sounds very tempting."

"It is definitely worth it! I think you will like it."

He waves the waiter over and orders his mom's coconut rice pudding for both of them.

"I would like to meet the fabulous cook of this meal," Felicia says, smiling.

"That can be arranged," Robby says with a grin and then adds, "I would like you to."

The pudding arrives in coupe dishes, and they both dig into it.

"Robby, that was wonderfully decadent!" Felicia exclaims after she scrapes the glass dish with her spoon, getting the last little bit of pudding.

"I agree," Robby says, laughing.

Then he adds, "Let's go see the chef and have a coffee."

"That would be lovely," Felicia replies.

Robespierre gets up and pulls out her chair as she rises. He offers her his hand. She takes it, and they walk through the dining area, which is not very full at this hour, through the double swinging doors into the kitchen. Lucienne is putting the garnish on two dishes for a waiter to take into the restaurant. The waiter takes the plates, turns, and leaves as Lucienne looks up and sees her son and Felicia. She is struck by how petite and lovely Felicia is. She smiles at them.

"I am sorry, young man, this is a restricted area," she says with a twinkle in her eye.

"Oh, I am sure it is, which is why I have come in," he says to his mom, and the two of them laugh.

"Mom, I would like to introduce you to Felicia, the woman I told you about."

Lucienne extends her hand, and Felicia takes it in both of hers.

"I am delighted to meet you, Mrs. Caracciolo," Felicia says.

"Oh my! No one has called me that in ages. Lucienne is fine," she replies with a big grin. "Come and sit down." Lucienne leads Felicia to the little table off to the side of the kitchen cooking area. She motions for Felicia to sit and turns to her son who is delighted watching the two women.

"Robby, would you mind?"

"With pleasure," he replies.

"Felicia, would you like espresso or American?"

"Espresso would be great."

Robby goes to the giant espresso machine to make the coffees for the three of them.

____

Joe DeFeo wants to settle this case badly. He has a severely injured client with serious head and back injuries from an accident on the entrance to the Brooklyn Bridge. It could mean some big money. He needs it. He has made some bad investments—not exactly investments; he gambles. The plaintiff's car went into the guardrail and then into an oncoming truck. The only problem is the defect in the road that the plaintiff claims caused her to lose control is minimal. Notice of a defect at that location was served on the city as required by law, but he fears that no one will believe that she lost control by hitting the small pothole. He sent Donnelly out to the location in the early morning hours with a photographer. They made fake photos of the defect, making it look much worse than it was. The pothole was repaired. He then sued the City of New York for negligence in failing to timely repair the defect in the roadway, alleging the large fake pothole was the cause of the accident and his client's injuries.

DeFeo expects this calendar call to result in the first conference on the case during which most judges will make an effort at settlement. He expects the case will be assigned to a judge handling city cases. DeFeo knows most of the judges in Brooklyn. He is hoping for a judge friendly to him. He brought the case in Brooklyn where his client lives.

The huge courtroom on the first floor of Brooklyn Supreme Court at 360 Adams Street where they call the calendar is jammed with attorneys for the call. Some are looking at their files. Others are talking to each other. Some attorneys are walking the aisles between the bench seats, calling the name of their case, trying to locate the other lawyer or lawyers on the case. Some lawyers are answering those attorneys. Some lawyers are sitting together talking and holding their Redweld folders containing the case files. Some are looking for papers in the Redwelds and taking them out and reading them. There is a cacophony of voices.

The clerks at the front start yelling out that the docket is being called and telling all attorneys to be seated. The attorneys in the packed room quiet down, stop calling out their case name, and quickly look for a seat. The clerk starts calling case names and the names of the law firms representing the parties in each case if no one answers. The attorneys on both sides of the case called stand and answer that they are present. If that happens, the clerk may just assign the case to a judge or send it out for jury selection. Sometimes one or more of the attorneys may yell out, "Application" or "Conference". The clerk will ask the attorneys to come up and approach the area where the clerks are sitting in the well. The attorney or attorneys making the application usually want an adjournment and will make their request for a new date whether it is consented to by any other attorney on the case or not. If an attorney objects, he or she will state the objection to the application. The clerk may grant it or deny it. If there is a further objection to that decision, the clerk will send it to the judge assigned to the calendar for a ruling. The clerks usually will send the case to a judge for a conference if both sides agree. If one side does not answer, or both sides don't answer, the clerk yells out, "Second call," and it goes on that list. That call will occur after the first call is completed, which takes some time. Attorneys coming late will answer the second call. If no one answers, the attorneys risk having the case marked off the calendar.

DeFeo walks in looking for a seat, acknowledging some of the lawyers he knows with a nod of the head or a silent mouthing of the word *hello*. He finds an empty seat near the front of the room and waits. George comes into the still noisy room full of the attorneys' chatter as the call starts. He has only one case to answer. Some lawyers have multiple cases. He represents the truck driver and the truck company that owns the truck that DeFeo's client ran into. He does not see any liability at all for his clients. He has cross-claimed against the city and counterclaimed against the plaintiff for the truck driver's emotional injury and the damage to the truck. In fact, the driver was very shaken up by the accident. He ran to help the woman, administered first aid, and flagged down a driver to call an ambulance for her. DeFeo sued George's clients to cover all possibilities. George does not expect the plaintiff will recover anything from his clients. He also does not expect to recover from the plaintiff, but he could from the city if the plaintiff proves her case about the pothole. He slides into a seat in the rear of the room and looks about. He always finds this huge courtroom full of regulars—that is, the cadre of attorneys who practice mostly in Brooklyn in this courthouse—as an alien place. He travels to all courthouses in all the boroughs and sometimes to Long Island, Westchester, and Rockland Counties. They all have their regulars, but this huge calendar call somehow makes it feel pretty clubby. He always sees the same attorneys walking about and talking to each other or the clerks. Nassau Supreme is similar but not as much.

When DeFeo's case, O'Neill, is called, George stands and calls out he is present. The clerk looks at his list of cases against the city and automatically calls out an adjourn date. DeFeo calls out, "Conference," and approaches the front of the courtroom where the divider is between the well and the gallery. George also moves up to it. No city attorney answers. DeFeo speaks, "Conference. Can we at least have a conference with the judge?" DeFeo says.

The clerk looks at George.

"That is okay with me," George says.

"I'll get a city attorney. Go to room 223," the clerk says.

———

Johnny Colrain puts down his brush and steps back. He looks at the large canvas on the easel. He steps close to the painting and then adds some more paint to two different brushes. He strokes one area of the painting with one color and then uses the second brush to apply a different color. He steps back again with one brush handle in his mouth and the other in his right hand. He looks critically at the painting. He is satisfied. He goes back to his paint tray and closes the tubes. He then begins to clean his brushes. Baloo is looking at him. He gives Johnny a baleful look. Johnny looks back at him and grins.

"Okay. Okay! I know it is time for a walk," he says as he finishes cleaning the brushes. The big dog gets up, puts his two front paws in front of him, and stretches his body while making a big yawn, showing his big teeth. Johnny puts the brushes down, grabs his leather jacket, a hat, and the braided leash off the pegs by the door. Baloo trots over to him. Johnny reaches down and snaps the lead on his collar. He gives the dog several pats on his side and on the top of his big flat head.

"Let's go," he says to the dog and opens the door.

As the two of them walk, Johnny is thinking about the murders. He has not helped Ashford very much. He walks toward Pier 25, and before long he is at Robespierre's. He was not planning to go there with Baloo, but here he is. He is not dressed very well and has paint on his jeans so he is a little circumspect about opening the door and looking in even though it is between lunch and dinner so it won't be crowded. He decides to go to the side door that leads to the kitchen. He knocks on the door. He waits and is about to leave when the door opens. Robby sees him and Baloo and smiles.

"I am sorry, sir. This is the door to the kitchen," Robby says.

"I am looking for my auntie, Lucienne, young man. Is she here?" Johnny replies, holding the dog close and noticing that Robby looks extra sharp.

Lucienne yells out to Robby.

"Who is it, Robby?"

"Someone who claims you are his auntie," Robby says.

"Is that Johnny, for heaven's sake?" Lucienne says.

"It looks like him, and he's with a big white dog!"

Baloo lets out a bark.

"Let them both in, son."

"Okay. Okay," Robby says with a chuckle.

Johnny starts in, and Baloo goes to Robby, tail wagging.

"Hello, big fella," he says to the dog as he bends over and scratches him behind his ear. He gives Baloo a few pats on his side then straightens up, and the two men and Baloo go into the kitchen. Johnny sees Felicia.

"Uh oh. I think I am interrupting," Johnny says.

"Don't be silly," Lucienne says, smiling.

"Hi, Felicia," he says. He goes up to Lucienne, gives her a big hug and kiss on the cheek, then smiles, looks at Felicia, and asks, "Am I interrupting, Felicia?"

Felicia smiles back at Johnny.

"Nope. I am just getting the lowdown on your friend here from his mom."

"Hmmm ... maybe I should hear this too," Johnny replies with a grin.

"Any coffee for a pal, Robby?" he adds, turning to Robespierre.

"Coming right up," Robby replies, going to the coffee machine and grabbing a mug.

The four of them sit around the small table chatting. They ask Johnny about Priscilla and then the investigation he is helping Ashford with.

"There is something I am missing about the deaths of Adrienne and Renée. I am also thinking that they are connected to the death of Burke Lambert."

"What does Ash say?" Robby asks.

"He is stumped too, but he has some new information about Lambert, and he is following a lead about a lawyer who was involved in the assault on a young model at a party in Brooklyn."

There is a pause as they think about what he has said, and then Felicia speaks.

"I would like to change the subject for a second. I am going to be singing at Tramps on Thursday night and would like you all to be my guests."

They all look at her, surprised. Robby speaks first.

"I can definitely arrange that."

He looks at his mom. She looks at her son and speaks.

"I would love to hear you, Felicia, but ..."

Johnny interrupts her.

"Auntie, when was the last time you were out at a jazz or blues club? You have to come. It will be fun." He looks at Robby.

"Robby, you can get a substitute chef for a night, right?"

"Lucienne can instruct the sous chef and prep some dishes with him," Robby replies.

"That would be great. I would really like Lucienne to come," Felicia adds.

"It's settled then, Mom. Okay?" Robby asks.

Lucienne looks at her son, then the others. She smiles.

"Okay. Sounds wonderful," she says, getting up and continuing, "Now I have to get back to work. We have people coming in for dinner."

"Speaking of which, I have to go also. It has been a wonderful afternoon, Robby. And the food was delicious," Felicia says, smiling at Lucienne and going over and giving her a hug.

Robby gets up and says, "I'll get you a cab."

Johnny reaches down and grabs the lead that is still attached to the big dog lying at his feet. They both get up. Johnny gives Lucienne his usual big hug and kiss on the cheek. He says goodbye and walks out with Robby and Felicia.

———

Aarika approaches the door to her apartment and hears the phone ringing. She opens it and dashes to the phone. She picks it up.

"Hello?" she says.

"Hello. My name is Muriel Lambert. Do you have a minute?"

Aarika puts down her bag on the table.

"Sure. But how did you get this number?"

"I found it in my husband's things. I would like to ask you a few questions," Muriel replies.

Aarika is not sure how to handle this but decides that she should talk to Muriel.

"Okay."

"Did you ever go out with my husband?"

Aarika hesitates and then answers, "Yes."

"Did he go out with other women that you are aware of?"

"Yes."

"How old are you?"

"Twenty-seven."

"Of course you are," mutters Muriel to herself. She then continues, "Are you a model?"

"Yes. You should know, Mrs. Lambert, that I only went out with your husband a few times."

Muriel wonders if she should ask this woman about sleeping with her husband but decides that it is irrelevant at this point. Aarika hesitates and then adds on her own, "For whatever it's worth, I never slept with your husband."

"Do you know who would want to kill him?"

"No. I really don't. I was shocked to hear about it."

Muriel is trying to process this call and says, "I think that is all I want to ask for now. Thanks for speaking to me so honestly."

Muriel hangs up the phone and thinks. She knew her husband liked models and young women and had not really wanted to know too much as long as he paid attention to her and their marriage. It wasn't really anything they discussed. It sort of just developed that way since he was the star of the marriage, very involved in politics and the necessary social events.

Stuart Schlussel enters Dave Morgan's office with some trepidation. Dave waves him in. His two senior investigators are there.

"I have the tape, Mr. Schlussel. You did well," Dave says to him, gesturing for him to sit. Dave continues, "I have referred the case to the Bronx DA. We know that Judge Katz in Manhattan also solicits kickbacks and that you have cases with him. We want you to wear the wire when you go to him also."

Dave looks at Schlussel. He knows that he has him, but Schlussel could protest. He waits.

"I can't do that," Schlussel says, staring at Morgan.

"Why not?"

"I just can't. Look, I did what you wanted with Judge Franco, but I cannot entrap Judge Katz. He is an old friend."

"The kind of friend that you are willing to go to jail for?"

Stuart says nothing and fidgets with his watch. There is a long pause.

"Do you know Joe DeFeo?" Dave asks.

Stuart looks up quickly into the faces of all three people.

"I do."

"Is he involved in paying kickbacks to judges?"

"I don't know," Stuart says.

"What about Simon Stone?"

"Same answer," Stuart replies, but his heart is beating fast.

"You know that you can get in a lot of trouble lying to a district attorney, Mr. Schlussel."

Stuart says nothing.

"Okay. You can go for now. We will be in touch."

"What about the deal we made?" Stuart asks.

"What about it? You are free to go right now," Dave says. He wants his phone tap to keep going for now without arresting this guy.

Jim Ashford and Johnny Colrain are in an unmarked car outside a brownstone in Brooklyn having gotten the address from the tap on Schlussel's phone. They watch the people going in, and occasionally Johnny takes a picture with his Canon camera equipped with a telephoto lens.

"There are Donnelly and Dugan," Ashford says.

"Party animals, it seems," Johnny says.

Some female and male models go into the building. They continue to watch, and then they see Stuart Schlussel and Simon Stone get dropped off in a cab. Johnny takes photos of them also. As they wait, Carole's ex Andrjez walks down the street and enters the building. More people show up and go in but no one else they know.

"Should I go in, Ash?" Johnny asks.

Jim thinks for a moment and answers, "No. It would not be good for Dugan to see you. You would get into it with him. I have seen enough. Dugan and Donnelly do not belong with this crowd. He must be providing drugs for someone putting on the party. My guess is the lawyers who showed up. Dave Morgan knows that Schlussel assaulted that model Susie Griffin at a party like this."

"Do you think there is a connection in terms of the murders of Adrienne and Renée?"

"I am not sure, but there may be."

"What about Burke Lambert?" Johnny asks.

"That is a tough one to figure. I don't see him attending a party like this, but his murder was not a robbery gone bad, so I don't know. Lambert did have two phone numbers in his phone book with the initials of both models. We are running the numbers, which have been disconnected, to confirm. Even if the numbers are theirs, it is curious but does not prove a connection to their murders. I can't seem to find anyone who would have a motive at this point."

———

It is 3:00 a.m., and a key turns in the door. Rita Schlussel is awake. She hears her husband come up the stairs and enter the bedroom. He is trying to be quiet but not doing that great a job. He takes his shoes and clothes off. He goes into the bathroom and turns on the shower. The smell of the perfume Obsession has come into the room. She rolls over, wondering exactly what her husband has been up to.

29

JOE DEFEO IS FEELING GOOD. He is sitting at his desk thinking about his accident case involving the pothole on the Brooklyn Bridge. That case could settle. The city comptroller has asked for a settlement demand, and he is musing what his initial demand should be. The comptroller is probably also dealing with George Fredericks. He figures that should be okay. He picks up the phone and dials. He asks for Mr. Schlussel. When the receptionist tells Stuart who it is, he wonders if he should take the call. He hopes it is not about Dave Morgan's investigation of DeFeo or some fraud. He decides he better take it and see what it is about.

"Joe?"

"Stuart, I want to run something by you."

"Okay," Stuart says as he stops looking over a pleading in a case, worrying that this is probably going to be a question about Dave Morgan. He listens as DeFeo proceeds to discuss the injuries his client sustained from the accident and asks what Stuart thinks he should ask for as his initial demand to the city comptroller.

George is sitting with Mr. Campanella. He is discussing the case involving the truck and the car on the Brooklyn Bridge.

"Something is not right, Mr. C. Look at these pictures."

Robert Campanella looks at them carefully. George watches him examine them. Mr. Campanella wears thick black horn-rimmed glasses. The lenses magnify and make his eyes look big. His long gray eyebrows are alive and moving as he examines the photos. He has a few wild hairs in those eyebrows like antennae of an insect that accentuate the movement. Campanella opens his desk drawer and takes out his big magnifying glass. He looks carefully at the multiple pictures of the pothole that is the basis of the plaintiff's lawsuit against the city.

"I see what you mean. Let's get hold of Ted Albert and see what he thinks. Can you get the negatives from DeFeo? Ted is going to want them."

"I should be able to," George says as he gets up and takes the pictures and the Redweld for the case.

"Thanks, Mr. C."

Robert Campanella looks intently at George and speaks, "If they are fake, you know what that does to any claim for our client against the city?"

"I do. Any claim for our driver and truck owner will be against the injured plaintiff who crossed into his lane, not the city. That means since she has the minimum insurance, the amount will be limited."

"Right."

"But it is also going to mean the case is exploded anyway, and DeFeo will be in trouble."

"Big trouble, George," Campanella agrees.

George leaves and goes to his office. He calls the professional photographer and exhibit maker that the firm uses, Ted Albert. He explains that he needs an opinion about the photos exchanged by the plaintiff's attorney, Joe DeFeo.

"I know him," Ted says.

"Why do I think, from the way you say that, you have a negative opinion of him?"

"Let's just say he asked me to do something on a case that I refused to do."

"Okay. Well, I am going to get some negatives in addition to the prints and will need your expert opinion as to their authenticity."

"Just bring them to the studio when you get them."

"Thanks, Ted," George says and hangs up.

———

Judge Franco is about to leave his chambers when his law secretary announces the two sheriffs. They are big guys. Much to his shock, they come in and arrest him and take him out in cuffs. He is charged with soliciting and accepting a bribe in the criminal complaint drawn up by a deputy chief investigator working for Bronx DA Rueben Torres.

———

Joe DeFeo's paralegal looks at the demand of the codefendant trucking company for copies of the negatives of the pictures of the pothole that have been produced in discovery in the O'Neill case. She does not see this as a problem, takes the negatives to a negative copying place, and has them copied. She sends the copies to George's office.

————

Felicia finishes her session with her pianist at the Carnegie Hall rehearsal space. She has decided which songs she wants to sing for Thursday night at Tramps. She feels a little nervous about this gig. She has invited a lot of people, and Robespierre and his mother will be there. She goes downstairs and hails a cab on Fifty-Seventh Street. When she gets home, she calls Carole. The phone rings, but she only gets the answering machine. She leaves a message. She has been thinking she should invite Carole and George to her gig. That will round out the group, is a way to thank Carole for the dinner and introduction to Robby, and will make the evening even more fun.

————

Simon Stone has his secretary get Stuart Schlussel on the phone.

"Did you hear that Judge Franco got arrested?"

"Yeah, Simon, I did."

"It's about taking kickbacks, I am sure."

"Yes."

"Do you think they know about Katz too?"

"I don't know, but I imagine they are looking to catch as many judges as they can."

"On a different subject I had fun at the party in Brooklyn, but I must say that it is too bad that Dugan and his buddy Donnelly had to be there," Simon says.

"I know. Dugan is a slug."

"How does he manage to get the models to come?"

"I don't know. I think he has his hooks into a booker at one of the agencies."

"Did the young model you like ever show up?"

"No. I am sorry about that. I miss those little get-togethers we had at Burke's. He controlled Dugan better than I can. I would have liked to get her at one of those parties for sure."

"Well, maybe we'll have to plan a smaller get-together for only a few people rather than the big parties you have been arranging."

"Yes. That sounds right. Anyway, I have to go, Simon. I have an upset client calling."

"Okay. Later."

Don Wilkins smiles as he listens to the two attorneys hang up. He thinks that his boss is going to pass this information on to his friend, Jim Ashford. *This might help Ashford's investigation.*

Ted Albert looks over the negatives and puts them on his special viewer. He has all the latest equipment and is a master at courtroom photographic and graphic exhibits. He is suspicious. He knows that DeFeo is unscrupulous. He magnifies the negatives. Sure enough, he spots that the negatives have been doctored to make a fake photo. It looks like a bigger hole was superimposed onto the location of the smaller pothole. It was a pretty good job, but it doesn't fool him. He frowns. *George will be angry about this. He is a throwback, straight and fierce. I would want him to represent me in any lawsuit,* Ted thinks. He remembers seeing George cross-examine a doctor defendant and make him admit to medical malpractice, seven times no less. *I thought the doctor was going to cry right on the stand,* he remembers, as George questioned him relentlessly with the records, the doctor's deposition, and expert medical textbooks and journals. He had never seen anything like it. He picks up the phone and calls George's office.

After hanging up with Dave Morgan, Jim Ashford is thinking, *This is the break that I have been waiting for. Obviously, both Schlussel and Stone have a connection to Burke Lambert. They went to small parties that Lambert had. How is that related to Lambert's murder?*

Is it related to the murders of not only Lambert but also the models? What did Schlussel mean when he said he would like to get the model from his party at one of the small parties that Lambert held?

––––––––

Dave Morgan is sitting in his office. George and Ted are in the two leather chairs in front of his desk.

"How do you want to handle this, Mr. Morgan?" George asks.

"We are going to look into him a little bit, then arrest him and turn him. We will also get the photographer who made the negatives and anyone else involved in making the fraudulent photos," Morgan replies.

"What do you want from us?"

"I will need you both to testify, first for the grand jury and then at the trial, but before that I am going to find out what he knows about kickbacks to judges."

"What about the case involving the pothole?"

"Don't do anything for now. After we arrest him, it will explode the case. We are going to let the comptroller know not to make any offers on the case."

CHRIS AT THE GORDON AGENCY hangs up the phone. She thinks for a minute and then calls Aarika.

"Hi, Aarika! How are you?"

"Good. What's up?"

"You know that ad campaign for L'Oréal we talked about?"

"Yes."

"Well, they want you for the redhead, and they asked for the books of several other models we handle. They are interested in that new girl, Susie Griffin, who is a brunette, and they are also very interested in Carole Lansdorf to be the blonde in the ads. They like her look. I know she is not modeling actively now so she can pursue her singing, but I am wondering if she might be tempted. The money will be very good; I am sure I can get her more than her normal rate. I know you guys are friends. Do you think she might be willing to do it?"

"I don't know, but maybe. It's hard to break into a singing career."

"Well, I haven't been able to reach her. I left a message at her apartment but haven't heard back. Do you know where she is?"

"I don't, but I will try to find out. I'll make some calls and get back to you."

"That would be great. Thanks."

Aarika calls Carole's apartment and gets the answering machine. She leaves a message. She decides to call Johnny Colrain.

―――――

Jenny Fernandez calls an investigator she knows at the DA's office in Brooklyn. She tells the investigator, Maria Popov, that Dave Morgan is onto a fraud in a civil case by Joseph DeFeo, a Manhattan lawyer, and that she should check DeFeo's cases on file there in Kings County for anything funny. She asks Maria to let her know if she finds anything. Jenny has looked up all his cases in New York County. She also has filed the paperwork necessary to get a tap on DeFeo's office phone. Before DeFeo is arrested in regard to the case brought in Brooklyn, DA Morgan wants other witnesses and further evidence of corruption that might be present.

―――――

Johnny Colrain answers the phone.

"Hello?"

"Johnny?"

He recognizes the voice on the other end of the phone.

"Hi, Riki! How are you?"

"I'm fine, Johnny. You?"

"Good."

"I am calling to see if you know where Carole Lansdorf is. I am trying to reach her."

"I don't know. You couldn't reach her at home?"

"I left a message, and my booker did also, but she did not get a call back."

"Oh. Is there something wrong?"

"No. Nothing like that. My agency has a job for her that they want to ask her about."

"Okay. I will call George and ask if he knows where she might be and get back to you."

"Thanks, Johnny. Talk soon."

Jim Ashford is sitting in his unmarked car outside a brownstone on East Seventy-Sixth Street between Lexington and Third Avenues. He watches Simon Stone, who is carrying a beautiful black leather briefcase, climb the stairs in front of the building and enter. Ashford gets out of his 1983 Plymouth Gran Fury, climbs the stairs himself, finds Simon Stone, Esq., Attorney at Law on the list of tenants, and he presses the button. He is buzzed in and enters the hallway that leads to the Stone office. When he opens the door, he is greeted by a secretary-receptionist sitting at a desk with a large IBM Selectric typewriter. She asks for his name, and he tells her and shows her his identification. She asks him to wait and walks into the interior office. She comes out in a minute and shows Detective Ashford in. Jim introduces himself and then sits down in one of the chairs in front of Stone's desk. The office is nicely furnished. There are framed newspaper clippings of some of Stone's cases with the amounts of the recovery either from a trial or a settlement in the headline.

Ashford pulls out his badge and gets right to the point.

"Detective Jim Ashford, NYPD. I'm investigating the murder of Burke Lambert, and I would like to ask you a few questions about him."

This prompts a subtle reaction of concern by Stone that Ashford notices, but he goes on.

"Are you okay with that?

Stone thinks for a minute. *I didn't do anything wrong, and I know nothing about Burke's murder. I can answer a few questions.*

"Yes. I have a question for you, Detective Ashford. Am I under arrest?"

"No. I am just asking questions as part of my investigation."

"Okay, ask your questions. I will stop you if I am not comfortable."

Jim looks at him and nods.

"Okay, you knew Burke Lambert, right?"

"Yes."

"Were you good friends?"

"I wouldn't say that. We were friends but not good friends."

"Did he have parties that you attended?"

Stone hesitates and looks hard at Ashford, thinking of how to answer. He smiles, but it is not a warm smile. He is thinking, *They will find out I have gone to a few of Burke's get-togethers. That is not a crime.*

"I have attended a few of his get-togethers."

"Where did he hold these get-togethers?"

Stone weighs answering this question.

"Usually at the gym or pool in his apartment building."

"Was Stuart Schlussel at any of the parties or get-togethers?"

"I prefer not to answer that."

This is a picture of Adrienne Wyatt. Was she at any of the parties that you attended?"

There is a longer hesitation this time.

"I don't know."

This is a picture of Renée Toulouse. Was she at any of them?"

"I don't know."

"Were there models at any of the parties?"

"There were women who looked like models."

"Did you bring any women to these parties?"

"No."

"Did Mr. Schlussel?"

"I prefer not to answer that."

"Were any of the women involved in slave/master behavior with any of the men at the parties?"

"I am not answering any more questions without counsel."

"You are going to have to come down to my office."

"I understand."

———

Stuart Schlussel is heading to court when he sees Jenny. She motions to him to stop. He tries to head up the stairs of 60 Centre Street before she can reach him, but she is too fast and catches up with him.

"Mr. Schlussel!"

"Yes."

"You have to come with me."

"I'm sorry, but I am due in court."

"I can't help that, Mr. Schlussel. I will arrest you right here on the courthouse steps if you do not come voluntarily."

Schlussel looks at Jenny, who looks back and says nothing. He then turns and heads down the stairs with her.

———

Jim Ashford has gone to Morgan's office and is talking to Morgan about his questioning of Simon Stone.

"Well, he admitted to going to some of Lambert's get-togethers but declined to answer whether Schlussel did too. He said women who looked like models attended, but he did not know if Adrienne Wyatt or Renée Toulouse had ever attended. I asked him about master/slave stuff, but he clammed up and wants a lawyer. He will be coming in tomorrow. I want to hear what Schlussel says."

Morgan's secretary buzzes and tells him that Jenny and Schlussel have arrived. He tells her to have Jenny take him to interview room number 2. Jim Ashford and Dave enter the room. Stuart Schlussel is standing and looks as upset as he feels. His gaze falls on Jim Ashford. Dave Morgan speaks.

"Sit down, Mr. Schlussel. This is Detective Jim Ashford. It seems that you have been involved in another matter. He has some questions for you."

Jim and Dave sit opposite Schlussel. Dave turns on the video tape recorder, and Jim explains that he is investigating the murder of Burke Lambert and the two models, and he wants to ask him some questions. He then reads him his Miranda rights. When he finishes, he asks if Schlussel understands what has been read to him even though he is a lawyer.

Stuart is upset by this but is trying to stay calm. He knows that detectives always have to read the Miranda rights to someone who is under custodial interrogation.

"I understand my rights."

"Mr. Schlussel," Jim begins, "we have reason to believe that you attended get-togethers that Burke Lambert held. Is that correct?"

This takes Schlussel by surprise.

"Uh ..." He tries to stay calm and consider his situation carefully. Dave Morgan and Jim Ashford wait. *I can answer a few questions about Burke that they obviously know about so I don't seem guilty of anything, which, of course, I am not.* Finally, he continues, "Yes."

"Were you there when Adrienne Wyatt and Renée Toulouse attended?"

This throws Stuart, and there is a long pause. He now knows he is in dangerous waters. He improvises, "I don't know who those women are."

"You know, it is bad form to lie to a detective in the presence of a senior district attorney for New York County, right?" Jim says handing him a picture of each model.

Stuart's mind is racing. He wants to be calm and make this line of questioning go away.

"Why are you asking me about these women?" he says, looking quickly at the photos.

"You read the papers, don't you, Mr. Schlussel?"

"Yes, but mostly I read the *Law Journal*."

"Do you watch the news on TV?"

"Occasionally."

"Let me ask you this. Were there models at any of these get-togethers?"

Stuart hesitates but is angry and answers.

"Yes."

"Are you aware that two models were recently murdered?" Ash says slowly, staring at Schlussel.

"Okay. Are you suggesting that I had anything to do with those murders?"

"I am trying to find out if you have any information that will help us solve the murders," Jim replies.

"I have no idea about who would have murdered anyone!" he says forcefully.

"Did you ever witness any S-and-M behavior at any of these get-togethers?"

Stuart is now very agitated.

"What kind of question is that?"

"We have reason to believe that at least one of the models was involved in that type of behavior. Who attended these get-togethers?"

"Different people."

"Can you give me any names?"

"Okay. I am not saying anything further. I want my lawyer."

Dave Morgan says, "I understand, Mr. Schlussel. That is your right. We are arresting you for sexual assault."

———

Aarika is watching TV in her apartment when the phone rings.

"Hello?"

"Hi, Riki! It's Carole."

"Carole! Where are you? Are you okay? Chris from the agency and I have left messages for you."

"I know. I just picked them up. I am fine. I am at home in Minnesota. My mom had to have surgery."

"Oh. I'm sorry. Is she all right?"

"She is now. She had to have a hysterectomy."

"When are you coming back to the city?"

"In a couple of days. I want to make sure she can manage by herself before I leave. What's up?"

"Chris wants me to talk you into doing a shoot for L'Oréal with me and this new model, Susie Griffin. She says that they want you and will pay more than your regular rate, so you should do well financially."

"It would be fun to work with you again, and I have to admit that it would be nice to have some additional income," Carole replies.

"I would love it if you would say yes. I think the shoot is at a beautiful estate."

"Do you know when they are doing it?"

"Next Monday."

"I will be back, and I have no singing gig scheduled so I should be able to."

"Great! Will you call Chris and tell her?"

"Yup. I will call you when I get home this weekend. Thanks, kiddo."

The two women hang up.

Joe DeFeo hangs up. He cannot figure out what has happened. The city comptroller had asked for a demand two days ago and was about to make an offer on the Brooklyn Bridge access motor vehicle accident, but now the comptroller has just told him he is not making an offer. He packs up his briefcase and puts on his suit jacket and overcoat. He leaves his inner office, walks through the office, says goodbye to the receptionist-secretary, and walks out to the elevator. Maria Popov is waiting for him as he steps out of his building. She arrests him for fraud.

Jim Ashford and Johnny Colrain are having breakfast together in Johnny's loft. Ashford fills Johnny in with the information he has gotten from Schlussel and Stone. He explains that the two lawyers confirm that Burke Lambert did have late-night get-togethers with models and a few friends in his building, using the pool and gym. Stone and Schlussel admit that they did attend two of them, but they don't know if Adrienne and/or Renée were there. Cocaine was used, but both say they don't know who supplied it. They claim that Dugan was not at either get-together they attended. Apparently, sometimes the get-togethers got a little kinky with some spanking and other such sexual play going on.

"Do you believe them?" Johnny asks, taking a sip of coffee.

"I do, although I am not sure about the cocaine supplier answers."

"How are we going to find out who was there when Adrienne and Renée were present?" Johnny asks.

"Maybe someone in the building, but the answer is I don't know yet."

"Why were they killed?"

"Yes. Why? That is the key to who did it."

"Where did the cocaine come from?" Johnny wonders out loud.

"Yes. Good question. I have an idea about that but am not sure yet."

Johnny gives him a look but says nothing. There is an unspoken thought shared between the two men. They finish the meal, and Ashford says goodbye.

"Thanks, John. That was good."

"Stay in touch, Ash."

31

LUCIENNE, ROBESPIERRE, JOHNNY, and Priscilla are standing outside Tramps waiting for Felicia. The street is alive with people and cars.

"She is really good," Johnny says to the group.

"A beautiful voice," Lucienne adds.

"I can't believe her range," Priscilla says.

Robby says nothing but just stands there, smiling. Felicia comes out and stands next to him.

"You were wonderful, Felicia. It was a real treat for me," Lucienne tells her.

"Really, Felicia," Robby adds, looking at her.

"I am glad you enjoyed it," Felicia says shyly.

"We loved it, Felicia," Johnny chimes in.

"How about we go back to Robespierre's for a few drinks before we call it a night," Robby suggests.

Johnny looks at Priscilla.

"We would love to, but it's late and a school night for Priscilla. I think we will let you three go," Johnny says.

"Are you sure?" Robby asks.

"Yes, but we want a rain check."

"My pleasure."

"Thanks, Felicia. I don't think I have ever really heard the blues before. Certainly, not the way you sing them," Priscilla tells her.

They all hug. Johnny and Priscilla head to where his motorcycle is parked. Robby hails a cab. One arrives, and he holds the door for Lucienne and Felicia and then jumps in.

When they get to the restaurant, there is only one member of the staff there just closing up. Robby thanks him, and they enter. He goes behind the bar and opens a bottle of champagne. He gets three flutes and pours the champagne into them. He raises his glass. Lucienne and Felicia do the same.

"Congratulations, Felicia. You were wonderful," he says.

Felicia looks at them both with a warm smile on her face.

"It was special for me knowing you two were in the audience."

Lucienne looks at Felicia and her son.

"It was special for me, Felicia, I can assure you," Lucienne says.

"And for me," Robby adds.

They all laugh.

Lucienne asks Felicia some questions about where she grew up. She tells them about her youth in South Carolina and her family. Felicia is thinking, *I normally don't like to talk about my life and family but this feels good somehow. These two are lovely people.* Robby is paying very close attention. He likes the way Felicia interacts with his mom. In fact, he likes the way she is in general. There is something very sincere about her. She is quiet, soft-spoken, and gentle, but there is a strength there for sure. This is very attractive to him.

Yes, she is very beautiful, but she also has depth, he thinks to himself. He definitely is smitten and wants to know more about her. He wants to mine her character, her likes, dislikes, but more than that. She has soul, and he wants to know it. *Will she want to know mine?* he wonders.

————

Priscilla holds tight on to Johnny's waist with her head close to his as they fly to his loft. She knows that is where they are going without him saying anything to her. She is a little scared, but she wants to go there. She wants to see where he lives. It will tell her more about him. She likes him, but she finds him mysterious. She can't really tell what he feels about her. Sure, he likes her enough to take her out a few times, and they can talk about art, but how does he really feel? She knows that he has been around and dated very beautiful women. That intimidates her. *Is he just experimenting with someone who is just a regular girl? A country girl, at that?* She hopes it is more, but she can't be sure.

They arrive, and she gets off the bike and takes off her helmet. He does the same and smiles at her. She is nervous. She goes with him when he puts the bike in the basement of the building. He takes her hand, and they get in the elevator. He opens the door to his loft, and there is Baloo greeting them. He is wagging his tail furiously.

"Hello, big guy! Have you been a good boy?" Johnny says, petting the big dog who then jumps up and puts his paws on Johnny's chest. Johnny laughs as he puts the dog back down on all fours. He grins at Priscilla, who has lost some of her nerves watching the two of them for some reason. She bends to pet the big white dog, being careful to avoid any drool. Johnny grabs his leash but does not clip it to his collar as he usually does because it is so late and no one should be about.

"Okay, let's go!" He opens the door, and the dog starts down the stairs with a clatter. Johnny and Priscilla follow. When they get to the first floor, the dog is anxiously waiting for them. Johnny opens the door and Baloo rushes out to relieve himself. He reaches for and holds Priscilla's hand as they walk down the street while the big guy goes about doing his business.

"What do you think of Robby with Felicia as a couple?" Priscilla asks.

"Well, it's obvious to me that he likes her all right. What do you think?"

"I agree, and I think she likes him. They go well together."

"I don't think I have to ask you about George and Carole," he says.

"Oh my gosh, they are definitely into each other. It is nice."

He squeezes her hand. She looks up at him and smiles. He calls to his dog.

"Come on, Baloo. Time to go home!"

When they go back in the loft, Priscilla starts to walk around. Johnny follows her as she examines the painting on the easel. She then walks around his workout space. As she walks by the heavy bag, she gives it a good hard punch. Johnny laughs.

"I better be careful," he says.

Priscilla gives him a look and smiles. She likes his loft.

"Would you like something to drink?" Johnny asks.

"No."

Priscilla turns to him. Something has happened within her; a line has deliberately been crossed.

"I want you."

He reaches for her, and they share a deep kiss. She is a good kisser, and it lasts a long time. He reaches for the zipper on her dress as he kisses her neck, but she reaches back and unzips it. She then steps out of it, and it falls to the floor. She is in her bra and panties. They keep looking at each other, and she reaches for his shirt. She starts to unbutton it. She finishes and takes his shirt off. She opens his belt and helps his pants come off. It all then becomes awkward trying to get them over his boots so he hobbles over to the bed with the pants down below his knees to sit down, and they start laughing. He pulls off his boots and furiously kicks off his recalcitrant pants. She steps out of her shoes and pushes him down on the bed.

They kiss for a long time with her on top of him. He reaches behind and unhinges her bra. She pulls it off and rolls on her back. He is surprised and turned on by the size and shape of her breasts. Then she turns on her side, facing Johnny, who is on his side. They kiss, and then he begins to caress her breasts. He kisses them, squeezes her large nipples before taking each one in his mouth. He bites them gently, which elicits an "Ooh ..." She throws her head back and just sighs as he moves his hand over her body. He caresses her stomach, feels the outline of her hip, and then quickly takes off her panties and moves his hand between her legs. He probes with his finger and finds her clitoris. He manipulates it slowly and carefully. Her wetness increases. She sighs louder in an increasing rhythm as she becomes more excited. He brings her to climax and then quickly takes off his boxers over his excited organ and moves on top of her. He kisses her and enters her. She moans, and he begins to move very slowly. He then slides off onto her side to put his penis at a different angle within her and squeezes her left breast as he continues to move. She reacts strongly to his move and becomes so aroused that she starts vocalizing her excitement. He keeps moving steadily that way and caressing her breasts with his right hand. As this continues, they both become more and more aroused, and then she climaxes again, and much to his surprise, she yells, "Oh fuck, fuck … yes!" He climaxes at that moment. He buries his face in her neck, staying in her. He feels her pulsing, squeezing his penis. After a while he just relaxes on top of her and then starts kissing her face all over multiple times until she starts laughing at him. This makes his organ withdraw on its own, but he continues kissing her face.

"Every freckle deserves a kiss," he says.

"You have a lot of work to do, then," she replies with a satisfied smile.

"Not exactly work," he replies, kissing her more.

———

The taxi arrives at the Beresford. Robespierre turns to Felicia and gives her a serious look but says nothing. She looks back at him and is also silent, but there is just the hint of a smile. He then pays the cabbie and opens the door and gets out. He reaches his hand into the cab and helps Felicia out. It suddenly starts to rain. She takes his hand and quickly leads him toward her building, letting out a scream and laughing with her little high- pitched sound as the outburst of drops starts hitting them. He laughs also. She acknowledges the doorman, who has come from deep in the lobby and opens the door for them. They get in the elevator together holding hands and smiling at each other, a little wet. The elevator stops at her floor, and she opens the door to her apartment. Robby is not exactly sure what is going to happen. He is excited but wants everything to go smoothly with Felicia because he really likes her. He follows her into the beautifully furnished apartment. Felicia is nervous. She likes this man but is not completely sure of what she wants to happen now. She goes to the kitchen, and he follows. She takes down two large red wine glasses. She pours them both some wine. Robby raises his glass.

"Thank you for inviting all of us, Felicia. It really was wonderful."

"It was wonderful for me too."

They sit down at the small table in the kitchen. They talk for a while about all their friends. Felicia is sorry that Carole and George could not come to her performance.

She gets up to put the glasses on the counter, and Robby watches her. She goes to him, leans over, and kisses him deeply. He marvels at her soft sweet mouth and kisses her back tenderly, but the kiss does not end. Their passion grows. He gets up slowly, still kissing her. He holds her face with both his hands. They break and look at each other inquiringly. She smiles at him, takes his hand, and leads him to the bedroom.

Sensing this is a serious, cautious woman, Robby looks at her and speaks, "Are you sure about this, Felicia?"

She has a little smile on her face that makes a dimple show on her right cheek.

"Do you think it is too soon for us?" she asks.

Robespierre looks at her with seriousness.

"I don't know you well, but I like you a lot, Felicia. I don't want to do something that will derail where I want this to go. I can wait if you think it is too soon."

"Thank you for saying that, Robby."

They kick off their shoes. She turns down the bed and lies down. He lies beside her. For some reason, he feels cautious and uncharacteristically passive, which surprises him. It has something to do with the feelings he already has for her, he guesses. She begins to take off his clothes. He assists when needed but remains very passive.

When she gets his pants off, she comes back to his black silk mini-boxers and gently takes them off past his erection. After she does that, she inspects his genitalia carefully. Robby can't believe what is happening and is holding his breath. He lets out a sigh with her first touch on his skin. Her hands are soft, smooth, and petite. Robespierre is looking at her and marveling at her face. She is concentrating, and he is fascinated by her careful examination. She slowly starts moving her hand up and down his erection. She brings her mouth down to it. She kisses the head, and then takes him in her mouth. Robby gasps. She moves slowly up and down, taking him deep with her hand holding him and moving upward at the same time, meeting her mouth. He can't believe how wonderful it feels. She is very focused on what she is doing. His sighs increase with each of her movements as his excitement increases even more.

He reaches for her face, but she suddenly stops and quickly takes off her top and bra. He looks at her small, beautiful breasts. Her face is intense. She quickly removes the rest of her clothes and sits on him. She then grabs his penis, lifts up, and inserts it carefully into her. He gasps again, feeling how wet she is. She starts riding him slowly. He leans forward and reaches out to touch her breasts. He strokes them and gently squeezes her nipples, which she reacts to with a little cry. She continues moving up and down but slowly increases her rhythm. Their breaths are synched to her movements. All of a sudden, she goes faster, harder, and harder. Suddenly she arches her back, stops, and lets out a scream. He feels her vagina spasm and then some warm fluid shoot onto his penis as he climaxes hard. He lets out a great groan as it keeps going and throws his head back. When it's over, he brings his head forward and looks at her; she is grinning. He starts laughing, and then she laughs. She waits for a few moments, then gets off him and moves up next to him.

She kisses him then rests her head on his shoulder as he hugs her and slowly strokes her arm. After a few moments she reaches down and pulls the covers over them.

"Robby, Robby, Robby, Robby ..." she says softly.

He smiles happily and responds, "Felicia, you, you, you ..."

———

Carole's plane taxis to the gate at LaGuardia. She is tired but feeling good and happy her mother has recovered so well from her surgery. She was thinking of staying another day, but her mother insisted that she felt good and sent her home to New York. She is also pleased about the modeling job with Aarika. She likes working with her, and it will be good to have some new income. Carole makes her way out of the plane, up the boarding ramp, and out into the terminal carrying a Louis Vuitton Keepall bag in her left hand and a Speedy over her right arm. She is wearing a pair of worn 501 Levi's, a thin black cashmere pullover under her raincoat, and white Adidas athletic shoes. Her hair is in a ponytail. As she enters the concourse, she sees a man sitting in a seat close to the gate smiling at her. Her heart jumps, and she grins at him.

"What are you doing here?" she says as she stops at his chair, and he gets up.

"What? A guy can't come to the airport to pick up his favorite girl?" George says as he gives her a quick kiss and a hug. He grabs her overnight bag.

"Favorite, huh?" she says, giving him a faux angry look.

He laughs at her.

"How is your mom?" he asks as she takes his arm and they walk toward the exit.

"She is good, thanks. She is tough."

"I have a feeling that her daughter is too," George says, smiling.

The two of them walk out the door and head to short-term parking and George's car. They drive into the city chattering away. Carole tells him about her mother, the modeling job with Aarika, and that she has a few auditions lined up. He drops Carole off at her apartment so he can take his car to the garage. When he gets back to her building, he talks to the doorman for a minute before going in. He does not see Andrzej watching from across the street.

32

PETER PICKFORD IS STEAMED and walking fast after exiting Judge Katz's courtroom. He strides through the hall past other attorneys toward the elevator and sees George Fredericks standing outside a courtroom looking at a legal paper as he holds a Redweld folder under his arm. Peter goes up to him.

"Hi, George. I hate that motherfucker!"

George looks at Peter with amusement.

"Who would that be, Peter?" George asks, somewhat curious, but then continues. "Wait. Let me guess. Judge Katz."

"That wasn't that hard, George, in this building and on this floor. Yes, that sneering son of a bitch!"

"What did he do?" George asks.

"He asked me for money!"

"What?"

"I have an order pending in front of him in a big infant's medical mal case in regard to setting the fees that I am to receive. He said if I wanted it signed, I had to give him $18,000 as a down payment. He wants a total of $100,000!"

"You're kidding!"

"No. I am not!"

George pauses and then speaks.

"I know that DA Morgan is investigating kickbacks and bribery of civil judges."

"Yeah?"

"Would you be willing to wear a wire when you go before Katz again on the case?" George asks.

"Damn right, I would!"

"Good. He will want you to come into his office."

"It's over by Foley Square, right?"

"Yes. One Hogan Place."

"Are you done here?" Peter asks.

"I am."

"Let's go over there now before I go back to my office."

"Okay. I will call over to make sure he is in."

They walk to the telephone bank. George slips onto the seat and dials the phone with Peter standing outside the open sliding door.

———

Carole is upset. She did not know that Andrjez was to be the photographer on the shoot with Aarika. She is mad that when she agreed to the shoot she did not ask who the photographer was. Apparently, Aarika did not know who it was going to be either. Carole was picked up by a limo with Aarika and Susie and taken to the location. When they arrived at a beautiful estate in Cold Spring Harbor on Long Island, they were taken to a large bedroom in the house to change into tennis clothes for the first photos. The three women then had hair and makeup done in the big bathroom off the bedroom. She learned at that moment who the photographer was. There was nothing she could do.

The stylist looks them over and approves the way they look. They are then taken by an assistant to the tennis court on the estate grounds. As they approach the tennis court, Andrjez is busy setting up his cameras and whatever supplemental lighting he wants. There are client personnel and assistants there with all the cases of equipment. An assistant takes the girls and gives them tennis racquets and a can of tennis balls. She takes them to the court opposite where Andrjez is at the tripod, looking through a camera. He looks up from the camera and says hello to the girls. He knows Aarika and Carole but not Susie. He comes over to them and introduces himself to Susie. There is no interaction between Carole and Aarika with him other than the greeting. Three male models come out of the pool house on the estate. They are also dressed in tennis whites and carrying tennis racquets. Andrjez instructs them how he wants them to pose and goes back to the camera, checks the light with his light meter, and decides what supplemental artificial light filling in shadows he needs since it is a partially cloudy day. He instructs his assistant which light to put on and then where he wants it placed. He then begins shooting.

Buttercup Pierce is listening carefully to this new girl. Her mind is whirring because she has heard some gossip about Burke Lambert.

"What do you know about Burke Lambert, Sara?"

"I know he liked to do some S and M with models."

"How do you know that?"

"He tried it with me."

"Where was this?"

"In the gym in the basement of his building."

"Did you go along with it?"

"No. That is not my thing."

Buttercup gives her a very fierce look.

"You understand, my girls do not get involved with that behavior."

"Yes."

"Who else have you told about this?"

"Just two of my friends who work for you."

"Who?"

"Olga and Dani."

"I don't want you to talk about it further to anyone else, and tell Olga and Dani the same thing. Do you understand me?"

"Yes."

After Sara leaves, Buttercup dials Robespierre's phone.

"Robespierre's."

"Robby?"

"Buttercup?"

"Yes. Tell your friend Colrain that Burke Lambert did his S-and-M thing with models in the basement gym of his building."

"Thanks. I will tell him. How are you?"

"I am fine. You?"

"Very good."

"I heard about Felicia."

"You have good sources."

"I do, and I heard she is a lovely woman, Robby."

"She is."

"Are you still your wild self?"

"What do you mean?"

"You know. Lots of girls?"

"No. That is not where I am at all."

"Good. I hope it works out for you both."

"Thanks, Miss B."

"Bye, Robby."

Robby hangs up and smiles. He calls Johnny.

———————

Johnny is sweaty but feels good. He has been jumping rope after hitting the heavy bag and speed bag. He answers the phone wearing the half gloves he wears when hitting the bags. He listens carefully as Robby tells him about what Buttercup told him.

———————

The shoot is over, and the models have changed back into their regular clothes. Carole, Aarika, and Susie are waiting for the limo to take them back to the city. Andrjez approaches them.

"Can I have a private word with you, Riki?"

Aarika looks at Carole with a quizzical look. Carole nods.

"Sure," Aarika says.

He gestures for her to follow him out of earshot of Carole and Susie.

"Riki, I'm sorry about the other night at the Vanguard. Is Carole still upset with me?"

"Honestly, Andrjez, I think she has forgotten about it."

He gives her an intense look.

"You mean she is interested in someone else, right?"

"Yes."

"That guy that pulled her out of the cab and punched me?"

"Yes, Andrjez."

"Is it serious?"

"Andrjez, I can only tell you that they are seeing each other."

Andrjez sighs and then speaks.

"On another subject, do you have Johnny Colrain's home number?"

"I do. Why?"

"I want to talk to him about something I think he is interested in."

She looks at him questioningly.

"I don't think Johnny would want me to give up his privacy. I'll tell you what. Give me your number, and I will have him call you."

"Okay. That is fine."

Andrjez reaches into his pocket and gives Riki his card. She takes it.

"Thanks, Riki," he says and then goes back to his assistants who are packing up his cameras and gear.

Riki goes back to Carole, who is looking at her nonplussed.

"What was that about?" Carole asks quietly, away from the others standing around.

"First, it was an apology about you and a question if you were still upset about it. I said no and that you had moved on. He asked if you were interested in the guy who rescued you, and if it was serious. I just said that you were seeing him. He then asked for Johnny Colrain's number. I asked why he wanted it, and he said he had something to tell Johnny that he would want to hear."

"What would that be?" Carole asks.

"I have no idea but I took his number for Johnny to call him."

———

It is late afternoon and Johnny is sitting at the counter in his loft with a mug of coffee reading *The New York Times*. The wind is rattling the windows in the loft. The phone rings, and he picks it up and says, "Hello."

"Johnny?"

"Hi, Riki, what's up?"

"I was on a shoot with Carole, and the photographer was Andrjez, Carole's ex. He wants to talk to you and when I would not give him your home number. He gave me his number for you to call him."

"That's the guy George decked, right?"

"Yes. He is a well-known photographer."

"And kind of an asshole. What does he want to talk to me about?"

"He didn't tell me, but he said you would be interested in it, and I said I would give you the number."

"Okay, thanks, Riki."

Riki gives him the number, and then adds, "If you want to talk to him in person, you can always come out to where we are shooting the L'Oréal campaign. We will be out there again tomorrow. It would be fun to see you."

"Where exactly?" Johnny asks.

"Somewhere in Cold Spring Harbor. They will know the exact address at the agency."

"Thanks. Maybe I will do that," Johnny says.

"Bring George; he can see Carole model. It is at a beautiful estate."

"I am not sure that the photographer would be happy to see him, but I'll see if he can get away."

"Okay, later."

They hang up. Johnny wonders what this guy Andrjez wants to talk to him about. *He is a photographer, and he knows a lot of models for sure. He also was at that party in Brooklyn. He probably knows that I have been asking around about Adrienne and Renée. Maybe he knows something that could be helpful,* Johnny muses.

He calls Ashford and tells him about this development.

"What do you think, Ash?"

"Call him and see what he has to say, John."

"Okay."

"And keep me posted."

Johnny calls his number. He gets an answering machine. It tells the caller that Andrjez will be out on a job for a couple of days and to leave a message. Johnny doesn't even like his voice. He hangs up. He dials a different number.

"Gordon Agency."

"Hi, may I speak to Chris, please?"

"One moment, please." There is a pause.

"Hello, this is Chris. Can I help you?"

"Hi, Chris. Yes, you can. Aarika told me to call you. I need to know the exact address where she is shooting, and she doesn't know it as she has been driven there."

"Hi, Johnny. Are you trying to get me in trouble? Like I told you before, I am not supposed to give out that information. Last time I did it there was a problem."

"Chris, it's me. I have worked through the agency. I am not an unknown stranger. You know me. I am not a stalker and not trying to do anything bad. I have to have the address. It can't wait. It's important, and she told me to call you to get it," Johnny replies.

"Hold on, I'll ask."

More than a few minutes go by, and finally she gets back on the phone and gives him the address. She adds, "You better get there early. Everybody stayed on the Island last night and the shoot is scheduled to start no later than seven thirty, and it's not expected to take too long."

––––––––

Donnelly opens the door of his house in Queens and walks out to his car parked in the driveway. He partially opens the driver's door when two investigators from the Brooklyn DA's office who have emerged from their car parked on the street approach him. He looks at them in disbelief. They confirm his name. There is a tense moment when they ask for his gun. He looks hard at them, hands it over, and asks what it is about. They arrest him for fraud, cuff him, lead him to their police car, and take him away.

33

THERE ARE HUGE CUMULUS CLOUDS in the sky with a background of bright blue. The road is dry. George is driving his dark gray Audi Quattro. He and Johnny are flying out the Long Island Expressway. George drives fast, and the two of them are talking away. They get off at Route 106 and then take Route 25A into Cold Spring Harbor. Johnny is wearing black jeans, a denim work shirt over a black T-shirt, and sneakers. George is dressed in a dandelion-yellow polo shirt, blue jeans, and running shoes. Because the weather is good, they have made excellent time.

George was excited by the prospect of surprising Carole and was able to take the day off. He also thought it would be fun to see her model. They find the address and slowly roll into the big circular driveway on the white peastone where there are a lot of cars parked. George finds a space for the Audi. Johnny and he get out of the car looking around where to go. They decide to forego ringing the front doorbell. They walk behind the big house and look down a huge lawn. It is like the description of Jay Gatsby's estate. The lawn has topiary plants, beautiful landscaping, and is rimmed by flowers. It drops down from the house where there is a big pool, a pool house at one end of the pool, and a tennis court. They see the models, assistants, the clients, and a camera on a tripod at the far end of the pool near the tennis court.

Johnny and George walk down the lawn toward the shoot. They approach slowly to one side of the pool, and with all the activity going on, they are not noticed. There are camera cases, tripods holding lights set up all around. The hair and makeup people are checking the models who are sitting in tall director chairs after the first set of photos. As each one is finished and stands, the stylists put the final touches on how the dresses and tuxedos on the models look for the next shot. George and Johnny sit down on two chaises and watch. The shoot is obviously supposed to be of a high-brow group of young adults enjoying drinks by a pool at a formal party. They move the models around into various poses and have them converse and laugh as Andrjez photographs them.

George is only interested in watching Carole. He likes the way she looks, of course, but also notices how she is interacting with the other people. She is friendly, smiling, and laughing. He gets the impression that she is also telling a few jokes to get the others in the shot to react as if they really are having a good time, which is what is supposed to be going on for the pictures. Aarika is absolutely gorgeous and a nice counterpoint to the blond Carole and the dark-haired Susie, who seems very much into what is going on. Andrjez is taking group shots and then close-up shots from several different angles. He is professional and obviously knows what he is doing. Sometimes he uses his Hasselblad camera on the tripod, sometimes a different smaller Canon. He has a light meter on a strap around his neck. He also uses a Leica that has a viewfinder that he looks through for other shots.

They finish and call it a wrap for the day. The assistants start taking the glasses and props. Carole is talking to one of the male models, then suddenly, as if she has an antenna and has detected someone looking at her not involved with the shoot, she turns her head and spots George and Johnny watching. She breaks out in a huge grin, waves, grabs up her gown with both hands, and walks along the pool over to them. George is grinning widely also. He gets up as she approaches as does Johnny.

"What are you guys doing here?"

"I have been watching you," George replies and then adds, "You look wonderful, by the way."

"You are bad," she says, giving him a quick kiss on the mouth. She looks at Johnny and addresses him, "No, really. What is going on?"

"Your ex told Riki that he wants to talk with me. I thought it would be better to do it in person and bring George along for company and to see you model," Johnny says, smiling at her.

Carole turns and looks toward Andrjez, who is taking one of his cameras off a tripod.

"What does he want to talk to you about?" she asks.

"I don't know, but I guess I am going to find out right now."

Johnny starts to walk toward Andrjez. Carole and George watch him for a minute, and then Carole turns to him with some concern.

"What do you think this is about, George?"

"I have no clue, but whatever it is, Johnny can handle it," George replies, looking down at her. Carole looks at him and then turns her gaze toward Johnny approaching Andrjez. She turns back to George and speaks.

"I have to go up to the house and change. Where are you going to be?" Carole asks.

"Right here," he answers.

"Great! I will be right back."

Carole lifts her dress up again and starts up the lawn toward the house.

—————

Andrjez looks up as Johnny approaches. They look at each other, sizing each other up again. Johnny reflects back to the Vanguard and the confrontation they had in Carole's apartment building lobby. He thought he might have to clock Andrjez then. The photographer standing with the Hasselblad camera in his hands, bends down, and puts it in a black case. He then stands up.

"Hello, Johnny."

"Hello, Andrjez."

"I didn't expect you would come out here to speak with me."

"I called your office but got the machine. I figured it might be best if we talked in person anyway. What is this about?"

An assistant approaches. Andrjez turns and tells him to start loading the lights and cases in the van. He then turns back and addresses Johnny.

"I heard you were asking about Adrienne after she was found. I shot a job with Renée after Adrienne's death. She was really upset, and it was hard to get her to do what I needed for the shoot, but I felt bad for her and did not want to fire her.

After the shoot I was not sure she would be okay, so I took her to Macquilken's to get something to eat. She did manage to eat something, but she drank a lot of wine. She was pretty sloshed and got talking. She told me that she and Adrienne had gone to Burke

Lambert's gym in the cellar of his building on a few occasions, got high, and had sex there. It got a little kinky, to use her words. She said there were other men and women there sometimes as well. Then she said that the last time there were supposed to be three men and women, but one girl did not show. They partied anyway, and that was all she said. She refused to tell me who the other men were. I wasn't that interested in who they were, actually, and did not push it. I am not sure it is connected to their deaths, but I have been thinking after Lambert was killed, it might be, so I thought I should tell you."

"I am glad that you thought to tell me. Did she say whether the other men were friends of Lambert or what they did?"

"No. She did not want to talk about them but wanted to get off her chest that she had been with Adrienne last when they were partying in the gym."

"Anything else?"

"I asked her what she meant by kinky. She said there was some slave/master role-playing, and sometimes masks were involved. That's all."

"Have you told anyone else about this?"

"No. As I said, I have been thinking about it, and when I heard you were looking into Adrienne's death and then Renée was murdered, I thought I should tell you. I was told you are helping a detective. I am not sure it means much or is related to why anybody was murdered. I wasn't interested in talking to the police, but I thought I should at least tell you."

"I am glad you did, Andrjez."

"And one more thing, Johnny."

"Yes?"

"Sorry I was such an ass the other night in Carole's apartment house lobby. I was drunk and upset. What happened outside the Vanguard was bad enough."

Johnny looks hard at Andrjez and reevaluates him.

"Apology accepted and appreciated. Thanks for the info, Andrjez."

Johnny turns to leave.

"One more thing, Johnny."

Johnny turns back to him again.

"Yes?"

"If I need a Great Pyrenees and a model like you for a shoot, can I call you?" he says with a smile. Johnny can't help but smile back.

"It can't hurt to call. If I can do it, I will."

"Good. See you," Andrjez replies and returns to his equipment.

Johnny walks up to where George and Carole are talking and laughing. He is deep in thought. They look at him, and he looks serious.

"What was that all about, Johnny?" Carole asks.

"It was about Adrienne and Renée."

"Was it helpful?" George asks.

"It might be. I have to go over it with Ash when we get back."

"Is the shoot over?" George asks Carole.

"It is. I have to go back down there and say goodbye and tell them I am going to the city with you guys. After that, I think we should stop off at the catering table and have something to eat before we leave. I am starved!" Carole says.

"Good idea," Johnny replies, smiling, then adding, "Go down and do that, and George and I will wait here for you, then we'll all go to the catering table together and grab something."

After eating the sandwiches they made from the cold cuts at the table and having some coffee, they walk to the dark gray Audi and get in. As they are driving, no one is aware that a black Ford Fairlane is following them. Johnny is silent and obviously thinking hard. George notices and says nothing. Several minutes go by, and Carole breaks the silence.

"Do you want to share, Johnny?" Carole asks.

"I would rather not right now," he replies, sharper than he meant to. George gives him a quick look of surprise. He looks over at Carole and raises his eyebrows. They all are silent again.

George is in the right lane as the road makes a sweeping turn to the right. He has a guardrail to his right protecting cars on the road from a drop-off into a ravine. Johnny is looking out the side window on the left from his back seat, thinking. He looks out the window idly lost in his thoughts. He sees a black car coming up fast in the left lane and then suddenly it starts to swerve to the right.

"Watch out!" he yells as the black car keeps swerving toward George's car. George has nowhere to go and pulls to the right. There is hardly any shoulder. He grabs the wheel extra hard and fights it as the right side of the car goes up onto the guardrail. The posts sticking up vertically above the horizontal metal railing rip into the front right tire, exploding it and then into the bottom of the car, making horrible loud noises and vibrations as the car progresses with its right side up on the rail for a short distance. The noises and vibrations feel like the vertical posts are about to go through the floor. Carole in the front passenger seat feels the vibration and actually picks up her feet. George fights to not go over the railing to the right into the ravine or tip over completely onto the road to the left as he slams on the brakes. He steadies the car, and the car comes to a halt tilted up on the guardrail at a precarious angle.

"Son of a bitch!" George yells, slamming his hands down on the steering wheel. He and Johnny on the left side of the car are leaning over toward the road at an acute angle. Johnny has recognized the man in the car.

"It was that bastard Dugan!"

Everyone is shaken up in the car. George and Johnny assess the situation and make a plan to get carefully out of the car. First, Johnny slowly moves over toward the right center of the car in the back seat to help keep the car balanced. Carole is on the right side of the car holding on to the door handle. The car will not go over the railing now that it is stopped on the posts and tilted left, but they do not want it to roll over completely on the road. George opens the driver's door. It scrapes the pavement but opens enough for him to get out from the driver's side on the left. The car does not move. Carole then scoots over past the gearshift and follows George, exiting out on the driver's side. Finally, Johnny moves back over to the left and quickly exits from the back seat through the left back door. The black car has sped on. George and Johnny look at the damage. The front right tire is demolished, and the posts have torn up the bottom of the car past the wheel to the back door.

"Obviously, the car has to be towed. You stay here with Carole. I will walk up the road to see if someone will let me use their phone. I need to call for a tow and a taxi to take us to a car rental place," George says.

"Nope, let's all go together. No one is going to steal the car," Carole says.

"I agree," Johnny adds.

As they walk, George notes the mile marker they pass to give to the garage to locate the car. The three of them walk down the road to the first house, go up to the front door, and ring the bell. No one is home. They try the next house, and this time a woman in her early sixties opens the door. She is wearing a print dress and house slippers. She looks at them questioningly, but then George introduces himself and explains what happened and that he has to make a phone call to get a garage to tow the car for repair. He also asks her where the nearest car rental is and whom to call for a taxi ride to the car rental agency. The woman's husband comes to the door. He is in his late sixties with thick gray hair, glasses, and a pipe in his mouth. He is wearing an old comfortable-looking green sleeveless cardigan sweater with tan buttons over a patterned cotton shirt. His wife explains the situation. He gives them the number of the local garage from a phone book he takes out of a drawer in a small telephone table in the hall with a small lamp and phone on it. George talks to the garage owner, explains what happened to the car, and tells him its location. He asks him if he can tow it in and assess the damage. He also tells the garage owner that he will call his insurance company to come look at the car. The man offers to take them to the car rental agency, and they agree to his kind offer. He drops them off and wishes them luck.

Evelyn Gordon feels she has been remiss, and she feels bad about it. She has not seen her friend Muriel since her husband's death. Finally, she has made it her business to find the time to invite her for tea. The two of them are in Evelyn's sitting room. It is a small feminine room painted in primrose yellow with swaths of colorful chintz fabric. Vlasta has brought in a beautiful Apponyi Blue Herend pot filled with Darjeeling tea and matching cups. There is also a dish of little pastries on the coffee table.

"This is lovely, Evelyn."

"How are you managing, Muriel?"

"I have been going through Burke's things. It is not easy."

"I am sure it has to be very tough."

"I can't figure out who would want to kill him."

"It is crazy. It makes no sense."

"I know he went out with friends and was not always the perfect husband, but I don't know of any enemies who would want to kill him or would even be capable of it."

"I can't imagine anyone who would," offered Evelyn.

"Has Joe mentioned anyone he can think of?" Muriel responds.

"He has not mentioned anyone."

"Does he talk about Burke and what happened?"

"No. But I am sure he misses him. I know I do."

Johnny, George, and Carole finally arrive in the city. Johnny has been mulling over what happened. He has made a decision. They drop the car off at the car rental agency on East Eighty-Seventh Street and start walking toward Carole's apartment building on East Eighty-Fifth Street. When they get to Lexington Avenue, Johnny says goodbye to both of them. Carole and George look at each other nonplussed.

"Don't you want to come up and have a coffee or something with us, Johnny?" Carole says.

"Thanks. That sounds nice, but I have something that I have to do," Johnny answers. There is no smile, and he looks determined. George feels the gravity in Johnny's manner. He senses something heavy is on his mind and is concerned.

"Does this have anything to do with what happened to us just now?"

"Yes. Dugan has tried something like this before."

"What are you going to do?" George asks.

"Look, George, I could be all wrong, but if I am not, I don't want you to get involved in anything dangerous."

George gives him a look like, *Are you kidding?*

"Johnny, you think I am going to let you go do something right now that could be dangerous by yourself?"

"I am not liking this conversation. I don't want either one of you to do anything dangerous," Carole exclaims, looking back and forth between the two men.

"Carole, I don't know if it will be, but this is the second time that someone has come after me when I have been with a friend or friends, not to mention at home with my dog. You don't know me really well, but I can't sit still for that. I have been going round and round in my head as to the why and who could be responsible for it. I have an idea in regard to both of those questions. You two should go home; I will be okay."

"No way!" says George.

Carole looks at these two guys whom she cares about. She understands that she can't talk them out of doing whatever it is that Johnny has in mind.

"Okay, what can I do to help?" she says.

"Tell us what you are thinking, John," George adds.

"Now I'm convinced no one followed me either of the two times this stuff has happened. The first time was at the studio where Aarika was in a shoot, and I went to talk to her about Adrienne and Renée. Now this time it happened again at another shoot. Only one person could have tipped off Dugan where I was then and where we were today—someone who doesn't want me to find out about him."

"John, we want to help. What can we do?" George asks.

"Okay. If you really are sure, I want you to be careful and not take chances. Carole, I would like you to call Detective Jim Ashford from the corner and tell him to meet George and me at the Gordon Agency on Seventy-Eighth Street. You will stay outside. This is his phone number." He writes it down on the receipt for the rental car and gives it to her.

He continues, "Jim is a button-down black detective. After you call him, watch the building without being obvious. When he comes, you can direct him into the building. If you see a big heavyset man rushing into the building before he shows up, tell Ashford when he arrives." Carole nods and gives a concerned look to both men.

"George, you should come in with me, and we'll see what happens."

They separate. Carole walks to a phone and searches in her purse for some change to make the call. When she is done, she walks to Seventy-Eighth Street and stands across the street from the large townhouse that holds the Gordon Agency between Lexington and Third Avenue.

Johnny and George walk fast to a large Seventy-Eighth Street townhouse familiar to Johnny without speaking. Johnny opens the gate and walks to the door on the side of the building that contains the offices of the agency. He presses the button and they get buzzed into the building. Colrain takes the stairs two at a time with George right behind him. They burst past the receptionist into the main office area. The bookers are startled, but a few say hello to Johnny and look with curiosity at George as the two men go by the Gordons' shocked secretary and barge into the Gordons' inner office. Johnny is relieved that Evelyn is not there. Joseph Gordon stands up and steps out from behind his desk. Johnny moves forward. He turns to George.

"George, I don't want you in here for this, but I would like you to stay outside the door, keep people out, and warn me if someone I should be concerned about, like a fat detective or a guy dressed in dark clothes, is coming in, okay?"

"Are you sure, John? I might be able to help in here."

"I am. This might not be pretty, and I don't want anything bad or illegal to come down on my lawyer, if you know what I mean. You will be helping a lot if you do what I've asked."

Johnny smiles at his new friend, who nods, and then gently pushes him out of the room, closes the door, and turns to face Joseph Gordon.

"Can I help you, Johnny?" Gordon says, looking at Johnny with a questioning outwardly calm look. He is hiding his disquietude.

"Why, Joe? Why?"

"Why what?" Gordon replies, trying to stay calm. His eyes lock on Johnny's, but there is just a little concern breaking through his usual cool facade.

"Joe, I know. I don't know the connection, but you have sent Dugan after me. You want to tell me about it?"

"I don't know what you are talking about."

"I'm a little angry at you, Joe. Denying it makes it worse. You knew I would be at the photographer's studio on East Twenty-Fifth because I called here to find out where Aarika was shooting a job. Dugan showed up and shot at me as I was finishing talking to her. Then I called here yesterday to find out where Aarika's shoot on the Island was today. Dugan showed up again and almost killed me and my friends."

Gordon is rattled but tries to keep his composure. He speaks.

"I don't know what you are talking about. I think you better leave."

Johnny moves toward Gordon.

"You like to inflict pain, don't you, Joe? But how do you like receiving it?"

In one swift motion, Colrain grabs Gordon's tie, yanks him close, and knees him in the balls. Gordon doubles over. Colrain grabs his head and brings his knee up again into Gordon's face. This drives Gordon backward and to the floor. He starts to rise wobbly. Colrain goes to help him to a chair by the desk.

"Don't make me really angry, Joe."

Gordon straightens up in the chair, his mouth and face bloody. He spits out a tooth. He wipes the blood from his mouth with the back of his hand.

"You can't do this to me. I am calling the police and my lawyer."

"There you go again, Joe."

"You are making a big mistake, Johnny!" Gordon says hysterically.

Colrain moves quickly closer to him, takes his two open hands, and slams them hard onto Gordon's ears at the same time. Gordon screams in pain. Colrain then grabs the back of Gordon's head by his hair with his left hand, snapping his head back. He violently jams the heel of his right hand up against the end of Gordon's nose and starts pressing. Gordon cries out again.

"Okay! Okay!"

Colrain lets him go, wiping the blood from the heel of his right hand on his pants, glaring at him. Johnny hears a commotion happening outside the door and George's preventing anyone from coming in.

"Talk to me, Joe."

Gordon lets out a big sigh and wipes his mouth again with the back of his hand. He is in pain and scared.

"Why were you trying to get rid of me? What were you afraid I would discover? Dugan is nuts. He could have killed not only me but also any friends with me!" Johnny shouts at him with his fists clenched. He starts toward Gordon.

Gordon looks down and gathers himself. The noise outside the door has subsided somewhat.

"Okay. Stop."

He lets out a big sigh and begins his story.

"I met Burke Lambert a long time ago. He had arranged for escorts for some dignitaries and business leaders from a woman named Miss Buttercup who ran such an agency. He and I actually took two of the women to a very private party. He told me about his slave/master parties with models, some from my own agency. He kept inviting me, and I kept declining, but I was intrigued and excited by the prospect of being with models like that."

He looks at Johnny, who just stares at him and says nothing. He runs his hand through his hair and continues with another big sigh.

"I liked Burke, his freewheeling style, his ability to escape the reins of marriage. We socialized a lot both by ourselves and with our wives. As time went on, I began to obsess on the idea of dominating a beautiful model. I knew Burke was doing that. I always had to be so businesslike around the gorgeous girls. I had that desire but was very afraid of being recognized. I owe everything to Evelyn. She is so involved in everything. I could not fool around except that time with the Buttercup girl. Finally, I decided to accede to one of Lambert's invitations when it was agreed that everyone would wear masks."

He pauses and looks at Johnny, who is looking at him in disbelief.

"Go on. What happened?" Johnny says.

Joe looks at the rich maroon walls in the office like he is lost and then at Johnny, who is staring fiercely at him. In a strange way he also looks relieved to be telling someone this story.

"The party was held late at night in the basement exercise room of Lambert's building. Dugan was there and supplied the drugs. I wasn't crazy about that, but the drugs were important. It was going to be a small group—three men and three women. One of the girls did not show, but two gorgeous girls, Adrienne and Renée, were there. Burke knew them. Everyone got high and naked except for their masks. Adrienne was tied to the tilted sit-up board on her stomach with her face toward the floor. Renée was tied to a wall with wooden dowels going across it that were used for attaching bands and other devices next to the pulleys, facing the wall. Riding crops were produced, and there was hitting. There was some yelling, groaning, nasty talk, and sex. Dugan got a little carried away with the hitting, and Burke and I stopped him. Nobody realized that Adrienne had vomited into her mask until it was too late. Burke tried CPR for a while, but she did not respond. When we realized that she had died, we were in shock. Obviously, we couldn't let this get out.

Dugan convinced both Burke and me that he could make it look like a suicide and keep Renée quiet. He took Adrienne back to her building. He got her up to her apartment through the basement, I guess. You know what he did then.

Lambert coked up Renée even more. She was really out of it. I am not sure she had any idea what happened to Adrienne. Burke then took her home to her apartment by cab. He warned her to keep quiet."

Joe looks up.

"No one intended for this to happen," he adds.

Johnny is surprised and absorbing what he has just heard. He is looking in amazement at Joseph Gordon, who continues, "Burke saw you talking to Randy Macquilken at his restaurant and then saw you take Renée home. I was concerned. Dugan assured me he could stop your investigating. I wanted him to do just that."

"What about Renèe and Lambert?"

"He went too far."

Johnny doesn't notice a side door behind the desk slowly opening.

"I am surprised Dugan didn't manage to fix the autopsy report," Johnny quips.

"I tried," Dugan says as he steps into the room with his gun drawn.

Everything slows down for Johnny as he looks at Dugan. He sees him and somehow is not scared. He evaluates the situation with a clear head and weighs what he can do with a strange calm.

"I am sure," Johnny says.

"You should've stayed out of it, Colrain."

"You always seem to say that to me."

"This will be the last time," Dugan says with a grin.

"Use your head, Dugan. Another murder is not going to help."

"Not you."

"Are you going to kill Joe too?"

"And say you did it. It crossed my mind."

Gordon gets up and shouts, "Don't be crazy, Dugan!"

"It's your gun, Dugan," Johnny points out.

Dugan takes out his knife from his pocket with his other hand, still holding the gun, and smiles at Colrain, his nasty malevolent smile.

"You're overrated in the brains department, Colrain. I caught you with this and had to shoot you. It ties you in with the deaths of Renée and Lambert."

"What about motive, Dugan?"

"Jealousy. Drugs. I'll think of something."

At this moment Gordon tries to flee. Dugan is forced to react. He takes the gun off Colrain and points it at Gordon, yelling at him to stop. Johnny Colrain leaps forward and lashes out with a karate chop to Dugan's wrist, causing the gun to fire as it is knocked out of Dugan's hand. The bullet catches Gordon in the left thigh and he falls as he gets to the door. The girls in the office scream. Dugan whirls around, slashing at Colrain with the knife. It cuts through Colrain's shirt and T-shirt, slashing his stomach as he jumps back. Dugan is rabid. Gordon slumps against the door holding his leg.

Dugan advances on Colrain, lunging with the knife. Colrain dodges his lunge and grabs the lamp on the desk. He feels the wet on his stomach. Dugan lunges again, and Colrain steps to the side and brings the lamp down on Dugan's shoulder, but it doesn't faze him. The fat man just smiles at Colrain, the adrenaline pumping as he moves to eliminate his enemy.

"You are done, Colrain."

Johnny tries to move toward the gun on the floor, but Dugan cuts him off. As he forces Colrain into a corner, George tries to force the door open against Gordon's weight. Evelyn Gordon is behind George, yelling her husband's name.

The door moves a little as George shouts, "Johnny, you okay?"

"Joe? Joe? Are you all right?" Evelyn yells out as George is moving Gordon by shoving harder on the door.

This distracts Dugan for a second, and Colrain grabs his knife hand with both of his, twists his body, and pulls Dugan's hand as hard as he can into the wall, which crumples the knife out of Dugan's hand. Dugan whirls around, swinging his arm with a fist in a backhand move that surprises Johnny and violently connects with his shoulder and chest, staggering him and moving him backward. He is still upright but momentarily shaky. Dugan sees the opportunity and moves forward fast, looking to finish Johnny off. Johnny steps backward, regrouping, facing the fat man. Dugan's mouth is contorted with hate. His eyes spew venom, and he attacks Johnny with both pudgy thick fists clenched, launching a haymaker right hand.

He is surprisingly quick for a fat man but not quick enough as Colrain steps to his left and forward, making Dugan miss. Johnny then unleashes a vicious left hook to the left side of Dugan's jaw, followed by a heavy right cross landing on Dugan's cheek and eye. This stops Dugan momentarily, but he keeps plodding forward heavily and again swings a roundhouse right fueled by his desire to destroy Colrain. This time Johnny ducks and buries a left hook into Dugan's ribs, followed by a thunderous right uppercut to his chin that snaps his head back and drops the large man like a sack of cement, his left foot twitching.

George finally pushes the door open. He steps in, looks around, and goes to where Johnny is standing, full of adrenaline, staring at Dugan, ignoring the blood on his shirt. George bends down to look how bad the wound is. Evelyn rushes to her husband bleeding on the ground. Muriel, who was behind the door with Evelyn, follows her in. She is in shock and confused. She stands looking down at the two of them as Evelyn is putting pressure on the wound in her husband's leg with her hand, trying to stem the blood. Evelyn yells for one of the girls in the office standing near the door to get towels from the bathroom to help stop the bleeding and the first aid kit.

Muriel heard her husband's name mentioned through the door. She turns to Johnny and points at Dugan on the floor.

"He killed my Burke?" she asks.

Johnny looks at her over George, who is still bent over looking at the cut on his stomach. This snaps him out of his trance. He nods. Muriel lets out a howl of rage. It looks like she might try to do something to the inert Dugan, but she does not move, just stares at him with anger and disgust.

At that moment Ashford arrives with two uniformed cops. All of them have guns drawn. Carole is behind them. She is relieved to see George with Johnny, who definitely looks like he has been in a fight. George stands up from checking the cut on Johnny's stomach, which does not appear to be too deep but is bleeding. Carole notices the blood on Johnny's shirt. Ashford and Carole immediately go over to Johnny and George.

"Are you okay, Johnny?" Ashford asks.

"I think so," Johnny says, holding his shirts against his stomach.

"It isn't very deep, but he probably needs a few stitches," George says.

George then goes over to where Evelyn is tending to her husband, picks up one of the towels, and brings it to Johnny to put pressure on the cut with it. Ashford directs one of the officers to call for two ambulances. He then turns back to Johnny.

"What happened here, John?"

"Dugan tried to kill all of us with his car coming back from the Island and followed me here to finish the job against me. After a little persuasion, Gordon told me what happened with Adrienne. He is responsible for her death. It is a long story. Dugan killed Renée and Lambert to cover up what happened. In the fight with Dugan his gun went off and hit Gordon who also needs to be charged."

"I need you to come down to the station and make a statement after you get patched up," Ash says.

Ashford has one of the cops cuff Dugan and bag his knife and gun as evidence. He is still unconscious, but they finally get him up and take him away. Evelyn, kneeling beside her husband, is putting pressure on the leg wound with a towel. She is all business. One of the police officers gets down and ties the towel around the leg. Ashford assigns that officer to go with Gordon to the hospital. He instructs the cop to make sure he goes to the NYU emergency room, which will have experience with gunshots, rather than Lenox Hill Hospital, even though Lenox Hill is closer, and to stay with him until he hears from Ashford. Gordon will have to be taken into custody and charged. Ashford directs that Johnny be sent to Lenox Hill for stitches.

Muriel is in shock. Ashford goes to her.

"Mrs. Lambert, I know this must all be very upsetting. Please go home now, and I will come and explain everything once I get it all sorted out." She looks up at him with a disturbed face.

"Promise me, Detective," she says.

"I promise," Ashford replies.

Muriel walks out, and Ashford turns back to Johnny, George, and Carole. He is shaking his head as he approaches them.

"Ash, how did you know to bring two uniforms with you?" Johnny asks.

"Your friend Carole said she thought you and her boyfriend George might be getting involved in something dangerous, and you had told her to call me to come. That didn't sound good. She sounded quite concerned, and she had reason."

Johnny and George look at Carole, who smiles a little sheepishly. Ashford makes a call to the precinct and instructs everyone in the next room to make sure no one goes into the office until the crime scene techs have finished their work. Johnny and Ash go downstairs first, followed by Carole and George.

"Boyfriend, huh?" George says quietly to Carole with a big grin, putting his arm around her and giving her a squeeze. She looks up at him quickly to check his face, sees his grin, and grins back.

34

ROBESPIERRE ENTERS THE OPENING at the Robert Easton Gallery with Felicia and Lucienne. It is quite crowded. They go to the bar, get three white wines, and join a group of people chatting and looking at a very large modern painting. The group is all their friends: Johnny, Ashford, Buttercup, George, and Carole. A well-dressed man approaches with Priscilla, stops, and tells her he is interested in the painting everyone is standing in front of. Priscilla looks at Colrain, who looks at Buttercup.

"Well, have you decided?" Johnny asks her.

"This is the one," Buttercup replies, smiling at him.

Priscilla turns to the prospective buyer.

"I am sorry, sir. It has been promised to someone."

The buyer sighs, takes one more look, and then walks away.

Robby turns to Colrain and the group and raises his glass in a toast to them all.

Acknowledgments

A SPECIAL THANKS to Victoria Carr for her friendship and insightful feedback in helping to shape this manuscript, Godfrey Clark Burns who set an example and encouraged me to write this book, and Bobbi Benson of Wild Ginger Press without whose guidance and input, this book would never have come together the way it has, and to Baloo, my magnificent Great Pyrenees.